CASALVENTO

GUDRUN CUILLO

CASALVENTO

House of the Wind

GREENLEAF
BOOK GROUP PRESS

Published by Greenleaf Book Group Press
Austin, Texas
www.gbgpress.com

Distributed by Greenleaf Book Group

For ordering information or special discounts for bulk purchases, please contact Greenleaf Book Group at PO Box 91869, Austin, TX 78709, 512.891.6100.

Design and composition by Greenleaf Book Group and Brian Phillips
Cover design by Greenleaf Book Group and Brian Phillips
Cover photography courtesy of Helmut M. Schuehsler
Additional imagery ©iStockphoto.com/Maria-Hunter, 2023.

Publisher's Cataloging-in-Publication data is available.

Print ISBN: 979-8-88645-065-1

eBook ISBN: 979-8-88645-066-8

To offset the number of trees consumed in the printing of our books, Greenleaf donates a portion of the proceeds from each printing to the Arbor Day Foundation. Greenleaf Book Group has replaced over 50,000 trees since 2007.

Printed in the United States of America on acid-free paper

23 24 25 26 27 28   10 9 8 7 6 5 4 3 2 1

First Edition

PRELUDE

———

Sometimes the angels lay the pathway on where to go

And it can lead to something high.

They bring with them "fate."

You can feel the angels—they come together.

They come to you and both of you start to shine.

And both of you start to swing,

First with the look that bonds you,

Then with the closeness of the body, the mind, and the soul.

You can feel the beat of the heart.

You can feel the heat that brings the body to life.

You start to swing.

You can hear the strings playing softly

On the instrument.

"The song of unity and love"—

The song lingering in the air.

Part ONE

1

ERIKA GERMOGLIO LIKED TO think of herself as a self-made woman, and anyone would be hard-pressed to disagree. Business was what she did best. She was proud of what she'd become—a high-powered professional specializing in turning distressed companies around, climbing the upper echelons of New York's social scene with her equally successful fiancé, Craig Bernhardt, a well-known real estate lawyer. Erika shared a high-rise condo on the Upper East Side with him. The breathtaking 180-degree view of the city didn't disappoint. Newly redone by Erika's old friend Todd, a sought-after designer, the condo showed off Craig's art collection and reflected their lifestyle—streamlined and elegant, a bit chilly. Exactly what she'd pictured years ago when they'd joined forces as a couple. Their home was a place to entertain and show off to friends, a setting that proved her life was very much on track.

These were the pleasant thoughts running through her head—she'd just woken up—on the morning after her thirtieth birthday. As she stretched in bed, she recounted the celebration dinner the night before. What had happened still came as a surprise, despite its inevitability.

"Honey, we've been engaged for a few years," Craig had told her. "I'm going on thirty-five, and you just turned thirty. I think we should set the date for this September."

"What?" His words had caught her off guard. "Are you really serious?"

"Yes," he replied. "I mean, yes, yes—let's do it." He leaned over, caressed her cheek, and handed her a glass of champagne.

"Here's to us," he said, smiling. "But drink carefully!"

Erika looked at the ring glistening in the bottom of the flute—the pale amber liquid magnifying the already large diamond. She stared in awe at it.

"I know you already have a ring," Craig went on, "but not the one you deserve. Five years ago I didn't have the money I have now. Our lives and income have changed. We need to change with it. Happy birthday!

"I know you and my mom will make the perfect wedding happen," he went on.

Craig smiled, and Erika considered for a moment his mother's knack for having things just the way she wanted them. He took after her in that way. "Just make her feel important," he added.

Erika slipped the ring onto her finger. "I love you," she said. "So much."

On Monday, Erika hurried to her office, coffee in her right hand, briefcase in her left. She'd dressed carefully, and for effect, as always. The black pencil skirt showed off her lean figure and long legs; her wavy auburn hair was loose and reached to her shoulders. She couldn't wait to break the news to her staff.

Molly, her assistant, would be pleased, but Erika wasn't so sure about Tiffany. The young woman was a good businesswoman—competent and attractive, with pampered, long blond hair. Tiffany always dressed well, her high heels accentuating her six-foot height. Erika relied on her to deal with clients. But there was something puzzling about Tiffany's personality. And her recent breakup with a boyfriend just added to the mystery.

"Good morning, Erika," Molly called out from behind her desk. "Tiffany's already in her office . . . and you look extremely happy for a Monday morning."

"I am! Craig finally asked me to set a date."

"That's great, Erika," Molly added, laughing. "It was about time, if I may say so. You two have been together forever."

The conversation drew Tiffany out of her office. "What's that I hear?" she said with a hint of surprise. "When will this wedding be? And where?"

"September second, in the Hamptons. At Craig's family's golf club."

"Fancy, fancy!" Tiffany said. "I guess all Hamptons society will be there."

Moments later, after numerous questions about what she had planned for her gown, the music, catering, and things of that nature—none of which she had answers for yet—Erika was back at her desk scrolling through emails when Molly buzzed her to say she had to sign for a registered letter from Florence, Italy.

"You know I hate being disturbed," Erika said, more to herself than Molly, who of course knew that. *What could possibly be that important from Italy?* she wondered as she signed for the letter and pushed it into her designer bag to look at later.

She remembered the letter when she met Craig for a drink and dinner after work. Even with their beautifully renovated kitchen, they rarely ate in and never cooked. It made her feel a tad guilty, but why bother, when they were surrounded by amazing restaurants with chefs competing with each other to turn out gourmet dishes from all over the world.

While they waited for their food, she opened the envelope and started to read. "This has to be a joke," she said. But no, the letter was real and seemed authentic, though the news it contained was barely believable—a relative of hers had passed away. As his only heir, Erika was to inherit his vineyard in Tuscany. She was to contact the lawyer Bernardo Morselli as soon as possible to set up a meeting in Florence.

"Since when do you have relatives in Italy?" Craig asked.

"It's news to me," she said. "I know my grandfather was Italian and my grandmother's family was from Italy, but she was born in the Bronx. And no one ever spoke about them. No one wanted to talk about it."

"Do you know why not?"

"A long time ago," Erika answered, "I found out that apparently my father's father immigrated from Italy in the early 1950s. He met my dad's mother in New York, and they got married. My father was born a year later. He was maybe one or two when his father left them. His mother—my grandmother—remarried, and no one ever mentioned her first husband after that. Years later, my father found out that the man his mother was married to was not his biological father. After that, my father and his mother never had a close relationship. She never even came to his wedding.

"And now there's no one to ask," she said. "With both my parents dead."

"What are you going to do?"

"I don't know . . . call the lawyer tomorrow, I guess."

After dinner, when they returned to their apartment, she went to the windows to admire the view. She loved having New York spread out in front of her. She could watch the pedestrians below and follow the lights of traffic that never seemed to slow down. This was her life. Sure, she enjoyed a good glass of wine in the evening, but what could she possibly do with a vineyard in Tuscany?

II

———

*W*ITH A SIX-HOUR TIME DIFFERENCE, Erika didn't wait long the next morning to call Italy. She was used to dealing with sticky or complicated situations in her line of work. Why put it off? Surely one phone call could take care of everything.

But she was surprised to hear the lawyer speak perfect English and even more surprised by his insistent tone as he quickly explained that she had inherited a small vineyard in the heart of Tuscany in the Chianti Classico region near Radda in Chianti. He did not go into details. Those would come when they met in person in his office.

"You can get a flight out tomorrow evening, Wednesday," Bernardo said, "and arrive in Florence or Rome on Thursday. Just let me know the airport and flight number, and I'll arrange for someone to pick you up."

"But that's impossible. I'm getting married in a few months," Erika explained. "I'm busy planning my wedding. Why can't we do this over the phone, or in a teleconference with you, me, and my U.S. attorney here in my office? I have no interest in owning and operating a vineyard. In any case, I'm sure I'll want to sell it."

"Signorina Germoglio," said Bernardo, "that is not how Italy works. I'll expect you on Thursday. Let me know where and when you'll arrive." He hung up.

"Who does he think he is?" Erika grumbled to Molly over lunch, not at all pleased at being ordered around. "I just need to get through today's meetings and see what Craig has to say about it tonight. I can't imagine he'll be happy about my little trip to Italy. Why couldn't I have inherited a winery in Napa? That I would love, but Tuscany? No way."

That evening, Erika met Craig for dinner at one of their usual restaurants. They talked about their work, the house he wanted to buy in the Hamptons, plans for the wedding. When she could put it off no longer, Erika told him about her talk with Bernardo.

"Honey, there is no way for me *not* to go." It was what she had finally decided was best. "The sooner I leave, the better. I'll have it all handled, give the property to a real estate agent, and come back home."

Craig frowned. "I don't like you going alone. But there's just no way I can take off right now."

"Look at it this way," she went on. "We could use the money from a sale to have an even grander home in the Hamptons."

He looked at her sideways and gave in. "When do you have to leave?"

"Tomorrow, late afternoon. I have to be in Florence by Thursday."

"Okay," Craig said, "but I'd really like you home by next week. We have so much to do."

That evening, Erika booked a flight for the next day, leaving JFK in the afternoon, changing planes in Frankfurt, and going straight into Florence. It seemed silly for someone to go all the way to Rome to pick her up.

But it was all so sudden. She couldn't quite believe it. She slept restlessly, getting up in the middle of the night to look for her passport, tossing in bed as she debated what to take, and suddenly beginning to get excited. Not just for the travel or the twist of fate that was the inheritance, but because, for the first time in a long time, she was doing something on her own.

Without Craig.

They had been together for years, since college, building their careers, getting ahead, not exactly planning the future, marriage, or kids, but still leaving it implied. Well, the ball had started rolling, and all that would come eventually, she guessed, as she finally fell asleep.

Erika awoke to the smell of fresh coffee.

"I'm a lucky woman to have you," she told Craig.

"No, Erika. I'm the lucky one. When do you leave today?"

"The flight boards at five."

"Let me get a car to drive you to the airport," Craig offered, "and I'll tell my secretary to call the phone company. You'll need a plan for cell service in Europe.

"Now, I have to go," he continued. "I've got early meetings. Have a safe trip and call me as soon as you land in Florence."

After they'd kissed goodbye and the door closed, Erika finished her coffee and looked at her closet. *How do you dress in Italy?* she wondered. *A little of everything, I guess.*

A couple of hours later, her Vuitton luggage was packed, her laptop was in its case, and her Chanel coat was thrown over her shoulders. As she got into the waiting cab, Erika assessed the luggage sitting on the curb. She was leaving for only four days, maybe a week tops, and it looked as if she was moving out. But she was going to a place she'd never been and didn't exactly know what to take.

From the car, she texted Bernardo her arrival information and went through her mental checklist: *Molly should be able to handle everything while I'm gone, and Tiffany can help. My mobile number is the same, and my computer is with me. The internet should be available, even in the hills of Tuscany.* All she needed to do was check in, get on the plane, go to sleep, and wake up in Europe.

On Thursday, by midmorning, Erika had landed in Florence more than a little exhausted. After collecting her bags and going through customs, she looked around for whoever the lawyer had arranged to pick her up. No one seemed to be waiting for her, though she'd told Bernardo exactly when she would arrive and even sent a photo so her driver would recognize her. And where were the porters? What kind of a country was this?

Grumpy and tired, she found a trolley, piled on her bags, and pulled it out of the departure hall. It seemed unusually hot for the beginning of May as she came through the sliding doors and searched for someone who could take her to Casalvento, the estate Bernardo had told her about.

In her designer coat and high heels, she was quite a contrast to the Italians, who were wearing jeans, casual shirts, and sneakers and paying little heed to the chaotic airport, where pedestrians were dashing in front of cars, creating a cacophony of horns and shouting.

She took off the coat and threw it over her luggage, causing the heavy trolley to take off on its own. Just as she grabbed it, she saw a man holding a sign with her name on it and waved him over. He was dressed in blue jeans and a blue shirt and looked to be in his early fifties, very suntanned and not tall, with silver-gray hair and a little beard.

He walked over and held out his hand for her to shake. "*Ciao, Signora. Io sono Santo. Sono qui, e vengo per portarla a Casalvento.*"

With a big smile, he added, "*Andiamo,*" and pointed to a blue van.

Erika just nodded as she realized that this man—Santo—didn't speak English. But the logo on the side of the van said Casalvento. He was definitely the right person. She followed him across the road, and, after he struggled to fit her suitcases into the back, he opened the passenger door for her.

As he started the car, Santo kept talking, trying to explain something in Italian. "I don't understand," Erika replied, but when he pointed to the air-conditioning dial, it dawned on her that he was telling her it was broken.

Oh, okay, not a problem. She rolled the window down to let some fresh air in and waited for a breeze. All she could think of, though, was how she would manage. She didn't want to make a bad impression with the people who worked at the estate, but this was not going to be easy.

She asked how long the ride was, but Santo just kept talking in Italian, waving his hands in the air rather than keeping them on the steering wheel.

Then she had a thought. "Radio . . . music," she said out loud. That needed no translation. Worn out as she was, she kept her eyes on the road as they drove out of the airport onto the highway toward Rome. But at the second exit, marked Siena, Santo got off the highway and began the trek up a series of narrow, uneven roads that didn't seem wide enough for two cars. All she could think, as they followed the signs for San Donato, Castellina, and Radda in Chianti—twenty kilometers—was that she'd never be able to drive on these roads. *How many miles is twenty kilometers?* she wondered. Before she could remember the conversion, she realized that, in all the airport commotion, she'd forgotten to call Craig.

She reached into her bag to get the cell phone, turned it on, and waited.

Benvenuti in Italia, her phone announced as the signal activated and messages in Italian popped up one after another.

At least my phone understands Italian, Erika thought. She dialed Craig's number, but almost immediately reception faded. She gave up. *I'll try again when I get there*, she thought.

Looking up from her phone, she saw that the roads were becoming increasingly winding. The frequent sharp turns and the heat were beginning to make her carsick, so she distracted herself by looking at the distant countryside. The Italian music on the radio played softly in the background, helping to soothe her. She had to admit, the view was beautiful, the landscape of trees and vineyards painted in deep, vibrant greens, with flowering bushes covering the ground like a natural carpet and unfamiliar flowers blooming bright yellow.

This must be Chianti, Erika realized.

At that moment, the view opened to a magnificent panorama. Here, high in the hills, she could see castle-like villas dotting the landscape. There were towns, too, surrounded by gray-green olive groves and the dark twisted forms of old grapevines. The landscape was a kaleidoscope of green and browns, with distant mountains rising to an amazingly blue sky.

Erika couldn't help herself. "Stop!" she called out.

Santo, startled, replied, "*Si, si, si,*" and pulled over to the side of the road.

Erika tapped the camera button on her phone and got out to take pictures. How else would Craig and her other friends in New York ever believe that she'd been in such an incredibly beautiful place?

A few minutes later, Santo drove them through a small town called Castellina, after which he took a sharp left and continued on. Here were buildings that seemed to be small hotels, interspersed with stone houses, some with barrels at the entrances with signs that read "*Vendita diretta.*"

Are those wineries? Erika wondered. Maybe one could just stop and buy wine directly from the winemakers.

After another fifteen minutes, Santo turned right at a sign that proclaimed, "Radda 6 km."

We must be really close, Erika thought, beginning to feel the prickles of nervousness, unsure of what awaited her. One more curve, and Santo was pointing out something straight ahead and speaking quickly in Italian.

Erika could see a massive stone wall and entrance with an iron gate embellished with grapes and leaves. Just beyond she could make out the bronze statue of a woman holding a basket of grapes.

This must be it, she thought, but, no, Santo kept driving. He was staring straight ahead, concentrating on taking each curve.

Suddenly, he said, "*Eccola*," and turned into a gate that closely resembled the first one. Next to the entrance stood a barrel and the now-familiar sign, *Vendita diretta*.

He drove up a hill, past towering cypress trees that grew on both sides of the road.

This must be the house, she thought.

Santo honked the horn twice, parked the car, and again said, "*Eccola*," with a delighted smile.

Erika got out of the van and stood there, breathlessly taking in the incredible view. She felt as if her heart could stop at the beauty of it. Then she heard a voice behind her.

"*Bella vista.*"

She turned around, and the voice said again, "*Bella vista*, is it not? That means 'beautiful view' in English."

A tall man with curly black hair and intense emerald eyes reached out his hand and, with a light Italian accent, said, "I'm Paolo de Alberi, the estate manager and winemaker for the late Signor Germoglio."

Erika just stood there, totally stunned, not only by the panorama but by the man who was standing in front of her.

Paolo was strikingly handsome, with a muscled body, a firm handshake, an oval face, and a smile that could melt any woman's heart. He did have rather strange taste in clothes, however, as evidenced by his checkered green-and-white shirt, khaki pants, and multicolored shoes.

But the thing that really took her breath away was the late owner's last name—Germoglio. It had been made clear to her that he had been a relative, and the last name indicated that he was on her father's side. But who was he? And why hadn't she heard of him—or from him—before now?

Erika was so surprised that she almost forgot to introduce herself.

"I'm Erika, Erika Germoglio. It's nice to meet you."

"*Benvenuta*. It's truly nice to have you here," Paolo replied. "We were all a little worried. Let me introduce you to everyone. Your grandfather . . ."

"My grandfather? This must be a mistake. This can't be my grandfather's place," Erika mumbled. But who would have chosen her to inherit this estate except a relative? But a long-lost grandfather, that would have never crossed her mind. She suddenly wished her father could have seen this—chances were he would have been as surprised as she was.

III

———

$\mathcal{P}$AOLO APPEARED SURPRISED by Erika's reaction, but he kept on talking. "Your grandfather was a truly amazing man. He took care of all of us like family. As you can see, here are the homes he had built for the staff, like the caretakers, Santo and Mirella." He pointed at a few small villas clustered together. They were stone-walled and surrounded by shrubs and small trees. The wine cellar appeared to be embedded into the mountain, as if part of the landscape and forest itself.

"You've already met Santo. Here is his wife, Mirella."

"*Benvenuta, Signora,*" said Mirella. A stocky woman with short-cropped brown hair, she wore pants and a shirt, and, with her staunch demeanor, it seemed clear who was in charge in that family. But a kind smile softened her masculine bearing.

"Mirella takes care of the wine cellar," added Paolo, "and this is her eldest son, Luca."

"*Benvenuta, Signora,*" the boy said shyly.

"And hiding behind Luca is Mirella's youngest, Robby," Paolo said, finishing up the introductions.

There was a big age difference between the two boys, Erika noticed, as her eyes teared up at the sound of the boy's name. "That's my dad's nickname," she said. "His name was Roberto, but everyone called him Robby."

"Yes, we know," Paolo said. "Signor Germoglio asked Mirella if she and Santo would name their son Roberto, and they had been with him so long they were honored to do that. But now, I'm sure you must be exhausted from the long trip, and hungry, too. Let's get you up to the house."

"This is not the house?" asked Erika, looking at the sizable stone building.

"No, this is the wine cellar. Your house is up the hill."

This must be a huge property, Erika realized as Santo drove the van farther up the road and made a sharp turn through another gate adorned with grapes and lions' heads. He came to a stop at some large, well-trimmed hedges.

In front of Erika was a beautiful rustic country farmhouse, all in gray stone with a portico supported by massive wooden beams. Terra-cotta pots of flowers flanked the entrance and graced the front of what seemed to be an enormous garage.

The smell of lavender and herbs was almost overpowering, and everything was green and lush. On one side of the house, Erika could see a vegetable garden as well as a patio with a table and chairs cushioned in yellow and white. On the left, a fountain and a few statues were set among English-style flower beds. A stone wall separated the house and its gardens from the vineyards, where a little dirt road lined with olive trees climbed up the next hill.

Erika stood there, speechless. Conflicting thoughts raced through her mind. She'd really had no expectations, no idea what this place would look like. Frankly, she hadn't had time to even think about it. All she knew was that someone had left her something she didn't want—especially now, with the wedding plans and her business. The timing could not have been worse. *But look at this place. It's heaven! What am I going to do with it, or the people who live here? My grandfather created a little family for himself here.*

Erika's mind was filled with questions. Why did her grandfather leave America? Why in the world did he leave his family, her father, behind? She needed to find out. She needed to know who she was. Someone had to know the truth. And how would she explain all this to Craig? How nice it would be to sit down and sip a glass of wine right now.

As if he'd read her mind, Paolo came out of the house with two glasses of wine in his hands.

What a handsome man he is, she thought, *a real Italian. He fits this place perfectly.*

"Ms. Erika." Paolo handed her one of the glasses. "Can I call you that?"

"No, just call me Erika."

He smiled. "Cheers, Erika! *Benvenuta in Casalvento*."

"Cheers, Paolo," she replied, taking a sip. "This is my granddad's wine? I don't know a lot about wine, but I do know what I like, and I certainly like this. What is it?"

"This is our Chianti Classico—a blend of eighty percent Sangiovese and twenty percent Cabernet. You know, you can't just make Chianti Classico like this. The property has to have the rights to do so, and Casalvento has had the rights for generations, since the early seventeenth century. But there will be time to explain all that," Paolo went on. "I don't want to overwhelm you with it now. Do you want to get settled in?"

"Yes, that would be great."

Paolo led her in through the door to the kitchen, which was rustic and spacious, big enough for people to cook together, but updated and efficient. The stove occupied the center of the room, with pots and pans hanging from a rack above. A tall Black woman was preparing a plate of *antipasti*.

"This is Doris," Paolo said, introducing her to Erika. "She was cook, housekeeper, and all-around helper to your grandfather for many years. At the end, she was the one who cared for him. He was to turn eighty-nine in October."

"Hello, Ms. Erika," Doris said with a lilting accent and a friendly smile.

"You speak English," Erika responded. "Thank goodness!"

"Yes, I was born in Nigeria," Doris said, "and came to Rome some years back. Then I married an Italian who lived in Radda. That is how I ended up here."

"Let me show you your bedroom," Paolo broke in, leading the way upstairs. "The house has an interesting history. It's a thousand years old and has been in the family for five generations. The stones for the building came from around the property. The walls are thick, to protect the owners and animals from the cold in the winter and from heat in the summer. In fact, in the old days, the first floor had no kitchen or living room. It was just for the animals, with stalls for the pigs, cows, and horses. The second floor held the kitchen and living quarters all together. Now there are two bedrooms with a living area in between, and when you look out the windows, you can see the vineyards. Here's your bedroom," Paolo added. "Santo brought your bags up. I'm sure you want to freshen up. The bathroom is there to your left. I'll wait for you downstairs."

Erika was only too happy to shed the clothes she'd traveled in. She took a shower, changed into some pants, and was about to go back downstairs when she remembered she had never called Craig.

She dialed his number, and he picked up right away.

"Darling," Craig said, "how was your trip? What does the vineyard look like?"

Erika started to describe Casalvento, but something stopped her from getting too excited over the details. *I don't want him to know how surprised I was*, she told herself. *I don't want to give him the wrong idea, and maybe I should leave out the grandfather part for now.*

Revived, Erika went downstairs and asked Paolo if he could show her more of the property.

"Sure," he replied. "We can take the little green tractor."

The John Deere was parked in the garage. Erika climbed in, Paolo started it up, and off they went, up the hill.

"The vineyards and the house are all fenced," he told her. "But the rest of the property isn't. It's too large."

"How large?" she asked.

"Seventy-nine hectares."

"How big is that in acres?" she said.

"Multiply by three. The property is self-contained. It has its own water wells, gas station, and generators. Here's the vegetable garden. And next to it are your truffle trees."

"Truffle trees?"

"Yes, your grandfather planted those trees some years ago, and now, every winter, someone comes with dogs to search for the truffles."

The next landmark was the chapel at the top of the hill. "The *cappella*," Paolo informed her, pointing at it.

"Everything is so well kept up," Erika said. "Who takes care of the grounds?"

"Mirella and Santo."

"Only them? That's amazing. In the States, we would need a small army."

Back at the house, Paolo parked the tractor near the garage and showed her the last surprise, a swimming pool tucked behind a row of hedges.

"I have to return to the cantina now," he said, "but if you need anything else, ask Doris to call me. Have a good night's rest, and we'll speak tomorrow. It's good to have you here."

"Thank you, Paolo."

Erika went into the kitchen. When she saw the small plate of prosciutto, cheeses, olives, and fresh bread Doris had assembled, she realized she was ravenous. She sat down at the wooden table and drizzled the plate with a bit of aromatic olive oil.

"That's from Casalvento too," Doris said. She brought out a plate of pasta and poured Erika another glass of red wine.

"This is delicious," Erika said, thinking that she and Doris would get along well. Truthfully, she liked everyone she'd met so far. They had all been so kind and welcoming.

Doris interrupted her thoughts. "I'm about to leave, Ms. Erika. I'll come at nine a.m. Is there anything you need me to bring for you?"

"No, Doris, I can't think of anything."

"Good night then, Ms. Erika. I'll lock up downstairs and leave your house key at the table by the front door."

"Thank you, Doris."

Feeling the effects of her long day, Erika went upstairs and found the suitcase with her toiletries and moved them to the bathroom. *What a lovely, relaxing space this is*, she thought, admiring the tan tiles and the mirrors framed in the same dark wood as the cabinets. It was modern and elegant, but with a rustic feel—so different from the sterile apartment in New York.

With a curiosity that overcame her exhaustion, she started to explore. Outside the bedroom, a wooden staircase rose to a third-floor tower that had been converted into an office. Folders and paperwork were lying around the room. She couldn't wait to see the view from the windows in the daylight.

Returning to the second floor, Erika admired the sitting area between the bedrooms. It had a coffee maker, a television, a small table, and three armchairs. It would be a good place to relax and read a book.

The other bedroom had the same layout as hers, but, whereas her room was all appointed in warm pink, this one was in green. It was all so tastefully done. She wondered if there had been a Mrs. Germoglio living here at some point.

She went back down to the main floor. The living area was basically one long room, divided by large arches framed in brick. The white walls made a beautiful contrast. At one end was a cozy sitting area with an open fireplace. Paintings on the wall depicted views of Tuscany. At the far end, another sitting area had cabinets of dishes, glasses, and knickknacks. Persian rugs warmed the floors, and ceramic pots were filled with plants and flowers.

In the center of the long space was the dining room, with shelves built into the walls for books and glassware. In one corner, a bass guitar leaned against a keyboard. Erika wondered who played those instruments.

Someone had had exquisite taste. What was strange, though, was that there were no photographs around. Not a single one.

She went back to the kitchen, poured herself another glass of wine, and carried it upstairs to her bedroom. She opened the door to a balcony and walked out. The breeze carried a rich scent of cypress trees and earth. Yesterday, at this time, she was in New York, boarding a plane, and today she was in the heart of Tuscany, looking out over the vineyards she could just vaguely make out in the darkness. Even the sky looked different here. It was like a dream.

Tomorrow, she would meet the lawyer.

IV

———

ON FRIDAY MORNING, she awoke to the unfamiliar sounds of birds chattering. It would be another warm day, she realized as she tried to figure out what to wear to meet the lawyer.

What was she thinking when she packed? *I don't think I have the right clothes with me. And my high heels are definitely not for this part of the country.* She dug through her suitcase until she found a light blouse and a simple pair of slacks. After she had dressed, she went downstairs, where Doris was already working.

"Good morning, Ms. Erika. I brought some pastries from the local shop," Doris said.

"Thank you," Erika said, taking one to have with her coffee. "This is yummy. But I can't keep eating like this. I'm getting married in September!"

"Would you like me to unpack your suitcases and put the clothes in the closet while you are at the cantina?"

"Oh no," said Erika. "I can do that when I get back."

"If you're sure. And what would you like for lunch today?"

"I don't eat lunch. I'm fine," Erika replied.

"And for dinner?"

"Isn't there leftover pasta? I can have that."

"Are you sure, Ms. Erika? I don't mind cooking something else for you."

"No, no. I'm truly good. See you later, Doris."

As soon as she was out of the house, though, Erika realized she wasn't quite sure how to get to the cantina. Take one of the cars? No, she'd walk.

Paolo was standing in front of the stone building, waiting for her. He waved as he saw her coming and smiled. Wait . . . was it her imagination, or was he looking at her with something like . . . admiration?

"*Buongiorno*, Erika," he said, looking into her eyes. "What an unusual color you have to your eyes," he said. "Hazel? Is that what they call it?"

"Yes," she said, feeling herself color. She knew she was attractive and had many compliments given to her about her cheekbones and thick hair, which she mainly kept tied up in a bun.

"How did the new boss sleep on her first night here?" he asked.

"Quite well. It's just very quiet. I'm not used to it, coming from the city."

"It will hopefully become easier. Please come into the office. I would like you to meet Elisa, our . . . your secretary. Elisa," he said, turning to the woman who rose from her desk, "this is Erika Germoglio."

"*Buongiorno, Signora*," Elisa said, reaching out her hand. Her voice was soft and motherly and matched her gentle face. "It's nice to meet you."

"And it's nice to meet you too, Elisa," Erika said. She looked at Paolo. "Does everyone speak English here?"

"Almost everyone in this part of the cantina. We do a lot of tastings during the summer especially, and most of our clients are American. It's almost a must. By the way, Bernardo Morselli called earlier. He should be here shortly. While we wait, I'll show you the cellar."

He led Erika through the tasting room to a huge back room, where Mirella and Luca were at work.

"Every vat, tank, and barrel is handcrafted in French oak," Paolo explained. "The estate grows Sangiovese, the grape of Tuscany, used for Chianti. We also grow Merlot and Cabernet. And, for white, we have Chardonnay, Sauvignon Blanc, and Gewürztraminer, a grape typically found in France or Austria. When you make Chianti, there are guidelines you have to follow. The length of the cork, the amount of aging . . . and you cannot ferment in small barrels. In the old days, Chianti wines were simple and cheap and came in straw-wrapped bottles. That all changed around thirty years ago, when wines around here became more sophisticated.

"Signor Germoglio really wanted to improve the quality of the wines. He followed the regulations but liked to think beyond what was usual. So we are also organic and vegan."

"Vegan?" Erika was surprised—wasn't wine naturally vegan?

"We don't clarify the wine with egg white," he replied. "We use pota- toes. I know it sounds like a lot to understand, but you'll learn."

But why bother? Erika thought. *He must know I can't possibly stay here.* She liked to drink wine—that was all she needed to know.

Paolo was about to go on with more details when he turned around and said, "*Ciao*, Bernardo."

"Erika, this is your grandfather's lawyer, Bernardo," he added, introduc- ing her to the tall, distinguished-looking man in his sixties who had just approached them.

Like a true old-school gentleman, Bernardo took her hand, kissed it, and said, "It's a pleasure to meet you, Signorina Germoglio."

"Please call me Erika."

"And how was your trip, Erika?" Bernardo asked. "Your impressions of Casalvento?"

Before she could answer, Paolo suggested that they go to the office, where they could speak in private. Erika followed the men, and Bernardo took a seat behind the desk and started removing documents from his briefcase and placing them on the table.

"We have a lot to go over and discuss," Bernardo said. "We especially need to talk about the future of the estate."

Erika broke in. "The future of the estate is simple. I want to sell it."

Paolo was taken aback. "How can that be?" he said. "You've just arrived, and you seem to like the place."

"I know," Erika said. "It's beautiful, and the people who work on the property are lovely and kind. I'll compensate them if they have to move after the sale."

Paolo started to say something, but Bernardo put his index finger on his lips.

Erika went on, barely taking a breath. "It's bad timing. I'm planning a wedding, my business is thriving. I can't possibly . . ."

"I know, Erika, that all this comes as a surprise," Bernardo said calmly. "Your grandfather was an amazing man. He worked day in, day out. Even in his elderly years, he was hands-on with Casalvento. But not all his decisions were good ones, especially when it came to family. We all knew he had a son who died tragically in a plane crash along with his wife, your mother.

Umberto had no other children and never remarried. Though you didn't know him, everything automatically goes to you."

"Yes, I know," Erika said. "But I don't want it."

Bernardo gestured around him. "Who would not want to inherit an estate like this? Erika, you should be proud of what your grandfather did. You can't just sell it without getting some little taste of Tuscany. And there is something else," Bernardo said. "There is also a second property called Livernano."

"What?" Erika exclaimed. "This is getting very confusing."

Bernardo continued calmly. "Yes, there are two estates—Casalvento, where you are now, and Livernano, twenty minutes away, with more vineyards and a hotel. It was a 1,500-year-old hamlet, called a *borgo*, that dated back to the Etruscans. Your grandfather bought it in 2002 from a friend, a local man who could no longer maintain it. It was in very bad condition, but your grandfather did not want more foreigners to buy property in Chianti, so he took it on himself."

Erika mumbled, "Well, I'll have to sell that, too."

"It's not that easy, Erika," Bernardo went on. "Your grandfather was a stubborn man, a *capotosto*, as we say here. He worked with a contractor on the buildings, but sometimes without official authorization. There are still open permits and other legal constraints. It would be hard to sell the property as it is."

"So what am I supposed to do?" Erika found her patience wearing thin.

"First, we need to go over all legal documents with the notary in town. I have fixed an appointment for next week. Make sure Elisa sends me a copy of your passport on Monday. Then I would recommend that you sit down with Paolo and Constantina—she's the manager at Livernano—and Bellini, the accountant."

"And then what?"

"Start by looking over the books and plans. See what was done and think about how you can resolve this issue. I'm sure Paolo will be of great help. After all, Casalvento produces world-class wines with some of the highest ratings in Tuscany, and though the hotel doesn't do badly, I believe it could do much better with the right guidance. Isn't that what you do back in America? Turn companies around and have them make a profit?"

"Yes," Erika said, "but that's in the U.S., and we are here in Italy. I don't know the laws. I don't even speak the language."

"Don't worry about the laws," said Bernardo. "I will help with the legal aspects."

Erika hardly heard what he was saying. All she could think of was how much she wanted to be back in her normal, comfortable life in New York.

"Erika," said Bernardo. "For almost forty years, your grandfather supported this community, and he was loved by everyone . . . except one person. And I have to warn you, that person is not easy to deal with."

"Could we sell the estates to him?" Erika asked.

"I wouldn't advise that," said Bernardo. "He was the contractor who worked with your grandfather, and he thinks he should have the property for free. He has no rights to the property legally, but we need to make some kind of an agreement with him."

Bernardo placed his documents in his briefcase and went out to talk to Elisa. "Please print out the financials of the companies," he told her. "We will need them next week."

Turning back to Erika, who had followed him out, he said, "Here is my number. You can call me anytime. Don't worry. It will be okay in the end. You have great people working for you, especially Paolo."

Erika followed him to the entrance. "Bernardo, wait," she said. "If I stay to sort this out, will you promise me something? Please."

"What is it?"

"You say that you knew my grandfather for almost forty years. I don't know anything about him. Can't you tell me who he was?"

Bernardo looked at her. "Of course, with pleasure. But, Erika, when you see the life he has created here, how he lived, and the people he had around him, I don't think I'll need to tell you much. The story will come on its own. I will see you next week."

"Before you leave," Erika insisted, "at least tell me where his grave is. I'd like to visit it."

"That's a question for Paolo," Bernardo said kindly. "He knows more about that than I do. Ask him."

V

A S ERIKA RETURNED to the office, still a little overwhelmed by all the deluge of information, Paolo walked up to her with a glass of red wine.

"Here, I thought you might want this after the meeting."

She took a sip. "This is not the same wine you gave me yesterday."

"No," he replied. "This is the Chianti from Livernano."

Elisa came in. "*Signora*, a gentleman from New York called. He wanted to speak to you, but I did not want to disturb."

"It's okay, Elisa," Erika said. "Did you get his name?"

"Yes, ma'am. His name was Craig. I can't remember the last name. I'm so sorry. He was speaking quickly, and my English is not perfect."

"No worries. I know who he is. And your English is fine!"

In New York, she would have jumped on Molly for missing a last name. Maybe the atmosphere in Italy was having an effect after all. She suddenly realized she was hungry, even if she didn't usually eat lunch.

"Paolo, can you get me a bottle of this wine? I'd like to go back to the house. I need to make some calls."

It was five in the afternoon. As she walked, it occurred to her that Doris had probably left and she was all alone for the weekend. Well, Doris had asked her if she wanted her to come in tomorrow . . . but she needed some time on her own. To think, and to catch up on email.

Then she remembered Craig's call. It was only about eleven thirty there, so she would try his office.

Craig's secretary, Suzan, answered the phone. "Hello, Erika," she said. And then, "No, he's not here. He took the day off."

That's funny, Erika thought. *He's always at work.*

"Is there a message?" Suzan asked.

"No, I'll call his cell."

But when she dialed, the call went straight to voicemail. That was strange too. As she warmed up some leftover pasta, she thought she should check on her clients. She tried to call Tiffany, but Tiffany never picked up either.

She sat in the kitchen and poured a glass of wine to go with the food. Something—the refrigerator or the ice maker—was making a weird sound, she realized as she took her plate to the sink. *I hope things don't start breaking down while I'm here.*

She carried a glass of wine upstairs and unpacked everything, placing her things neatly in the armoire. It wasn't that late, but jet lag was taking its toll. Erika took her glass out to the balcony. It was just starting to get dark, but here, without city lights, the sky was already filling with stars. As she stared at them, they seemed to dance.

Or was that just the wine, tricking her?

Why didn't Craig pick up his phone? And where was Tiffany? Yes, maybe she should have called New York earlier, but there was so much going on, and Tiffany was always such a drama queen.

I'll call them again tomorrow, Erika thought as she crawled into bed. *I can't do anything now anyway.* Within moments, she was in a deep, deep sleep.

The first thing she did when she woke up on Saturday was to check her phone to see if Craig had called or texted. There was nothing from him and no reply from Tiffany either. *How odd*, she thought.

There was coffee by the coffee maker in the upstairs sitting room, and she brewed a pot while she showered and got dressed, then took a cup out on the balcony outside the green bedroom.

It really doesn't matter where you sit, she thought. *The views are amazing anywhere you look.*

It wasn't long, though, before the things she needed to do crowded out all thoughts of the landscape. There were emails to answer and write. And if she had to stay longer than planned, Tiffany would have to deal with some of her clients. Then there were Livernano and Casalvento to think about. Bernardo had said that with Paolo's help, she'd be able to make them really profitable. That would help with a sale.

And what about the wedding? Well, Craig's mother wouldn't mind taking that over. She loved to plan things. Like her son. Maybe it was better to stay out of her way. She would go back to New York as soon as she understood things here and when she felt she had Paolo on board. Then she could handle things from a distance. That would work. At least until she could sell the properties. She'd go over the books with Paolo and get a feel for what needed to be done, and how quickly it could be done, before she told Craig. Either way, he definitely would not be happy with her extended stay.

Erika got her laptop and took it up to the tower room, which she already thought of as her office. Thank God she'd bought a converter at the airport—she connected the cables and turned the computer on. She looked around at the piles of papers and documents. It would take a while to go through those, and who knew what she'd find? Not today, though.

Lost in her emails, she forgot about the time. Finally, she sat up, stretched, and checked her watch. Past three—no wonder she was hungry. She went downstairs to see what there was to eat.

Why on earth did she tell Doris to stay home? She could have at least asked her to prepare something quick and easy.

It turned out quick and easy was just a step away—Erika opened the refrigerator and saw cheese, ham, prosciutto, olives, and tomatoes. Perfect. She put a little meat on a plate, cut a wedge of cheese, and added slices of tomato. She found bread and toasted a couple of pieces, then carried everything to the table outside. She made another trip for oil and balsamic vinegar. *Don't forget the olives,* she thought. Now the only thing missing was a nice cold glass of white wine.

That was easily fixed. She found a bottle in the refrigerator and poured a glass.

Just as she was about to sit and enjoy her feast, she thought, *No, wait. I have to take a picture. No one will believe I did this for myself!*

She took a photo to commemorate the occasion and a selfie for good measure. A few minutes later, she heard the phone ringing. It took her a few seconds to realize it was the house phone before she ran inside to answer it.

"Hello?"

"*Buongiorno*, Erika. How is your day?" It was Paolo's voice.

"It's been perfect, thanks."

"I'm calling you to invite you to our family's house tomorrow. It's a tradition to spend Sundays together. Why don't you join us? It will be fun. I'll pick you up at a quarter to noon. You'll like it, I promise."

Well, I have nothing better to do, thought Erika as she accepted. And she would meet his wife and kids. She wondered how old he was.

Back outside, Erika finished her lunch and glanced at her cell phone. Why was no one calling her?

She missed Craig. Surely, he was up by now.

Erika dialed his number, and this time he picked up right away.

"Darling, how are you?" Craig asked. "How is everything going? It sounds like you're next door!"

"I'm okay," Erika said. "There's a lot going on, and I have to sort things out in my head and figure out what we want to do with this place. Being here is completely different than I thought it would be. It's so lovely, and everyone has been friendly and welcoming. I even saw fireflies last night. I remember them from my childhood—my dad always told me to go out and catch them and put them in a small jar. He said I could sell them to my friends as flashlights."

"You're being silly," he said.

"I know," she said, "but it just brought back old memories that I'd totally forgotten."

"When are you coming home, honey?" Craig asked.

"Well, I have a meeting on Monday," she said. "I'll be able to tell you more then. But why didn't you call me last night? And where were you Friday? You never take a day off. Are you okay?"

"I have a very complicated deal, honey," he said. "It's taking a lot out of me. I have to finish the documents this weekend. The closing is next Thursday, and I have meetings all week. I really need to be prepared. I even ordered in for this weekend so I could work in peace."

"I guess I'll let you go then," she said, adding, "I love you," as she heard Craig hang up.

Erika suddenly felt as though something was off. She had called him expecting to feel happier after speaking to him, but instead felt more alone and left out. His voice sounded odd, almost as if he didn't miss her as much as she thought he would. Here she was, ready to spend the rest of her life with him, so why did she think something wasn't right? Maybe she was overthinking it? It *was* her first time away from home, and away from him.

"Let Craig do his work, then," she said aloud in the empty space. "I'll spend Sunday with Paolo and his family."

Restless, Erika decided to explore more of the house. This time she went downstairs to the cellar, where bottles of wine filled the racks, not only from Casalvento but also from other wineries throughout Italy.

There were cigars in boxes too. *My grandfather's, I guess. He had a nice lifestyle, that's for sure.*

She reached for a bottle of red and peered at the label. Casalvento 1966.

No, she couldn't take that one. She put it back and pulled out another. Janus 2004. Bottle in hand, she wandered down the hall and into the laundry room. Along with a washer and dryer, she found cabinets filled with clothes in all sizes.

"Here's a jacket that fits me," she murmured, "and some rubber boots. Those will come in handy."

Lining the walls were shelves of jars—homemade tomato sauces, marmalade, and other unfamiliar fruits and vegetables, all labeled in Italian.

She went back up to the kitchen, opened the wine, took another serving of cheese, and went out onto the patio. It was a beautiful evening, but maybe a bit chilly.

She ran down to the room with the clothes, grabbed the jacket, and came back to sit under the entry's massive wooden beams. She breathed in the smell of grass and the trees that wafted on the cool breeze. The wine had a faint aroma of tobacco.

It was very quiet, with only the sounds of birds and crickets. As the automatic lights came on, Erika felt a chill. She went inside and locked the front door behind her. Then she locked the kitchen door and poured another glass of wine.

This is the best one yet, she thought.

What to do next? A soak in the tub, of course.

A little while later, she was relaxing in the bath, sipping the wine. *How rich I feel*, she thought. *How decadent this is. How perfect.*

VI

———

HE PEAL OF SUNDAY CHURCH BELLS woke her. A glance at her watch told her it was eight o'clock. Too early to get up, but when she turned over and tried to go back to sleep, the fresh grassy scent that came through the open window was too delightful to ignore. She jumped out of bed, found some jogging clothes and her running shoes, washed her face, and poured a glass of water.

From my own wells, she remembered. *How amazing is that?*

Her thoughts wandered. She hoped that Craig would be understanding about her needing to stay longer. Maybe he'd want to come and see Casalvento for himself after Thursday. But why did he assume she wouldn't be back right away?

He must be completely into this deal.

Erika hurried down the stairs, unfolded the shutters, and opened the front door. It smelled as if it had rained overnight, but she never heard anything. *I can't believe how deeply I sleep here*, she thought. *It must be the air . . . or the altitude. We're 1,800 feet up.*

She looked for her iPod for some music to jog to and wondered which way to go first. It really didn't matter—she was running on her own property, not in Central Park, not along 57th Street. Actually, why bother with music? It was a gorgeous day. She would just enjoy it.

She jogged out the door, following the road uphill. She passed pines and towering cypresses, saw the truffle trees Paolo had pointed out, and came up to the chapel slightly out of breath.

She opened a little wooden gate and walked straight into a spiderweb. Startled, she waved her arms, trying to make sure the spider wasn't in her hair. The view stopped her mid-wave. Before her was an endless expanse of vineyards and woods. She could even see the top of the cantina.

When Craig comes, she thought, *we'll have to drive around Tuscany.*

She turned around and saw a large Madonna placed over a little marker. *That must be my grandfather's grave*, she thought as her heart beat a bit faster. But no. The gravestone bore a picture of a dog. It read: "To my beloved friend and dog, Monk Monk. Rest In Peace."

That was his dog? She tried the chapel door, but it was locked. Erika shivered. This place was giving her the creeps. She jogged back down the hill and past the Casalvento gate, which opened as she went by. She realized that it must operate on a sensor, and turned back to see if the gate closed on its own. *Yes, good.*

A few minutes later she was at the house.

She went upstairs to shower, then opened the armoire to pick something to wear. *Not an easy choice*, she thought. *It's difficult to find the right look for a family gathering, especially without knowing anyone there.*

As she tried and discarded one outfit after another on the unmade bed, the room began to look as though a storm had passed through. But she finally decided on black Chanel pants, which still fit perfectly, even after a couple of days of pasta. She added a silk blouse and slipped into her flats, applied a little makeup—not too much—and put her hair up in a ponytail.

She looked at her image in the mirror, almost expecting to see something different in her face. A week ago, she was still in New York, celebrating her birthday with Craig, a perfect future all lined up. And now? She was in Tuscany, alone. Her clothes were tossed all over the place. If Craig were to see this, he'd be all over her. In New York, their apartment looked as if no one lived there most of the time.

Forget it. It's Sunday, I'm in Tuscany, and I'm heading to an Italian get-together. Which reminds me. I need a hostess gift. She had some chocolates that she'd bought at duty free and could bring those for Paolo's kids. She didn't have flowers for his wife, but she was sure they'd understand. Maybe a bottle of wine?

On her way to the wine cellar, Erika saw a glass door with a wrought-iron grille of grapes and grape leaves that she hadn't noticed before—all handcrafted, no doubt, and very expensive looking.

She took a bottle and was starting upstairs when she heard a car pulling slowly into the driveway. It was 11:45 sharp.

Paolo blew the horn, and Erika made sure the windows were shut. She took the house keys and her gifts and went out.

Paolo greeted her with a kiss on her right cheek and another on the left. "*Come va, Erika, oggi? É una bellissima giornata.*"

"Paolo, you know I don't speak Italian."

"I know," he said. "This is my way of giving you lessons. You have to start somewhere. I was saying hello and that we have a beautiful day. Don't you agree?"

"That I have to learn Italian?"

"No, or, yes . . . that too. But that we have a beautiful day."

"Yes, it is a beautiful day," she agreed as she turned and locked the front door.

My keys, my door, my house, she thought. *How strange is that?*

"Paolo, I have a question," she said. "I went for a run today. Are there any wild animals I need to be aware of?"

Paolo started laughing. "Yes, there are plenty of wild animals here, but if you leave them alone, they won't harm you."

"What kind of animals?"

"Let me see! We have hare, deer, porcupines, badgers, red foxes, wolves, and, most important, our famous wild boar. The wild boar is only dangerous if she has a little piglet with her. And it's rare that you will see wild animals during the day. They mostly come out early in the morning and late in the evening."

"Paolo, where I come from, wild animals are fenced in. At the zoo. I guess it makes me a little bit nervous."

"You're funny!" Paolo said.

"I don't think I'm being funny at all," she went on. "What if a boar came charging at me? I could scream my lungs out, but with no one around, what would I do? Climb up a tree?"

"That's a thought." He laughed. "Let's not imagine the worst. I don't know of anyone ever being attacked, and I'm sure you won't be the first."

"One more question. Where did you learn to speak English so well?"

"It's a long story, Erika," he said carefully. "One day, I will tell you, but not now. Let's go. My family is waiting to meet you."

Erika jumped into his blue pickup. They drove out of the property, across the main road, and down yet another dirt road.

Two minutes later, Paolo was turning into a gravel driveway. "*Eccola*," he said.

By now, Erika knew what that meant, but she was surprised to see so many cars. She took a close look at the structure. With its two stories, it resembled a square box, with five windows upstairs and down. It was painted yellow and had a slate roof and a wooden front door. All very simple, but well kept, with old barrels in front planted with red flowers.

At one side of the house, she saw a grape-covered pergola with tables and chairs. On the other was a vegetable garden and a wire-fenced chicken coop.

"My mother is very proud of her chickens," said Paolo, "and especially of their eggs. It's all organic."

Everywhere, it seemed, flowers were blooming—roses, the yellow ones Erika had seen everywhere since she arrived in Tuscany.

"What's their name?" she asked.

"They are called *ginestre*," said Paolo.

"So beautiful," she murmured, adding, "Is this a restaurant?"

Paolo looked at her and smiled. "You're really funny, Erika. This is my family's house. As I told you, it's a tradition for Italian families to spend Sundays together. So you'll see many generations here, starting with my grandmother. My grandfather passed away three years ago."

"I'm sorry, Paolo," Erika said.

"Don't be. It was better like this. He smoked like a chimney and suffered terribly from lung cancer at the end. My grandfather grew up in this house, my father grew up here, and I grew up here too. We all still live here."

"You live with your parents?" Erika's voice betrayed her surprise.

"Yes. Here in Italy, you stay with your parents until you get married."

"You're not married?"

"No."

"And you don't have children?" she asked.

"No," Paolo said. "Why are you so surprised?"

"Oh . . . I guess I just assumed you would be. I'm sorry—that was silly of me."

"Well, I came close once, but it was not meant to be. Let's go into the house. Everyone's waiting."

Erika could hear the laughter as soon as they walked through the front door. Inside, the kitchen, living room, and dining room all ran together in a huge space, which was filled with people of all ages. Kids were playing with their toys on the floor. Men were sitting or standing near a door that was open to the backyard, smoking and drinking out of a balloon-shaped bottle. Most of the older men had caps on, shading faces aged from the sun. They looked as though they had worked all their lives and were happy to spend a relaxed Sunday drinking, eating, and mulling over whatever had happened that week.

The women, with aprons tied around their waists, were in the kitchen on the opposite side of the house. One was cutting vegetables. A second was stirring a pot on the stove. A third woman was pointing, evidently doling out instructions. Bottles of wine stood on the table and countertops along with piles of greens, bowls of meat, and several containers of fresh pasta.

As soon as the ladies saw Erika, the chatter stopped. They looked at her expectantly, appraising her from head to toe.

The woman in the center burst out, "*Ciao, cara mia. Vieni a incontrare tutti.*"

Completely taken aback, Erika looked over at Paolo. "What do I do now?"

"This is my mother," he explained. "She is welcoming you and wants to introduce you to everyone."

He turned to his mother. "*Mamma, per favore, la signorina non parla Italiano. Lasciami fare.*" To Erika, he said, "Here, I'll make the introductions. This is my mother, Elisabetta, and her mother—my grandmother, Sienna. Next to my grandmother is my sister, Constance. There are my cousins Anna and Paula, and next to them is Katharine, my uncle's wife."

They all smiled at Erika, who smiled back, a bit overwhelmed.

"I won't go into the names of the kids," Paolo continued, "but the dog's name is Fammi—means 'hungry' in English. He's always hungry! The cat near the window is Gatto. One day, she showed up and never left."

Paolo gestured to the men. "This is my father, Paolo, and his brother, Giorgio."

"You have the same name as your father?" Erika asked.

"Yes, I'm the oldest. That's the tradition."

He pointed to the next man, whose smile revealed a lack of teeth. "That's Stany. He's from Hungary. He's been with us a very long time. He takes care of a lot of things around the house. He doesn't say much, but he's a good soul. And this is one of my father's best friends. We call him 'the mentor.'"

As Paolo spoke, the man peered closely at Erika and nodded a quick hello. Paolo had already moved on to the next group.

"This is my younger brother, Luigi. His three kids are in the corner playing with Constance's kids. Her husband, Joe, is there too."

"What a big family," said Erika. "I'll never remember all the names."

"You don't have to for now. It'll all be clear after you've been here for a while. My father and uncle and almost all of their friends worked, or still work, at Casalvento or Livernano. My uncle takes care of all the bees in Livernano as well as the grounds. My father drives the tractor for both estates. They all knew your grandfather well. He spent most Sundays with us. Just like this."

Paulo's tiny grandmother approached Erika with a wooden spoon in her hand. Dressed all in black with dark stockings, heavy black shoes, and a black scarf on her head, she looked a little foreboding, but her smile was so broad she was anything but scary. She waved the spoon at Paolo, grabbed Erika's hand, and led her over to the stove.

Anna tied an apron around Erika's waist and said, "*Andiamo, Signora.*"

No knowledge of Italian was needed. It was clearly her job to stir the sauces. She smiled inwardly—if only they knew that she hardly knew how to boil water, they'd never trust her with this pot!

As the women gestured with their hands and kept talking to her in Italian, she answered in English and tried to follow the instructions they mimed. Somehow, it worked. The tomato sauce slowly simmered. Sausages cooked on the grill, along with a huge piece of steak. Peppers roasted in the oven. Green salads were dressed with Casalvento's oil and vinegar.

The kids set the table with an assortment of china. Water glasses were set out for the wine. Finally, around three, all preparations were finished. The pasta went into boiling water, and the women carried all the different dishes to the table.

The men put out bottles of wine, and everyone took their seats. Paolo gestured to Erika to take the chair next to his, and the feast began. Plates circled the table, with everyone talking at cross purposes, as one course swiftly followed another. It seemed like chaos, but no one seemed to mind.

There was bread and focaccia, several types of pastas, lasagna, then the meat. There was fruit for dessert, and cake.

It was more than she ate in a week. Fortunately, Fammi came to her rescue, eating whatever she could sneak under the table. She was sure Paolo had seen, but he didn't say anything.

She sat back and sipped the wine, and though she had no idea what anyone was saying, she loved the whole spectacle. Paolo tried to translate, but it was hopeless. She couldn't help laughing at the whole crazy scene.

How long had it been since she'd laughed out loud like this? She was like a different person here.

By seven, dinner was over. The women had cleaned up, and the men were smoking cigars and drinking grappa. "Try some," Paolo told Erika. "It's a typical after-dinner drink, made from pressed grape skins."

Erika took a sip and grimaced. "Not for me. It tastes like gasoline!"

Before she left, Erika hugged and kissed everyone, Italian-style, right cheek and left. Again and again, she said how wonderful the day had been. "I promise I'll be back," she said.

As Paolo drove her home, she spotted a couple of deer on the side of the road.

"Look at that," she said. "I've never actually seen a wild deer before."

The lights had come on by the time they got to Casalvento, which had taken on an air of mystery in the dark.

Paolo escorted her to the front door. As she unlocked it, she said, "Thank you for the day. You are so lucky to have a close family like that. I didn't understand anything, but somehow it didn't matter. I truly had fun. And I've never ever eaten so much in one afternoon. Do you really do this every Sunday?"

"Yes, we do," Paolo said. "It's always the same. It's a day you talk, drink, and eat. Of course, we also have our disagreements, but on Sunday we get along. They loved having you there, Erika."

He kissed her on both cheeks. "*Buona notte*, Erika. I'll see you tomorrow morning." He headed toward his car.

"*Buona notte*, Paolo." Happy and a little tipsy, she closed and locked the door and went upstairs.

She took her clothes off, and ignoring the chaos she'd left behind that morning, she got into bed. Was that what it would be like to have a big family? Aunts, uncles, cousins . . . how sad that she never even knew she had a grandfather. She wondered what it would have been like, to have sat at that big table with him, to have laughed and shared stories with him. She would never know.

VII

———

$\mathcal{E}$ RIKA AWOKE WITH THOUGHTS of family still in her head. She couldn't think of anyone she knew in America who did anything like that. She had really enjoyed herself. But that was yesterday. Today, she had to get down to business. That meant getting Livernano and Casalvento attractive enough—profitable enough—to sell.

And she needed to make sure she got the respect she needed. She was here to make decisions and to act. She wasn't just Umberto Germoglio's granddaughter—she was the boss. She needed to forget about Paolo and his sweet and wonderful family for the moment. He needed to see what she was made of . . . that she was a true businesswoman and a successful one. She'd been on her own for a very long time—without a big family to support her—and she'd made something out of her life nonetheless. Paolo and everyone else around here needed to understand that. Of course, she also needed Paolo's help. She didn't speak the language, and then there was the issue of those open permits for Livernano. So somehow she had to strike the right balance. She needed to be the turnaround expert that she was, the person that people were a tiny bit afraid of. As a friend had once told her, "Honey, being nice in business doesn't get you anywhere. Being a bitch gets you everywhere!"

As she got moving, she heard the front door open. *That's right*—it was Monday, and Doris was back.

A half hour later, Erika was dressed and ready for the day, and she went downstairs to greet the housekeeper. "Doris, where can I find the keys to the Toyota outside?" she asked.

"All the keys are underneath the upstairs stairwell," Doris said. "There are cabinets behind the wooden door. I can get them for you."

"Let me come with you," Erika said. "I'll need to know for the future."

She got the keys and was almost out the door when Doris said, "Ms. Erika, what about breakfast? You need to eat!"

"No worries—I made myself coffee upstairs. I don't have time for breakfast today. I don't want to be late for my first day at work."

She got into the Toyota, which definitely had seen better days.

Oh, she realized, *it's a stick shift.* How did that go? Right foot was the gas, brake in the center. What was the left one? Oh, yes, the shift. She put her foot on the brake and started the car, then slowly eased the car into first gear and pressed the gas pedal.

Okay, I'm moving. Great! Now for second gear, she thought. *I guess I still remember my first driving lessons with Dad. Oh, if only he could see me now.*

She found her way to the cantina, parked, and went through the tasting area to the office. Paolo was waiting for her.

"*Buongiorno,* Erika," he said.

"Good morning," she replied, as sternly as she could muster without sounding rude.

He gave her a look that told her he'd picked up on her tone, but said nothing. "Let me introduce you to someone," he told her, taking her back to the tasting area.

"This is Erika Germoglio, the owner of Casalvento," Paolo said to the girl behind the counter.

"Nice to meet you, Ms. Erika," she said. "My name is Hanna. I do the wine tastings and tours here."

"It's good to meet you as well. Can you tell me how many people normally visit each day?" Erika asked as she shook the girl's hand.

"It depends. Sometimes I have twenty or thirty a day, and sometimes a lot less. This is still the beginning of the season. I just started back to work on the Easter weekend. I only work around six months. In late fall and winter, we don't really have customers coming."

"What do you do during your months off?"

"I visit my family," Hanna answered, "and study for my master sommelier's test. The classes are usually during the wintertime in Florence."

"Sometime, in the next few days, I'd like you to give me a wine tour," Erika said.

"With pleasure, Ms. Erika."

What an easy lifestyle they have here, Erika thought to herself, frowning a little. She didn't think that would work in the States. "What's on the agenda today, Paolo?" she asked.

"We have to start with the winery books," he said, "and we should go to Livernano. I need you to meet Constantina—the manager and marketing director there. She will have lunch ready for us."

"Hm. I don't really do lunch," Erika said. "Not usually."

"No? But don't you want to see what the chef does? Taste his cooking?"

"Yes, I know that's important, but it doesn't need to be today. We have a lot of work to do, and sitting down, having lunch, and maybe sipping wine is definitely not part of my plan."

"Okay, you are the boss," Paolo said, following her into the office.

"Good morning, Elisa," Erika said. "Here's my passport. The lawyer said he needs a copy sent to him by email."

"Yes, I remember," Elisa said. "And I've printed out the financials from last year and placed them all on the table."

Erika looked at the first page. "Elisa. These are all in Italian. I don't understand any of it."

"I know," Elisa said. "We are trying to set a date with Bellini the accountant for this week. He and I will help you go through them one year at a time. We can explain them to you."

Erika felt her face grow hot—this was starting to feel a little bit over the top. "I don't have the time to wait," she said. "Tell him to come tomorrow morning. We need to get going on this. Plus, I need to meet the director of the bank the winery does business with. And just one year of financials will not do. I want the last three years."

"But we just went digital on the winery books last year," Elisa said.

"Do what you have to do. I need them ASAP."

"Excuse me, Ms. Erika. What does ASAP mean?"

"As soon as possible," Erika said. "We have no time to lose. The faster we work here, the faster I can go back home. I have a lot of work waiting for me in the States, plus a wedding to prepare. I'm not on vacation here."

Paolo and Elisa exchanged startled looks. He shrugged.

"Come on, Paolo," said Erika. "We can go to Livernano now."

As he drove, she checked her watch. It was now noon here—six in the morning in New York. Should she call Craig in an hour to wake him up? No. Wait a minute. Why should *she* call *him*? He should be the one calling to find out how she was doing. The fact that he hadn't . . .

She was also having second thoughts about the best way to relate to her new employees. Maybe she was being a little too hard on Paulo? She didn't want him to quit. What would she do without him? But could she really depend on a guy who probably never finished high school? She had no idea if he even had any real education. But where would he go if she fired him? She was sure he had no money. Why else would he live with his parents? That seemed odd to her, even if it was typical here.

Paolo broke into Erika's thoughts. "This is the beginning of the Livernano property," he said as he made a series of turns and crossed a bridge that seemed barely wide enough to fit the car.

Erika noticed a massive stone inscribed with "*Per Aspera ad Astra.*"

"What does that mean?" she asked.

"It's Latin. It means 'through hardship to the stars.' It was your grandfather's favorite phrase."

They continued up the steep dirt road to a gate in a stone wall with "Livernano" written on it.

"I can't believe this," Erika said, stunned by the beauty of the property. "All this is Livernano?"

Paolo nodded and pressed the gas to power the car up the hill. Abruptly, he stopped and reached over Erika to open her window.

"Look up through the cypress trees at the top of the hill," he told her. Can you see the vineyards, with trees and a house in the center? That's Casalvento."

"So we are higher than Livernano?"

"Yes, Casalvento is six hundred meters elevation. Livernano is just around five hundred and fifty."

"It looks so small," she said.

"I know, but you're only seeing one side of the mountain from here. The cantina is on the other side. You own from Casalvento all the way to this hill and Livernano. Your granddad bought all the land in between."

Erika sat quietly—that was a lot to absorb. All of this . . . hers?

Paolo pointed to the vineyards. "Here, to the left, we grow Merlot, and on the right, Sangiovese. See the vines? There's a difference between the way we do them here and at Casalvento. In Livernano, the vines are grown Alberello-style. Like a little tree. In the woods below Casalvento, we use the Cordone Speronato style that's typical for Tuscany. And at Casalvento the vines are in Candelabro style, like a candle holder."

Erika became curious. "How many hectares of vineyards are there?"

"Between Livernano and Casalvento, around twenty-two hectares. What all the vineyards have in common is the high density and low yield. We have 6,660 plants per hectare. And we get one-third less production, but the quality is the best."

Paolo started driving up the hill, but a few minutes later he stopped again. "Here's the entrance to Livernano," he said finally.

Erika took in the stone wall, the barrels planted with flowers, and a metal sign with the crest of Livernano.

"It looks like a village from centuries ago," Paolo said as he drove slowly past a small stone building. "But a lot of love and labor went into this project. We were under construction for almost eighteen years. This house was the last one we finished. It's the Royal Suite. Below there are quarters for the workers."

He pointed out a patio with lounge chairs and a sitting area. "There's the pool. And here we have our little church. We do a lot of weddings.

"*Eccola,*" he said as he pulled onto the gravel parking place.

After a moment, she asked, "When was the land valued last?"

"I don't think it has been evaluated for a very long time. Why?"

"I need to have a starting point," Erika said. "I want to know what Livernano and Casalvento are worth. Please put that on your to-do list, Paolo."

He looked at her questioningly.

"Don't you have a to-do list?" she asked.

"No, I have everything memorized," Paolo said.

"Of course you do," Erika murmured to herself as she got out of the car. "Come on, Paolo. We have work to do."

"Yes, yes, I'm coming," he said. "Let me show you the rest of the village. This is the event tent. We use it for weddings or other get-togethers, like birthdays . . . and reunions."

He led her between the houses, through a rose-trellis arch, into a piazza. In the center of several buildings was an open-sided tent and a table that could sit at least two dozen.

"The steps here go down to the pool," Paolo said, "and to the building we passed coming in. Here's our vegetable garden. The produce—all organic—is for the kitchen."

As they were standing there, a woman in her forties with curly reddish hair came out to greet them.

"Erika, this is Constantina," Paolo said.

"*Benvenuta*, Signora Erika," Constantina said with a warm smile.

"Hello, Constantina," Erika replied. "It looks very quiet around here. How many clients do you have staying tonight?"

"Three rooms are occupied," said Constantina.

"And how many rooms in total?"

"We have twelve suites."

"So just one-quarter full?" Erika said.

"Yes, the weather before Easter was rainy and cold. The sun only came out last week. But we are getting requests every day now. Last week, I booked thirty rooms for the summer."

"How do your clients find you?" asked Erika.

"They use a variety of popular booking websites, word of mouth . . . and our website," said Constantina. "We have amazing ratings."

"Yes, but they haven't done much for you so far this year," Erika noted sternly. "You need to be more creative when the weather is bad. Maybe drop the rates for those days or make packages available online. Can you print out the bookings and reservations you have so far for this season? And the ones from last year. I want to compare them. Actually, please print the calendar for all of last year."

"Yes, ma'am." Constantina nodded.

"Paolo and I are going to walk around a bit more," added Erika, "and then I want to meet the staff. We'll see you later."

"Does she know what she is doing?" Erika asked as they walked away. "She doesn't seem very competent as a manager."

"She has been with Signor Germoglio since he bought the place," Paolo said.

"I don't care about that," Erika said. "What did she do before she came here? Before she worked for my grandfather? What kind of degree does she have?"

"I honestly don't know, Erika, but of course I will find out. But you should know that Constantina is fluent in four languages, and the guests love her. We have a lot of repeat visitors, and she is great with events. I hope you realize," he went on, "that Livernano is not exactly a hotel. It's more like a luxurious bed-and-breakfast."

A while later, after a closer look at the rest of the village and some stiff introductions to the Livernano staff, Paolo drove Erika back to the cantina at Casalvento.

"I'll be honest," Erika said. "I'm not really impressed with the people working at Livernano."

"This was the first time you met them," Paolo replied. "They are trying their best, but they don't know you, and they're worried that they may not have a job next week."

"Why wouldn't they have a job? That's nonsense, Paolo."

"Erika, you are now in charge, and they don't know what to expect. Sometimes, when people try too hard, it comes across the wrong way. Come here more often and get to know them. You'll understand who they are and what they do. Most of them do multiple tasks. The waiter, the chef, and the maid sometimes put in twelve-hour shifts. The clients—especially the Americans—are demanding. They are used to good service, and we truly try to provide it. The rooms are the best. And so are the people who work here. Your grandpa was very proud of them."

"Don't worry, Paolo," Erika said. "I wasn't going to fire them tomorrow. And, yes, I'll make an effort to go to Livernano and get to know them. Now I have some work emails I need to answer. I'll drive myself back to the house."

"All right," said Paolo. "I'll see you tomorrow."

As Erika took the Toyota back to the house, she thought that tomorrow she would try to drive herself to Livernano. She needed the practice.

She turned the engine off and took a deep breath. This would not be easy, she thought. But she couldn't make enemies here. She had never dealt with a hotel or even a bed-and-breakfast before and depended on these people, who had. Maybe she had come across as too hard. What did Paolo say? For her grandfather, they were family.

She grabbed her handbag and got out of the car. Santo must have cut the grass, she realized. The smell was delightful, as aromatic as one of her wines.

VIII

ORIS WAS IN THE KITCHEN as Erika came in.

"Hello, Ms. Erika. I made some food for you. You must be starving."

"Yes," Erika said. "I just realized I had nothing to eat all day long. What did you make?"

"There's a frittata with potatoes and eggs," Doris said, "and I have some stuffed peppers for you. Dessert is ice cream from Radda—the best in Tuscany."

"That sounds like too much food to me," Erika said, "but let's try it. First, though, I need to go for a quick run around the grounds."

A run would help clear her mind.

She went down to the vineyards, passing a statue of a farm girl holding a basket of fruit. She jogged carefully between the rows, dodging stones here and there.

So far, she had not seen a single grape. She wondered when they would be fully grown, and when the harvest would be. Suddenly, it dawned on her that Craig had never called.

A half hour later, she was back at the house.

"Your food is ready!" said Doris.

"In a few minutes," Erika answered. "I need to take a shower and change—I'll be quick, so it doesn't get cold."

While she was getting dressed, she heard a car coming into the driveway. She peered out the window but couldn't make out anything. But when she came downstairs, she saw a stranger talking to Doris, who didn't seem pleased with the conversation. The man was tall but on the heavy side, with a substantial beer belly. His green pants and shirt were rumpled and a bit dirty, and his short hair looked as if it hadn't been combed in a week.

"I'm Franco," the man said to Erika, narrowing his brown eyes in an unfriendly squint. "I was the contractor for these properties, the architect's right-hand man, and the person in charge of the estates."

"Oh, really?" Erika said. "I'm Erika Germoglio, granddaughter of the late Umberto Germoglio, and I believe I'm now in charge of Casalvento and Livernano."

"We will see," said Franco. He turned around and walked out.

"What an unpleasant person. Is he always like that?" Erika said.

Doris sighed. "Yes, I'm afraid so. He thinks he knows everything. Before he came, I set the table for you outside," she said, changing the subject.

"Thank you, Doris."

"Of course."

Doris poured a glass of wine for Erika, once she had made herself comfortable on the patio and invited Doris to join her for the meal.

"Doris, what wine is this?" she asked.

"I brought up one of Signor Germoglio's favorites, Janus 2007."

Erika swirled the glass and held it up to the light. The wine was a deep red color, with the aroma of black currant, a hint of wood, blackberry, and, yes, that grassy, earthy smell.

Tuscany is in this glass, thought Erika. *How wonderful it must be to go home and open a bottle of our wine and have the genie of Tuscany come out of the bottle.*

She swirled the glass around and inhaled the aroma again and again. Every time she detected something slightly different. She finally took a sip.

"Oh, I love this," she said. "This is the best one so far. Maybe I'm beginning to really appreciate the different tastes. But I should definitely order some books about wines. And some to help me learn Italian. Another thing for my to-do list!"

She took a bite of the frittata. "This is yummy, Doris," she said.

Erika looked around at the garden, with its fruit trees and backdrop of cypress. *I wish I could share this moment* with Craig, she thought. *No, I don't,* she corrected herself. *This is my moment.*

She finished the frittata and tasted the stuffed peppers. Doris had pre-pared them with ground beef and rice and covered the peppers with a light tomato sauce that had just a whisper of spice. The wine went perfectly.

"Doris, I wish I could cook like this," she said.

"I can teach you, Ms. Erika."

"No, I don't think so. I'm not good in the kitchen. I'm not domesticated."

"What do you mean?"

"I mean that I'm useless in the kitchen or for cleaning the house. And forget about washing clothes!" As Erika finished the peppers, she said, "I can't believe my appetite here. But I think the ice cream will have to wait."

She leaned back, sipped her wine, and listened to an unfamiliar sound.

"Doris," she said, "what is that sound?"

"Oh, that," Doris said. "I'm so used to it I hardly hear it anymore. Those are *cicale*, cicadas. They make that sound to attract the females. They are mating."

"Really? How funny."

She brought her plate into the kitchen and went into the living room. It was too warm for a fire. Too bad, as it would have been nice to sit in front of the fireplace in the evening. When that time of year came, she would no longer be here.

She took the remote control and tried the TV. An Italian newscast was on.

"Doris, can you come here a moment?" she asked. "Do you know if we can get American stations?"

"I'm not sure, but we have Sky." Doris took a second remote in her hand. After a few minutes, she had located other channels.

Erika settled in to watch the news, in English this time. As Doris got ready to leave, she had one more request. "Please close all the shutters," she said. "That Franco gave me an unpleasant feeling."

After the news, Erika found a movie in English. A couple of hours went by before she looked at her watch again. It was already midnight. She had to get herself to bed. She turned off the television and lights and went upstairs. She checked her phone one more time. Craig still hadn't called. Should she call him now? *No, wait until tomorrow.*

She was about to fall asleep when she thought she heard a car pulling out of the driveway. *That's silly. Doris left hours ago. I'm the only one here.*

The next morning, she threw on the one pair of jeans she had brought as an afterthought, put her hair in a bun, added lip gloss and mascara, and she was ready.

Doris was already in the kitchen as she came downstairs.

"Today I feel like having an egg," Erika said. "Just three egg whites, please. No salt."

A few minutes later, Doris put down a plate with two eggs over easy, toast, honey, marmalade, and orange juice.

"This is not exactly what I wanted," Erika said, laughing to show she was not terribly offended.

"Ms. Erika, what you wanted I don't know how to make. Besides, this is so much better."

Erika looked down at the plate. Defeated, she smiled. "You're right— and it *does* look better than three egg whites."

It was time to drive to the cantina. This time no one was waiting to greet her, so Erika took her laptop and some papers and went through the tasting room into her office. *I'm sitting in my office at my desk*, she thought. Her desk! It was hard to believe.

She turned on the computer and sent some emails to Molly and Tiffany. She would call Tiffany later and let her know what was going on.

Elisa and Paolo were busy working when she went in to see them an hour later. "Good day, Ms. Erika," Elisa said.

"Good morning. When do we have our first meeting?"

"Well, we asked for an appointment with the accountant today, but all they said was maybe."

"What do you mean? They are not coming?"

"Maybe yes, maybe no."

"This is unbelievable," Erika fumed, "and not acceptable at all."

"But, Ms. Erika, it's not because of us," Elisa said.

"I don't care whose fault it is. I need to have this meeting ASAP. Elisa, I can't be here all summer long. Get it done. Please!"

She stormed out and got in the car, determined to find her way to Livernano.

Two hours later, after many frustrating twists and turns and dead ends, she finally arrived at the village. She found Constantina in her office.

"Good day, Ms. Erika."

"Good morning, Constantina," Erika said, taking a chair. "Now that I'm finally here, can you tell me about Livernano?"

"Sure, what would you like to hear?"

"Just start from the beginning. Tell me everything you know."

"This is what we call a *borgo*," Constantina began. "It's a village or a hamlet, and it's about 1,500 years old. The first inhabitants were the Etruscans and then the Romans. But after the Second World War, Tuscany had a very hard time getting back on its feet. Most people left here to try their luck in other countries. Livernano was completely abandoned in 1953. Then, in the 1960s and '70s, there was a buying boom. A lot of properties were bought by the Swiss and English. Livernano was bought by a man who had been born here in Chianti but later moved to Switzerland to earn some money. When he came back, he planted grapes here, and in 1997, he made the first bottle of wine. Livernano had no Chianti Classico rights, so he could only make super Tuscan wines, and he also made a blend of white wine. That was very unusual for this area."

"What is a super Tuscan wine?"

"They are red blends from Tuscany," Constantina said. "But they use grapes that are not indigenous to Italy—like Cabernet Franc, Syrah, Merlot, or Cabernet Sauvignon. Winemakers were frustrated with the bureaucracy, and they started to mix unsanctioned varieties, like Merlot, into their blends. Eventually, they succeeded in creating the IGT. That stands for *Indicazione Geografica Tipica* for good-quality wines that didn't meet the regulations. Those are the super Tuscans."

"You know a lot about this area, Constantina."

"I was born and raised here. I know every hill, road, and family here in Tuscany. Especially in Radda, Gaiole, and Castellina. My family goes back to the Medici period."

"And when did Livernano become a bed-and-breakfast?" Erika asked.

"When Signor Germoglio bought Livernano," said Constantina. "The village was a ruin. He restored each house, one by one."

"He did a lot in eighteen years," said Erika.

"Yes, he did," continued Constantina, "and he only used local masons. The furniture in each room is from this area too. His idea was to bring old Livernano back but with modern amenities and style."

"Who did all the construction work?" asked Erika.

"A local company by the name of Stucca," Constantina said.

"And the owner's name is Franco?"

"Yes," said Constantina, looking puzzled that Erika knew that.

"He came by my house yesterday."

The phone rang. "*Buongiorno*, Livernano," Constantina answered. "Yes, she is right here. One moment, please."

Constantina placed the call on hold and said, "Ms. Erika, a Mr. Bernhardt is on the phone."

Erika took the receiver and motioned to Constantina for privacy.

"Of course," Constantina said. "Just call me when you need me."

"Hi, Craig," Erika said.

"Hi, darling," said Craig. "How are you? It was hard to get you on the phone. Where are you?"

"Yes, Livernano has almost no reception for cell phones. But you got me now. How is your closing coming?"

"Is everything okay, Erika? You sound so . . . so distant to me."

"Craig, I *am* distant. I'm 4,200 miles away from New York."

"Erika, don't be like that," said Craig.

"Like what?"

"You know what I mean."

"Craig, I'm far away from home," said Erika with an edge in her voice. "I have no one here I can lean on, and the only person I have is you. And you are too busy to even call me."

"But, honey, I'm calling you now."

"Sorry, that's not good enough. You call me every day at work to see how I'm doing, and now that I'm in Italy, thousands of miles away, you have a hard time finding me or you don't call at all."

"Now you're being unfair."

"That's what you think, Craig. Listen, I have a lot to do today. Call me after your closing on Thursday."

"Honey, please—"

"Bye," Erika said as she ended the call, feeling a little less awful than she thought she would.

IX

ERIKA MOPED FOR A FEW MINUTES after the phone call, then told herself to forget about Craig for now. She would talk to him after his closing. But was she too hard on him? No, surely not.

She dialed Tiffany's number next. "Hi, Tiffany. It's Erika."

"How are you?" Tiffany answered. "What's happening in Italy? I've tried calling you over and over again, but you've been hard to connect with."

"I know, Tiffany. A lot has happened," Erika added, filling in the details of the last week.

"Oh, boy!" Tiffany said. "What are you going to do?"

"I don't know. For now, I'm just taking things one step at a time. Looks like I'll be here three more weeks."

"Did you tell Craig?" Tiffany asked.

"No, not yet. He has a difficult closing, and I don't want to burden him with all of this now. Plus, I wouldn't even know where to start. But can you do me a favor?" Erika continued. "Call Craig and see if he wants to have dinner. I'm sure he'd like that. And please don't tell him any of what I just told you, okay?"

"Okay, I promise."

"There's one more thing," Erika said. "Can you please take care of my client, Mr. Levine? Molly has all the paperwork on what he needs. He's becoming very impatient, and the six hours' time difference and internet lag's not helping. I don't want to lose him."

"No worries," said Tiffany. "You concentrate on your issues over there. I'll take care of everything and everyone here."

"Thank you again," Erika said as she hung up the phone.

She got up and thought, *While I'm here, I should probably take a closer look at Livernano. Paolo only showed me the basics.*

She went into the kitchen, where the chef was beginning to prepare for dinner. There was plenty of space, and it looked as if it was stocked with everything he might need.

The adjoining dining room was large but still cozy, with an open fireplace and a large panoramic window. She remembered that Constantina had said it was used as the breakfast room, too. It was a lovely and warm space, especially with the yellow walls and wooden tables and chairs. And the veranda looked comfortable too, with more tables and a sofa. She saw Constantina tidying something.

"Any chance you can make me an espresso?" Erika asked. "I'm dragging a bit. And I would really like to see the rooms."

Twenty minutes later, the two women were entering one of the suites.

"This is Baronale," Constantina said. "It was the first suite we did. When we started this project, this room didn't have a roof. There was a large tree in the middle of the space!"

"You're kidding," Erika said. "I can't imagine that."

"This is now the sitting area," Constantina continued. "And up the few stairs is the bedroom and a small balcony."

"It's beautiful," Erika said, adding, "those beds seem awfully large for here, aren't they?"

"Yes, it's unusual," Constantina acknowledged, "but Signor Germoglio wanted to have the best, most comfortable beds. So we got the mattresses from the U.S. and had the beds made locally. See the painting on the frame and the cabinets? That was all hand-painted by a friend of your grandfather's. She did that in all the suites, and she also painted the decorations in the church. She was a very talented lady. Your grandfather knew her for a long time. She was from Austria, and she came each summer and finished another room."

"That's incredible, Constantina."

"Yes, it's very cool. Let me show you the Sauvignon Suite next door."

As they went in, Erika saw the fireplace in the corner and another large bed with a painting of angels. The spacious sitting room had silky red curtains, and the bathroom was huge.

"Are all the rooms this grand?" she asked.

"Yes," said Constantina. "Each one is different, but all of them elegant. Upstairs, we have three smaller rooms: L'Anima, Sant'Andrea, and San Giovese. Below the pool is the Royal Suite, which was the last addition. Above the kitchen, in a little tower, is the Livernano Suite, which has two bedrooms. And downstairs, across from the kitchen, we have the Chardonnay Suite. Above that are Cabernet and Merlot."

"I love the way the rooms are named after grapes," Erika said.

Constantina led her to another patio. "Here is the pizza oven," she said. "Once a week in the summer, we have a pizza fest."

They continued along the walkway and down a few steps.

"This is the old storeroom," Constantina said, "where we keep the oldest vintages behind lock and key. There's also a poolroom and a little place to just hang out. And there is one more building, with the Janus and Katarina Suites. Would you also like to see the church?"

"Yes, please," said Erika.

Constantina led them to the chapel and unlocked it, pushing open the heavy door. Inside, all was stillness and beauty. Erika couldn't help standing and staring at the benches, the paintings, and the fresco of Sant'Andrea.

"This place is amazing," Erika said. "In fact, all of Livernano is amazing. My grandfather did a great job. And I guess the contractor did as well, even though I don't like him. He's a strange man."

"Would you like to stay for dinner?" Constantina asked.

It was a tempting idea, until she realized she'd have to find her way home after a nice meal and a glass or two of wine.

"Maybe tomorrow," she said. "I still have a lot of work to do tonight. Have a good evening, Constantina. And thank you for showing me around. This is a very special place."

As she drove home, Erika reconsidered her first impressions. She'd been wrong about Constantina. She did know the area and the business and her clients.

"But I better concentrate on my driving," she murmured to herself. The dirt roads were so narrow. Most of the time you couldn't tell if a car was coming or not. And everyone here seemed to drive like a maniac. And she couldn't believe that this was a main road. Paolo had told her it connected Radda to Siena, but because it was a historic road, it was not allowed to be paved.

Twenty minutes later she was passing the cantina. Robby, Santo's younger son, was leaning on his bicycle and waved as she drove by.

She was getting used to Doris having everything ready for her when she came home, Erika thought as she finished dinner. First there was that nice sparkling rosé, Dream. Then there was that ragout with the mystery meat. The only thing Doris would say was that it came from the Casalvento property. But she didn't remember seeing any livestock. Then there was a bottle of Puro Sangue, which Doris said meant "pure blood." She would have to ask Paolo what the grapes were.

Erika refilled her glass. She took it to the living room and turned on the TV.

I guess this is my new routine, she said to herself.

Doris cleaned up and started closing the shutters. "How did you like the dinner, Ms. Erika?"

"I loved it! You are an amazing cook. But now, tell me, what was in the ragout?"

"You had *cinghiale,*" Doris said. "Wild boar!"

"I had what? Oh, no!" Erika cringed.

"But you liked it," Doris said. "You ate every bite."

"Yes, I did," Erika said, laughing out loud.

"I'm all finished for tonight," Doris said. "Is there anything else you need?"

"No, Doris, good night. Just please lock up."

Erika was still laughing at herself when the phone rang, startling her. It was Bernardo Morselli, calling to tell her that the appointment with the notary was set for Friday in Siena.

"I can't wait to get this all done," Erika said. "This place is beautiful, but I need to get back to the States. Do I need to do anything to prepare?"

"No, Erika, everything should be in place," the lawyer said. "I will pick you up around nine, and I'll drive you to Siena. Don't forget your passport. Have you been keeping busy?"

She told him about getting to know Casalvento and Livernano. "But it's so difficult to get appointments fixed!"

"That's normal, Erika," he said. "I assure you, it will all fall into place. Good night for now. I'll see you on Friday."

Erika turned off the lights and moved to the sitting area upstairs. As she got comfortable there, it felt as if someone was watching her. But when she looked out the window, all she saw was darkness.

You're being crazy, she told herself. *There's no one around. It's just you. Mirella and Santo are by the cantina, but they never come over here.*

In New York, she would run around in the middle of the night and was never afraid, but here in the middle of the countryside, it seemed a little scary. And yesterday, she could have sworn she did hear something.

But you're just imagining things. Just drink your wine and watch an old movie.

She fell asleep before the movie ended and woke with a start. It sounded as if a car had just driven off. *But no, I guess I was just dreaming,* she reassured herself.

She looked at her phone. It was one in the morning.

She would ask Santo tomorrow if anyone could have been here, and for now she would go to bed. *Maybe,* she thought, *I should get an alarm for the house.*

X

———

*S*HE WOKE UP WITH the same feeling of uneasiness. Was there really someone out there? She was far away from everyone, but anyone in a car would have to drive through the gate, and they'd need an opener . . . and to come in through the south gate, not only would they need an opener, but they'd have to pass the cantina. And then Santo or Mirella would hear them.

You're being crazy, she told herself. *Remember, you are your own boss, and you're not afraid of anything. You can overcome any challenge. Now get out of bed and get on with your day.*

She got up, made herself some coffee, showered, and got dressed.

Why do I feel like I'm in a boxing match? she thought. Maybe she had won the first two rounds, but she'd been wrong about Constantina. She did know what she was doing, and Livernano was a real jewel—she needed to have dinner there sometime this week.

As Erika sat down to breakfast, her mind kept racing with things to do and places to go. She wanted to know where her grandfather was buried, so she could pay her respects. Bernardo had told her Paolo would know, and she would ask him today.

She looked at Doris at work in the kitchen and realized again what a pretty woman she was, with her dark skin, curly reddish hair, and dark brown eyes. But it was more than looks that made her attractive, Erika realized. The woman had an attitude toward life, a happiness, that made her personality shine.

"Doris, do you have any children?" Erika asked suddenly.

"Yes, Ms. Erika. I have a daughter, who is fourteen."

Erika paused to consider that. Maybe something was missing in her life, and she didn't even know what it was. Was she even happy?

Yes, of course she was. She was going to marry a wonderful man in September, and they would have wonderful children.

She stopped herself. Did Craig even want children? It occurred to her that they had never discussed this very important thing. Wasn't that something that two people got clear on prior to an engagement? But enough with that line of thinking—it was time to go to work. As she stepped outside, she saw it had rained overnight, leaving everything with the clean, fresh smell of wet grass.

How many shades of green there were in Tuscany!

When she got to the cantina, Paolo was already there.

"Good morning, Paolo. I have a question for you," she said.

"Sure, what is it?"

"Last week, I asked Bernardo where my grandfather's grave was, and he told me to ask you. I want to pay my respects and maybe bring him something from Casalvento's garden."

"Yes, I understand, Erika. You don't have to go far."

"What do you mean by that?" Erika asked. "Was he cremated?"

"Oh, no. He is up at the chapel."

"I was there, Paolo," Erika said, "when I went for my run, but the only grave that I saw was for a dog."

"Yes, that was your grandfather's beloved Monk Monk. That dog was with him for sixteen years, and they were inseparable. He loved that dog more than his life. No, he is inside."

"Inside the church?" Erika was surprised.

"No, Erika. It's a long story and a slightly complicated one," Paolo went on. "Your grandfather wanted to greet his master—that's what he called God—standing up. We really wanted to grant him that last wish, but we knew that it was no longer legal. No one is even allowed to be buried on their own land anymore, but we promised him. In the end, we had to bury him at a cemetery nearby. But we like to believe he is here at the chapel, and for us he is. His spirit is there. You can feel his presence at the church and also in your house. You know upstairs, in the sitting area, there is a heavy armchair with a lamp next to it?"

"Yes, I know that chair."

"That was his favorite place at night to have his grappa and read his books. He was an avid reader, in Latin, too. He was also very religious," Paolo continued. "I think that's why, when he found out that he was ill, he became very, very angry at God."

Erika nodded. "I understand his spirit is here on the property. Sometimes I have the feeling I'm not alone in the house, but that's probably just my imagination. Where is his grave? I mean, the real one?"

"It's near Radda, at a cemetery in the woods," Paolo said. "In a very old and dark cemetery. Spooky. No place for Umberto Germoglio's spirit, if you ask me. We don't even know which grave it is. It's unmarked."

"How can you not know where exactly his grave is? Weren't you there when they buried him?"

"No, none of us were. We had the funeral in Casalvento."

"This is too strange to understand, Paolo," Erika said. "But I still want to pay my respects. Who has the keys to the chapel?"

"Doris knows where they are. She goes up there every Friday to clean. She dearly loved him."

"They really are a family," Erika said, sighing. "My grandfather must have been an amazing man. I wish I had known him."

For the next few hours, Erika and Paolo and Elisa met with the accountant and the director of the local bank. When the meetings were over, Erika was surprised by what she'd found out. The situation was not bad at all—with a few minor cutbacks, the winery would be very profitable, and attractive to a buyer. She'd been faced with much worse than this.

"Did you call a realtor?" she asked Paolo.

"Why?"

"We need to get the land appraised," she insisted. "I want to know what Casalvento is worth, and Livernano too. I also want to know the exact hectares of land and how many are planted with grapes and what kind. And I need to know how many houses there are in Livernano. You can email me that later. That should not be too hard."

"Of course not," Paolo replied a little somberly. "I guess you truly are thinking of selling it." He smiled. "What a shame—I hope Bernardo has better luck in changing your mind."

"I wouldn't count on it," Erika said lightly. Who was he to guilt her like this? "But, before I forget, I also need a list of names of the people who work in Livernano and Casalvento, their positions, and what they earn."

Paolo started to walk away.

"I'm not finished, Paolo," she said. "I need an inventory of machinery, cars, and bottles of wine. How do you expect me to make this company really profitable if I don't know what comes in and what goes out?"

"No, you are right. I'll get right on it."

Erika returned to her desk and opened her computer. There were hundreds of emails, but not a thing from Craig.

I'm not sending him an email, she thought. *I'll wait until tomorrow, when his deal is over.* But what about Tiffany? She was curious to know if they had dinner, but if she asked, Tiffany would know she hadn't heard from Craig. Better just to ask her about business.

She sent Tiffany a note and then emailed Craig's mother to find out how the wedding plans were going.

How quiet it seems here today, she thought. *I don't think I've seen any customers today.*

She went to the counter. "Hanna, have you sold anything?" Erika asked.

"Only four bottles of Chianti so far," the girl replied. "It's very slow today."

"So, what do you do all day?"

"I answer the requests for tours that come in via email overnight and the wine orders," Hanna said.

"I'd like you to give me a wine tour, like you do with the clients," Erika said.

"I'm happy to, *Signora*. We can do it now if you wish!"

"No, not now. Maybe tomorrow."

"I'm off tomorrow. It's Thursday," said Hanna. "I'm always off on Thursdays."

"Okay, then Friday."

Hanna nodded.

Erika returned to the office and looked around again carefully, wondering what it could tell her about her grandfather.

The decor was simple. A desk and a chair in the center of the room. A small TV next to the door. A bookshelf against the wall with some objects and books but no pictures.

She looked out the window and saw the Italian flag and, next to it, an American flag, which she hadn't noticed before.

What did Bernardo say? she wondered. *When you are here and see the life he has created and the people he had around him, you won't need to know much more.*

She took the computer and said good night to Hanna, then drove back to the house.

She left the car running and ran inside.

"Doris," she called out.

"Yes, ma'am? I'm upstairs."

"Where can I find the keys to the chapel?" Erika asked.

"They're in the key box under the stairs, to the left. It's the one with the Madonna keychain," Doris said.

Once she had found the key, she jumped back in the car and drove up to the chapel. As she opened the gate, she couldn't help but admire the view. What a beautiful spot this was! Of course her grandfather would have wanted to be buried up here.

The air inside the building smelled like honey. There was a little altar at the front with a lantern and a candle. Next to that was an open bible and a large wooden cross sitting on a hand-embroidered cloth. Religious paintings decorated the walls, and the stained-glass windows had images of the Madonna, Jesus, and the saints.

Erika knelt and dipped her fingers in a bowl of holy water and took a seat.

"Grandfather, I'm Erika, your granddaughter. How are you?" Perhaps it was a silly thing to ask. "I just wanted to let you know that you have created a little paradise here on earth. The people are so kind, and they all love you so much. But I never got to know you! I have so many questions, questions like, why did you leave my father and us? Why did you never contact us when you found out about our existence? Maybe one day I'll get my answers. I also wanted to let you know that I'm working with Paolo. I've been giving him a hard time, but I think I can learn a lot from him. To my surprise, he's quite smart. Elisa is very helpful too, and she does a great job.

"I know I never met you, but I'm here with the people who were your other family."

Erika struggled to lock the heavy wooden door but finally managed. As she put the keys in her pocket, she looked up.

There was a rainbow directly overhead. *You never get to see those in New York*, she thought. It gave her goosebumps all over. Surely that was a sign that her grandfather was here!

Her parents were gone so early in her life that she never felt as though she had much of a family. She believed Craig was her family, but right now she didn't feel very close to him. How could she describe what the difference was? What was the effect this place was having on her?

XI

—————

EXHAUSTED BY THE UPS AND DOWNS of a long day and slightly hungry, Erika drove slowly back to the house thinking about food. Her first words as she came into the kitchen were "What are we having for dinner tonight?"

"*Sono sorpresa che lei sia cose affamata,*" replied Doris.

Unsure what that meant, Erika just nodded.

Doris smiled. "*Oggi abbiamo frittata di patata e melanzana parmigiana.*"

"I have no idea what that is," answered Erika, "but it sounds amazing! I'm just going to freshen up and be back in a flash. Can we eat outside, by the kitchen?"

Refreshed by her shower, Erika put on comfortable clothes and hurried back downstairs. A glass of wine was waiting for her on the table.

It was six o'clock—early for dinner—but she was hungry, and Doris would go home soon. Even though it was a little cool, it was still a good night to be outside.

Erika sat there and savored the play of colors in the early evening. She liked the way the white patio furniture and yellow cushions contrasted so beautifully with the garden's varied greens. Sunflowers were growing around the kitchen door. *I can't wait for them to bloom,* she thought as she watched butterflies flitting around the garden.

Everything was alive, yet so tranquil. Overhead, the Tuscan sky was changing color from a clear blue to the pinkish yellows of sunset.

She suddenly realized that she hadn't done any meditation since arriving in Italy. She supposed, in these surroundings, that she didn't need to.

She felt balanced. *I can feel my breath and my heart beating easily and slow. I'm as calm as the sunset giving way to the night.*

While Doris cleared the table, Erika took her wine glass and walked around to the front of the house. Going down the stone stairs, she went through the olive trees. From there, she could see the front of the house, with its wooden shutters and yellow umbrella in front. If only those stone walls could talk, she was sure they would have a lot to say.

As she watched, a dark red car pulled into the driveway.

She wondered who it could be and hurried back to the house. Just as she came up the stairs, she heard the front door close, followed by the sound of a car pulling away.

"Who was that?" Erika asked Doris.

"It was one of your neighbors. He wanted to talk to you, but I told him you were out."

"Why did you do that, Doris?"

"I did not want him to stay with you alone. Once you let him in and give him a glass of wine, you can't get rid of him." Doris turned around and went back in the kitchen.

What a strange thing to say—there had to be more to that story. She would ask Paolo tomorrow. For now, though, it was time to relax.

"Doris," she said out loud, "how do I turn on some music?"

"Let me show you, Ms. Erika."

Doris led her to some cabinets by the stairs leading to the laundry. "This is the heart of the house," she said, opening one of the cabinets to reveal a disastrous tangle of cables.

"Wow, is this legal?"

Doris smiled. "Maybe yes, maybe no. It's Italy. But it's working, and that is all that really counts. This one is for the telephone at the big front gate. When someone pulls up, they call, and we can open the gate from here. But it's not working at the moment. The ants ate the wire."

"We need to get that fixed." She mentally added it to her to-do list.

"This cable," Doris continued, "is for the telephone and the internet. And below it, the yellow and red lights are very important. The red one is for the *caldaia*."

"What?"

"The *caldaia* is the boiler, for hot water. If the red light is on, you don't need to do anything. But if the *caldaia* breaks down, which it does sometimes, there's no hot water. If that happens, Santo comes, and he can fix it. Now, see the yellow light," Doris went on. "That comes on when the power goes out and the generator is on. It happens a lot here, especially after the storms."

"Storms?"

"Yes, Ms. Erika! We have more lightning here than anywhere else in the world. When that happens, this is what you have to do."

Doris turned around and opened another door underneath the stairs. "Here are the plugs for everything that's electric and the telephone. We need to unplug them all. We don't want to burn out all our electronics."

"Doris, that's a lot to take in at once. For now, can you show me how to turn on some music?"

"Ah, the music . . . yes, it's here." Doris pushed a button, and a local talk station came on. She tried again and this time found some music. "Here are the controls for the music around the house, the gardens, and the pool. They each have their own on and off buttons."

"Thanks, Doris. I just want the living room on for now."

As Doris went to close the shutters, Erika began to stop her, then remembered the engine she heard a few nights before. It was probably a good idea to keep them shut.

"Ms. Erika, I'm finished here," said Doris. "I hope you have a good night. Do you need anything for tomorrow?"

"No, Doris, thank you. Oh, wait, can you buy fish here in town?"

"The best time is on Friday. That's when the fish truck comes from Sorrento, south of Naples, to the center of Radda. The fish is super fresh."

"Okay, Friday it is. Good night, Doris."

With the shutters closed and front door locked, Erika felt completely safe. The house was like a fortress. She switched off the music, watched the news, and went up to bed. "I'm not calling the U.S.!" she vowed.

Nothing disturbed Erika's sleep that night, and, the next morning, she had breakfast and went straight to work in the cantina. There were no emails from Craig, but her computer had messages from her office in New York. Molly and Tiffany reported that everything was under control with Mr. Levine's company and had copied her on all the correspondence.

She was lucky to have them at the company and to have a good friend like Tiffany. She decided to send a note asking if she'd had dinner with Craig.

Erika spent the next few hours with Elisa and Paolo, going over inventory. The winery books were nothing like what she was used to looking at. The rules concerning vineyards were both unfamiliar and strict. But Paolo assured her everything was in order.

"Really, you have no worries there," he said, handing her the list of employees and wages she had asked for. "And, later today, I'll have the information about Livernano and Casalvento you wanted."

"Okay," Erika said. "Did you speak to a realtor?"

"Yes, I did. There's someone I have in mind. He works for a real estate company based out of Geneva. They have an office in Castellina. His name is William Gotthold. He's English, I think, but he lives here and has been married to an Italian woman for a long time. I left word with him. If he doesn't call back, I'll call again."

Erika returned to her office, but a few minutes later she asked Paolo to come in and close the door behind him.

"Paolo, what's wrong with that contractor and my neighbor? Both of them came to the house. I met Franco. He certainly wasn't very nice. He told me that he was the person in charge here. The neighbor I haven't met yet. When he arrived, I was out in the vineyard. But he did speak to Doris."

Paolo nodded. "Franco has been in charge of all the construction—from the house to modernizing Casalvento's cantina and rebuilding Livernano. He did an amazing job, but I think he has just realized that there's nothing more to do on the estates. Maybe he hoped to be in Signor Germoglio's will. You can never know what's in people's minds. The neighbor is a different story. His name is Vincenzo, and he is very jealous. I'm sure you'll meet him soon."

"I can't say I have a burning desire to," Erika said.

"He has a reason to be jealous," Paolo went on. "We have better wine than he does and higher ratings. We have more tourists. I also think there's another reason he came to see you—he wants to build a new vineyard, and it would cut into your land. He can get the permission only if he has a full hectare in that spot. And he does not. Your grandfather would not allow him to use it, and he was right, because after a certain time that piece of property would be his and not yours anymore."

"Could we sell the piece of land to him?"

"The property that he wants is just below your garden and the vineyard. It would ruin your view, Erika. You'd see tractors and people working on the vines. You wouldn't want that. And we are organic, and he is not. We don't spray pesticides or herbicides, but a west wind would bring all his chemicals onto your property."

"Yes, you are right," Erika conceded. "When the time comes, maybe we can meet with him and defuse the tension."

"That would be a good idea."

"I have another question, Paolo. A few nights ago, I heard a car engine right in front of the house. I felt like someone was watching me. Do you know who or what that might be?"

Paolo looked at her thoughtfully. "Sometimes during hunting or birding season, local people come up to the property, but they wouldn't be so close, and I'm not sure this is the right time of year. I'll have Santo walk around at night, and I'll ask him to close the north gate so that if someone drove up to the house, they'd have to pass by the cantina—Mirella and Santo would hear that. Would that make you feel better?"

"Thank you, Paolo. That would help. There are some other little things too. Funny as this sounds, Doris told me that the phone that rings when people drive to the gate isn't working because the ants ate the cable. Can we get that fixed?"

"Sure. I'll have Santo look into it when he closes the gate."

"This is probably an easy question for you," she added. "This morning when I came in, I saw Mirella and Luca in the back room next to the main office working on something with a large machine. What were they doing?"

"They were putting labels on bottles," Paolo explained. "We don't do that until they are sold and ready to be shipped out. One reason is that the labels would be scratched when the bottles age in the racks. But also, every country has its own label for the back of the bottle, and we don't know in advance where the bottles will go or how many. When an order comes in from abroad, the wines are pulled, labeled as requested, placed in boxes of twelve, and put on a pallet and wrapped up. The load they did this morning will go to Japan."

Erika nodded. "It's amazing to me how organized everything is. You know," she said, "I went up to the chapel yesterday, and there is definitely a presence you can feel there. I stayed for a little bit to pay my respects, and after I locked up, there was a rainbow right over me. Isn't that amazing?"

"Maybe your grandfather wanted you to know he was with you, Erika. I told you this is a special place! But now it's my turn to ask a question," Paolo said.

"Sure, ask me."

"I was just thinking that you have been up at the house all week long. Maybe I could take you out to dinner tomorrow night to a nice local restaurant. We have some really nice ones, or we could go to Florence."

"Paolo, thank you, but I don't think we have time for that now. We have so much to do, and—"

"But you have to have a little fun, Erika, and you have not seen anything of Tuscany."

"Let me think about it. I'll let you know."

"Okay," he said, dropping his hand to his sides. "Is there anything else you need from me?"

"No, thank you. I really appreciate everything you have done."

When he had gone, Erika leaned back in her chair and considered his invitation. Dinner out did seem like fun, and Paolo was good to have around—he made her feel safe, or comfortable, or something . . . but she didn't want to start having dinner dates with employees.

She looked out the window and saw cars coming and going. Even with Hanna off, Elisa was doing a great job with the customers. She and Paolo were a good team. All of them were. It was really quite an operation. And it could be even better.

Her business sense kicked into gear. *I need to find out how much it costs to make one bottle of wine. Another thing for my to-do list.*

She looked at her watch. It was after four, time to call it a day. Erika waved to Elisa on her way out and got into her car.

Instead of heading home, though, she made a detour. Paolo was right—except for getting lost on the way to Livernano, she hadn't been anywhere. It was time to see what Radda was like!

XII

___

$\mathcal{I}$T WASN'T LONG BEFORE ERIKA found herself at the edge of Radda. Signs made it clear that no cars were allowed into the middle of the town, so she pulled into a parking spot and got out to explore.

Radda wasn't big, but there were lots of little shops selling all kinds of goods. Wine, of course. A *macellaio*, which she realized was a butcher shop when she saw the sausages and prosciutto hanging on hooks inside. A place that had local soaps made from goat milk. A few doors down, a tiny tobacco shop was selling newspapers and postcards along with cigarettes.

Erika walked in and saw the clerk sitting behind the cash register, smoking. "Do you speak English?" she asked.

He nodded.

"Do you have a guide to Radda or Chianti?"

She paid for the booklet and continued on till she found herself in a piazza in the center of the town. A bar had set up several tables with umbrellas, and people were enjoying glasses of wine and other aperitifs with a few snacks. It was a perfect spot, and she took a seat and opened the guidebook. In front of her was the church, and to her right was the city hall, another old building, with crests embedded in its wall. Tourists were taking advantage of the front steps to rest.

Just then the waiter came up. "*Ciao, bella signorina. Cosa posso prenderti?*"

She looked at the next table, where a rather good-looking man was sipping a reddish cocktail. "I'll try that." She pointed at the drink.

"Ah, Campari soda," said the waiter.

Erika said, "*Sì,*" and sat back to get used to the idea that she was finally a tourist in Italy. She was turning back to her guide when the waiter returned with some chips and olives along with her drink.

Erika took a sip and grimaced. "What did I order?" she thought aloud. The drink was really bitter. "How can anyone drink this?"

The man at the next table laughed. "You never had Campari soda before?"

"No. This is my first one ever, and I'm not sure I like it."

"You'll see," he said. "It's refreshing on a hot summer day. Are you American?"

Erika nodded.

"Me too, sort of," he went on. "I'm German, but I live in New York!"

"I live in the city too," said Erika. "How funny to meet here."

"Are you on vacation?"

"It's half pleasure, half work," Erika said.

"For how long?"

"For a while. I have to finish something first, then I can go back."

He raised his glass. "*Salute.*"

"*Salute,*" she answered, lifting her own and taking another sip. It tasted a little better the second time.

"By the way, I'm Maxemillian Stronghorn, but everyone calls me Max."

"I'm Erika Germoglio. You can call me Erika."

She looked closely at him. He was handsome for sure, probably in his mid-forties, with steel-blue eyes and blond hair cut short in the back but long enough in front that he had to keep pushing strands behind his ears. She couldn't help noticing his lean fingers as he did that, along with the fact that he didn't wear a wedding ring. Well dressed in jeans and a white shirt, with a sweater over his shoulder, he looked cool and self-confident, and was probably very aware that women found him attractive.

"How long are *you* staying in Italy?" Erika asked.

"I'm here in Chianti for four days for a wedding, then off to Naples and the Amalfi Coast to catch up with friends from Florida, then to Rome and back to the Big Apple. But I've been in Europe a couple of weeks. Before I came here, I went to Germany to visit family. I work for a German bank in New York. And you, what do you do?"

"I'm a partner in a consulting firm in New York," said Erika. "We specialize in companies in distress. We analyze strategies and try to make them profitable again."

"That's interesting," he replied, smiling. "I guess I'm one of the people lending you money to do that. Where are you staying, Erika?"

"Just a mile from here, toward Castellina."

"What's the name of the hotel?"

"Oh, it's not a hotel," she said. "It was my grandfather's place."

"So you are Italian?"

"Well, I guess half of me is, but I don't speak the language. I can hardly say good morning."

"I'm lost with this language too," said Max. "I always think the Italians are fighting when they speak because of the way they use their hands—their whole bodies, actually—when they try to express themselves."

They chatted for a couple more minutes before Erika turned back to her guidebook, but after a few minutes Max again broke the silence.

"Would you like to join me for dinner tonight? The wedding isn't until Saturday, and I'm the first to arrive."

"That's very tempting, but I have to return to the estate."

"Your husband is waiting?"

"No, I'm not married," Erika replied, wondering why she didn't feel the need to mention that she was engaged.

"I'm no longer married," said Max. "Sadly, it didn't work out for us. Thank God, we never had children."

They continued to talk over another Campari soda, followed by a glass of Chardonnay. Max was funny, and it was nice to sit here and not worry about business or New York or Casalvento. Italy was bringing out a side of her she never knew she had. But her responsibilities weren't just going to go away—she looked at her watch.

"Max, I really have to go."

"All right, but first, why don't you change your mind about dinner?"

Erika considered for a moment . . . why not? "Max, where are you staying?"

"Right here, Palazzo Leopoldo. They have a great restaurant, but it doesn't open until eight."

"You know what," she said. "I'll drive home and get changed, and I'll meet you at eight in the lobby."

"That would be great, Erika."

She pulled out her wallet to pay for her drinks, but Max waved her hand away.

"Thank you, Max. Until later." As she walked off, she looked back and waved, and Max smiled. Suddenly, she had her doubts as to whether this was a good idea.

She was debating with herself as she walked to the car. *He doesn't know where I live. I can just go home and stay home. No, I want to go. I'm going!*

As she walked into the house, she could smell something cooking. Doris was in the kitchen.

"*Ciao*, Ms. Erika. *Buonasera. Come fa?*"

"I'm doing well, but tonight I'm going out for dinner."

"*Perché?*" Doris asked.

"Because I ran into a friend who came for a wedding. He is staying in Radda at the Palazzo Leopoldo."

"Invite him to the house, Ms. Erika. I can cook for two!"

"Doris, he is not that close a friend!"

"That's okay. I'll stay until he leaves," Doris offered.

Erika thought for a moment. Why not? Then she wouldn't have to drive back to Casalvento in the dark. What was his name again? She searched her memory . . . Max Stronghaft . . . no, Stronghorn.

"Doris, if you don't mind staying, then let's invite him. Can you call the hotel for me?"

A minute later, Doris was handing her the phone. "*Eccola.*"

Max was on the line. "Oh, Erika, you're calling to cancel, aren't you?"

"No, Max, on the contrary. Doris, my housekeeper, had already started to prepare dinner, and she's an amazing cook. She thought it'd be better if you joined me here. You could come around eight. What do you think?"

"I'd love to," Max said, "but I'll need directions."

"Max, ask if they have a driver. That will be easier for you."

"I'm sure they do," he said, and she gave him the address.

"Okay, Doris," said Erika. "We're in your hands."

"Ms. Erika, go ahead and change. I'll set the table in the living room. It's too cold outside for dinner. I'll call Santo, too, and tell him not to lock the gate."

By the time Erika came back down, wearing a simple black dress and high heels, music was playing in the background, and the fireplace was already warming the room.

I hope this setting isn't too romantic, she thought. *I don't want him to get the wrong impression!*

She heard someone at the door. Max was standing there, holding a bottle of wine.

"Wow, Erika, this is an amazing place," he said. "You did not tell me how grand it is or that it is a winery. I would have brought something different."

"Don't worry, Max. It's always nice to taste someone else's wine. Don't just stand there . . . come in!"

"With pleasure, Erika. By the way," he added, "I have the driver for the whole evening. Is it okay if he stays in the car in your driveway?"

"Sure. Or if Doris is okay with it, he's welcome to stay in the kitchen. Let me check."

Erika escorted Max past the dining room table to the sofa near the fireplace, then went to talk to Doris.

She came back with two glasses of her own Medoc sparkling rosé. "The driver is all set. He'll keep Doris company. And now, *salute!*"

"*Salute,*" he echoed. "How long have you been making wine, Erika?"

She almost choked laughing. "Since last week!"

"That's funny!"

"It's not a joke, Max. Three weeks ago I didn't even know that I had a grandfather. He died a few months ago, and I only learned of his existence this week. He left me two estates. I'm here to take over Casalvento and Livernano."

"Livernano? You also own Livernano?"

"Yes, why?"

"Because that is where the wedding is. My friend rented the whole place. What a coincidence!"

"That's right. I forgot there is a wedding in Livernano this weekend.

And I remember hearing that the couple was German. I didn't put two and two together."

"Actually, the bride is German, but the groom is from England. We used to work together in London. I introduced them five years ago. I'm their best man."

"What a small world," said Erika. "How long have you lived in New York?"

"On and off almost nine years, but part of that time I was in London and Hong Kong. We have banks all over the world. It means a lot of traveling, but I don't mind. And you? Do you travel a lot?"

"No, not really. This is my first time in Italy."

"Even though you had family here?"

"I didn't know that I did. My parents never spoke about my grandparents, and then they died in a plane crash when I was eighteen. But I see that Doris is ready for us. You're in for a nice surprise."

A bottle of white wine was on the table, and Erika poured them each a glass.

"This is our white wine from the Livernano vineyard, L'Anima. That means 'soul.' It's a blend of Chardonnay, Sauvignon Blanc, and Gewürztraminer. Cheers!"

"Cheers," said Max. "This wine is very good, Erika. Fresh, crisp, and the hint of Gewürztraminer gives it a nice aroma. Well done—I'm impressed!"

"Well, I didn't make it," she said. "My grandfather did."

"It's clear you are a fast learner."

Doris came out with the first course and put the plates on the table.

"Max, let me introduce you to Doris, our chef."

"*Buongiorno*, Mr. Max. This is homemade lemon pasta."

"Oh, I love lemon pasta. There's a restaurant in Capri that's famous for that dish. Let's see how this compares."

Doris waited for his response.

"I'm impressed," he said after taking a bite. "This is delicious, and the wine goes perfectly."

Doris started to explain what went into the dish: "Fresh pasta, lemon juice and lemon zest, a little cream, a lot of Parmesan cheese, two eggs, and . . ."

"It's okay, Doris," Erika broke in. "You don't need to tell us how exactly you made it."

Doris turned around and walked away, mumbling to herself. When she returned to clear their plates, she didn't say a word.

"I think I hurt her feelings," Erika said.

"I'm sure it's okay," Max said as he got up and added a log to the fire. "Who plays all the instruments?"

"I think my grandfather did. I'm trying to find out more about him."

Doris, still silent, came out with two fresh glasses and a bottle of red wine.

"This is our top wine," said Erika. "Janus, vintage 2011. It's one hundred percent Cabernet."

Erika was about to pour it when Max said, "Please, let me do that."

They both took a sip.

"I don't know what to say," he added. "One wine is better than the other. I should buy some and have it shipped home."

Doris brought in the main course—*bistecca alla fiorentina*, finely sliced steak over lettuce and lemon with thyme-roasted potatoes on the side. The aroma of the meat and herbs filled the room.

"Bon appétit, Max," Erika said.

After the steak came dessert—*castagnaccio*, Tuscan chestnut cake.

Conversation flowed easily along with the wine. They talked about theater, art, music, and how much they hated golf. Max told Erika about his ex-wife and how long it took for him to get over her.

Erika found herself telling Max about Craig and her wedding plans and that she hadn't yet mentioned that she'd have to remain in Italy longer than she thought. Before they knew it, it was eleven.

"Erika," Max said as he was leaving, "I don't know what the plans are for the weekend or the wedding, but I would like to take you out for dinner or lunch. Here's my card. You know where I'm staying. This was an amazing evening. Thank you!"

He got into the car and rolled down the window. "Please thank Doris for the delicious meal. *Ciao*."

Erika went back into the house and found Doris.

"I'm sorry if I hurt your feelings," she said. "Please forgive me."

"*Non è importante*. It's all good."

It was shortly before midnight when Doris left. As Erika got ready to go to bed, her phone rang. She heard Craig's voice on the line.

"Hello, darling. How are you feeling? Better, I hope."

"Hearing your voice does make me feel better," she said carefully, not wanting Craig to realize she was a bit tipsy. "How was the closing?"

"Everything went perfectly. Thank goodness!"

"Do you miss me?"

"Of course I do, honey. You told me you'd be back in a flash, and it's already been a week. Do you even know when you will be back? Tiffany told me she's handling some of your clients. Do you think that's wise, Erika?"

"I have no choice. The time difference makes it hard to manage New York, and I need to focus on Casalvento and Livernano."

"What is Livernano? You never explained about it."

"Livernano is another one of my grandfather's estates."

"It's kind of weird, don't you think, that you never knew any of this?"

"Yes, I do," she said, "and I'm going to find out what has happened and why. Tomorrow I have a meeting with the notary in Siena, and the lawyer will drive me there. He knew my grandfather for forty years, and he's promised to tell me the story."

"So, if you get the place signed over tomorrow, then you can come home soon," he insisted.

"As soon as I have it all under control, Craig. It's a bit of a mess and difficult to explain on the phone. I'll give you all the details when I'm back home." Changing the topic, she asked, "Did you have dinner with Tiffany?"

"Yes, I did."

"And . . . ? Was it fun?"

"Erika, you know she's not really my thing. She talks about herself too much. My ears were falling off by the time we reached the main course. But, honey, I've got to go. I'm going out with the boys tonight to celebrate the closing."

"Okay, good night. I was just about to go to bed when you called." She hung up.

That was better. *I do miss Craig,* she thought, though it was certainly fun to be with Max tonight. Was it wrong for her to be having these thoughts?

He was so good looking, and so interesting, too. She allowed herself to wonder what it would be like to have him in her life—after all, she wasn't married yet. Images of the two men flitted in and out of her mind as she drifted off to sleep.

XIII

---

*E*RIKA WOKE UP ON FRIDAY overcome with emotions and torn by conflicting thoughts. She had come to Italy exactly one week earlier, assuming she would be able to quickly and easily assess the situation and arrange for a sale of the properties. After all, she had no ties to this place.

Seven days later, how different everything looked. The winery, the house, the people . . . everything now meant something to her. They were part of her family, one she never knew she had, and when she actually became the owner of Casalvento and Livernano, they would come into play even more. The only thing missing was her grandfather's story. But Bernardo had promised to fill that in as well.

Someday, after she and Craig were married, she'd be able to tell their children about the place she had once owned in Italy. It made her sad, though, to think that the history of generations of her family would disappear with the sale of the estates. And what would happen to the workers—her grandfather's other family?

Craig expected her to arrange a sale as soon as possible, but contemplating that didn't make her very happy. Maybe if Craig could see the place for himself, he'd come to understand that selling right away wasn't the best idea. And the decision was hers, not his, to make.

Erika dressed herself in a black dress and high heels. She found her passport and lucky pen, put them in her handbag, and went downstairs to wait for Bernardo.

He rang the doorbell at nine thirty sharp.

"You look lovely," he said when Erika opened the door. "Are you ready?"

"Yes, I guess so."

"*Andiamo, cara.*" Bernardo opened the car door for her, and together they drove off.

Determined to find out more about her grandfather, Erika was nevertheless shy about asking questions, and she was relieved when Bernardo broke the silence.

"I knew your grandfather for forty-six years," he began, "and was his lawyer for forty of them. He was a very proud man, very stubborn and set in his ways, and the older he got, the more stubborn he became. His marriage to Concetta, his wife, was everything to him—he loved her so much. He was heartbroken when he had to return to Italy, and she stayed in New York with their son, Roberto, who was only a year and a half old."

Erika was surprised. "He *had* to return?"

"Yes. The estate here was run by Umberto's older brother, Gabriel. They never got along, unfortunately, and when your great-grandfather passed away, the property went automatically to the oldest child. That was Gabriel. Without a way of making a living here, Umberto had few choices. He left for the United States in 1953. When Gabriel died in a tractor accident, he was called home to Italy. Again, he had no choice. Your father was just a baby . . . But here we are, in Siena. I'll tell you more about your grandfather's story later. For now, I need to go over some details with you before we see the notary. First, you need to understand that, in Italy, the notary is very important. I faxed your passport with all your information already, and he has everything prepared. According to the will, you'll inherit everything your grandfather owned. He also had in his will that you must take care of Mirella and her family, pay for education for Robby, and provide housing for her, as well as for Paolo and Doris. If you decide to sell, please promise me that you will honor his wishes."

"I will, I promise."

"Also, you have a contractor, Franco, who is very angry because he thought he was getting part of the winery in the will. Umberto was not very pleased with the contractor in recent years, especially when his health began to fail. Franco kept trying to change Umberto's mind and alter the will. But your grandfather was determined to leave everything to you. At one point, he discovered where your father lived in the United States and what he did, but Umberto never shared that secret with anyone but me. He never contacted your father, either.

"Later, Umberto found out that he had a granddaughter. He was surprised and pleased. It was shockingly clear how much he loved your father and you. And when your parents died, he lost his son a second time, just as you lost your parents. Umberto could never make up for what was lost. But he wanted to think of something for the future.

"Without your knowing about it, your grandfather opened a bank account in your name in New York. Whenever he could, he had money wired to that account. I found your late father's lawyer in New York, and he helped me find you. It wasn't easy. You had changed colleges and then moved in with your fiancé. Now the lawyer has the details of the account."

Erika could barely believe what she was hearing. "Bernardo, you are telling me that I have money somewhere, and I don't know it. How much money is there?"

"I honestly don't know. You'll need to contact the lawyer. But I have more to tell you about your inheritance here. Your neighbor, Vincenzo, also had an issue with your grandfather. He claims that some of the property is his. That has been going on for generations. But now, since Vincenzo took over the vineyards and winery, it has become a real fight. He needs that piece to make up a full hectare of land so he can plant a new vineyard. I'm sure he has already contacted you."

"Yes, he was on the property a couple of days ago, and when I asked Paolo about it, he explained a little about the issue."

"You should also know," Bernardo went on, "that Vincenzo's father, Giuseppe, was married to Umberto's sister, Josephine. Vincenzo and his brother, Massimo, are your cousins."

"I don't understand! I have living relatives here?"

"Yes, you have two cousins."

"Do they know about me . . . that I'm their cousin?"

"Yes, and of course you'll meet them."

"Does Paolo know about this?"

Bernardo nodded.

"I can't believe he didn't say anything about it when I told him that Vincenzo had come to the house," Erika said. "I've had some scary nights this week. I thought I had someone watching me in the evening, and then I heard what I thought was a car in the middle of the night."

"Erika, these are people who are set in their ways, but I don't believe that they would actually harm you. Especially your cousin. I'm sure there is an explanation for it all. But I haven't finished. There is one more important thing in Umberto's will."

"What is it?"

"Erika, before you decide what you want to do with your inheritance, you have to stay here for five more months and learn more about Casalvento and Livernano and the lives of the people there. After that time is over, you can decide to sell it, sell part of it, or keep it. Whatever you wish. And I will help as much as I can."

Bernardo had been driving while he talked. Now, in front of the notary's office, he parked the car and turned to Erika, who couldn't believe what she was hearing. She stopped breathing as she struggled to fight back tears.

"Erika, are you okay?"

"How can I be okay, Bernardo? For God's sake. My life has just done a one-eighty! First, I have the most amazing birthday and my fiancé gives me an incredible ring and tells me to set a date. Then I find out I had a grandfather who loved me enough to leave me his precious estates, and then I hear that there are people who wish I didn't exist. And, finally, I discover that I have to stay for five months before I can make any real decisions. My head's spinning, Bernardo. What am I going to do? I'm supposed to be getting married in a few months."

By now she was sobbing openly. She felt dizzy, as though everything around her was unstable. A grandfather she never knew had suddenly taken charge of her life.

"And what about my business? I have a company to run. How can I do that from here and also learn everything I need to about Casalvento and Livernano?"

"Erika, let me try to reassure you. I knew your grandfather for decades, and he had a heart of gold. I want you to know him and understand him. He only had this one wish. And you'll find out more about who you are. It will be important for the future, for you and your children. I'm sure that your fiancé will understand."

"I'm not so sure about that, Bernardo. Craig hates surprises and change that he hasn't planned for." She was still crying but less intensely.

"Erika, take a deep breath, and put your life in New York out of your mind. Think of everything you've seen and done in the last week. Think about the people you've met here. Think about Casalvento and Livernano. Those properties are a jewel here in Tuscany.

"I can imagine you here. And maybe a time will come when you can too. Who knows!"

Erika looked at him. Was it true that her grandfather hadn't wanted to abandon his family in New York? She remembered the rainbow she'd seen at the chapel. Wasn't that a sign? There was so much more to find out about her family and Casalvento. No, she couldn't just walk away now, but there were still so many questions, so many things to explain.

She took a deep breath. "Okay, Bernardo, I'll give in to my grandfather's wishes and stay at least five months. I'll stay, but I need to go home to New York as soon as possible. I need to explain everything to Craig and postpone my wedding. I need to arrange to take care of my business while I'm here, and I have to contact my father's lawyer. I also need to get clothes, shoes, everything. I don't think you understand how confusing and upsetting this is and how much I have to do."

"Of course, Erika," Bernardo said. "Please, try not to worry too much. I know this is a shock, but it will work out. Now let's go up to the notary and sign the papers. I'm sure he has been waiting for us quite a while."

They spent the next hour in the notary's office with Bernardo translating as Erika sat dazed and signed paper after paper.

Bernardo drove back to Casalvento in silence. Just as he dropped her off, he said, "You know how to contact me. I'm here to help whenever you need me. When you get back from New York, I want to show you Florence." He walked Erika to the front door. "There's one more thing, Erika."

He took an envelope out of his jacket pocket. "Your grandfather left some letters for you. This is the first one. Read it when you're alone. You'll begin to understand your grandfather and this place."

XIV

———

$\mathcal{C}$ONFUSED AND SHAKEN, Erika still had the envelope in her hand as she went into the house and dropped into a chair in the living room. Her head buzzed with questions. How would she explain to Craig everything that Bernardo had just told her? How could she do without him for the next five months? How soon could she get a plane to New York, and how in the world could she arrange to take care of her clients? How could she learn everything she needed to know about Casalvento and Livernano quickly?

Doris had turned on music in the house, and the beauty of the room added to the sense of calm. Slowly, Erika began to relax. She looked at the envelope Bernardo had given her. With trepidation, she opened it and began to read:

Dear Erika,

I think beginning to write to you was the hardest step. I'm not sure how many letters I have started and never finished, but I really wish you to get to know me and the circumstances that led me to my life.

I wish I could have known you when you were a baby. I tried to find you and finally was successful. I know your path has not been easy, especially after you lost the only family you knew. You don't know how many times I wanted to reach out to you, but my lawyer, whom you have met by now, decided that would not be the best thing to do.

We came up with this plan: In case of my death, we wanted you to come to Italy and see the property that has been in our family for more than five generations.

I was the second of three children. Your uncle, Gabriel, was the oldest. Your aunt, Josephine, was the youngest. I was always my father's favorite. Gabriel was different. We knew by law he would inherit our property, so I learned to be a mason. That was important for my future. Nevertheless, I was hoping my brother would let me stay at home, and I could help him run the farm. Unfortunately, that was not the case.

When our father passed away, Gabriel inherited everything. Josephine had already married our neighbor by then, and they had a small farm and vineyard. But I was at Gabriel's mercy. I had to make the difficult decision to leave home and go to America.

My father's brother, Sonny, had already left Italy during hard times in 1910. He became a well-known, respected man. When I left in 1953, my uncle and his family took me in with open arms. I started to work in his construction company in the Bronx.

I had a very difficult time at first. I was used to living in the country. The city was so different and new to me in every way. I had to learn the English language very fast. But I lived in an Italian neighborhood. Most of the older people had come around the same time as my uncle, while most of the people my age were first-generation Americans. They did not even speak Italian.

Uncle Sonny and his wife had seven children. One of his sons, Maurizio, was my age, and we spent most of our time together. He, like his other brothers, worked for my uncle. He also had a band. I learned to play the bass, and I became a part of Mau's band, which he named The Trio.

Uncle Sonny was my hero. I wanted to become like him—a self-made man—and I worked very hard to do that.

Before long, I met your grandmother. Her name was Concetta Uva, and she was a sweet young woman with a lot of suitors. I had to be very creative to get her attention. As a first-generation Italian American, she knew only limited Italian. We spoke only English together.

Concetta became my wife, and soon after, she was pregnant with your father. It seemed nothing could destroy our happiness. When your father was born, we named him Roberto, like my father.

Erika had to stop reading for a minute and wipe her eyes. It was almost impossible for her to believe she was sitting in her grandfather's house, reading about relatives she didn't know she had. Part of her was angry that all of this had been kept from her. "I must have cousins in New York too," she said to herself. "Why were we so isolated from them?"

She continued reading his letter, which was written in ink on beautiful stationery in clear, old-fashioned handwriting.

I slowly got used to my new life in the States. We bought a townhouse and had a typical Italian-American life. We ate things I was used to in Europe—sausages, prosciutto, pasta. Concetta was a great cook. She had learned from her mother.

We had meals with my cousins and their wives on Sundays and drank wines we made ourselves. They were okay, not like the ones I had at home in Italy. I still have most of the recipes in the drawers of the desk in my office. Don't hesitate to look through them. It's important for you to go through everything.

The biggest difference from home was the scenery. I missed Italy a lot. I missed the rolling hills and the fresh air, especially after it rained. I missed the roses in the garden and seeing the grapes grow. Those memories started to fade one by one, and I believed I would never see any of that again.

Concetta had never been to Italy. I always told her about Tuscany— the simple life, the winemaking. But she did not really care.

When Roberto was a year and a half, I received a letter from Italy. It was very unexpected, and it contained sad news. My brother, Gabriel, had died in a tractor accident on the farm. He was not married and had no children. I was the one next in line, and I had to take over. My sister had her own life with her own children and their own farm.

I had no choice but to go back.

Your grandmother, however, did not want to come with me right away. She was concerned about taking little Roberto, and she had never been far away from her parents. We decided that I would go first, and she would follow when Roberto was three years old.

I flew back to Italy three weeks later. It was so difficult to leave my wife and child behind, and I was afraid what I might find when I returned. And I was not at all sure if I had made the right decision. But I had missed the land where I was born, and again I had no choice.

When I arrived, I couldn't believe what had become of the estate. The vineyards were neglected, and so was the house and the garden. It was a total disaster. My only thought at that moment was, thank God that our father did not live to see this. And it was good that Concetta and Roberto weren't with me.

I had some money saved, and that came in handy. I wanted to restore the estate and make it livable and comfortable for my wife and child. I hired new people and started from scratch. It was a new beginning for me. My mission was to once again make the best wines of Tuscany.

Here we are, years later!

I'm very proud of you, Erika, and happy that you have followed my wishes so far. How I would have loved to see you living in my house and enjoying the countryside.

I'm sure you will fall in love with Italy. You have Italian blood in you. You are a Germoglio!

Paolo is a very good man. He has been working for me for a long time. You can trust him with your life. The same is true of Bernardo. They promised me that if you decided to stay, they would take care of you, guide you, and help you in every way.

Paolo can teach you a lot about winemaking and about the land. Go to the vineyards with him. Make yourself at home in the cellar. Drink our wines. Let him show you how to taste them properly.

Elisa and Constantina are also great people, as are Doris, Mirella, Santo, and their children. You don't need to worry. They will all welcome you with open arms.

This is the first letter I have written to you, but there will be others. Bernardo will give them to you when the moment is right. Now, enjoy a glass of wine tonight, and have Doris spoil you with her good cooking! I send you my love.

Your grandfather,
Umberto

XV

———

ERIKA SAT THERE STUNNED. Though the explanation of why her grandfather didn't contact her still didn't settle with her, she could almost hear his voice in the letter, as if he was right there, sitting next to her. But how was that possible, when she had only found out of his existence barely a week earlier? Her whole life had changed in that time. And it was clear that it was about to change even more.

She looked around the room. How different this place was from her apartment in New York. The warm colors, the fresh flowers, the welcoming feeling the second she stepped through the door. In New York, the apartment had a gorgeous view, sure, but the rooms were all black, white, and gray. A little sterile, with just paintings to give the place some life.

The clothes in the closets were similarly dull. Craig wore a starched white shirt every day of the week with his gray suits. Her clothes were all black and white. Like her life in New York.

Every day was the same—get up early, work out, take a shower, have coffee, go to the office. In the evening, she would meet Craig for a drink, go out for dinner, go home, go to bed, read a book, and fall asleep. One day was like another. Sometimes, she found it difficult to get out of bed and face the day.

Maybe this is a sign, Erika thought, *that life could be completely different.* For the last week, she had enjoyed getting up in the morning. And when she went to bed, she thought about the next day with a renewed sense of energy and purpose.

She went into the kitchen, where Doris greeted her warmly. "*Ciao, Signora. Com'è andata oggi?*"

"Doris, please, no Italian now. I've got so much to do. I'm going to be here for the next five months, but I need to go to New York right away to arrange things."

Doris looked surprised. "Let me get a glass of wine for you."

"Yes, please."

Erika went outside to think. She wouldn't have to pack clothes. She had a closetful in New York. All she needed was her laptop and phone. A carry-on would be plenty.

She sipped her wine, heard the music playing inside the house, and began to relax. But how would she break the news to Craig regarding her extended stay and all the complex legal aspects? She sighed. At least they would have some time together, but he was not going to be happy. It would be best if she told him over a nice dinner.

Decision made, she went up to shower and change and came back refreshed.

Doris was waiting for her downstairs. "Ms. Erika, Mr. Max came by in the afternoon. He was hoping to see you. He brought you the flowers that are in the living room, and he told me again how much he loved my food. He also said that he bought lots of wine from Hanna in the cantina."

"How thoughtful," Erika said.

Erika walked outside. "Why is the table set for two, Doris? I'm not expecting anyone."

"I know, *Signora*, but you have a guest tonight."

"Who could that be? Max is with the wedding party in Livernano."

"Me!" came a man's voice from down below.

Erika turned and saw Paolo coming up the stairs from the garden. He looked really good—she liked the blue-striped shirt with his blue sweater and jeans. It was hard to believe he didn't have a girlfriend, and she wondered why that was the case. Maybe there was something wrong with him? Oh, what difference did it make? She was engaged!

"Bernardo stopped at the cantina after he dropped you off," said Paolo, "and he told me that you agreed to stay. I wanted to keep you company and celebrate." He held up the bottle of wine he'd kept hidden behind his back.

"With all due respect, Paolo, I really had no other choice, did I!"

"Probably not. But I'm happy anyway. Let's open the bottle of wine, shall we!"

They sat at the table and toasted.

"*Salute!*" said Erika.

"To a great summer!" added Paolo.

It was Friday, and Doris had remembered to buy fresh mussels and prepared them with a white wine sauce. She also served salad, fresh from the garden. Since Paolo was there, Erika told Doris she was free to go home. Who didn't like to leave a little early on a Friday?

The meal was simple and delicious, and the time passed quickly. With fruit and cheese, they opened a second bottle, a Chianti Classico from Livernano, a Riserva.

"Paolo," Erika said, "I'm really enjoying this wine. Can you tell me what the difference is between a regular Chianti and the Riserva?"

"The blend is the same, but the Riserva has to age for at least eighteen months. We let it stay up to twenty-two months in the cellar in small French oak barrels." He gave her a little smile that made her wonder if he was flirting with her, but a moment later, his tone was more matter-of-fact. "Bernardo told me that you will need to go back to talk to your fiancé and organize things in New York. When will you leave?"

"I thought I would go to Florence tomorrow morning and see if I can fly standby. I tried to look for flights after I got back but couldn't find anything. And if I tried to search now, after all the wine, I'd probably end up on a flight to Abu Dhabi."

They both laughed at the idea.

"I tell you what," Paolo said. "I'll drive you to Rome tomorrow. From there, it will be easier to find a flight, and you can probably get a direct one, with no connection."

"But Rome is so far away."

"No, it's only two hours, but we'd have to leave early—around five, since all the flights to the States leave in the morning."

Erika hesitated. "Wow, that *is* early."

"Yes, but if you want to get out tomorrow, that's the best way."

"Okay, Paolo, and thank you!"

"We're the ones who are thanking you, Erika—all of us from Casalvento and Livernano. You're earning a lot of respect by doing this. We know that it's not easy, and many of us thought that you might not agree to stay."

"I thought the same thing myself," Erika said.

Paolo smiled. "Your grandfather had a saying, and today, after enjoying this meal, it's especially good to remember it: One must live in the present, not the past and not the future. The ones living in the past will never have a future, because they can't see the present. *Salute!*"

Now it was Erika's turn to smile. "I like it," she said.

"Now, we should clean up. You'll have to get up early tomorrow."

As Erika helped bring things to the kitchen and watched Paolo load the dishwasher, it struck her how well he knew his way around.

"Did you have dinner here a lot?" she asked.

"Yes, Umberto loved to cook, but he did not really like having a lot of people in his private zone—that is what he called it. But he didn't mind me, and I loved his company. It was fun with him, and I always enjoyed our time together, like I have with you tonight. I learned so much over the years from him. He was the one who helped me with my English and pushed me to go abroad."

"Where did you go?"

"I went to California, to Napa, and I stayed for two years. I worked at a vineyard there and fell in love. I truly thought she was the one, but, as you can see, it did not end happily. So I came back home heartbroken. And now I'm happy I did." After a few awkward seconds, Paolo said, "Santo told me you had a visitor last night for dinner."

"I guess news travels fast," said Erika. "He was just someone also from New York who happened to be part of the wedding party this weekend at Livernano. Why are you asking?"

"No reason. But it's getting late. I'll pick you up at five thirty. You should probably go to bed. Be sure to lock up after me."

"I will. Good night, Paolo."

Erika closed up the house and turned off the lights downstairs. As she got ready for bed and washed her face, she looked in the mirror. *You are engaged*, she scolded. *Yesterday it was Max. Today it's Paolo. Your life is not here—it's with Craig in New York. And tomorrow at this time you will be at home in your apartment. In Craig's arms.*

She could picture his face when he saw her. Why not surprise him? That would make the reunion even sweeter.

She set the alarm and quickly fell asleep.

It seemed like only moments later that the shrill sound woke her. It was still dark outside, but she pushed herself to get out of bed and turn on the coffee maker. While it brewed, she showered and dressed, then sat down with a cup of coffee and used the laptop to check for flights to New York.

There was one leaving Rome at ten, with an open seat in business. Perfect.

At five thirty sharp, Paolo was there with his pickup. She gathered her things and met him downstairs.

"You're in a cheerful mood this morning!" he said, after they had exchanged a greeting.

"Yes, I found a flight. It leaves at ten and arrives just after one, New York time. That's great because it means an easier ride from the airport to the city. And check-in should be easy. I have no luggage."

"You have your passport?"

"Yes, I do!"

"Then *andiamo.*"

There wasn't much traffic at that hour, and they passed the time talking about the cantina, the wine cellar, and Livernano.

"How long are you staying, Erika?" Paolo finally asked.

"I told Bernardo that I would need a week, and he said that was fine. I booked a return flight for next Saturday that arrives in Rome at eight on Sunday morning."

"I'll be there to pick you up."

"Thank you so much, Paolo!"

"*Far niente.*"

"That reminds me," said Erika, "I definitely need to order some books on learning to speak Italian. It's the first thing on my to-do list, which is getting longer all the time. There's a lot to do, but I think I can get it all done in one week. Monday morning, I have to go straight to the office. They'll all be surprised to see me—I have never done anything like this. I'm really not a very spontaneous person."

Paolo glanced at her. "Maybe you are, at least more than you think. Look at everything you've done in just a week."

Soon after, Paolo was pulling up to the terminal. Erika grabbed her laptop and carry-on. "I can handle it from here, Paolo," she told him.

"Okay, then. Have a safe trip, and I'll see you next Sunday." He kissed her on both cheeks.

He got in his truck and drove off, and Erika headed to the check-in counter.

Two hours later, she was in her seat for takeoff. When the flight attendant served lunch, she ordered a glass of Chardonnay. It wasn't like her L'Anima, she thought, then smiled—she was already thinking of it as her wine.

She slept for most of the flight and was almost startled to hear the flight attendant announce that they would be landing in a few minutes.

On the taxi ride home, she began to wonder if she'd done the right thing—Craig wasn't the kind of guy who liked surprises. But it was *her*, his *fiancée*, and not just anybody. He'd likely be thrilled to see her and all this worrying—

Suddenly, the taxi was pulling up to her building, and the doorman was helping her out of the car. "Welcome back, Ms. Germoglio," he said. "How was Europe?"

"Amazingly great!" she found herself saying, with more enthusiasm than she had intended. It *had* been great, she realized as she stepped into the elevator and pushed the button for the thirty-seventh floor.

A little hesitantly, she opened the door to their condo. "Hello, honey. Surprise! I'm home. Craig?"

There was no answer.

This was strange. Where could he be? It was Saturday, so definitely not at the office. She hoped he didn't drive out to the Hamptons, to his parents' house. She tossed her handbag on the sofa. She would shower and freshen up—she wanted to look great when he came back.

A few minutes later, she stepped out of the shower, with a towel wrapped around her head. When she reached for her toothbrush in its usual place, she stopped and stared.

Whose toiletries were those? Whose decidedly *female* toiletries?

She heard the door open and voices in the living room, so she threw on her bathrobe and went into the other room.

"Tiffany?" Erika said. She stood there frozen, barely breathing. No way was she really seeing this. She heard Craig's voice, but it came to her from far away, as if from another planet.

"Erika? What are you doing back? I thought you were in Italy."

"I came to surprise you, to explain what has been going on in Italy and . . . but who cares? You, Tiffany, of all people . . ."

"Erika, it is not what you think! You told me to take care of him."

"Yes, but I didn't expect you to move in with him."

"What are you talking about, Erika? You have this all wrong."

"Tiffany, how stupid do you think I am? What are your toiletries doing here? Explain that, please."

"Erika—" Craig tried to break into the conversation, but Erika silenced him.

"Quite honestly, Craig, there is *nothing* you could say that could explain this. You complained about Tiffany to me, so I would have never guessed . . . and yet, here she is. I guess everything happens for a reason."

Erika closed the door to the bedroom and went to get dressed. It didn't escape her that Tiffany had stood naked in just the same place as she was standing right now. All she could feel was disgust—Craig was waiting for her when she stepped outside the bathroom door, and the sight of his face heightened that emotion.

"So Tiffany left?"

"Yes, she was upset."

"Seriously? *She* is upset? How do you think I feel? I thought you'd be happy to see me. That you'd take me in your arms and kiss me, ask me how I've been. Instead, I find you and Tiffany together."

Craig moved to embrace her. As if.

"Get out of my way, Craig. I need to get my stuff."

"What do you mean, get your stuff?"

"Do you honestly believe I'll stay here?"

"Erika, please forgive me."

"Forgive you? So then you did sleep with her!"

"It wasn't like you think. We both were drunk, and you weren't here, and one thing led to another. It was stupid, a big mistake. I'm sorry, Erika. It will never happen again."

"Oh really? I guess Tiffany travels around with her toiletries wherever she goes." She was practically shouting, and she didn't care. "A big mistake you were planning on repeating today, it seems."

"Erika, I promise! Please believe me. It was only that one time. Please, Erika!"

"Craig, I'm leaving now, and I don't know when I'll be back. I need to think, and I have to be back in Italy in any case for the next five months."

"You need to go back?" Craig stepped closer to her, as if to block her escape.

The thought that he might touch her sent new waves of disgust through her. She felt nauseated.

"Please leave me alone, Craig. I don't really feel like explaining anything to you right now, and I have to get some things together. Just get out of my way!"

"What has gotten into you? Are you *totally* getting crazy? What will my mother think? She's been busy planning the wedding—you have no idea the work she's put in."

Erika took a breath and stood still. She gave Craig the coldest stare she could muster. "Craig, I don't think you get it. There will be no wedding, at least not anytime soon. I'm going back to Italy, and I'll be there for five months. For now, I need to sort things out on my own. I've got to think about my future, here and in Italy. Now, please, Craig, leave me alone."

Craig turned on his heel, and Erika watched as the door shut behind him. Did that really just happen? First, him and Tiffany. Then her throwing him out so she could pack her things—she couldn't believe it. She blinked, willing her eyes to focus and the dizziness to subside. Maybe she was getting a little crazy?

What was she going to do now? And where should she go? She took a deep breath and started throwing things into a suitcase.

Part TWO

XVI

---

*S*TILL TOO NUMB TO PROCESS everything that had just occurred, Erika filled her suitcase with things she thought she might need in Italy, then went into the bathroom and tossed Tiffany's toiletries into the trash. Finally, she stopped to take a breath and contemplate her next move. Where could she go?

Todd had been a close friend since college. He and his partner, James, had an apartment in SoHo, and they had never let her down. She certainly needed them now.

She took her suitcase and her laptop and went downstairs to get a taxi.

"The corner of Mulberry and Hester Street, please," she told the driver. Then she pulled out her phone and called Todd.

Luckily, he answered right away. "How are you, darling? How's Italy?"

"I'm in New York, Todd."

"You're back already?"

"That's a rather long and complicated story. Where are you?"

"I'm having a drink at the Rooftop bar with James. I've been busy working on an apartment uptown. Driving me insane. People with too much money are crazy. Please promise me you will not become one of them after you are married."

"As of today, I'm not sure if there will be a wedding."

"Whoa. What are you saying?"

"I'm in a cab on my way to your apartment right now—I'll explain once there. Can the doorman let me in? And can I stay, maybe a couple days?"

"Of course, darling. We'll just finish this drink and be right there."

"Thanks, Todd. I knew I could count on you."

An hour later, the three of them were sitting in the couple's tastefully decorated apartment, drinking vodka tonics—not really Erika's drink of choice, but she needed something stronger than wine as she spilled out her sorrows. Todd and James hung on every word as she told them about her unknown grandfather, her inheritance, the beauty of Casalvento, and the stipulations in the will. When she got to her discovery about Craig and Tiffany, there was no holding back her tears.

Todd handed her a box of tissues, and both of her friends waited quietly for her to compose herself.

"You know, guys," Erika finally said, "there's a silver lining. Craig has made it easier for me to go back to Tuscany. There's a lot to do and think over, and I guess I can stop worrying about the wedding! Can I stay with you until I go back? It won't be too long—I have a ticket for next Saturday."

Todd and James chimed in together. "Of course, darling. Stay as long as you wish."

"I'll put your things in the spare bedroom," Todd added. "Are you hungry? We could order something for dinner."

"I'm just tired," Erika replied, putting her phone on silent. "I think I'll go to bed . . . but maybe I'll have one more vodka tonic."

"Coming right up," said Todd. "What about you, James?"

"Yes, that sounds good."

As Erika took her drink, she glanced at her phone. She didn't want to speak to Craig, but she was curious to see how many times he had called. She was surprised to see there were no missed messages.

"Can you believe it?" she said. "Craig never even called to apologize."

"Darling, you know he was never my favorite. I only designed your apartment because you convinced me to. I never liked his arrogance," Todd said. "You know his reputation—he's slick as an eel. And he always bossed you around."

"I didn't like him," said James, "but it's still hard to imagine him doing something like this."

"I know," said Erika, "and not even one phone call to say he's sorry."

"He'll call," said James. "You'll see. But for now, don't think too much about it."

"That's not so easy. I lost my fiancé today along with my best friend and business partner."

"She was never your friend, so nothing's been lost. A friend doesn't do what she did . . . I don't care *how* drunk they were, Erika."

"But how am I going to keep the business going?"

Todd tried to reassure her. "You said she's already taking care of your clients with Molly, right? And it's definitely in Tiffany's interest that the company remains a success, right?"

Erika nodded thoughtfully.

"Look," Todd continued, "tomorrow's Sunday. Go to the office and check out how things are going. Go through the books while no one's there. Assess. Then, on Monday, talk to Molly. You don't need to go into gruesome details—just make it clear that she has to report to you if she thinks anything is going wrong. Have her send you a weekly update every Friday. That should be okay for the next five months."

Erika finished her drink. "You're right. I just need to take things one step at a time. And now my first step is to get my tired body into bed. Thanks again, guys—I love you both. I'll see you in the morning."

The smell of fresh coffee woke Erika up the next morning. She put on a robe and went into the kitchen, where the table was set for breakfast. Todd and James had made pancakes, her favorite. She was hungry, too. She looked at the two of them, grateful to have friends like these.

They were so well suited to each other. Todd Harrison—skinny as a stick, even though he ate like a horse—was of average height but with a nice head of brown hair that set off his green eyes. And, like all designers, he dressed really stylishly—colorfully but stylishly. Blond, blue-eyed James Cooper was taller, six foot something, with a perennial suntan and muscles that were the result of regular gym workouts. His office uniform was invariably a tailored suit that made him look like a poster boy for Brooks Brothers.

Todd had more interior design clients than he could handle, and James was a rising star in the trading world.

They lingered over breakfast and coffee, until Todd said, "I'm headed out to meet some clients, but James could come with you to the office if you're still planning to go in."

"That's a good idea," said Erika. "I just hope Tiffany isn't in today!"

Todd laughed. "She doesn't strike me as a work-on-Sunday kind of a girl. And besides, you'll have your private security detail," he said, winking at James.

Thirty minutes later, the three of them were sharing an Uber heading uptown. Erika and James got out at 65th and Park and took the elevator to Erika's office. She unlocked the door, turned off the alarm, and breathed a small sigh of relief. No one was there.

"James, you can sit in my office while I check the mail—this shouldn't take long. I need to see how far she's gotten with the Levine project."

"That's fine, I have email to check," he said. "Take your time."

The paperwork was right there on Molly's desk, and Erika paged through it. "This all looks good," she said as she went to her desk. One by one, she opened the envelopes that were stacked there. Nothing really urgent—she'd go through them more carefully with Molly on Monday.

"All done, James. We can go."

She turned the alarm back on and locked the doors, but as they got into the elevator, she had another thought. "Do you feel like going shopping with me? I need some comfortable clothes for Italy, and it would be fun to have a fashion consultant for this afternoon."

"It would be my pleasure," James told her.

Two hours later, they were walking out of Bloomingdale's burdened with several shopping bags. "Thank you, James," Erika said as they headed downtown. "That was great. I feel like a new me."

Back at the apartment, she examined her purchases and changed into jeans and a T-shirt, adding a spritz of just-bought perfume. The scent of roses and thyme reminded her of Tuscany.

"James, can we have some wine?" she asked. "Is there a bottle of white? If not, I'll run and get one."

He handed her a glass and peered at her closely. "You seem better today, Erika."

She smiled. "I guess yesterday I used up my tears. Now I need to focus on me. I've got to figure out what I want and need. Life has certainly thrown me a curveball, but I think in the end I'll be okay. You know what, James . . . why don't you and Todd come and visit me this summer? I could show you Casalvento and Livernano, and we could all explore Tuscany together."

Todd happened to open the apartment door at just that moment. "What do I hear? Did someone say Tuscany?"

"Yes," Erika answered. "You guys have to come. Plus, you can help me decorate the place a little. What do you think?"

James and Todd stared at each other for a second, then turned to Erika.

"I need to go to Europe anyway," said Todd, "to shop for antiques for my clients."

"You'll love it. I promise." Erika suddenly remembered she'd taken photos. She got her phone and scrolled through the pictures.

"Oh, darling," Todd said. "It looks amazing, and it sounds like you're beginning to fall in love with the place."

Erika hesitated. "Yes and no. My life has been in New York, and now . . . all I can say is I'm confused, but it is an amazing place."

"When do you want us there?" asked James.

"I'll be there all summer long. Come whenever you want, and stay as long as you can. I bet Paolo could help you find just the right antiques, Todd. He knows everyone."

"Who is Paolo?" James asked.

"Oh, nobody. He's just the winemaker and looks after the property."

"Oh *really?*" Todd teased her. "*Just* the winemaker?"

"He *is* kind of cute," Erika said.

"Oh, darling, maybe your summer has more in store for you than you know."

XVII

———

O N MONDAY, IT WAS ERIKA'S TURN to get up early. She set the table for Todd and James, who were still asleep, and sat down with coffee to make a list of everything she had to do before she left on Saturday.

First, contact the lawyer. She scrolled through her contacts list to find Peter Schaffenhausen, her father's lawyer, but it was not even eight in the morning, still too early to call. Meanwhile, she saw that there was nothing on her phone from Craig—not a single text or call. "Forget him for now," she told herself, speaking the words out loud so that they would somehow sink in. "Stay focused and get everything done."

It was a good time to go to her office—if she moved quickly, she could get there before Tiffany arrived. She wasn't exactly relishing that meeting.

Erika showered and got dressed and was heading out the door when Todd got up.

"I'm going to the office," Erika told him. "Can I meet you and James for drinks at the Rooftop after work? Maybe around six?"

"Sure, darling. Have a great day!"

By a quarter to nine, she was sitting at her desk in the still-empty office.

Fifteen minutes later, Molly walked in. "Erika, what a surprise! I thought you were in Italy! Did you get everything organized? Do you have pictures? I'd love to see them."

"Later, Molly. We've got a lot to go over in the next few days. I leave again by the end of the week."

Molly set her bag down, a look of disbelief on her face. "What? You're leaving again? Why?"

"Yes, and this time for much longer. I'll explain everything, Molly, but first can you help me get things in good shape? How is Mr. Levine's company doing?"

"I think quite well, Erika. But you can't keep me in suspense. What happened in Italy that you have to go back?"

"Okay, Molly. Here's the short version: The person who left me Casalvento was actually my grandfather."

"Your grandfather? I thought you told me he disappeared."

"Yes, he did. It turns out he went back to Italy. I'm still finding out more about his story, but that will take time. Also, one of the stipulations of the will is that, before I can do anything with the estate, I have to stay in Italy for a number of months. So you can understand that I'll need your help."

"Of course, Erika. I'll do whatever I can. But what about the wedding?"

"That's on hold for now," Erika said carefully, not wanting to share any other details for the moment. "Molly, you'll be my eyes and ears while I'm gone, so I need to know that I can trust you. First, I'd like you to send me an update every Friday. And you'll be taking on more responsibility, so if you need to hire someone to do some of the routine work, you can do that."

"Thank you, Erika. I won't let you down."

"You're welcome! Now let's get to work."

An hour later, Erika realized the rest of the office was still quiet.

"Molly, where's Tiffany?"

"Oh, I forgot to mention that. She called me this morning and said she wasn't feeling well. She was going to work from home."

What a coward, Erika thought. "Too bad," she said. "I hope she feels better tomorrow." She changed the subject. "Molly, I need to make some calls. Can you please close the door?"

Taking a deep breath, Erika dialed the lawyer's office, and his secretary put him on the line.

"Erika, how are you? And how was Italy?"

"Well, Peter, as I'm sure you know, it was full of surprises."

"Erika, I've been as surprised as you. All I know is that not long ago I was contacted by Bernardo Morselli, who said he was a lawyer for Umberto Germoglio. He said your grandfather had been putting money into an account for you here in New York since your parents died. Your grandfather wanted to transfer the funds to your account upon his death."

"You know, Peter," Erika said, "this has all been so confusing. I just wish I'd gotten to know my grandfather years ago. I would have loved to have some family after my parents died. And now . . ." She choked back tears—now was not the time, and she would hold it together.

"What's going on, Erika?"

"You know about the stipulations in the will, right? That I've got to stay in Italy for five months? Before I could do that, though, I needed to come back and make arrangements for my company and also explain things to Craig. We'd just begun to plan our wedding for September. Bernardo said I could take a week, so I decided to surprise Craig. Instead, *I* got the surprise. I found him with my best friend and business partner, Tiffany."

"Erika . . ." Peter paused, seemingly at a loss for words. "I'm so very sorry. What can I do to help?"

She pulled herself together. "Well, I was told by Bernardo that you now have access to the account my grandfather set up. Can I come to your office tomorrow to go over those details? Around eleven?"

"Of course. We can have lunch afterward—and meet with the bank manager, too."

"Thanks, I would like that."

Erika spent the rest of the day touching base with clients and working out plans for the next few months. By five, she was ready to leave the office behind. She got a taxi and headed to the Rooftop restaurant to meet Todd and James. She was the first one there, and she took a minute to check her phone. Craig had called while it was on silent but hadn't left a message.

"What white wine do you have by the glass?" she asked the waiter, who had just walked up.

"We have a nice Pinot Grigio from Friuli, Italy."

Minutes later he was back with her drink. He waited until she'd taken a sip and nodded her approval.

"Are you expecting more people?" he asked.

Before she could answer, she spotted Todd and James and waved them over.

Todd pointed to Erika's glass. "I'll have that," he said.

"So will I," echoed James. "Or better yet, can you bring us a bottle?"

"So, darling," Todd asked as he settled into a chair, "how was your day?"

"I got a lot done. And Molly's doing a great job. I don't think I realized how capable she was. I'm glad she's there. And guess what? Tiffany never showed up today. She called Molly's cell and said she was coming down with something."

"What a coward," said Todd. "Did Craig call?"

"Yes, but he didn't leave a message. You think I should call him?"

"No!" Todd and James answered almost in the same breath.

"Don't call him back this week," Todd went on. "Send him a text telling him that you're busy, that you need to get the office organized, and that you'll contact him when you're back in Italy."

"You know what, you're right." She toasted to her friends. "Cheers!"

"Why don't we just stay here and order food," James suggested. "It's a beautiful evening, and it's nice to sit outside."

"Sure," she agreed. "We could start by sharing a *pizza margherita*. And we should get a bottle of red—a Chianti Classico from Tuscany."

"Look at Erika, our new wine connoisseur," laughed Todd.

"I learned a lot in my first week," she agreed. "Did you know that for a Chianti, you have to have a minimum of eighty percent Sangiovese grapes? *And* your property has to have the right to call it Chianti Classico."

"I'm impressed!" said James.

"Who taught you that?" Todd asked.

"Paolo," Erika replied with a smile.

"We need to meet this Paolo," Todd said.

After the pizza came a spinach salad, spiced shishito peppers, sliders, and crispy fries.

"Guys, I can't eat any more," said Erika.

"No worries, darling," Todd said. "We can burn some calories on the walk home."

"Sure, Todd, the three-minute walk will do a lot!" Erika laughed and looked at her friends. She was lucky to have them. "So, did you think about Tuscany? Will you come?"

"How does the first of June sound?" Todd asked. "James's birthday is the fourteenth, and we can all celebrate together. We'll invite Paolo, too!"

"Todd, you are so bad!" Erika said.

"Erika, darling, what else is new?"

They were still laughing and joking by the time they got back to the apartment. Reluctant for the evening to end, Erika and Todd had a tequila nightcap before turning in—with James shaking his head at them. The next morning, she woke up with her head spinning and her stomach queasy. What she needed now was an aspirin or two and a cup of strong black coffee.

James was already at the kitchen stove with an apron wrapped around his boxer shorts. "Good morning," he said cheerily. "A little hungover, are we? I'm making you and Todd my special hangover omelet. You'll see how fast you feel better."

Todd emerged from their bedroom and sank into a chair.

"What happened to you, Todd?" Erika asked. "You look like a truck ran over you."

"Good morning," he replied. "Coffee, please, and your killer omelet, James."

After quickly throwing some ingredients together and a few minutes at the stove, James put the omelets on the table. "Here you are," he said. "You two need to learn when to stop drinking."

He came back with the coffee as Todd and Erika each slowly took a bite.

"James, what's in here?" Erika said, perking up. "This is really spicy."

"My secret. You don't want to know. Just eat it, and you'll feel so much better."

"I'm not going into the office today," Todd said. "I'll work from home, and, tonight, no tequila!"

"Well, I have to go to work," said James. "The market opens up in two hours."

"Todd told me about your new firm," said Erika. "How does it feel to be the new star in the trading world?"

"I can't complain! But it's hard work to build up a company like ours. We've recruited some great talent, and we're now in ten states, but there's still a lot to do. I'll tell you more later. I really have to get ready and go."

A half hour later, Erika and Todd were still hanging around the kitchen table, commiserating about Craig.

"You two are still here?" asked James as he was about to leave. "Don't you need to get going, Erika? Aren't you meeting your lawyer?"

"Yes, you're right," she said, slowly getting herself showered and together. *No more tequila,* she vowed.

As she walked to the corner to hail a cab, she had the eerie feeling that someone was following her, but when she checked around, all she saw was a person walking in the other direction. Maybe the hangover had made her paranoid.

She raised her hand, and a taxi stopped. As she got in, she took another look around, but there was no one. *Get a hold of yourself*, she thought. First, there was someone watching her in Italy, and now here. What was happening to her? She considered how many things had changed in her life, and how quickly. She missed her mother, who always encouraged her to go with her instincts, to listen to her inner self and not overthink everything. But what would she have said about Craig and Tiffany? She was so sure she'd found her soulmate in Craig and that they had the perfect life together. That she'd have the perfect wedding. Did he ever really love her? There were so many questions still to answer.

XVIII

———

*A*T ELEVEN SHARP, ERIKA WALKED into Peter Schaffenhausen's office. The lawyer came from around his desk and gave her a hug.

"Erika, it's so nice to see you. Considering what you're going through, you look radiant."

"Thank you, Peter. I appreciate that."

Holding her at arm's length, he went on. "So, tell me. How was Italy? What was your first impression?"

"I honestly had no idea what to expect. I assumed I'd go to Italy and sell the place. Obviously, that did not turn out as planned. I was amazed—I'm still amazed—at what my grandfather built with Casalvento and Livernano. And the people that work there welcomed me with open arms."

"So, you liked it?"

"Peter, what is there not to like? And after what happened with Craig and Tiffany, I'll be very happy to go back to Italy. I want to find out what my grandfather was like and what my father missed out on by not knowing him. There must be answers."

"I'm sure there are, Erika. Everyone has a reason for what they do. In the meantime, we need to find out about the bank account your grandfather set up. I had it transferred to the bank we've used in the past, and we have an appointment with the manager after lunch."

An hour and a half later, they were sitting in leather chairs across a heavy wooden desk from a rather professorial-looking banker. Very politely, he went over the details of Erika's accounts. First, there was the trust fund her mother and father had set up. That had about $800,000 and would become available to her soon. She already had access to everything else she'd inherited and had sold the family home years ago. James was over-seeing that money.

"Now, let's talk about this other account," said the banker. "The one set up by Umberto Germoglio now contains half a million dollars."

Erika involuntarily raised her hand to her mouth. She stared across the desk, speechless, doing the math in her head. With her trust fund and her grandfather's account, she was worth close to $1.3 million.

Finally, she managed to say, "What do I do now?"

"As I said," the banker answered, "the trust money you can't touch yet. But you can withdraw funds from your other account whenever you want."

Struggling to come to terms with what this meant for her future, Erika fought back tears.

"Aren't you happy, Erika?" Peter asked.

"Of course, but it's just so . . . so unexpected, that's all!"

The three of them shook hands, and as Erika left the bank, her mind was racing—she needed to talk to James.

"Erika," Peter said, giving her a hug. "If you need anything, anything at all, please let me know. And, Erika, I wouldn't mention the money to Craig or Tiffany."

She smiled ruefully. "I know—I'm not stupid. Thanks again, Peter."

"Have a safe trip back."

As her cab made its way downtown to Todd's apartment, Erika watched the streetscape. The storefronts, the people rushing wherever they were going . . . it was all so familiar to her. She was part of it, and it was part of her life. Could she really let it all go?

She got out at Todd's building and walked into the lobby, only to find yet another surprise.

"Tiffany! What are you doing here?"

Erika tried to walk past the other young woman, but Tiffany put her hand on Erika's arm to stop her. Repulsed, Erika shrank back.

"Erika, please! Can we just go over to the Rooftop for a drink? I really need to talk to you!"

"What is there to talk about? For me, it's simple. You were my best friend, and you slept with the person I was supposed to marry in the fall."

"I want to explain," Tiffany pleaded. "I couldn't face you on Monday in the office, but I wanted you to know what happened."

"What *happened?* Let me guess. As always, you took the easy route. You break up with your boyfriend and take the first new opportunity that presents itself. "

"Please, Erika, give me a chance to explain. Come have a drink with me."

"I've had a long day—a drink with you is the last thing I need now."

"I've waited all day to talk to you," Tiffany went on. "I saw you leaving here this morning, and I wanted to talk then, but when I saw you going up the street, I lost my nerve and turned around."

"So that was you this morning," Erika said. "I'm not losing my mind after all. Look, Tiffany, I'll have dinner with you tomorrow. Meet me at Milo's uptown at seven. But no games and no Craig."

"Understood. Thank you," Tiffany said.

Erika left her standing there as she got into the elevator. She was still trying to calm herself as she opened the door to her friends' apartment.

Todd was at his desk, poring over plans for his new design project. Looking up, he said, "Hi, darling. How was your day?"

"You won't believe it," Erika said. "First, I met with my lawyer, and there's a lot to tell you about that. And then, just now . . . Tiffany was waiting for me downstairs. She wants to talk."

"And?"

"I agreed to meet her for dinner tomorrow. Is James back yet?"

"No, he'll be back around six thirty. I thought we would stay in and order pizza."

"What a splendid idea."

Erika went to change into some new sweatpants and a T-shirt. Craig had always hated sweatpants—even her nicer and more feminine pairs fell under his scrutiny. But that didn't matter now.

"Okay, I'm ready for a glass of wine," she said as she came back to the living room.

"Sure, darling. What should it be, white or red?"

"Red, please!"

"I hope this 2012 Napa Cabernet will be up to your new standards," Todd joked.

It was close to seven when James came through the door. He tossed his suit jacket onto the sofa and dropped down next to it. "I'm pooped. How was your day, dear?"

Todd started to reply, but James broke in. "Not yours—Erika's!"

"You won't believe it," she said, filling him in on Tiffany and their agreement to meet the next day.

"That's a good idea, Erika. You two need to work this out somehow if you're to continue working together. And I'm sure she also needs to tell you her side of the story. See what she has to say."

"You're right, I guess. But there's more. I also need your advice on a financial matter."

She told them what had happened in the lawyer's office and at the bank.

"Your life is getting more and more exciting every day," said James.

"I think it's wonderful," added Todd. "I love it."

James went to change. "Can you be a dear and order our favorite pizza? No anchovies."

"Sure," said Erika, smiling.

"Not you, Erika!" said James, sharing the laugh. "You still count as a guest, for at least another day!"

A half hour later, they were putting slices on their plates and clinking wine glasses.

"I wanted to thank you again for letting me camp out here this week," Erika told them. "Now, in all seriousness, James, what should I do with the money?"

"Maybe you should buy some more clothes," suggested Todd.

Erika rolled her eyes.

"Do you need any extra money right now?" asked James.

"No, not really. I might need some when I get back to Italy, but there's no way to know yet. Having these financial cushions, though, will certainly make my life easier."

"I'll tell you what—I'll put together some options for you, and you can think about them when you're back in Italy. You don't have to do anything right away. Okay?"

"Perfect, James. I knew I could count on you."

"Do you guys feel like watching a movie?" asked Todd.

"Yes, but I think I've had enough drama and action for one day," said Erika. "How about a romance?"

"There's *Under the Tuscan Sun*," Todd said. "That seems appropriate!"

They never got to the ending, though, all three of them falling asleep on the sofa. Erika woke up during the credits and slowly made her way to bed. As she drifted off again, all she could think of was how grateful she was to have friends like these.

She woke up the next morning still groggy. What was on her list for the day? she wondered. Oh, yes . . . Tiffany. She dragged herself to the bathroom, brushed her teeth, and took a good look in the mirror. She was a mess, and there was no way she could meet Tiffany looking the way she did. She needed something . . . maybe a facial or a massage. Or maybe she would splurge on both. She tended to get busy with work and neglect self-care, but it wasn't every day that her engagement was broken off in the midst of handling two new estates overseas! She had to stop for a moment and slow down.

Two hours later, she was in a dark room having all the kinks in her muscles massaged out. As she waited for her facial, she picked up a travel magazine. Tuscany was on the cover. How funny—that was where she'd be next week. And for the next five months. Who could have imagined that two weeks ago?

There was plenty of time before dinner, and she didn't want to go to the office. Instead, she window-shopped her way up the east side, stopping in at Chanel and Louis Vuitton but not buying anything. She used the time to think about what she would do when she met Tiffany. What could she say that would convey how betrayed and hurt she felt?

As Erika was about to enter the restaurant, she heard Tiffany's voice calling her name. Once, they would have hugged. But not now. They greeted each other with a simple hello.

"Do you want to have a drink at the bar," Tiffany asked, "or do you want to go straight to the table?"

"Let's just go to the table."

They sat in uncomfortable silence as the waiter brought menus and took drink orders. Finally, Tiffany took the lead. "You look good, Erika. Italy must agree with you."

"Thanks, but you look tired."

"I haven't slept well, Erika. I'm sorry. I was wrong, I know. I betrayed our friendship, and I also put our business partnership at risk. What more can I say?"

"I don't know, Tiffany. I've lost a fiancé and a friendship all at once. How do you think I feel? Mostly, I'm disappointed. How long have we known each other, Tiffany? Ten years? Twelve? We shared our deepest secrets. Whenever you called, or needed me, I was there."

"Erika, I swear to you I will never see or talk to Craig again. I promise!"

Erika stared across the table, weighing Tiffany's words, reluctant to believe them. "Let's order," she finally said, steeling herself for what she had to say.

"Tiffany, when I think back to everything we shared . . . birthdays, ski trips, special getaways, it's hard for me to forgive you for what happened. You betrayed my trust. I haven't even heard from Craig. But, you know, I'm okay with that right now. Italy is a new opportunity for me to learn about my history and myself, and I'm going to grab it and see what comes. For now, I don't really want to talk any more about the personal side of things. But I do need to ask you to take care of our business while I'm away."

"How long will you be gone?"

"Until I'm ready to come back," said Erika, not wanting to reveal any further details.

"Can I come visit you? When things settle down?"

"I don't think that's a good idea. Let's just take it step by step."

As they finished their meal, Erika got up. "You can get the bill, Tiffany. I've got to go. My friends are waiting for me."

She looked back as she left and saw that Tiffany was still sitting in the same place, crying quietly. She felt sorry for her, but she also didn't really feel that bad. She also knew the two of them would never be close again. That chapter was definitely over.

James and Todd were waiting for her with a glass of wine when she got back, curious to hear what had happened.

"I love you guys for being there for me, but I really don't think I can talk any more tonight," Erika said. "I'll tell you more in the morning." She took the wine into the bedroom and sipped it as the emotion of the dinner finally hit her and tears rolled down her cheeks. She would be happy to leave New York for a while.

Erika was up early the next morning and once again sat at the kitchen table with a cup of coffee and her to-do list. There wasn't that much more to do. She walked over to the window and looked down at the city scene. People were going to work, walking dogs, stopping to talk to friends. A few weeks earlier, she'd been a part of that scene, but now it seemed very distant. She was ready to go back to Italy.

Saturday seemed to come quickly. That morning she stood in the foyer surrounded by five bags of varying sizes, hugging Todd and James goodbye. "I guess I overdid it a bit in the luggage department," she told them, "but I've got everything I could possibly need." She ticked off the contents—books on winemaking and learning Italian, lots of new clothes and shoes, a few keepsakes. "I'll see you in June!" she sang as she walked out the door. She wanted to leave them with the feeling that she was strong and would be okay.

Before long, she was sitting in the airport, looking at the planes outside the window. *Okay,* she thought. *I might as well text Craig before I leave.* She began to type: *I hope this text finds you stressed out, lonely, and lost . . .*

"That's ridiculous," she said to herself. "Make it short." She started again: *Craig, I've gotten my affairs in order. On my way back to Europe. Will contact you later next week.*

She stared at the message for a while, then pressed send.

The last three weeks had presented her with more challenges than she'd had in the last thirty years of her life. She loved this city, but she needed to let whatever was going to happen take its course. She was looking forward to being back at Casalvento.

Goodbye, New York. Goodbye, Craig. And hello, Italy.

XIX

———

At the rome airport, Erika had collected her luggage, cleared customs, and found a porter to help her to the exit when she heard someone call her name. Max was standing in the check-in line for New York, and he waved at her. She asked the porter to wait a few minutes, and she walked over to talk to her friend.

"Erika! So great to see you. What are you doing here?" Max asked.

"I just came from New York. I guess you must be taking my plane back to the city."

"I didn't know that you were going back so soon."

"Well, a lot changed very quickly—basically overnight—and I had to go back to take care of things. It looks like I'll stay in Tuscany for some time, and I've come to the conclusion that I don't really mind. By the way, I never had the chance to thank you for the flowers. They were lovely."

"My pleasure—I'm glad you like them."

"And how was the wedding at Livernano and your time at the Amalfi coast? I can see you got some sun."

"The wedding was amazing. What a gorgeous property you own! It was romantic, the food was delicious, and so was the wine, plus it was sweeter because I knew the owner."

There was no more time to talk. Max had to check in, and Erika had gotten a text from Paolo that he was waiting for her outside.

As she walked to the exit, though, she thought how handsome and confident Max seemed and what a crazy coincidence it was that their paths should cross again. Under other circumstances, who knew what might have happened? But she certainly didn't need any kind of remote romance. The situation with Craig was problematic enough. And she was still trying to figure out what to think about Paolo.

At that moment, she saw him leaning next to a big black car, and she headed over to him. He laughed when he saw her mountain of luggage, then gave her a hug and a kiss on both cheeks before loading the bags into the trunk.

"Thanks for picking me up, Paolo."

"*Con piacere, cara.* I'm glad I brought your grandfather's car to pick you up. I thought it would be appropriate, but it's handy that it has such a big trunk."

"This is his car?"

"Yes, it was his treasure. It's a 1962 Lincoln Continental. He took great care of it—it was his baby."

"It's beautiful. Believe it or not, I've never ridden in a car that was older than me."

"Well, there is a first time for everything! But how was your week, Erika? Did you get everything taken care of?"

"Yes, I was busy, and the time flew by," she said, not quite ready to share everything that had transpired.

"How did it go at the winery?" she asked. "Has it been busy?"

"It's all good," he said. "The hotel's filling up, and Constantina booked another wedding for later in October. Hanna is doing well with direct sales. Elisa is getting all the paperwork ready for you. We also started to work on the outstanding permits. I asked the real estate agent, William Gotthold, to come to Livernano and Casalvento so I could show him around. He wants to meet you."

"Paolo, I'm impressed. It sounds like you had a busy and productive week too."

When the car finally pulled through the gate and up to the house a couple of hours later, Mirella, Santo, Luca, Robby, and Doris were all lined up to meet her. Suddenly, Erika felt a wave of emotion pass through her—this was home now, and she was happy to be here with all these people.

"*Benvenuti*, Signora Erika," she heard on all sides as she shared hugs and kisses.

When she walked inside, there were fresh flowers everywhere and the welcoming aroma of Doris's cooking.

"*Grazie, grazie tutti.*" Erika tried out the phrases she'd been practicing. "*Sono felice di essere tornata qui.*"

Paolo looked at her appraisingly. "Now it's my turn to be impressed."

"Thank you," she said. "I guess the CDs and books I bought will pay off. I'll try some lessons, too. But right now I need to freshen up."

She ran upstairs and washed her hands and face, and by the time she came back down, the car was unloaded and everyone besides Paolo and Doris had gone.

It occurred to her that she hadn't brought anything back for anyone from the States.

Why didn't I think of that? she wondered, *especially for Robby.* She turned to Doris. "Could you please help me unpack my luggage? I brought back a whole wardrobe from New York—a new style for the countryside. It will be fun to organize it together."

"Of course. And I thought you might be hungry. I prepared something for you to eat. Just a few *antipasti*, with our own cherry tomatoes and a small plate of pasta pesto."

"Super, because I'm starving! I didn't eat anything on the plane. And can I have a glass of our white wine with it?"

Erika noticed Paolo standing in the kitchen. She'd completely forgotten about him.

"Oh, Paolo, thank you so much for picking me up today. That was very nice of you, and I can't believe how well the car drove. Do you want to join me?" she added. "Doris made pasta pesto."

"Not today, but thank you. My family is waiting for me. Remember, Sunday is family day! Here are your car keys," he went on. "We usually park it in the garage below the entrance to the cantina. But I think from now on it should stay here with you."

"Thank you, Paolo."

"Okay, then, I'll see you tomorrow. But you can take it easy. We have no appointments planned. We thought you'd need a day to recuperate."

"That was thoughtful, Paolo. Thank you again. And I've been thinking . . .

maybe this week you can start to show me around Tuscany, and we can have dinner somewhere close by."

"*Con piacere.* I would love to, Erika. *A domani.* See you tomorrow."

"*A domani,*" she replied, then turned to Doris. "Can you bring the food outside? I'm starving."

Erika sat down on the patio. As she sipped her wine and started on the *antipasti,* she finally began to relax. So much had happened in such a short time, and it was all due to someone she'd never met.

"Grandpa, I will make you proud," she said quietly. "The money you gave me will go toward the property to continue your legacy. What you've done for me took foresight, and I'm very grateful." She lifted her glass to the sky and promised to visit his grave.

Doris came out from the kitchen to refill her glass.

"How I missed your cooking, Doris. This is delicious."

Afterward, while Doris cleared the table, Erika went upstairs to shower and change. She put on a pair of jeans and a sweater, thinking, *Oh, if Craig could see me now!*

But she caught herself—why should she care what Craig might think? She needed to put him out of her mind.

As she came back down, she decided that a walk would do her good, but her cell phone was buzzing. Craig. She debated for a moment on whether to answer or not, but decided she would have to confront him sooner or later. It might as well be now.

She picked it up and heard, "Erika, how are you? How was your trip?"

"Everything went smoothly. Did you get my text?"

"No. What did it say?"

"That's strange," Erika said. "I sent it yesterday before I boarded the plane."

"I'll check," Craig answered. "But I missed you! I stayed away last week because I knew you needed space and time to get things organized. But I really wanted to talk to you."

She answered him with silence. The truth was, she had not wanted to talk with him at all. And she didn't want to now.

"Erika, are you still there? Please talk to me. I'm so sorry. I didn't want anything like this to happen."

"Maybe not, Craig," Erika finally said. "But it did, and with my best friend and business partner. I can't just close my eyes and pretend that it never happened. As I told you back at the apartment and in that text you say you never saw, I need time to think. And, quite frankly, I'm beginning to believe that maybe you and I are not the right match for each other, that we only built our relationship on convenience."

"That's not true. I love you, Erika."

"Really, Craig? Do you really love me?"

"You know I do. I've been with you from the moment your parents died."

"Yes, I know that. But what does love mean to you?"

He didn't answer, and they both were silent for a moment.

Then Erika broke in. "Craig, I just got back from New York. I have work to do here for the next five months, and that will give me time to think about us. You should do the same! Goodbye for now."

She took a deep breath and played over the conversation in her head. What she needed was a walk. She would go up to the chapel, and perhaps that would help to clear her head.

She was almost there when she realized she'd forgotten the keys. Oh, well, there was always next time.

She went through the gate, paused to look at Monk Monk's grave, and stopped at the front of the building. From there the view was spectacular. She could see the cantina below and a vista that extended to the mountains. Beyond that? She could imagine Siena and eventually the ocean. The colors were so vibrant. Her eyes took in all the green, and she breathed in the smell of the flowers and trees. The sound of the crickets added to the perfect harmony of nature all around her. If only her life was like that!

But harmony would have to wait, and she guessed it might come, eventually. In the meantime, she needed to know more of Tuscany. There was so much here to explore—she wanted to see Florence and visit the Uffizi, Michelangelo's *David*, the Accademia, and the Duomo. Go to Siena, Pisa, and San Gimignano.

She could have done all that with Craig. What a liar he was! She was sure he had received her text. She was so mad at him that she could hardly think straight. And all of this made her wonder if he had been unfaithful to her before. She knew Todd never trusted him at all, and now clearly his intuition had been spot on.

It was hard to believe that she had been with Craig for thirteen years. That was a long time. So, yes, it was time to rethink their relationship. She wasn't the same person she was when she met him. In fact, she wasn't even the same person she was two weeks ago. And she wasn't used to being by herself.

Perhaps her grandfather was sending her a sign that life had something different in store for her.

Erika looked at the chapel and started to cry in spite of herself.

"Dear Grandpa," she said quietly, "help me make the right decisions. I need you, even if I know I'm strong enough to do this. I need help remembering how strong I was in New York. That I can be that way here, too."

She wiped away her tears. Yes. She could do this! And she would.

She closed the wooden gate and hurried back to the house feeling stronger and more confident.

XX

---

*O*N MONDAY MORNING, Erika was determined to show off her new wardrobe style. She put on blue jeans, a white T-shirt with the Casalvento logo, and sneakers and made her way to the cantina. The stone-paved path took her through the trees and vineyards to where Santo was on a small tractor between the rows of grapes.

She stopped for a moment to inhale the fresh air and give herself a little pep talk. She would take one day at a time, and she would start writing a daily log, as she used to when she started her business. That would help her when the time came to make some decisions about Casalvento and Livernano.

Hanna was not at the counter when Erika walked in, but Elisa was already behind her desk.

"Good morning, Elisa."

"*Buongiorno, Signora.* Welcome back."

"Thank you. Where's Paolo this morning?"

"He went over to Livernano with Marco, the agronomist, to look at the vineyards. He should be back in a couple of hours. Can I help you with anything?"

"No, Elisa. Everything is fine."

Mirella and Luca came in and greeted Erika as well as they headed toward the room with the labeling machine.

"We got an order from Russia," Elisa explained, "and they are preparing the bottles. It's for fifty cases—one pallet—a mix of Chianti Classico from Casalvento and Puro Sangue. The Russians love Puro Sangue!"

"That's great," Erika said.

"Hanna had a good weekend too," added Elisa. "I'm preparing all the documents for shipping now. That's why my desk looks a little messy."

"Don't mind me," said Erika. "Please go on with your work. The only thing I need is the passcode for the computer in the office."

"The code is under the keyboard."

Erika logged in and started going through her emails. There were dozens, including several from Craig, who kept saying how sorry he was and how much he wanted to talk. There was one from his mother, too. She clearly had no idea what had happened and was demanding answers. She would respond to those later—right now she had no idea what to say to them. She wished that Craig would just let her know that the wedding—and engagement—was off. It didn't seem like something that should be hers to tackle.

She emailed Todd and James to say the trip back had gone smoothly and thank them again for the fun moments and for being such good friends.

Finally, she carefully read the emails from Molly and Tiffany. They were handling the Levine project well, she realized, and she just sent a few suggestions before logging off the computer.

"Elisa, do you have Signor Bernardo's number?" she called out. "Could you get him on the phone for me?"

As she waited, Erika thought how much she liked working in this office and not just being on her own laptop by herself. She was beginning to prefer being around more people in the evening as well. In New York, she used to spend evenings alone with Craig or they'd meet his friends on weekends. *His* friends, not hers. Craig hated James and only tolerated Todd because he was a famous interior designer. Otherwise he would never have allowed him to do the apartment. She knew Craig had taken her into his world, but maybe it was just an empty, selfish world after all.

"Erika," Elisa called out. "Signor Bernardo is on the phone now."

"Thanks, Elisa." Erika gathered her thoughts and picked up the phone. "Hi, Bernardo."

"*Buongiorno*, Erika. How was your trip? Did you get everything done in your short week?"

"It was a good trip. Thank you. Everything went smoothly."

"What can I do for you?"

"Honestly, there's nothing in particular. I just wanted to check in with you and let you know that I'm back."

"I knew you would be, Erika. Listen, I promised that I would show you Florence and take you out for dinner with my wife. This week there's a baroque festival in Florence, and I have tickets for a concert on Friday night at the Anglican church in Piazza San Marco. We would very much like you to join us. It only happens once a year, and it's a beautiful place."

"I would love to come, but I don't know how to get into the city."

"Why don't you see if Paolo wants to come?" suggested Bernardo. "I'm sure we could get two more tickets. And we could have an early dinner before the concert."

"I'll ask him when he comes back to the cantina and email you later on with his answer."

"That's fine. Call me if you need anything. I'm happy that you're back, Erika."

"*Grazie*, Bernardo."

"*Ciao, Erika, a dopo.*"

She hung up the phone and yawned. Maybe she was a little jet-lagged after all—perhaps it was a good time to go back to the house and rest.

Elisa was deep into her work as Erika came to say goodbye.

"What are you doing, Elisa?"

"I'm double-checking the number of weekend sales from Casalvento and Livernano. We have to be very precise."

"Oh, of course. I didn't mean to interrupt you. But I'm going back to the house now. Can you ask Paolo to call me when he gets back?"

The aroma of the lemon trees at the cantina entrance hit her as she walked out. How beautifully they went with the pots of roses and lavender, she thought. Someone had done a lovely job here.

By the time she had walked back to the house, she was really sleepy. It was such a warm day that she thought she would just take a nap in the lounge chairs by the pool.

Sometime later, she woke up to the sound of Doris's voice. "Ms. Erika, Ms. Erika," she called, "Paolo is here."

"Okay, I'm coming."

Paolo was leaning against the kitchen door, dressed in his work clothes—khaki pants, a blue shirt with the sleeves rolled up, and heavy boots for the vineyard. His arms were crossed, which emphasized his muscled arms.

He knows he looks cool, Erika thought. *Men can be so full of themselves.* Nevertheless, she couldn't help smiling at him.

"*Ciao*, Paolo."

"Ciao, Erika. How are you? Tired?"

"Yes, a little. It was a busy week—that and the trip back must be catching up with me. I fell asleep by the pool. What time is it?"

"It's four thirty."

"What? I dozed off for three or four hours. I must really have been tired! And now I'd love a glass of wine. Will you join me?"

"Sure, what would you like?"

"I feel like white wine," Erika said. "Is that okay?"

"Yes, I'll get some for us. And I'll ask Doris for a snack—some olives, cheese, a little bread."

The bottle emptied fast as Paolo told her about his visit to the vineyards with the agronomist. "It looks like a good year for the grapes," he said.

Doris came out with one of her simple pasta dishes, and Paolo retrieved a bottle of Chianti Classico from the wine cellar.

"Do you know the story behind the wine label?" he asked her, pointing to it. "There was a coin that was found generations ago in one of the fields. Your grandfather thought it was a sign from God and would look good on the bottles. The coin turned out to be from 300 B.C. You can see it has a head that faces both forward and back. That's the Roman god Janus—the god of beginnings, gates, doorways, and passages. His name is where the word 'January' comes from."

"That's a lovely story," Erika said, thinking that this was a new beginning for her, and maybe it was good to have Janus watching out for things.

"Paolo, I almost forgot. I spoke to Bernardo today, just to tell him that I was back, and he invited me to come to Florence on Friday, to have dinner with him and his wife and then go to a concert at one of the churches there—I don't remember the name. I'd love to go, but I don't know my way around the city. Bernardo thought that maybe you would want to come as well. It was his idea, and I'm sure you already have plans for Friday night, but if you don't, I would love for you to come. Maybe we could go a little early and walk around. What do you think?"

Paolo didn't say anything right away. He looked at her. "Erika, I have a lot going on this week. The tractor needs some work, and we have to get the wine books in order, and the best time for that is always after work. Let me see how the week goes."

Erika nodded. "Okay, but I told Bernardo I'd let him know tomorrow, because he would have to get other tickets. So maybe let me know by then?"

"It seems you are not the strict businesswoman who left for New York a week ago. I'm glad you are looking to enjoy your stay a little. Do you really want me to come?"

Erika waited a minute, then realized that she honestly did. "Yes, Paolo, I do," she told him.

"Okay, then, the boss has spoken. Tell Bernardo tomorrow that we'll be there."

"Actually, Paolo, it's probably better if you contact him. He needs to let you know where to meet."

"Yes, ma'am! Now let's clean this up. Doris has already left."

They took the dishes to the kitchen and put things away. Paolo closed the shutters as Erika excused herself and made her way upstairs.

"I'll lock up for you," he called up. "Good night!"

XXI

$\mathcal{O}$N AN UNUSUALLY HOT Thursday afternoon, Erika drove to Livernano bristling with anticipation. The hotel was full, thanks to a wedding scheduled for later in the day. It was the second ceremony that year but the first time Erika would get to see the preparations. As she waited impatiently for the main gate to open, she looked around. The only sign of Livernano was the flagpoles that rose above the cypress and olive trees lining the road.

It was hard for her to believe that she'd only arrived back in Italy on Sunday. The days seemed to bleed into each other, and there was so much to do that she barely had time to think. But she welcomed the challenge.

Once she was through the gate, the long dirt road brought Erika past the church, and she pulled into the parking area at the top near several other vehicles. She made a mental note to make sure the cars were moved before the wedding took place, then walked back down to the entrance of Sant'Andrea. The thousand-year-old sanctuary had no air-conditioning, which was why the ceremony had been rescheduled to five in the afternoon, but it was as beautiful as she remembered. Sunflowers had been added to the arch of roses at the entrance, and just inside was the alabaster statue of the Virgin Mary that had come from Medjugorje, in Bosnia-Herzegovina, where she was said to have appeared to believers.

Sunflowers had been placed throughout the church too, at the edges of the pews and on the altar in front of a painting of Sant'Andrea. The sun that streamed through the stained-glass windows left bits of jeweled light everywhere. It was a serene place to say "I do."

Back outside, Erika saw the bride and groom posing for photographs while Constantina watched.

"*Buongiorno*, Signora Erika," Constantina said as she came over. "The heat today is killing us. We have been spraying the cut sunflowers with water. We don't want them wilting before the wedding starts. It's also been a little hectic. The air-conditioning in the Livernano and Chardonnay Suites isn't working correctly. A few guests are complaining, but I can't do anything about it right now."

Erika nodded her concern. "We need to address this as soon as possible, but, yes, after the wedding. How have you arranged the dinner?"

"We've placed the table outside and strung lanterns. We won't add the flowers till later—grapevines with sunflowers intertwined. We're keeping them in the little cantina near the party tent for now. That's the coolest place. We have white tablecloths, and the chairs also have white covers—with a big bow in the back that will hold a sunflower. Right after the ceremony, there will be a champagne reception below the pool."

"That all sounds perfect, Constantina," Erika said. "I'm not sure what I'm doing here—you have everything under control."

Constantina smiled gratefully. "Thank you. It's a hard job, but I love it."

"Is there anything I can do for you?"

"Yes, I do have a favor to ask. Could you introduce yourself to the bride and the groom? They were so excited when I told them that the owner was from New York. They are a lovely couple, teachers from New Jersey."

"It will be my pleasure," Erika said. "I'll let you get back to work . . . Oh, wait, what are their names?"

"Nicole and Vern."

As she went over to say hello to the couple, Erika felt a little wave of sadness. She was supposed to have her own wedding in September. She had begun thinking about a dress and imagining what the party would be like, but now—who knew what the future had planned for her. She could only hope it was for the better. It was funny . . . she didn't really miss her New York life, with everyone rushing everywhere and not paying attention to what was around them. But she did miss some romance—and it had taken her best friend and her fiancé's betrayal to see that she hadn't even truly had it. Where was *her* true love? Someone who could overlook her flaws and make her laugh? She looked at the wedding couple, who were holding hands and smiling at each other. You could see they were in love. Maybe one day . . . The new her had to believe in hope, love, fate, and the future.

She hadn't always been a nice or kind person, but that time seemed like a million years ago. Things were changing. For once, she was excited to get up in the morning. She looked forward to learning and doing new things, even if they were a challenge. She was going to keep taking the next step forward.

She was smiling at that idea when she introduced herself. "Hello, you must be Nicole? And you're Vern, right? I'm Erika, the owner of Livernano. I'm so happy you chose our little village for your wedding. You're in the best hands with Constantina."

"She is just amazing," said Nicole, who was wearing a simple, long white dress and holding a bouquet of sunflowers. "There are so many little details I'd never have thought of."

Her face glowed with happiness. At her side Vern was wearing a dark gray suit. His arm circled Nicole's waist. "Isn't she beautiful?" he said. "Am I not the luckiest man!"

"You certainly are," said Erika, "and you two make a handsome couple. I also heard that you made your own blend of wine for the wedding and bought a whole barrel to ship home. What a fun gift you've given your-selves . . . I wish you a great life together. Congratulations."

She left the couple to go on with their photo shoot and did a quick tour to see what else was happening. The kitchen looked like organized chaos. At the pool, children of the wedding guests were playing. Here and there, adults were sitting in the shade, reading, chatting, sipping a drink. She over-heard one of the guests asking what was in an Aperol spritz. "A mix of Aperol, Prosecco, and orange juice" was the answer. "It's very refreshing on a warm afternoon."

As Erika crossed the piazza, she heard the phone in reception ring sev-eral times. Evidently no one was there at the desk, so she ran over and picked up the phone.

"Livernano, *buongiorno*."

There was silence for a second, then the voice said, "Erika, is that you? It's Paolo.

"I have the owner of Pesce Winery here at Casalvento. He'd like to say hello, but I said that you were not here. What do you want me to tell him?"

"Is he important?"

"Yes, he comes from one of the oldest estates in Tuscany. His family is very well known and respected, and he's spending some time showing friends from New York the different estates in the area."

"Paolo, can you give them a tour and a wine tasting, if they want one? Then ask him to leave his number, and I'll call him next week. Just make sure you don't give out any secrets!" she joked, adding, "I know you can handle him. I'll see you later, Paolo. I have to go."

"Okay, *a dopo*!"

Constantina came into the reception area and told Erika that the ceremony would start in ten minutes and the bride and groom were asking if she wanted to join them.

"Constantina, I would love to, but I'm not dressed for a wedding. Please tell them that I have to meet someone at Casalvento, and say I'm sorry to miss it. Just make sure to take pictures. I would love to see how the table looks when it's completely set."

Twenty minutes later, she was back at the cantina in Casalvento. The tasting room was busy with both Europeans and Americans.

"*Buongiorno*, Signora Erika," Hanna greeted her, motioning her over. "This is the owner of Casalvento," she said to the couple at the counter. "She also is from New York."

Complimenting Erika on the beautiful property and the amazing view, the visitors said, "You're living the dream here. And Hanna is amazing. She gave us a great tour. And this tasting has been the highlight of our trip."

"Thank you! We're very lucky. Enjoy the wine." Erika turned to Hanna and asked quietly, "Is Paolo in the office?"

"No, he's giving a tour right now."

"I'm going up to the house. Please ask him to call me before he goes home."

Erika was barely in the door when Doris said, "Ms. Erika, Mr. Craig Bernhardt called again today. He is asking you to please call him back at the office."

"Did he ask where I was? What did you tell him?"

"That Signora Germoglio is at work!"

"You are an angel." And, for the first time, Erika gave her a hug.

Moments later, Paolo was knocking on the kitchen door. "*Ciao*, Erika," he said. "How was your day?"

"It was good." She smiled. "Everything was going well with the wedding, but Constantina told me there was a problem with the air-conditioning in two of the rooms."

"We need to get that fixed before August, Erika. I'll make sure it's done next week. We expect a hot summer."

Erika nodded, then changed the subject. "For tomorrow, Paolo, how do I dress?"

Paolo smiled. "Comfortably, above all. Wear shoes you can walk in all day—that is important. I have the day planned out. I'll pick you up around eleven. We can have a light lunch in the center of Florence—then we have tickets for the Uffizi Gallery."

"Sounds really nice! I also want to do a little shopping."

"There's plenty of time. No worries. We're meeting Bernardo and his wife—her name is Gloria—at a restaurant at five thirty."

"Perfect," Erika said. "Do you want anything to drink, Paolo?"

"No, thank you. I have to finish up some things at the office, then home. I'll see you tomorrow morning. Remember, comfortable shoes!"

"Okay, okay, I got it!"

Doris asked if she wanted anything.

"Yes, I'd like to try an Aperol spritz, but I can get it myself." She found a bottle of Aperol and opened some Prosecco, then got orange juice and ice from the refrigerator and took the drink outside where she could sit in a lawn chair and look at the vineyards.

Yes, those two tourists had been right—a vineyard in Tuscany *was* a dream. She had never wanted it, but she was learning to like it—like the Aperol spritz in her hand. Who knew!

Erika watched as a butterfly flitted close by, trying to land on the rim of her glass. She took a sip and raised her drink. "To new dreams!" she told the butterfly.

XXII

——

ERIKA OPENED HER EYES the next morning to bright sunlight that felt like a kiss on her cheek. Who would have thought that this was where she'd be for the next five months? She turned over to check her phone for the time and saw there had been a call from New York. The number was unfamiliar, so she dismissed it, though she wondered who it was.

Hearing Doris coming through the door downstairs, she jumped out of bed and made some coffee in the lounge, then washed her face and went out onto the balcony. The vineyards had a yellow glow from the sunrise and a startlingly fresh country smell. What a beautiful day! Perfect for going to Florence. Sightseeing, shopping, dinner, a concert . . . all the things she used to love so much, or at least thought she did. Here everything seemed a bit different.

She took her coffee and went downstairs.

"Good morning, Doris! No breakfast for me today. I want to get ready for the trip to Florence, and I still want to squeeze in a quick run before Paolo picks me up at eleven."

"But, Ms. Erika, you will be walking all day today!"

"I know. I just want to go up to the chapel to say good morning to my grandfather."

She was back soon and, after considering several choices, dressed in jeans with a white blouse and comfortable sneakers. She grabbed her denim jacket and handbag and was ready as Paolo pulled into the driveway at eleven sharp.

"Okay, Doris, I'm off," Erika said as she walked out the door. "Can you please make sure all shutters are closed when you leave—I'm not sure what time I'll be home."

"No problem, Ms. Erika. Do you want me to prepare some food for you for the weekend?"

"Yes, your simple pasta would be nice . . . Or better yet, could you make that delicious tomato sauce, the one that's a little spicy? You can just leave it on the stove. I will try to do the rest."

"No problem. Everything is here. I went shopping this morning before I came. I also bought fresh bread. I can cut it in slices and put them in the freezer. You can take them out and just place them in the toaster. And you remember how to turn on the stove?"

"Yes, you showed me," Erika said. "I think I've got it. I'm still not comfortable cooking everything on my own, especially if I have to cut up onions or garlic or whatever else goes into that amazing sauce of yours, but I can certainly manage to boil the pasta."

She went out the door and got into Paolo's truck. "*Buongiorno*," she told him.

"*Buongiorno*, Erika! You look very nice today. I see you're wearing sneakers. Good choice."

"I'll take that as a compliment. You don't look so bad yourself."

"I take that as a compliment, too," he said. "*Andiamo*."

About an hour later, he stopped the car at the edge of the city.

"This is Piazzale Michelangelo," Paolo told Erika. "It's a famous lookout point with a panoramic view over the heart of Florence. Look, you can see from Forte Belvedere to Santa Croce. There's the Ponte Vecchio over the Arno, and there is the Duomo. Beyond the city are the hills of Settignano and Fiesole."

"Oh, Paolo, this is breathtaking," Erika exclaimed as she stared at the city laid out before her and tried to identify the landmarks Paolo was pointing out.

"We'll drive to the Santa Maria Novella train station and park. It's in the center, and from there we can go everywhere on foot. We can't really drive anyway. Only taxis and buses are allowed."

"It sounds perfect. Let's go!"

"This is a new side of you," Paulo said teasingly. "It's nice to see you having fun."

Back in the car, they drove over a bridge and into a maze of traffic, with Vespas and mopeds passing them on both sides.

"Paolo, this city traffic is insane," Erika said, a little bit terrified at how disorganized it all looked. "I'm amazed that no one gets killed. Where there are two lanes, three cars are trying to squeeze through. Thank goodness the cars are small here."

"Erika, believe me, it looks worse than it is."

She was finally able to breathe again when Paolo finally pulled into the garage.

"Are you hungry?" he asked. "I thought we'd get something to eat before we go sightseeing and shopping. But make sure you hold on to your purse. Pickpockets love to rob tourists. Just be careful and stay close to me."

As they made their way through the streets, Erika enjoyed window-shopping at the boutiques with luxury goods—leather, perfumes, watches, clothes. When she looked up, they were standing in the piazza in front of the Duomo, a view made famous in postcards.

"Paolo, this is amazing. How old is this church?"

"I believe they started building it in 1296, but it wasn't finished until 1496. The official name is Cattedrale di Santa Maria del Fiore—the Cathedral of Saint Mary of the Flowers. The outside of the basilica is made of green and pink and white marble. We can go in later. But first, let's have lunch. I know the owner of a nice little restaurant, Trattoria Nonna. I went to school with him, and he's bought some of our wines."

The owner turned out to be a funny-looking character. Not very tall, rather overweight, with shiny black hair and a black apron sprinkled with flour wrapped around his waist. He had an open smile and kind eyes.

"Erika, meet my dear friend Fabrizio."

Fabrizio wiped his hand on the apron, shook Erika's hand vigorously, and kissed her cheeks, left and right. He winked at Paolo as he showed them to a table. "*Mamma mia, una bella donna. Fantastico.*" Even Erika understood what that meant! Feeling her face warm, she turned away.

"*Prego,* Fabrizio," said Paolo, "*una bottiglia di nostro Vino Casalvento Chianti Classico.*"

"*Ma, certo. Sta arrivando!*"

He disappeared into the kitchen—five minutes later, there was prosciutto, bread, olives, and olive oil on the table, along with the bottle of red wine.

Erika was delighted. "Paolo, do you know this is the first time I've had my own wine in a restaurant. I need to take a picture I can send later to my friends in New York." But she couldn't contain herself. She sent one right away to Todd and James, with a short text explaining the photograph.

She broke off a piece of bread and tasted it. "Paolo, the bread here tastes so bland. Why don't they put salt in it?"

"In the old days," he said, "salt was like gold, very rare for farmers. And then, they had salty prosciutto. They really only used to use salt for preserving food. I guess that is still the tradition—no salt in our Tuscan bread. Tuscany was and still is very simple. We cook from the land. We hunt a lot, pick wild asparagus and portobello mushrooms, and hunt for truffles. All that goes into our traditional dishes. Is it okay if I order for you?"

"Of course. I wouldn't have any idea what to order anyway."

One by one, the dishes were served: pizza without crust, risotto with radicchio, then red snapper with crushed cherry tomatoes, and finally an espresso and almond biscotti.

Afterward, Erika leaned back with a hand on her stomach. "I'm stuffed, like a turkey for Thanksgiving."

Paolo laughed. "I'm pleasantly surprised. You eat a lot for a woman!"

"Thank you! I'll take that as a compliment."

Paolo called over to the owner. "Fabrizio, *il conto, prego.*"

"*Subito, mi amico! Eccola!*"

They paid, hugged, and kissed again for goodbye.

"What a nice man he is, Paolo," Erika said. "And the food was really good."

"Yes, it's a simple kitchen, but everything is very fresh. Now we should start walking toward the Uffizi. We have a private tour starting at two, but that gives us about a half hour to just roam around."

They walked to the Ponte Vecchio, where small shops lined the bridge over the Arno River, and arrived at Piazza della Signoria. A life-size copy of Michelangelo's *David* was surrounded by tourists taking pictures. Erika couldn't resist.

"Paolo, please, can you take a picture of me and David?"

"Sure, give me your phone." As he held it, Erika could see him checking out the screensaver—she hadn't yet changed it. "Erika, is this Craig? He's a good-looking guy."

"I guess he is, in his own way. But please, Paolo, focus on me and David!"

The Uffizi Gallery was only steps away, and the line of people to get in was endless. Paolo guided Erika to a woman waiting a little apart and introduced them.

"Erika, this is our guide, Nunzia."

"*Ciao*," the young woman said, extending her hand. "Are you guys ready for the tour? We can go in this entrance and avoid the crowd. The Uffizi Gallery is one of Italy's most remarkable museums, and it made Florence famous, too."

For the next hour, she showed them the museum's treasured works of art and regaled them with interesting facts about the paintings and sculptures—masterpieces by Giotto, Paolo Uccello, Botticelli, Michelangelo, Raffaello, and Leonardo da Vinci. Before she ushered them back out to the piazza, Nunzia said, "These are the paintings that forever left their mark on the world of art. I hope they have also left their mark on you."

"Nunzia, this tour was amazing," Erika said. "There's so much to take in, much more than is possible in a single visit. Thank you!"

She turned to Paolo. "Where to now?"

"I think we've had enough sightseeing and museums for today. Did you want to shop a little? Most of the Italian brands, like Gucci and Prada, have factories right here in Florence, and the shops carry all the luxury brands."

"Yes, perfect."

Before long, Erika had shopping bags filled with a Prada handbag and some designer jeans. "I'm getting tired, Paolo," she said, stifling a yawn. "Thank goodness I'm wearing sneakers. Can we sit somewhere and have a glass of Campari?"

"I think we should start going toward the place where we'll meet Bernardo and Gloria for dinner. We can take a side street. It will be faster." He reached out to take her shopping bags.

"Do you come to Florence a lot?" Erika asked. "You know it so well."

"I used to come more, especially for the night life, but now that I'm older, not so much."

"That's funny, Paolo. You are *not* old!"

As they passed an outdoor bar, he said, "Let's take this table over here. Do you want anything besides the Campari soda?"

"Just that. I want to save some room for dinner. Do you know the restaurant we are going to?"

"Yes, you'll like it. They are known for their Florentine steak. If you like, we can share one."

"I'll let you know later. Right now I don't want to think about food. I just hope I don't fall asleep during the concert."

She added, "Thank you for showing me Florence. I like it here. It's so alive."

"Next weekend we could explore Siena if you want," Paolo offered. "It has its own history."

"Yes, why not? Let's see how the week goes."

Erika sipped her drink and suddenly asked, "Paolo, did you hear back from the real estate guy about the appraisal of the property?"

"Are you still thinking about selling it?"

"I don't know, Paolo. Mostly I want to know what it is worth. That's important, whatever I decide to do."

"I will follow up with him on Monday. In the meantime, have you heard any other strange noises at night? Do you still feel like someone is watching you?"

"I forgot about that, Paolo. No, it's been quiet since I got back."

"While we're sitting here," Paolo said, "I need to tell you about your unhappy neighbor, your cousin. We can go over details next week, but he's been calling the office. Last week you were in New York, so we had an excuse to put him off, but he knows you've returned. We need a plan to deal with him."

"Have him come to the office, Paolo. I don't want him at the house."

"I agree. Also we should talk about the contractor. We're going ahead with the open permits, but it would be good to settle things with him before too much time goes by. And now we should probably leave. We're meeting Bernardo in about twenty minutes."

They were there in plenty of time, and Bernardo, looking distinguished as always, greeted Erika warmly with a hug and a kiss on each cheek, then introduced her to his wife, who Erika couldn't help but think looked so unlike him. *He's so tall, and she's petite, with short gray hair, a simple dress, and hardly any makeup. I guess opposites do attract!*

Gloria spoke about as much English as Erika spoke Italian, but they smiled at each other as Paolo and Bernardo kept up the conversation during dinner.

The concert at St. Mark's capped off the evening. The acoustics of the Gothic-style Anglican church accentuated the delicacy of the baroque instruments and the ethereal voice of the singer.

Afterward, Erika was effusive in her thanks. "Bernardo, I loved it all—especially the harpsichord and the singer. He sounded like a bird."

"Yes," Bernardo explained. "Centuries ago it was a castrato who sang that music—a man who had been emasculated as a boy. But today, that very high male voice is a countertenor."

"Thank you so much, Bernardo, for the wonderful evening," Paolo said. "I'll find a taxi to take us back to the garage at the station. Erika can stay with you for the moment."

Erika took advantage of the time alone with him. "Bernardo, while we are waiting, can we meet and talk about my grandfather soon? You promised me that you would tell me his story."

"Erika, everything has its moment, and that moment is not yet come. I will tell you more, I promise, when the time is right."

"Here's the taxi!" Paolo called out from the street corner he stood on.

Erika gave Bernardo and Gloria the Italian-style kisses she was getting used to. "*Ciao. Buona notte!*" she told them.

Paolo was soon driving out of Florence back toward Casalvento. He had the radio playing softly.

"Paolo," Erika said. "You know, every time I ask Bernardo to tell me about my grandfather, he keeps postponing the conversation. I really want to know more about him and his life."

"Bernardo is an honest man, and he always keeps his word. Maybe he has a reason."

"I hope he has a good one," Erika said quietly before she dozed off. She woke up to the sound of Paolo's voice.

"Erika, wake up. We're home."

"Oh, I'm sorry, Paolo. I fell asleep. What time is it?"

"It's eleven."

"Do you want to come in for a nightcap? I just had my beauty rest, and I don't want to go to bed just yet."

"Okay. Let me just turn the car around. I'll bring in the shopping bags."

As she went into the house, Erika realized that she hadn't watched the news since she'd been back or done many of the things that had seemed so important in New York.

When she heard Paolo come in, she called out, "I'll go to the kitchen and get some cheese. Do you want to pick out a bottle of wine?"

A few minutes later, they were sitting on the sofa with a plate of cheese and a newly opened bottle of wine. Paolo had turned on some music.

"Let's have a toast," Erika said. "To my grandfather and to the future—whatever it may hold." She was quiet for a moment before asking, "So, Paolo, where did you learn English so well? Was it your time abroad?"

"Erika, it's late, and I told you it's a long story. I'll tell you another time."

"What is wrong with everyone? No one wants to tell me anything. Not Bernardo, not you. Why does it feel like everything is one big secret?"

"I promise I'll tell you, just not tonight." He picked up the plates and took them into the kitchen.

Erika leaned back on the sofa and held up her wine glass against the light. This was her wine, and she still just couldn't believe it.

"Okay, Erika. I cleaned up a little," said Paolo. "It's late, and it was a long day. I'm going. I'll lock you in."

"Good night," she said, heading up the stairs. She had barely undressed and gotten into bed before she fell asleep.

She woke up to the sound of her cell phone buzzing and leaned over to look at the time. It was eight thirty in the morning, and her head ached. *I need a jumbo-sized aspirin and coffee*, she thought as she wondered who was calling her at this hour. The number was from someone in New York. But if they couldn't leave a message, who cared? She just hoped she didn't make a fool out of herself last night . . . but if she did, so what! It was about time she let go a tiny bit.

XXIII

---

*T*HE MORNING SUNLIGHT, the fresh breezes, the smell of grass and flowers—all of Tuscany's seductive qualities—were slowly becoming irresistible to Erika. After waking up late on Saturday, she took her coffee outside, enjoying the way the feel of terra-cotta tiles on her bare feet gave way to the carpetlike caress of the grass. The stone wall that separated the house from the vineyard was the perfect place to sit and contemplate the rustic elegance of the house and the colorful English-style garden.

Among the flowers were two bronze cherubs, one with a flute and another with a harp. Nearby was a fanciful fountain with water spouting from the mouth of a fish, adding its music to the sounds of the day. Erika could only marvel at the vision and the work that went into creating this magical scene.

She looked over to the vineyard and thought about what Paolo had once said: "You never know what you'll get each year. You are at the mercy of the gods and the weather." Maybe that's why her grandfather had become who he was. Alone—as she was in this unfamiliar world—he had cultivated a new family, surrounding himself with people who cared for him deeply. And who seemed to care for her as well.

She heard her cell phone ring in the house and ran in to get it but missed the call. It was the same unknown number. *Okay, I need to find out who this is,* she thought and pushed redial.

A male voice answered.

"Erika?"

"Yes, who is this?"

"It's Craig, my darling."

"This isn't your number. Where are you calling from?"

"You wouldn't return my calls, so I hoped you'd pick up if I used a different number."

"What do you want?"

"Don't be angry. I wanted to talk to my fiancée and see how you were."

"Craig, we broke off our engagement."

"You did that, Erika, not me."

She sighed into the phone. "This is a waste of time. For what it's worth, I truly, truly cared for you and loved you. For a long time after my parents died, you made my life worthwhile. And I wanted to be perfect for you, so I let you mold me. I became part of your world, with your friends and your ambitions. But you also sometimes made me feel small and insecure in the way you made assumptions about us, the way you spoke to me. That became normal to me. I got used to it. And now, here I am, across the ocean and a world away from you, and I'm functioning perfectly well. I like the person I'm becoming. I think I was always afraid that you'd leave me, and I'm no longer afraid—of you, of not being perfect, and of being without you. I wish you all the best, but it's over."

"Erika, you can't do this to me."

"Yes, Craig, I can. I loved you the way you wanted me to love you, but that time is past, and I hope you find the perfect person for you. That will never be me. Goodbye."

"Erika, stop it. I love you. It was Tiffany's fault—she was always coming on to me. You can't just—"

She hung up.

Was it a mistake to do that? She certainly wasn't sorry, though she would have loved to talk to Todd and James about it. She hoped that they'd really be able to come and see this place for themselves. She needed old friends around. And she needed a shower to wash off all that negativity!

A half hour later, she felt more relaxed and back in tune with her surroundings. With no plans for the day, she decided to do nothing—no Italian lessons, no work, no worrying. Maybe she could start keeping a diary again? She went up the stairs to the office and found an empty booklet on a shelf.

There was something next to it that looked like a photo album. When she opened it, a bygone world appeared in black-and-white images.

It looked like the pictures were taken in front of the house.

Everyone looked so serious. Well-dressed women sat with babies on their laps, and the men stood stiffly behind them. As she paged through, she saw men in uniforms, but it was unclear who they were. Was her grandfather one of the babies? After the wartime photographs, the pictures stopped, adding to the mystery.

She knew this was something she wanted to look at again. She carried the album to her bedroom and placed it on her nightstand. Then she put on a swimsuit and sun hat, grabbed the blank notebook and a pen, and headed for the pool.

She lay down on a lawn chair under an open umbrella and considered the last few days. The wedding at Livernano had been unexpectedly beautiful, and Florence, with its art and museums and concert, was unbelievable. And then there was Paolo. Being with him all day was fun, and after they got back . . . Well, it was odd to see how uncomfortable he had been before he loosened up over the glasses of wine. It was a good feeling to just talk though—she could sense that he respected her, and there was no question that he was a handsome man.

She dozed off for a while and woke herself up with a swim. Then she took her notebook and tried to put down on paper all the conflicting emotions that had threatened to overwhelm her in the previous weeks. Hours passed as she filled one blank page after another, sometimes smiling, sometimes tearing up for a moment. It felt good to let everything go, and it was helping her think more clearly, too.

It was four thirty in the afternoon by the time she realized she was hungry and remembered the sauce Doris had left on the stove. She went into the kitchen and, mentally repeating Doris's directions, filled a pot with water, added a little salt, put the pot on the stove, and turned on the burner. Then she put the tomato sauce over a low flame on another burner.

She found a box of spaghetti in the pantry and, when the water was boiling, added the pasta. *Don't cook it for more than four minutes*, she told herself, watching the time. Four minutes later, she drained the spaghetti, put the pasta into the sauce, added just a little of the boiling water as Doris had shown her, and stirred.

She set the table for herself outside, got Parmesan from the refrigerator, and went to the garden to pick some basil and parsley. The aroma tickled her nose as she pulled apart the leaves with her hands.

Spooning pasta onto her plate, she topped it with some grated Parmesan and took it to the table. The only thing missing was wine, and that was quickly remedied as she retrieved a bottle of Chianti Classico Riserva and poured herself a glass.

The occasion called for another photo. After all, this was her first home-cooked meal cooked by her, something definitely worth commemorating.

As she sipped her wine, a breeze animated the trees. *Well, this is Casalvento,* she mused, *the House of the Wind. It's a magical place. Could life be any better?* She still had a lot to learn and to do, but she liked her new work. She had to believe that her grandfather put that clause in his will on purpose—he wanted her to stay here long enough to learn how he had lived and to get to know the family he had created. The photos in the album, they were part of her history. She was a Germoglio, and she couldn't ignore that.

But what about her company in New York? She wondered if Tiffany would be able to buy her out. Or would she even want to? She had time to think about that and needed to be sure that she wanted to stay. And what would Todd and James think? There were so many questions, so much to work out. She just had to trust that she'd make the right decision when the time came.

XXIV

———

*O*N MONDAY MORNING Erika looked for Paolo at the cantina. "I'd like to visit my grandfather's real grave. Will you bring me there?" she asked.

"Yes, I can do that, but remember, I'm not sure exactly which one it is."

"That doesn't matter, Paolo. I just need to go there. It may sound strange, but I feel I need to be near his spirit. Sometimes, at night, I think I can still hear that car engine. And, once in a while, I also feel a presence in the house. I can't explain it. It's not scary, but it does make me a little uneasy. I thought if I went to my grandfather's actual grave, or somewhere near the site, and brought him some roses or grape leaves and maybe let him know that I'm here and that I'm trying my best to make it work for me, then maybe it would stop. Sorry . . . I know it sounds crazy."

"No, Erika, I understand. You have to remember the house has been here for generations. Maybe there are things in it that aren't rational. We can go and visit him. None of us ever went, because, for us, he is here at Casalvento. Why don't we have lunch in Radda, at the local bar, and afterward I'll take you to the cemetery."

"Oh, Paolo, thank you so much. I'll go up to the house and see what I can bring."

"Take some roses, Erika. He loved them."

Doris was in the kitchen when Erika walked in. "Back so early, Ms. Erika?"

"Yes, Paolo's going to take me to my grandfather's grave."

"Up to the chapel?"

"No, to his actual burial site."

Doris seemed puzzled.

"Never mind. Paolo understands. But there's something else I wanted to ask you. Over the weekend I was in the office, just looking around, and I came across some recipes. One of them really caught my eye."

"Which one? Signor Germoglio loved to cook. It was a hobby for him."

Erika laughed. "That is something I definitely did not inherit. I'm useless in the kitchen."

"I disagree. The only thing you need is practice. If you would like, I can show you some simple dishes."

"I'd like that, Doris. But here's the one I was talking about. I think you'll do it better without me." Erika showed Doris the pages with the recipe for *penne della Nonna*, which called for red peppers, cream, Parmigiano-Reggiano, parsley, and boiled ham.

"I never saw Signor Germoglio cook this dish, but I'm happy to try it," Doris said. "Not today though. I don't have the ham or the heavy cream in the house. Is tomorrow okay?"

"Of course, Doris. I'm not going anywhere soon. Except to Radda for lunch. So for dinner, can you make something light? I need to stop eating quite so much! Now I must be off. Where can I find some garden clippers and a plastic bag?"

"Why do you need those?"

"I want to cut some roses," Erika explained.

Doris gave her the clippers, and Erika cut the flowers, added a little dirt from the garden—along with a few grape leaves and a small piece of olive branch—and walked back to the cantina. Paolo was in the truck waiting for her.

"*Andiamo*," she said as she hopped in. After a moment, she showed him what she'd brought. "Paolo, I cut some leaves off the grapevines. How do you tell the Sangiovese leaves from the Cabernet or the Merlot ones?"

"The Sangiovese leaves are lighter green. In the summer they turn yellow, and after harvest, they get darker and a little red. The leaves are also bigger than the ones from Merlot or Cabernet vines. We can go through the fields tomorrow, and I can show you firsthand if you would like."

"Yes, absolutely. I want to learn."

"*Eccola*," Paolo said as he parked the truck in Radda. They walked over to the bar, and he introduced Erika to the owner as Signor Germoglio's granddaughter and the new owner of Casalvento. He ordered a panino for each of them, with Campari soda for Erika and a coffee for himself.

An hour later, they were back in the truck and on the steep winding road to the gravesite. Along the way, Paolo pointed out the vineyards of some of the most famous estates of the Chianti Classico region. Finally, they came to a brown sign with the word *Cimitero* and an arrow pointing ahead to a dark wood. A few meters farther on, he stopped the truck at the side of the road. Erika could see a low stone wall enclosing the area and a partly ruined stone structure farther on. The place looked as if it had been abandoned years before.

"*Eccola.*"

"What, here?" Erika asked, wrinkling her nose at the smell of moss and damp earth. Carrying her bag of flowers and leaves, she followed as Paolo led the way through an iron gate and down some stone steps. The few gravestones scattered around appeared old and neglected.

Erika looked up to see an owl sitting on a branch watching her. With a rush of wings, it suddenly flew straight at her head. She suppressed a scream as it came at her, but the bird flew directly over her and landed on an iron cross that seemed to be marking a grave, but there was no name, no picture, nothing.

Shaking, she whispered to Paolo, "This must be it."

"I'm not sure."

"Paolo, it's an omen," she insisted. "I'm sure this is the one."

"It looks like no one has been here for a long time," he said. "It's hard to tell the graves apart. They're so overgrown."

"I know," she said, "but I feel this is the right place. I'll clean it up and get rid of the weeds."

Paolo was looking at some of the old gravestones when she called him back over to see how she'd arranged the roses and leaves.

"You did a nice job, Erika," he told her.

"Yes, and before we go, I want to say a prayer." She composed herself before the grave, folding her hands together. "Dear Grandpa, we brought you some roses from the garden at Casalvento and a little dirt from your beloved vegetable garden. We also brought you an olive branch and grape leaves. I want you to know that your garden looks amazing. The way you would like it. Mirella and Santo are doing a wonderful job, and Paolo is here with me. He takes great care of the vineyards. The longer I'm here, the sorrier I am that I never met you. But believe me, we all still feel your presence all the time. Grandpa, I'm new here and trying to live the life you left me. But, from time to time, I get really scared in Casalvento, especially when I'm alone at night in the house. If your spirit is there, please watch over me, and don't let anyone do me harm. I promise we'll take good care of your property and continue to run it as you would have. I like it here and am thinking of staying even a little longer than you had asked me to. So, if you can, look out for me. Goodbye, for today. We will bring you some grapes when they are ripe."

They drove home in silence, but Erika couldn't shake the eerie feeling she had in the cemetery. She asked Paolo to close the shutters and lock the house. But it was a long time until she could fall asleep. As she tossed and turned, she couldn't help wondering if ghosts really existed.

XXV

———

ERIKA WOKE UP PONDERING the same questions she'd gone to bed with. Were there ghosts? And where was her grandfather's spirit? At Casalvento, or at the cemetery where he was buried? Those thoughts kept spinning in her head, threatening to overwhelm her. It would be so much easier, she realized, if she had someone to talk to, a friend who understood her and the situation she was in.

She hoped Todd would call soon. He and James would give her honest advice. And she needed to be more appreciative toward Paolo—he was trying so hard to be helpful.

Maybe a swim would clear her head?

Erika put on her swimsuit and appraised her figure in the mirror. Even with all that she was eating, she didn't seem any heavier. How could that be? Was it that the food was so fresh and prepared with olive oil instead of butter? Or was she simply more active all the time, instead of working at the computer all day and just going for a run in the park or to a gym for a workout a couple of times a week?

She opened the front door and stepped outside into a fresh new day. The stone paving was freshly cleaned, the dead leaves all gone, and the cars were washed. Santo must have taken care of it all. The flowers in the terra-cotta pots had been watered. Paolo had told her that vases like these, called *anfore* or *orci*, had been used as much as six thousand years ago for winemaking. Now they served as flowerpots. There were lots of them at Casalvento—at the entrance to the house and by the garage.

She appreciated that Paolo was trying to teach her about Tuscany and winemaking. Learning things about a business had always been part of the way she ran her company. It helped make her a success, and she liked to absorb information. She wanted to know about everything here, from the way the grapes were grown to the names of the flowers in the garden.

She put down her towel and eased into the pool. The water was chilly, but, after a few laps, she appreciated how refreshing the water was.

When she heard Doris driving up, she hurried back to the house, went upstairs, and jumped into the shower. Now she was ready for the day. Paolo would be arriving soon to show her more about the vineyards.

Doris was working in the kitchen when Erika came down. "Good morning, Doris. It's another gorgeous day!"

"Yes, it is, Ms. Erika. I bought all the ingredients for the *penne della Nonna*. I'll make that for dinner. But when I came in a few minutes ago, the front door was open. Please don't forget to lock it."

"Don't worry, Doris. I woke up early and went up for a swim."

"In this cold water?"

"Yes, it felt good! You know, Paolo's coming this morning to take me through the vineyards. I'll need those rubber boots from the cabinets in the laundry room."

Erika was putting on the gear as Paolo drove up in the truck.

"Ready?" he asked.

"Ready as can be."

They drove straight into the vineyards, with Erika holding on tightly as the already narrow path got even more narrow and rose precipitously.

"Don't worry, Erika," Paolo tried to reassure her. "Nothing will happen. I drive through here all the time, if not with the truck, with the tractor."

"I believe you, Paolo, but I'm not used to mountain driving."

"Erika, these aren't mountains. They're just hills. And on this side of them, we grow Merlot. The next two months—June and July—are a very important time. You can already see the bunches, so we need to control diseases like mildew. We only spray with natural products. To hit the target better, we use our hands to push the branches up the wire on the sides of the vines. That way, we also create a wall of leaves that works like a photovoltaic panel—the more the leaves stay in the sun, the more they'll nourish the grapes. Leaves that are in the shade are in competition with the grapes. That's why we will prune away some of the branches later on."

"That sounds like a great deal of work."

"That is only a small part. We also do what's called a green harvest. We take off some unripe clusters of green grapes from the vine. It is a form of crop thinning to help manage yield. Every winemaker does it a little differently. Your grandfather knew exactly what he was doing. I miss him. He taught me so much. I learned a lot in school and in California, but he gave me my real education."

"I'm grateful that you're trying to pass his wisdom on to me. But honestly, it's too much to take in all at once. I'm worried I won't remember it all."

"Of course, but every time we talk about the grapes, something will sink in. One day you'll be able to teach someone else."

Paolo turned off to take the dirt road to Livernano, passing the entrances to other farms from the area, roller-coasting up and down the hills, and going through the gate into the vineyards, where he parked the truck.

"Let's walk a little," he said. "I will show you the chestnut trees on the other side of the vineyard. Those attract game, and because of that we have a lot of hunters in the fall on the property. They are allowed to come without asking for permission from you, but they're supposed to give you ten percent of whatever they catch on your property. Only locals are allowed to come in—they have permits. Most of the time you can't see them, but you definitely can smell them."

"Smell them! Why?"

"Most of them smoke *gorgonzole*. That's what the locals call the Tuscan cigarillos. They stink. That's why they have that name."

"You are funny, Paolo!"

"No, really, I'm not kidding you. The hunters can only come after we have picked the grapes, not before, but they don't always respect the rules."

Paolo took her farther toward the edge of the vineyard. "Over here are old airplane hangars, where we store equipment and materials. And over there we have the beehives. We make our own honey, but we also need the bees for natural pollination. We also have a lot of fig trees on the property, along with plum and cherry trees."

"I'm impressed."

"It's important for the vineyard to be organic, and that affects the hotel. We serve what we grow on the property, and whenever we buy something, we buy organic products and do our best to support local producers. It's not always easy." He paused and turned to her. "Are you hungry?"

"Starving."

"Perfect, let's go up to Livernano and have a bite to eat."

By late afternoon, Erika was back at the house, catching up on emails. Craig was filling her inbox with angry, whining messages—she decided to just ignore them for the moment. The aroma of sweet peppers cooking distracted her. The smell made the house come alive, she thought, wishing that she had friends to invite for dinner.

A huge clap of thunder interrupted her thoughts and sent her running down to the kitchen.

"Ms. Erika, a big storm is coming," Doris said. "Can I go move my car closer to the house?"

"Sure, Doris, go! But tell me what I can do."

"First, we need to make sure all windows are closed."

As Doris went out the door, Erika could see the clouds moving in quickly, changing the sky from light blue to an ominous gray. The smell of rain was in the air, and as the wind strengthened, she saw a flash of lightning, followed by a roll of thunder.

The kitchen door opened with a gust of wind, and Doris hurried in with Paolo close behind. "We need to close all windows and shutters," he said.

"I already closed the windows."

"Good," Paolo said. "Now you and Doris should start on the shutters. I'll unplug the electricity and the phone lines."

Minutes later, they were standing in the kitchen, out of breath but relieved to be ready to face the storm.

"Erika, can you believe Tuscany is the lightning capital of the world in the summer?"

"That's strange. I would have thought Florida. The weather is certainly unpredictable. Paolo," she added, "would you like a glass of wine?"

"Sure! I think we earned it," he said with a grin on his face.

"Why don't you stay for dinner and ride out the storm with us? Doris already made the pasta sauce. I'll get a bottle of the Casalvento Riserva 2011 to go with it."

"I'll go. Is it in your cellar?"

She nodded.

As the storm raged, they set the table, lit some candles, and enjoyed the pasta.

"I found the recipe up in the office," Erika explained. "There were many others too."

"Yes, Umberto loved to cook, but I never had this dish."

Two hours later, the sky was back to Tuscan blue, and, except for a drop in temperature, it was as if nothing had happened.

"Luckily, we didn't get any hail," said Paolo as they reopened the shutters and windows and plugged in the phone and the electric lines. "That would have been really bad for the grapes."

They could hear the phone system rebooting and the TV coming on automatically.

"Good, it seems like everything is working—nothing got hit. It can get really ugly, especially when we get hail the size of golf balls. At least you know what to do if we are not around. I have to go and check on everything at my house now," he said. "Thanks as always for the good food, Doris. And the wine, Erika."

"Good night, Paolo," Erika said, adding, "Doris, you go home as well. I'll manage the rest."

After Paolo and Doris had gone, she refilled her wine glass and was on her way to the living room when her cell phone rang. She smiled broadly as she recognized Todd's number and answered the call.

"*Pronto, chi parla?*"

"Erika?"

"Yes."

"It's me, Todd."

"I know! I saw your number on my screen."

"So you're an Italian already?"

"Yes, why not? I have to fit in if I want to stay."

"Well, you sound great."

"I feel great. I just had my first experience with a real Tuscan storm—it was exciting. What's happening in New York?"

"We've been busy. I'm still working on the same job with my difficult client. I've never worked for a crazier person. First, she wanted a fireplace and an antique look. Now, she wants it all Art Deco and wants me to rip everything back out. It's insane."

"I know, my dear friend, but she's paying for it, so try not to worry."

"Darling, it will take another four months, at least, to redo everything. I'm not sure I can survive this everyday drama. Listen to this—last week her hair was long and blond. But yesterday, when I came to check on the job, I didn't even recognize her at first. She had cut her hair off and colored it black. She told me she wants a 1920s look, to match her new apartment! But enough about her. How is Tuscany treating you?"

"*Molto bene.* I'm learning to love it here. The people who work for me are amazing, and every day I learn something new. This morning, Paolo took me through the vineyards and explained the differences between all our varieties of grapes. Last Friday I got to explore Florence with him, did a little shopping, and later went to dinner and a concert with my lawyer and his wife. And the weekend before last, I helped organize a wedding at Livernano. If I want to relax, I can swim in the pool and lie in the sun with an Aperol spritz."

"That sounds like a wonderful, laid-back life."

"I found an old photo album in the office upstairs, and it made me remember the photography courses I took in college. Do you remember that?"

"Yes, and I also remember that you were quite good at it. I honestly could not understand why you stopped."

"Craig thought it was a waste of time and that I needed to concentrate on business courses. I guess it made sense to me at the time."

"And how *is* Craig?" Todd asked carefully.

"He can't accept the fact that I broke the engagement, and he wants me back. I think he's afraid of what people will think and say. I spoke to him a couple of days back and told him again that it's over between us. But he didn't take it well. Now he is bombarding me with emails, and I'm not sure what I should do. Reply or not! Todd, what do you think?"

"It's not an easy question, but I think you should lie low for a while. Don't reply."

"You know, he even called me from a different number, because I wouldn't answer."

"That sounds like Craig, darling. You're much better off without him. Look at you—you remind me of the Erika I used to know. When you came into a room, you lit it up. When you and Craig got serious, your energy was all gone. So, darling, we need to find you someone new—better to get your mind off Craig and to have some fun. What about Paolo?"

"Todd, stop it. I'm changing the subject. When are you coming to Italy?"

"That's the other reason for my call. I need to find Art Deco furniture for Mrs. Crazy, and there's a source in Berlin. So, I thought I'd go to Berlin at the end of May or beginning of June, and then I could come to Tuscany right after."

"That would be great! And that's only a couple of weeks away. Will James come with you? We could celebrate his birthday together."

"He's trying to get a week off."

"That's not enough time. He needs to stay longer."

"I'll let you know, Erika. But now I have to go. I love you, darling."

"Todd, I can't wait to see you. We'll talk soon. *Ciao*."

Erika sat and sipped her wine as her mind raced with thoughts of everything she wanted her friends to do and see. She hoped the next few weeks would go quickly. And Todd was right about the photography. She wanted to start taking pictures again. Maybe Paolo could help her shop for a camera and that would rekindle her old passion. It had been way too long.

XXVI

⎯⎯⎯

*T*HE NEXT MORNING, Erika walked over to the cantina to look for Paolo. She found him working with Mirella in the barrel room.

"*Buongiorno*, Mirella," she said. "*Ciao*, Paolo. You look very busy. What are you doing?"

"We're racking the wine. We have to do this once in a while," he explained. "Using gravity, we transfer the wine from one barrel to another in order to remove the sediments. We usually do this three or four times, first after the fermentation and then again a couple of months later and before we bottle. A lot of work goes into winemaking—and a lot of passion!"

"I can see that, Paolo. And the result is our wonderful wines," she said. "Will you be working all day? I think I'd like to go to Siena. I need to buy a camera. A good one. Do you know of a shop that sells professional photographic equipment?"

"I do. I bought all my gear from them."

"You take pictures?" Erika asked with surprise in her voice.

"Yes, since I was a child. It's a hobby—something else to do besides winemaking. But I should be done in thirty minutes. Then we can go."

"Perfect."

Paolo smiled. "You surprise me, Erika! When you first came here, you were stiff and all business, dressed in black, your hair pulled back into a bun. But today you're standing in front of me in blue jeans and a sweater, and you look really happy and ready to learn."

"I guess this place is having a positive effect on me," she said. There was much more she could have said but . . . well, she was technically Paolo's boss. The lines felt a bit muddled as it was, with their dinner and sightseeing.

Sometimes it felt a bit as if he was flirting with her, but it was hard to tell, with the cultural differences and how warm everyone was here.

A half hour later, they were on their way to Siena, following the winding roads past vineyards and olive groves and through an old village where the streets were barely wide enough for cars.

"What happens when there is a truck or a bus trying to come this way?" Erika asked.

Paolo laughed. "So far it's always worked out, but there are close calls. You can see the scratch marks on the walls and the missing stones on the corners between the houses."

As the landscape changed, Erika became curious about the plants she saw, which were so different from those at Casalvento.

"Paolo, what is that cactus? It's the size of a bush, and those thorns are enormous, but the flowers are beautiful."

"We call them *fico d'India* here, but I think the name is prickly pear in English."

"What don't you know?" she said, laughing.

"You forget I grew up in Italy, and over time you learn. And I had good teachers. Italy is a country with a complicated history. Did you know that we have thirty-four languages and dialects? Here in Tuscany, we don't understand people from the south. But they say Florentines speak the true Italian."

As they neared Siena, Paolo gave Erika a quick history lesson.

"You can see that Siena is surrounded by brick walls, and the buildings in the center are made of the same red bricks. The Etruscans were here, and then the Romans. It's like Livernano—the basic history is the same. This was always a big banking center, too. And during the Renaissance, great artists created the Duomo and the Palazzo Pubblico with the Torre del Mangia. But for centuries there was a power struggle between Florence and Siena. In the 1500s, Florence got the upper hand, and Siena was incorporated into Florentine territory. When Italy formed a republic, Siena became a part of Tuscany."

Paolo parked the car just inside the walls, and as he and Erika joined the throng of tourists crowding the narrow walkways, he urged her to hurry a little. "The stores close at noon," he said, "and open again at four. That's why we say, if you want to invade Italy and rob us, do it between twelve and four."

"That's funny," she said, slightly out of breath as she followed him up and down the stairs that connected the streets of the town. "How much farther is it?"

Paolo looked back at her. "I thought you ran every day? Are you telling me you're having trouble keeping up? We're almost there."

Five minutes later, they were at the shop. Erika was impressed by how well the owner knew his business, and she soon was the proud owner of a Leica camera with several lenses.

"It's amazing how much cameras have changed," she said as they said goodbye to the shop owner.

"But the basics are still the same," Paolo assured her. "It's just the computer part that's new."

"It'll probably take me some time to learn to use it."

"I have a similar camera," said Paolo. "Let me know if you need any help. But now, how about lunch? I know a small trattoria near the Piazza del Campo."

"Yes, please. I'm famished!"

They went down some stone steps and came out into a huge piazza.

"*Eccola*," said Paolo. "This is the famous Piazza del Campo, known for the horse races called the Palio. They've been going on for five hundred years—on July second and August sixteenth."

"They have horse races here?" Erika was astonished.

"Yes, it's the most important event in Siena. The city is divided into areas called *contrade*, and they challenge each other. It's very dramatic and colorful. Tickets, good tickets, are very hard to get."

"I'd love to see that while I'm in Tuscany."

"Let me see what I can do."

After they found seats at the trattoria and ordered pasta and white wine, Paolo explained more about the Palio. "Every *contrada* has its own banners," he told her, "and the riders all ride bareback. It's not unusual for a horse to lose its rider and finish the race by itself. And it's very fast. There are three laps, and each one only lasts about ninety seconds. But it's an intense ninety seconds."

As they finished the meal, Paolo asked, "Do you want to stop and see the Duomo? It's very close."

"Let's save that for another day. I'm ready to get home and practice with the camera."

Erika was quiet as they drove back to Casalvento. *This is a different me,* she thought, *a bit of a dreamer, learning new things, seeing things with fresh eyes.* She was looking forward to using the camera to show that.

Paolo dropped her off at the house and said he'd see her tomorrow at the cantina. "Don't forget our meeting. The accountant and someone from the bank will be there with Bernardo. We need to show them all the improvements you've been working on."

"I won't forget, Paolo. *Ciao,* and thank you!"

Doris was in the kitchen as she came in. "*Ciao,* Ms. Erika," she said. "What did you think of Siena?"

"It was amazing. So much history, and I got a camera! I just want to freshen up, but then I think I'll start learning how to use it. Have you made anything for dinner?"

"I'm sorry, Ms. Erika. I was doing laundry and ironing, and I lost track of time. But I can make a simple pasta."

"You know, Doris, I had pasta for lunch. A simple *antipasti* plate would be great."

Erika mixed herself an aperitif and took the camera and the accompanying manuals to a lounge chair by the pool. She knew she would need to read the manuals carefully, because it would be nothing like using a cell-phone camera. Still, she was so glad Todd had encouraged her to take up photography again.

And it would be so good to see him and James here. Somehow, she knew summer would be exciting. She would have houseguests, which she'd never had before—that hadn't fit in with her and Craig's life at all. Here, it seemed natural. It was a place you wanted to share with friends. She needed to talk to Doris about what they needed to do to prepare.

With that in mind, Erika went to get her *antipasti* from the kitchen and poured herself a glass of her white wine. She thought about her grandfather and how he had changed her life so suddenly.

Grandpa, I'm happy here, she said to herself. *I just wish I knew more about you and your story . . . how this all got started and why I'm here now by myself.*

If Bernardo or Paolo wouldn't tell her more, then she would go through every drawer in the office until she found the answers.

XXVII

———

ERNARDO ARRIVED AT THE CANTINA exactly at eleven in the morning, and Erika was there to greet him with a hug and a warm smile. He grasped her by the shoulders and peered at her.

"Erika, you look different. Happy and even refreshed. I would say Italy is agreeing with you."

"Thank you, Bernardo—I feel good. Thank you for coming. I think you'll be pleased by what Paolo and I have accomplished."

"The accountant and the director of the bank should be here any moment," Bernardo added.

Paolo helped her to bring a couple extra chairs into the office, and half an hour later, the five of them were seated around the desk, going over the books for Casalvento and Livernano. Both the accountant and the bank director seemed pleased and surprised.

"I'm impressed by what you both did in this short time," said the banker. "You seem like an ideal team. How did you manage it?"

"It was a combination of things," Paolo explained. "We began by getting several bids for things we used in the vineyard and also for the hotel and restaurant. That was Erika's idea, and it allowed us to cut some costs. And we're using our own people more efficiently in the fields, thanks to a weekly schedule that Erika drew up."

Erika interrupted him. "I could do that because Paolo was aware of what each person was capable of doing. And when we met with each person individually, we found out that many of them had many other skills as well. Carl, the tractor driver, used to be a plumber, so we can rely on him for that. And it turns out that Simone, the chef, also knows how to service the pool. Everyone has pitched in. If they finish their work early, they've agreed to help out at Livernano. So far it's all working well."

Paolo picked up the story. "Erika has organized a staff meeting at Livernano once a week to go over what's happening and what each person needs to do. Now the waiter is also seeing that the dining room is clean and restocking the wine racks, which needs to be done every evening. As an incentive, we've authorized a bonus for their extra work, which they'll get at the end of the season."

Erika continued, "We check our bookings each day, and if we're not full, we take advantage of that to clean around the property. We also make sure that the bedrooms of guests who had a late checkout are made up immediately—we don't want to turn any walk-ins away. And the restaurant is now open to the public, and there are tours that people can book online. One, called the Sunflower, includes a tasting and set-price lunch at Livernano. In the evening, we call it the Sunset tour—same tour, but the meal is a set-price dinner."

"This was Erika's idea too," said Paolo.

"Once we posted these on our website, we started getting some bookings right away. It's all extra income—'after-sales,' we call them in the States."

"These are very good ideas," said Bernardo. "I can see they've been productive."

"I think we'll be able to reduce costs by twenty percent in the next three months," Erika said.

The bank director smiled. "Another reason why I am increasing the company's line of credit," he said.

"Thank you," said Paolo, "that will particularly come in very handy during the winter, when Livernano is closed."

The meeting ended on a high note, with handshakes and congratulations all around.

As he was about to leave, Bernardo took Erika aside. "Erika, I'm very proud of what you and Paolo have done here. You're really your grandfather's granddaughter. And, as you know, I mentioned that I had other letters for you from him. I brought you the second one today. It will tell you more of Umberto's story."

Bernardo handed her an envelope. "Read it later, when you're by yourself."

Erika's hands shook a little as she took the letter. Much as she wanted to tear it open right away, she knew Bernardo was right about waiting. And she needed to finish up the business at hand. She turned to Paolo, who was putting away the books.

"Paolo, thank you for all you did today."

"No, Erika, I have to thank you. We're a good team, don't you agree?"

"Yes, I do, Paolo. I could not do it without you. I've majored in business, and this is what I do for a living—I help companies turn themselves around. That's what I do best. But to do that, I need an enthusiastic staff. And that's what I have with you and Elisa and everyone else here at Casalvento and Livernano." She smiled. "And you never resented the fact that I am a woman. Not many men want a woman telling them what to do. Especially not the Italian ones."

"You know, Erika, everything you said made sense. So why disagree?"

Erika didn't linger at the cantina. She thanked the staff for all their good work and walked back to the house, intent on looking closely at the landscape around her. How would the vines look in the months to come? she wondered. Would she be able to see what Paolo had described? The grapes turning into wine in the bottle? Could she document that process with her new camera?

As she came into the house, she greeted Doris and went upstairs, taking the letter up to the office, where her camera equipment and manuals were scattered over the desk.

She sat down, opened the envelope, and began to read.

Dear Erika,

I hope this second letter finds you well and happy. I'm sure the days are filled with a lot of work for you. The vineyards and gardens always need attention. I hope the hotel has filled up with tourists from all over the world, and Casalvento is busy with wine tours.

I'm sure you are managing everything just fine with the guidance of Paolo and the team. Santo and Mirella have always been a great asset to the estate. You know they named the youngest after your father. That was a great honor for me. We lived together like a family. We cooked together, laughed together. It made my days worthwhile.

Doris has probably told you that one of my passions was cooking, especially during the spring and summer, when the vegetables are growing and the tomatoes are hanging off the vines, red and ripe. The ones from the garden taste so sweet, and I loved having cucumbers, melons, and greens fresh from the garden. When anyone asked, "What is there for dinner tonight?" I would reply, "Whatever the garden has to offer." Doris is a great cook. Let her teach you.

Paolo loves to cook too. We had many great moments together in the kitchen. Perhaps you can invite him for dinner from time to time. I would not want you to be alone in the evenings all the time. That is not good for a beautiful young woman.

I asked you to go to my office and look around. I hope by now you found some recipes and have tried them. Some of them are very old. They come from your great-grandmother.

Now, let's continue with my story!

I came back to Casalvento in early spring and started immediately to rebuild the farmhouse. The roof and windows had to be done first. Then we modified the kitchen and added new appliances. At the same time, we started working in the vineyard and hiring people to work on the farm. That is where Paolo's family came in. His grandfather started to work with me first, then his father, and now Paolo.

I was in constant contact with your grandmother. She and Robby seemed to be doing well. That first summer went by fast. Then the harvest came. It was a good hot year, but due to the neglect of the vineyard, we did not have the quantity I hoped for, nor the quality. It was not up to the standard that our farm had once had. But at least it was a start.

We planted the vegetable garden in front of the house, and I planted cherry trees and chestnut trees. We also planted all the cypress trees around the house. In the fall, we worked in the cellar, fermenting the wines, racking them. I hope you're beginning to understand what is involved in winemaking.

Your grandmother sent me pictures of Robby, who was growing fast.

We missed each other a lot. She had promised to come as soon as I was finished remodeling the house.

I made a room for Robby. I redid our bedroom, and gradually the house became beautiful. The fireplace in the living room downstairs was one of my favorite places, along with my chair upstairs, where I spent hours reading my beloved books.

I did most of my work and planning in my office. You may already have found some pictures there, mainly from my side of the family. Your great-grandmother was left on the church steps as an infant, and no one knew where she came from. She grew up in a convent near Florence. During the summer and for harvest, like everyone else, she came to work in this area in the fields. That is where she met your great-grandfather.

They fell in love instantly. He was eighteen, but she was only four-teen, too young for marriage. So it was decided that she would return to the convent. That was where she learned to read and write, how to run a household, how to cook. She was very beautiful, with thick hon-ey-colored hair and a beautiful round face with high cheekbones and bushy eyebrows. She had large, almond-shaped brown eyes. Your pic-tures remind me of her. You can see the resemblance for yourself in the old photographs.

My mother was a great cook and wrote most of the recipes in her little book. That cookbook is with the pictures in my—now your—office.

Your great-grandfather waited patiently for her. The very day she turned eighteen, on July 5, 1926, they got married. Soon after, she was pregnant with Gabriel, my oldest brother. Three years later, she had me, and two years later, my sister, Josephine. Josephine and I were always very close, but Gabriel was different. I did not get along with him at all. I truly never understood the reason why.

Josephine also married very young. At eighteen, like her mother. She married our neighbor's son, Giuseppe. Have you met your aunt's sons, your cousins? We called Massimo, the younger boy, the smart one. He became a doctor in Milan. Vincenzo, the oldest, stayed and ran the farm. He can be angry and difficult at times, but underneath he is all right. Try to get to know him.

My parents were a very happy couple. They worked hard. Then the war came, and in 1940 my father had to join the military, like all the other men. My mother was left to run the farm and raise us. It was a difficult period in our lives. I was ten years old by then, and Gabriel was thirteen.

Everyone was so scared our father would not return. The Italian military was poorly equipped, and a lot of good men never made it home. Our father, however, did return. He had no visible scars, but mentally he was not the same man who had left. He never spoke about that period of his life.

But slowly, things came back to normal. We worked the farm and the vineyards. When I turned sixteen, I started to learn to become a mason. It was not my first choice of work, but my father insisted. He always told me I was the second in line, and Gabriel would take over the farm one day. I had to listen. It served me well when I came to the United States.

Our parents died very young. My mother had a heart condition that no one knew about. She passed away at forty-eight. Our father passed away when he was fifty-eight years old from lung cancer—too much smoking.

The rest you already know. When he died, I left for America.

It is important to me that you understand how we grew up. I loved my parents deeply.

After I returned here and worked on the house, I was ready to have my wife and son come and join me in Italy. I had done everything I could to give them a comfortable and loving home in Tuscany. That was not to be. There is much more to the story, but it will have to wait for another time and another letter. For today, my dear Erika, I'm finished writing. It tires me, and it also is sometimes difficult to remember and write down the memories, some painful, others good.

Enjoy a glass of our good wine, Erika, and don't forget to invite Paolo from time to time.

Sending you much love.

Your grandfather,
Umberto

XXVIII

———

*E*RIKA READ AND REREAD the letter, eager to absorb every last bit of meaning, trying hard to hear her grandfather's voice in the written lines. The more she knew, the more her perspective changed. She went to find the picture album she'd left in her bedroom and searched through it, looking for the one that showed her great-grandmother. She tried to see if there was a family resemblance.

One thing hadn't changed much. Though eighty-some years had passed, the house behind her looked very much the same. *We humans are really only here for a split second,* Erika thought. She had to begin making every moment count. She took a deep breath and went downstairs to find Doris.

"I'm making *pasta e fagioli,*" Doris told her. "It's a pasta-and-beans dish, something like a soup. Your grandpa liked it with sausage, so that's how I make it."

"I can't wait to taste it. Doris, I really want to learn more about cooking. Can you teach me some simple dishes? I could watch and help you."

"I would love to do that. And we can start tomorrow. We have a lot of strawberries from the garden, and I was planning to make marmalade. If you have the time, we could do it together. It's not hard."

"That would be perfect."

Erika opened a bottle of red wine, poured a glass, and took it out to the table, where the low sun was casting a glow over everything. Breathing deeply, she could smell the basil and the fragrant rosemary hedge. She looked up to the sky and raised her glass. "To you, Grandpa. Thank you."

Doris brought out the *pasta e fagioli.*

"That looks delicious," Erika said as she dipped her spoon into the creamy dish. "I love the fresh rosemary and parsley you put in. And the sausage gives it a wonderful flavor."

"Oh, wait," Doris said. "I forgot to add one thing. It's important."

She disappeared into the kitchen and came back with a small bottle.

"This is vinegar," she said. "We add just a splash. Your grandpa told me it's a must."

The days were flying by. Erika made strawberry marmalade with Doris and Mirella and read both her grandfather's letters again and again. She went to the cantina to work with Paolo and Elisa and visited Livernano every few days. In the evenings, she studied the camera manuals and practiced with the Leica, taking pictures of the garden and the paths through the vineyards.

One late Friday afternoon, as she was about to try to take some sunset photos, she stopped to talk to Doris, who was preparing dinner.

"That smells yummy! What are you making tonight?"

"*Linguine con cozze e vongole*, linguine with mussels and clams. I bought a whole bag of them at the market today. And I know it's Paolo's favorite dish. I thought you might like to call him and invite him for dinner."

Erika considered that. "I don't mind having company tonight. I can call him and ask if he can come."

Doris nodded.

"Do I still have time to take some photos?"

"Yes, this won't be ready for another hour."

Paolo accepted the invitation when she called him, and Erika went out to the back of the house. She used a zoom lens to highlight some decorative columns in the distance, then switched to close-ups of the many-hued roses in the garden. Marveling once again at the sculptures her grandfather had installed among the blooms, she took a picture of the fawn in the center of the flower bed, then another of the work that adorned the steps leading down into the vineyards—a pretty farmer's daughter with a basket of grapes.

She was heading into the olive groves when she saw a car coming down the driveway. Thinking it was Paolo, she capped the camera lens and walked back to the house. But this wasn't Paolo's car, she realized, and when she went into the kitchen, she saw a stranger talking to Doris.

He turned around and introduced himself. "I'm Massimo Ovietti, brother of your neighbor. Your grandfather's sister, Josephine, was my grandmother, so your grandfather was my uncle. I'm your cousin. Welcome to Casalvento!"

Massimo put out his hand, then decided to envelop Erika in a hug instead. "I'm so pleased to meet you. When I heard that you had decided to accept the will and stay here, I was surprised but delighted, especially to have such a good-looking cousin!"

"Thank you for the compliment." Erika smiled at him, appreciating Massimo's charm and his perfect English. His hands were very soft and clean, she noticed, and decided that he was clearly not a farmer.

"Massimo, Doris made dinner," she said. "Why don't you stay and eat with us?"

"Yes, I would love that. I guess it was perfect timing."

"Paolo will be joining us at seven," Erika said. "In the meantime, would you like a glass of wine or Prosecco?"

"I would not mind having a glass of your white wine."

"Let me get some. Please go outside and make yourself comfortable."

A few minutes later, she came out with wine, glasses, and some olives and sat down next to Massimo.

"Paolo and your grandfather make the best white wine around here," he said as he took a sip.

"And do you also make wine?" Erika asked.

"No. I'm a doctor, a neurosurgeon. I live in Milan and just came home for the weekend. From time to time, one needs to get away from the city."

"I actually have a cousin who's a neurosurgeon . . . I'm impressed."

"Thank you, and you?"

"I majored in business. I have a consulting firm in New York, and I specialize in turning distressed companies around."

"Also impressive."

Erika peered closely at Massimo. "You know, besides my parents, I have never met any of my relatives—in the United States or here."

"Well, you have now. Hasn't my brother, Vincenzo, come by yet? He is the one who runs the farm next to yours."

"He was here, but I missed him. I know he had some disagreements with my grandfather."

"He may be jealous, too, because Casalvento makes such good wine." He smiled at Erika. "And how do you get along with Paolo?"

"Very well. He's helping me a lot. It's a little much for me to absorb all at once, but we make a good team. And I can help him on the business side."

"He was my best friend growing up. We're the same age, and we went to school together. Then I went to the university in Bologna, and we drifted apart. Now, when I'm here, we see each other, and we have some good times together. I'm happy that I'll see him tonight," Massimo added. "We did some really stupid things together."

"Like what?"

"Like going out in the fields and pushing sleeping cows over. Or taking the tractor for a spin. Chasing girls. Neither of us married."

"Where did you learn English so well?"

"I was in the States for one year as an exchange student and then in England for three years. And I worked at a hospital in Jacksonville, Florida, for two years. That helped me a lot. And with your grandfather, we only spoke English. Paolo and I spent a lot of time with him. He was funny and always had so many stories to tell. But he never told me I had a cousin!"

They heard the sound of Paolo's truck in the driveway, and a moment later he joined them on the patio. When he recognized Massimo, he laughed out loud, then came and hugged him like a brother, clapping him on the back.

"What are you doing here?" Paolo asked.

"Escaping the city, and I was curious about the cousin everyone was telling me about. So I decided to come and look for myself!"

"Paolo," said Erika, "please sit down and have a glass of wine with us."

"Of course. Here . . . I brought us something different to try. You need to explore different wines from Italy. This one is from Verona. It's an Amarone, typical for that area. What are we having for dinner?"

"*Linguine con cozze e vongole.*"

"Fantastic. My favorite! *Salute!*"

Doris came out to set the table, and Paolo opened the Amarone and decanted it. By the time dinner was served, Erika and Massimo were talking and laughing as if they'd known each other forever.

After dinner, they opened a second bottle, and as the garden lights came on, they turned on some music. Paolo took Erika's hand, and they started dancing, then Massimo cut in, then Paolo again. They danced and talked till midnight under an almost full moon.

Erika was awakened on Saturday morning by the sounds of someone working in the kitchen. *How can that be?* she wondered. *Doris doesn't come in on the weekends. Who could be down there?*

She put on her robe, went down to the kitchen, and was surprised to find Paolo making breakfast and Massimo setting the table outside.

"Paolo?" she asked.

"*Buongiorno*, Erika."

"What time is it?"

"It's ten thirty."

"What are you doing here?"

"You told us to come back in the morning after you so kindly asked us to go last night."

"I did? I guess I had a little too much fun!"

"How are you feeling?"

"I'm not sure yet. I need coffee." She poured herself a cup and nodded at Massimo. "You guys are cheery this morning!"

"Yes," said Paolo. "And we've made you some eggs and bacon, with tomatoes and toast."

Massimo opened a bottle of Prosecco. "We can celebrate finding new cousins!"

"I'll celebrate," said Erika, "but just with coffee for now."

"Okay," said Massimo, "so what are we going to do today?"

"We can go to the seaside," Paolo suggested.

"Paolo, that's a great idea. What do you think, Erika?"

"I think I'll stay home. I want to hang out at the pool."

"You can hang out there anytime," Paolo reminded her. "Today you're coming with us to Grosseto. It's not too far. No argument. We leave in one hour."

"I guess I have no choice," she said, smiling.

An hour later, the car was loaded with beach gear, and they were on their way to Grosseto, where they found a sandy beach backed by pines, with a concession that rented them umbrellas and sun beds. Dinner was at a local fish restaurant where they feasted on grilled calamari followed by *dentice*, snapper, prepared on the grill with olive oil, salt, and lemon. The Italians sure knew how to live it up, thought Erika. She considered their immense fondness for food and wine and the company of good friends and felt lucky to have this new chapter in her life.

Exhausted by the end of the day, she fell asleep on the ride home and was again asleep in bed almost as soon as Paolo and Massimo drove away.

In the middle of the night, she woke up thirsty and went downstairs to get some water. It occurred to her that since she had visited Umberto's grave, she hadn't been disturbed by the sound of a car engine or any other strange noises. Paolo might have thought her foolish, but maybe her appeal to her grandfather had some effect.

XXIX

HE NEXT WEEK ERIKA was busy with work at Livernano and Casalvento. She helped to run the staff meetings and with organizing bookings and tours, and she made sure everything was ready for the tourists, who were increasing by the day.

On Friday, she pitched in as the staff bottled some eight thousand bottles of Chianti Classico, paying close attention as Paolo explained the process to her. The red wine had already been stabilized, clarified, and filtered and had the sediments removed. After a minimal amount of sulfites had been added, the wine was ready to be taken out of the tank. She watched as Mirella placed an empty bottle on the assembly line, and then marveled as the bottling machine went to work—washing each bottle, infusing a bit of nitrogen to keep any oxygen out, filling the bottle, and, finally, corking it.

Santo and Luca took the filled bottles and placed them in what Paolo called the cage, which held five hundred bottles. The Chianti would rest there for another three to six months before it could be labeled. Then it would be ready for sale.

It was amazing to be able to see the entire process of winemaking, from the grapes in the vineyard to the bottles about to be shipped. She had never imagined, when buying a bottle of wine, how much work went into it.

By the end of the day, she was tired but looking forward to the evening. Massimo had returned for the weekend and had invited her and Paolo for dinner, and though she was nervous about meeting her other cousin, she was curious, too. As she left the cantina, she asked Paolo, "What should we bring tonight?"

"I would bring a couple of bottles of the L'Anima Gold. They love that wine, plus they don't make any whites, so there's no reason for your cousin to be jealous."

He picked her up an hour later and drove the short distance to the neighbor's place, where Massimo greeted them with embraces and Italian-style kisses. Like Erika's house, the building was old but seemed more forbidding. The stark stone architecture had not been softened with greenery or flowers. As they walked inside, Massimo introduced Erika to his brother, Vincenzo, who nodded and brusquely shook hands but said nothing else.

Erika was startled by his coldness, but Massimo took her aside and said quietly, "Don't worry about Vincenzo. He is like this all the time—a bitter man. Now you know why I don't come home often. There's no way to change him. He's been like this since his wife left him and took the kids."

"How long ago was that?"

"Six years ago. It's sad, really. He hardly sees his children at all. His wife went back to her family in the Veneto, near the Austrian border. She also came from a winery. Life does not always turn out the way you thought."

"Oh, Massimo, it's funny that you should say that to me. Two months ago, I thought I had the perfect life and was getting married in September. Now I'm in Italy. I've broken off my engagement and found a family I never knew I had."

"You look pretty happy."

"I am! It's been unexpected, but so far it has worked out for the better."

"Let's go in for dinner," Massimo said. "We're having chicken curry. We thought you'd enjoy a change. Your L'Anima wine will go perfectly."

All during the meal, Paolo and Massimo did their best to lighten the mood and keep Erika entertained, but Vincenzo remained silent till the end. Finally, he invited them all outside to try some of his own wines.

As he poured a glass for each of them, he suddenly blurted out to Erika, "You know I own land inside Casalvento!"

"Vincenzo," Massimo interrupted him. "Not tonight, please. You've just met Erika. You should be getting to know her."

"It's okay," Erika said. "I know about your situation. But I've just arrived, and I need to understand more about the property. We're neighbors and cousins, and we'll take it up after I'm the official owner. That won't happen for a few more months."

Paolo added, "Vincenzo, that's only fair."

"But I need to know this year," Vincenzo insisted. "I want to start planting next spring."

"I won't forget. I promise," said Erika.

"Let's have some more wine," said Massimo, "and enjoy the rest of the evening."

Vincenzo relaxed a little and poured everyone another glass of wine, but before too much longer, the party broke up. As Paolo drove Erika home, she couldn't help saying, "How different Massimo and Vincenzo are. It's hard to believe they're brothers."

"I know, Erika. It has not been easy for Vincenzo. He stayed here while Massimo went out in the world and studied. He was the oldest and had to take over the farm. Maybe he feels like he deserved some fun too. And I think he misses his kids."

"We do need to resolve this nonsense with the property somehow," Erika said.

"You handled it well. When the time comes, I think Bernardo will be able to take care of it once and for all."

"I hope so. I just found out I had cousins. I want them as friends, not angry neighbors."

As May drew to a close, the cantina hosted more and more visitors for its Sunflower and Sunset tours, and the rooms at Livernano were almost always filled. Everything had begun to run smoothly, and Erika recognized that it was thanks to the people who worked for her. They made a strong team . . . and a good-looking one, too. The image of Paolo, suntanned and muscular, popped into her mind. She realized he probably knew how handsome and sexy he was in the white or yellow polo shirts with the Casalvento logo that he always wore, and she wondered again why he didn't have a girlfriend. Then she reminded herself that she was his boss. She shouldn't think of him any other way. And there was no question he knew what he was doing when he was working. Even the tone of his voice made it clear he was in control.

The grapes were entering a new stage in the vineyards, Paolo had told her. Because no irrigation was allowed with Chianti Classico, everything depended on nature. But so far nature was cooperating in a gorgeous way.

The properties were in full flower, with roses blooming in terra-cotta pots and lavender planted in open barrels. Ivy climbed the old stone walls, and the herb garden provided a bounty of basil, parsley, oregano, and thyme for the Livernano kitchen and Erika's own table. The vegetable garden was also starting to produce tomatoes, peppers, and eggplant.

Erika finally found time to meet with the real estate agent to talk about a possible sale. The value was still important to her, but the idea of selling the estates had faded, and when he heard she had changed her mind, his face betrayed his disappointment.

She continued to work on her photography and go through the papers her grandfather had left in his office. Most were in Italian, and even those in English didn't always make sense to her, but it was clear that he hadn't left his family because he wanted to abandon them. It was his duty to take over Casalvento.

One afternoon her phone rang as she was at the desk. Craig's name was on the screen.

"I'm doing amazing," she told him when asked how she was. "How are you?"

"I miss you. And our friends are asking about you. I told them that you're in Italy and very busy, helping to make the vineyards and the hotel as profitable as possible to sell them."

"You told them what? How dare you, Craig! You never change, do you?"

"What do you mean?"

"Craig, I'm not *selling* anything. I'm running the estates with Paolo and Constantina." Her voice got louder and angrier. "And get this in your head. I'm not coming back to the States anytime soon, and I'm never coming back to you. You and I are finished!"

She shut down her cell, feeling angry. She wanted Craig out of her life once and for all.

Maybe a run would calm her down.

In minutes, she was out the door, running past Santo and Luca working in the vegetable gardens on her way to the chapel. There she paused to catch her breath, admire the view, and say a quick prayer. Then she ran back down and waved to Santo and Luca as she passed them again. In this direction, a field of sunflowers, just beginning to open, caught her eye. Standing straight and already tall, the blooms looked like a row of saluting soldiers. She slowed down to a walk, taking time to admire the loveliness around her—the cypress and pines along the road ahead and the vineyards below. Through the trees, she could see the back of the house with the pool and the garden, and some of the other small buildings. They looked like an island surrounded by vineyards. It was unlike anything at home in New York, achingly beautiful. Why would she ever sell a paradise like this?

XXX

---

*I*T WAS LATE THE NEXT AFTERNOON when she got a text from Todd: *On my way to JFK. Will leave Berlin Saturday morning and arrive in Florence at midday. James will arrive from Frankfurt one hour later. I can wait for him. Please let me know who will pick us up. Thanks, darling! Love, hugs, and kisses.*

She couldn't wait to see them—and the weather was so gorgeous they would never want to leave! She called the cantina and asked for Paolo.

"*Ciao*, Paolo. Remember that I told you some friends will be coming soon? They arrive in Florence on Saturday. Is there someone who can pick them up?"

"Of course, Erika. Santo will do it. Do you have their arrival information?"

She read him the details and added, "Please make sure he has a sign with 'Casalvento' on it."

"No problem. I'll take care of it. Have a nice evening."

Suddenly Erika thought of her grandfather's second letter. Before she could second-guess herself, she said, "Paolo, if you have nothing planned for tonight, do you want to join me for dinner? Maybe even help me prepare it?"

"You are cooking tonight?"

"Yes!"

"What are you making?"

Erika suddenly realized what she had said. She had no idea what to make, or even if she could prepare a meal. Before she could say anything, though, Paolo went on, "It doesn't matter. I'll be there at six."

"Paolo, seven would be better."

"Okay, seven then. *Ci vediamo fra un po.*"

"*Ciao*," she answered and quickly answered Todd's text.

Then there was the question of how to make dinner. She had made pasta with Doris's sauce but never prepared a whole meal on her own. Her cooking lessons hadn't progressed that far. She obviously needed some help.

"Ah, here you are, Doris," Erika said as she went down to the kitchen. "I was just on the phone with Paolo and invited him for dinner. But I'm afraid I told him I was cooking."

Doris laughed. "Okay. What were you thinking of making?"

"I have no idea. What do you think? Can you help me?"

"Well, I was planning on making *pasta e fagioli* for dinner. Remember that dish? I already soaked the beans overnight. It's easy to make, and Paolo likes it too. Come on, we can do the rest together."

Erika got an apron, turned on some music, poured herself a glass of white wine, and smiled at Doris. "I'm ready. Where do I start?"

"First, get a large deep pot. Then we need to chop up a big onion."

Erika followed the directions, digging out the biggest pot she could find. "What's next?"

"We need to peel some garlic cloves and mince them, then chop a couple of carrots and stalks of celery and mince the tomatoes."

Once Erika had done those things, Doris continued, "Now drain the beans, but leave a little juice behind. Then chop the parsley. We'll need some broth and pasta, too."

"Doris, what about the sausages?"

"Well done, Ms. Erika—I just wanted to see if you remembered."

Doris guided Erika through the rest of the steps, and they were just finishing up as Paolo walked in holding a bottle of red wine. "What are you making, Erika?" he asked. "It looks great."

"*Pasta e fagioli*. It will be done in a few minutes, and we can eat outside."

"I can't believe what I'm seeing," he teased. "Erika in the kitchen with an apron on. Who would have ever thought?"

Erika put her hands on her hips and feigned a stern face.

He smiled. "I'll take the wine to the table," he told her.

Doris set the table, and Erika followed with the *pasta e fagioli*. She added a splash of vinegar as Paolo watched. "I see you know your grandfather's secret ingredient," he said, smiling approvingly.

Erika nodded and asked, "Paolo, what wine did you bring to have with my first cooked meal?"

"I brought a Brunello. This wine is full bodied, fruit forward, and with a long finish. It should go perfectly with dinner." As he opened the bottle, she thought he looked very handsome. He was all dressed up, and something else was different. Maybe he had a haircut? She couldn't help but wonder if maybe he liked her a little bit.

At that moment, he looked up at her. "Shall we see what kind of a cook you are?"

He lifted a bite and tried it, but gave no reaction. In fact, it looked as if he was frowning a bit.

"You don't like it?" Erika asked.

"I'm kidding around. I love it. I'm impressed. But it's probably beginner's luck."

"Paolo, you're mean!" Erika tasted the dish and felt proud of what she had accomplished in the kitchen.

Paolo raised his glass and proposed a toast. "To a new Erika that cooks! Do you like the wine?"

"Yes, it does go well with the meal. You were right."

"If you want, we can go to Brunello di Montalcino and do some tastings. It's only sixty kilometers south of Siena. It's another region of Tuscany, and Brunello's red wines are also DOCG."

"What does that mean?"

"It stands for *Denominazione di Origine Controllata e Garantita*— Denomination of Controlled and Guaranteed Origin. Brunello's grapes are also a hundred percent Sangiovese, but they taste a lot different than ours."

"How many kinds of Sangiovese are there?"

"More than forty-eight. If you want, we can go for a day trip to the top ten wineries."

"That sounds wonderful. I would love that."

After dinner, Paolo helped Erika clean up, then they went back outside and kept talking, mostly about Livernano.

"We should go there tomorrow," said Paolo, "and see how everything is going."

"You know, Paolo, I've never had dinner there. Maybe we should have an early meal there."

"Dinner for a second night in a row?" he said. "I must be a better conversationalist than I thought."

"Strictly business, of course, Paolo," Erika added quickly, blushing at his joke. "I need to learn how good our chef is."

"Okay. I'll see you tomorrow in the office, and we can drive over together around four p.m. I want to check the vines over there, too."

"That sounds perfect. But now, I'm tired. Cooking has exhausted me." She laughed.

"It was delicious, Erika. Thank you."

He gave her a quick kiss on the cheek, left and right.

"Thank you, Paolo," she told him, a little sad that their evening couldn't go on a bit longer. But there was so much to do in the morning. "Can you lock up for me?"

"Sure. *Buona notte*," he said, and with that, he was off.

Part THREE

XXXI

―――――――

*E*RIKA WAS WEARING white jeans and a light blue shirt when Paolo picked her up the next day to go to Livernano. She had decided to wear her auburn hair loose and had her sunglasses hooked onto the large bag on her shoulder. "Very sporty," Paolo said cheerfully, "but still the elegant boss."

"Thank you for the compliment," Erika told him. "Let's go."

"You may need a sweater or something for later."

"Not to worry. I've got one in my bag."

He looked at her white shoes. "You can't go with those shoes. We'll be walking in the fields first."

"I know. I've got rubber boots in here, too." She jumped into the truck. "*Andiamo!*"

As they walked through the vineyards, Paolo inspected the plants, pointing out how the various grapes were progressing. Erika was fascinated by the small clusters under the leaves.

Then it was on to Livernano, which was bustling with guests. Hanna had come over to help out with wine tastings, and Constantina was busy supervising the staff and making sure diners were happy. Erika still found it hard to believe that all this belonged to her. As she and Paolo sat down at a long table, she asked Constantina if she wanted to join them for dinner.

"With pleasure!"

Moments later, Hanna came to take their drink orders.

Erika looked at Paolo. "Should we start with the L'Anima Gold?"

He nodded. "And some sparkling water."

The waiter arrived with a basket of freshly baked bread and focaccia and followed up immediately with an amuse-bouche of stuffed zucchini flowers. One after the other, the courses flowed out smoothly: fried green tomatoes with balsamic glaze, fresh pasta with white rabbit sauce, and finally the seared Florentine steak called *tagliata di manzo*.

"This food is amazing, Constantina. I'm really impressed."

"He is a true chef. He worked at Trattoria Quatro Lioni, in Florence."

"I don't think I want any dessert, but I do want to thank the chef." Erika got up and went to find him, and though his English was as limited as her Italian, he beamed at the compliments.

After dinner, as Paolo drove Erika back to Casalvento, he complimented her on how comfortable she now was, how much she seemed in her element, and how different she appeared from her first week in Italy.

"Don't forget," Erika said as she got out of the car, after thanking him for his kind words, "my friends are coming tomorrow. Please make sure Santo remembers to get them at the airport in Florence. And I want you to meet them, too. *Buona notte*, Paolo."

Erika had a bottle of Prosecco chilling in the refrigerator as she waited for Todd and James to arrive. As soon as she heard a car in the driveway, she rushed out the door.

Todd and James emerged from the van looking as though they'd stepped out of a fashion magazine.

"Darling," Todd exclaimed. "What a drive! All those curves. But we made it! And how wonderful it is to see you." He took a step back. "You look positively radiant."

"You must be happy here," James said. "It shows."

"Welcome to Casalvento," she said, rushing over in time to be enveloped in a huge hug from Todd and James together. "Guys, I can't breathe!"

James let go, but Todd kept his arm around her waist. "Oh, darling, you not only look fantastic, you also smell like a rose. Tuscany agrees with you."

"Yes, I love it here. It has become my new home." She turned to Santo. "*Prego di prendere i bagagli e portarli nella camera degli ospiti.*"

"Oh, I *am* impressed," said Todd. "You're really taking this Italy thing seriously."

"I'm trying. Learning this language is not as easy as I thought, but slowly I'm improving. Now I want you to meet Doris. She's my Girl Friday, and she made us lunch. She takes care of everything, even teaching me how to cook and helping me with my Italian."

Todd and James grinned at each other and said in unison, "You cook?"

"Yes, I do. You'll see!" She led them inside and introduced them to Doris, who said, "Welcome to Tuscany. Please, if you need anything during your stay, let me know. Lunch is outside today."

Erika took Todd and James to the table, set with pretty lemon-patterned ceramic plates. "Here we are—with everything that Tuscany and my garden have to offer. Fresh mozzarella with tomatoes and basil, fresh from the garden. Cucumber salad with fresh oregano, marinated with a little yogurt and our own olive oil. And some local prosciutto, several cheeses, a zucchini frittata, bread, and Parmesan."

Todd was effusive. "Darling, I want to marry you and move here. No wonder you love it here. This is simply paradise. Everything is done with so much taste—the stone walls with the climbing roses, the terra-cotta tiles." He looked up. "James, look at the angels sitting on each corner of the roof."

Erika tilted her head. "You know, Todd, I never noticed them before!"

"Darling, that was the first thing I saw."

"Why don't you go look at the back. I'll get the Prosecco."

Todd and James walked to the back patio, and when Erika found them, they stood taking in the view of vineyards and olive trees.

"Oh, my God!" Todd said. "I have died and gone to heaven."

"Todd, you are always so dramatic," said Erika, who was bringing three glasses and the bottle of sparkling wine. "But that was exactly what I thought too when I first came here."

Todd was still admiring the view. "James, look at the roses and lavender. This part looks like an English garden. And are those rosemary hedges?"

Erika smiled and nodded.

"Who planted this?"

"I believe it must have been my grandfather." She handed the glasses to Todd and James and poured the Prosecco. "*Salute!*"

"Erika, to you!"

"Let's go and eat."

The afternoon passed quickly as they sipped the wine and leaned back in their chairs to savor the view of Tuscany's rolling hills.

"Erika," James said, "you have a jewel here. No wonder you look the way you look now. You bloomed like that red rose there."

She took a deep breath. "I thought I had the perfect life in New York, but fate had something different in mind for me. I've fallen in love with this place and what it has to offer. I wake up in the morning happy to get up. I hated Mondays in New York, even though I liked what I did. I welcome the challenges here. Paolo's teaching me all about winemaking, and the longer I'm here, the more I appreciate the lifestyle and what my grandfather did. I get why he added this clause to his will. He wanted me to know about my roots. I keep finding things in his office—pictures, old documents. He even left handwritten letters for me. It's amazing but also strange at the same time. Now I'm here, where he wanted me to be, and it's relaxing and rewarding. I smile and laugh like I haven't done for a long time. No one tells me what to do, how to dress, or how to wear my hair. No one puts me down. It's making me completely rethink my life before."

Just at that moment, Paolo came around the corner. "*Buongiorno,* everyone."

Erika introduced him. "This is Paolo, my right-hand man and manager of the properties."

As they assessed the newcomer, Todd and James exchanged a sly look that clearly meant, "Not bad looking."

Erika, worried he might notice, gestured to Paolo. "Come have a glass of wine with us."

Todd chimed in. "Erika just told us how helpful you've been and how much she loves it here."

"Oh, she did?" Paolo said as he sat down and poured himself a glass of wine.

"She also told us how much she's learning from you," James added.

Paolo's eyes met Erika's for a second. He held up the glass. "Cheers, everyone. *Benvenuti.*"

"Paolo," Todd said, "maybe you can help me. I have a mission while I'm here—I was hired by one of my clients to shop for her new apartment. I need to buy some antique furniture. I would love to hire you to help me if it is something you would be interested in—I know it will take some time out of your work here."

"No need to worry—I have the free time and would love to help a friend of Erika's. Erika already told me, and I have some antique stores lined up for you to visit next week. There is also a local furniture market nearby, every Saturday."

"And if I find furniture, can you help me get it to the States?" Todd asked.

"Yes, we just sent a container with twenty-four pallets of wine to New York, and everything went well. I'm sure we can do that."

"Paolo," asked James, "where did you learn to speak English so well?"

"I worked at a vineyard in California for a few years. I fell in love with the owner's daughter, and we got engaged, but her father had other plans for her. Long story."

"You were engaged?" Erika set her wineglass down a touch too hard, and James caught her eye.

"Yes. Why? Does that shock you?"

"No, no, it's just you never told me, that's all."

Paolo's glass was empty, and he stood up. "It's time for me to go home. It's almost dinnertime. It's nice to meet you. I know you'll enjoy Tuscany."

"Have a nice weekend, Paolo," Erika said.

"I'll check in tomorrow. I need to get some samples of our wines. We hope to bottle the Chianti Classico from Livernano and Casalvento next week. *Buona notte, tutti.*"

As soon as he'd left, Todd turned to Erika. "Oh, he is a hot cookie, darling."

"I know, Todd, but not for me."

"Are you sure, Erika?" James asked. "He seems to like you."

"Guys, he is my *employee.* Now stop it and pour me another glass of wine."

Lunch had evolved into a light dinner, and Doris came out to tell them that their rooms were ready and their suitcases were upstairs. "Is there anything else I can do before I go home?" she asked.

"No, but can you come in tomorrow for a couple of hours? I don't think I can handle these guys on my own."

"Sure, should I bring some *pasticcino?*"

"That would be perfect. *Buona notte,* Doris."

"*Buona notte.*"

"What is *pasticcino?*" James asked.

"Pastry. You'll love it. The Italians have the best! Now let me show you your little home away from home."

"Yes, please. And I need to take a shower," said Todd.

"And so do I," added James.

"You guys get settled in, and then we can relax."

An hour later, they were making themselves comfortable in the wicker chairs in front of the house. Chips and olives were on the table, along with another bottle of wine and fresh glasses. Italian music was playing softly in the background as the sun went down. The lights around the property gave the garden a lovely glow.

James raised a glass. "Cheers to our darling Erika. And thank you again for having us!"

"What does Casalvento mean?" asked Todd.

"Translated into English, it means 'House of the Wind.' Feel the breeze? It comes up every evening."

"Who named the property?"

"I don't know, James. The house is a thousand years old. It used to be a simple farmhouse, with space for cows and pigs on the ground floor and rooms for the family upstairs. The people here ran the farms for the Medici, one of the oldest families in Tuscany and the founders of the oldest bank— the Monte dei Baci."

James looked over at Erika, eyebrows raised.

"I know it's hard to imagine," said Erika. "At least we have no pigs or cows in the house."

They all burst out laughing, and she added, "Oh, God, it's so good to have you two here. I really missed you guys. I've got all kinds of things planned for you."

"Don't forget, we're on vacation," said James. "We want to sleep in and do what comes. Let the day tell us what we want to do. Drink good wine and eat good homemade pasta. I want to enjoy my ten days here—it was difficult to get time off. I need some time to reenergize for work. Do you have a pool here?"

"Yes, over near the garage. I'll show it to you both tomorrow."

"Perfect! That is where you'll find me."

"And Doris and I will be in the kitchen cooking, using all the wonderful things from the garden."

"I want to help too," said Todd.

James started to laugh. "Erika, if I were you, I wouldn't let him into the kitchen."

Todd changed the subject. "I don't want to sour the moment, but what is happening with Craig? Is he still in the picture?"

Erika took a breath. "Well, you remember that when I was back in New York, I had already decided to honor my grandfather's wishes and stay the five months. I had to call the wedding off. At this point, I don't want to marry Craig at all. He, of course, is trying to patch things up, but ever since I've been here, I've begun to realize how controlling and manipulative he was."

"Oh, well, darling, I knew it from the beginning," said Todd, "especially after I did the apartment for him. He never asked you what *you* wanted."

"I guess that's true, Todd, but it seemed normal to me. I felt totally different then. As I said this afternoon, here in Casalvento I feel free and happy. I cannot go back to my life in New York. And I realize now that Craig was cold. He never hugged or kissed me with any kind of passion. He never held my hand, because he thought showing emotions in public wasn't cool."

Erika stopped, overcome by old memories. "I think I've had too much wine. Let's call it a night. Tomorrow I want to show you around Casalvento and maybe go over to Livernano for lunch or a drink. But we'll have dinner at home. If you want anything special to eat, let me know."

"I want to try a Florentine steak," said James. "If possible."

"And you, Todd?"

"I don't care—just feed me."

"Okay. You two are welcome to sit out here longer. But I have to go to bed. I can't believe that you aren't tired after your trip."

"Are you kidding, Erika?" said Todd. "Who could be tired in these surroundings? But you're probably right. Come on, James, let's all call it a night."

They helped carry the dishes and glasses into the kitchen, and Todd looked at Erika in disbelief as she loaded the dishwasher. "Darling, you are doing dishes now, too?"

"Of course! I don't want Doris coming to work tomorrow morning to find a dirty kitchen."

Todd smiled. "You really are a new person, Erika, embracing a new life. See you in the morning."

XXXII

———

$\mathcal{J}$AMES WAS SITTING OUTSIDE reading a book when Erika came down for breakfast. She gave him a kiss on the cheek and sat next to him.

"How did you sleep?" she asked.

"Like a log. The air is so fresh, and it's so quiet. I think the birds finally woke me up. You don't hear them like this in New York. I walked around the house and the vineyard a little. Erika, this property is huge and so beautiful."

"Yes, isn't it just? But where's Todd?"

"He's still sleeping. He won't be down before ten."

Doris was in the kitchen, and Erika went in to ask her to serve breakfast outdoors.

They were sampling the *pasticcino* when Todd came downstairs.

"Good morning, sleepyhead," said Erika. "You're just in time to try these with my strawberry marmalade. I made it myself."

"You made this?" asked Todd. "It's fantastic."

"Well, Doris showed me what to do. But I'm learning. Now are you two ready?"

"Ready for what?"

"I want to show you the whole property. We can take the John Deere, but one of you guys will need to sit in the back." She led them around to where it was parked.

Todd took one look and exclaimed, "Erika, can we please take the car?"

"You guys are too much. This is better for going into the vineyards and up the hills. It'll be fine. Hop in!"

One hour later, they were back, and Todd and James couldn't stop talking about the views from the hills, the rows of grapevines, the little chapel. "I still cannot believe that you never knew of this place," said Todd. "How is it possible no one ever mentioned your grandfather and his story?"

"No one ever spoke about him, and I never gave that a second thought. It just seemed normal."

"I guess you're right. I remember in college, we never asked each other about our parents or grandparents."

"Anyway," Erika went on, "I thought, if you wanted, I could show you Siena, and after lunch, on our way home, we could go to Livernano for a drink."

James smiled at her. "Erika, I'm a little tired. Todd came in from Germany, but I had a long trip. Why don't we just hang out. Then later Todd and I can go into Radda and buy groceries for tonight's dinner. I would love to go to the local shops."

"That's fine, James. You can take one of the cars. Radda's only two kilometers from the house. But the shops are closed until four. Why don't we hang out by the pool till then?"

"Darling, that sounds like a wonderful idea!"

At the stroke of four, James was dressed and ready to go into town. "I always have to wait for Todd," he complained.

"Oh, James, let him be our prima donna. And here he comes . . . Mr. Handsome!"

Todd walked out dressed in white pencil-style pants with a red belt, an orange polo shirt, orange-colored socks, black pointy shoes, and a red scarf around his neck.

Erika had to hold back a laugh. "Todd, where do you think you're going?"

"Shopping!"

"Dressed like that? You're not in the Hamptons. This is Radda—simple, casual Radda."

"You don't like it?"

"Of course we do. It's just that you're so . . . colorful."

James rolled his eyes. "Okay, Todd, let's go."

"Have fun, guys. I'll see you back around six."

"Do you need us to bring you anything?"

"No, just whatever you want to have for dinner. And remember we have lots of vegetables from the garden. Have a good time."

Erika went back into the kitchen. "Doris, in case they don't bring anything back, is there something we can cook now as a backup?"

"We have plenty of vegetables in the garden. I could make eggplant parmigiana."

"Great idea. Can I help? I've never made that dish, and I'd like to learn."

"Of course, Ms. Erika. And if you don't need it tonight, you can put it in the freezer."

Erika put on some music and got an apron while Doris pulled vegetables and herbs from the garden and cleaned them. Erika took notes as they prepared the eggplant and assembled the dish.

Todd and James returned exactly at six, carrying half a dozen bags full of food and snacks.

"Darling, let me tell you, those little shops are amazing," said James. "You can't just choose something. You have to experience it before you buy. And it all looks so delicious. We bought a little bit of everything. We're here for ten days, after all!"

"And the people in the shops were so nice," Todd said. "Of course, we had to tell them we are your friends and guests from Casalvento. Here, sweetheart. There's a little something for you." Todd handed Erika a little brown paper bag, and she pulled out a yellow cashmere shawl.

"Oh, Todd, James, thank you. I love it! It's beautiful."

"Come on, throw it over your shoulder," said Todd. "That yellow suits you perfectly. Now you look like one of the sunflowers in the field."

She turned right and left, modeling the shawl for them. "This is perfect for the evenings here. I don't have anything like this in my closet. You guys are so great. Now, are you ready for a drink?"

"Yes, I would like a vodka tonic," said Todd.

"Oh, no," Erika protested. "This is Tuscany. Your choices are Prosecco, white wine, or red. Or, if you are adventurous, Campari soda or an Aperol spritz."

"Okay, Prosecco for me," he said.

"For me, too," added James.

Erika went to get the wine and glasses and asked Doris, "Can you please unpack the goodies? We can have a little bit of everything for dinner and save the eggplant parmigiana for another time."

Moments later, all the food that they had bought was arranged on the table, and the three of them sat down to enjoy it.

"Everything is so fresh here," said James.

"That's the beauty of it," Erika said. "The Italians love to eat and drink, and most of them are skinny. In the States, we gain weight just by looking at the food. I have been on diets all my life, but here I've been eating like never before in my life and have not gained an ounce. My hair and my nails have gotten stronger, and I feel full of energy. My stress level is much lower here. And you know what I love the most? I can walk to my office."

"So, you would recommend we all move here?"

"Sure, James. Why not? What do you think, Todd?"

"I could stay and start decorating Erika's house. Just kidding, darling. It looks great as it is."

"You could see what it's like by coming to the cantina. We'll start bottling the wine tomorrow or the next day. You should come and help."

"Darling, I'll pass. I'm not groomed for physical labor," said Todd.

"Well, I'm just happy you both made it here," said Erika, raising her glass for one more toast. "Cheers!"

On Monday morning, Erika was dressed and ready to leave when Todd and James came down to breakfast.

"Good morning!" she told them. "I think today would be a good day for you two to go to Siena. I have to work—Paolo called early and said that we're bottling last year's vintage today, and I want to be a part of that. If you come to the cantina, Elisa in the office can tell you how to get to Siena. I'll see you back at six tonight."

When Erika got to the cantina, Hanna was already at the counter.

"*Buongiorno*, Hanna. How is everything going?"

"Very well, *Signora*. We had a busy weekend here with a lot of wine tours. But I love it like this."

"That's good to hear. Where are all the others?"

"They have already started bottling."

Erika walked into the bottling room and saw Paolo working, making sure that everything was going smoothly. He motioned her over.

"*Buongiorno*, Erika," he said. "I'm glad you came to help. But you also need to know that Franco, the contractor, has been here a couple of times, asking questions and being unpleasant. We need to talk to Bernardo about dealing with him once and for all. For today, though, let's concentrate on the bottling. I'll show you what to do."

Hours later, she was finishing up with the others when she looked at her watch. It was already six, and she realized that Todd and James would be back soon.

"Paolo, I've got to run," she said.

"No problem. We'll be done in a few minutes."

As she walked back to the house, past the olive trees and the vineyards, she realized how much the vines had changed. When she first arrived, there were hardly any leaves; then there were tiny grapes, and now the fruit was almost fully grown. Paolo had said they would soon turn color. *They're turning from gray to green*, she thought, *like me*.

Todd and James were waiting for her on the patio, enjoying a glass of wine.

"How was your day?" she asked. "I'm worn out. Bottling is hard work." She fell into a chair and let out a sigh.

"Are you telling us that you've not been back since you left this morning?"

"Yes, Todd, I have been at the cantina. It was rewarding but exhausting. James, can you hand me some wine, please?"

He poured her a glass.

"And how was your day in Siena?"

"Don't ask," said Todd. "First, we couldn't find our way to the city center. James was driving in circles, literally. He saw a sign that said '*sensa unica*,' with a blue arrow facing in one direction. He insisted that would take us to the city center."

"Oh, no!" She broke out laughing. "That means 'one way.'"

"Yes, we know that now," said Todd, "but before we figured that out, we'd been going in circles forever, passing the piazza and the Duomo I can't tell you how many times. We finally found the parking lot—which, by the way, we had also passed many, many times."

"Later, we visited the Piazza del Campo and the Duomo," added James, "and had lunch in a wonderful restaurant. Then we had to shop. Todd, give her our gift for today."

"You don't need to bring me gifts every time you go out," said Erika.

"Oh, yes, we do," said Todd. "We need to spoil you, darling. Here it is."

He handed her a little bag. Inside were an apron, an oven mitt, and dish towels with a sunflower design.

"You don't expect me to really use these in the kitchen, do you? They're too pretty."

"Yes, you will, darling. The sunflowers enhance your kitchen beauty. Now, what's for dinner tonight?"

"Doris bought us a steak for *bistecca fiorentina,* and we have potatoes and a fresh salad. And later we can watch a movie outside. I found a projector upstairs in the office, and we can project the film on the garage wall."

It was a perfect night, clear with stars, warm and a little breezy. The events of the day—the physical exertion and contractor questions—all faded away as Erika watched the scenes flickering on the garage wall. Afterward, she sat and talked for hours with her friends.

XXXIII

―――――

*W*ITH THE ARRIVAL OF Todd and James, Erika's days became a mix of sightseeing with them, continuing to make Casalvento and Livernano as profitable as possible, and checking in with her New York office, though the latter seemed farther and farther away. One day, she went with her friends to the little town of Castellina, spending the whole afternoon there before heading to dinner in Radda.

The next morning, Todd and James wanted to see Florence. Since she had to work, she arranged for Luca to drive them there. "The inner city is tough to get around," she explained. "Most of the roads are closed off and can only be used by taxis or buses. You'll have to park at the train station and then explore on foot. It'll be much easier to go with Luca."

She spent her own morning in front of the computer in her office. From time to time, she'd take a break and look at the pictures of the relatives she never knew, wishing she could fill in the missing details. She couldn't wait for the next letter from her grandfather and wondered how many there were.

Then she'd turn back to the emails, which were cluttering her inbox. *I've got to catch up with Tiffany and Molly*, she thought. At some point, she needed to tell them she wasn't coming back home and that she wanted Tiffany to buy her out. It was still too soon, though—maybe after she had taken care of Mr. Levine's business and felt more secure in her decision to stay in Italy and the properties had been fully transferred to her after the five months.

Erika was having lunch in the kitchen when Paolo stopped by.

"I just came from Livernano," he said. "They're having a *festa* tonight, firing up the pizza oven and welcoming a *pizzaiolo*. He's a chef who specializes in making pizzas. Everyone can create their own version. Plus there will be live music. I thought you and your friends would like to go. I already told Constantina to save places for you, just in case."

"That sounds great. You'll be coming with us, Paolo?"

"Yes, and I can drive you. I'll pick you all up at seven."

By late afternoon, Todd and James were back from Florence, full of enthusiasm.

"Florence is such an exciting city," said James. "While Todd was shopping for furniture, I did a little sightseeing, but there were a lot of tourists—on the Ponte Vecchio I had to use my elbows to get through. I also did some major damage at Gucci and Prada. The clothes here are so different than in the States. They fit so beautifully."

"And they look so good on you," added Erika.

She and James were dressed and ready for the *festa* at seven, but Todd, as usual, was taking his time.

"You look pretty tonight," James told her, "especially with your shawl."

She beamed at him. "Thanks to you and Todd for the special touch. But where *is* Todd? Paolo should be here any moment to pick us up. He is as on time as a watch."

"Let me go and fetch him."

At seven sharp, Paolo rolled into the driveway, and Todd emerged as colorfully dressed as ever. She thought he looked a bit like a bird of paradise, but that did fit his bright personality.

Without any recent rain, the unpaved road to Livernano was dry and dusty. As Paolo sped along the many curves, he left clouds swirling behind him. Todd, who was sitting in the back seat, piped up, "Erika, please have him slow down. I'd rather not die on a back road in Tuscany, and especially not *before* the *festa*."

"I heard that, Todd!" said Paolo. "We are almost there. Don't worry. I grew up on these roads."

As they arrived at Livernano, preparations for the *festa* were almost finished. The musicians were tuning up. The pizza oven was already on, and there was a long table with an array of toppings to choose from. Constantina introduced Erika to the *pizzaiolo* and showed her to the seats that had been reserved at the head table. Soon the space filled up with the hotel guests, who lined up to create their personal pizzas.

Todd and James came over and sat down as the waiters began to pour the wine, and Paolo soon joined them.

"Todd, what did you two do in Florence today?" he asked.

"I found some great antique shops and bought furniture. That reminds me. Can they deliver the furniture to Casalvento? If so, I will have the furniture I bought in Berlin sent to Italy as well, and we can fill an entire container. And are we going to that market on Saturday?"

"Yes, if you want. As for the container, Erika will have to approve it."

"It's fine with me," she said. "I don't know how to arrange it, but it seems like Paolo has it all under control. For now, though, let's go and choose our pizza toppings. We can see who creates the best one."

No one was surprised when Todd designed the most colorful pizza.

"You win," declared Erika, before turning to Paolo and gesturing at the dance floor. "Okay, let's see how good you are." She kicked off her shoes and stood up.

Paolo led her toward the musicians and swung her around so that her dress billowed out and her hair brushed her shoulders. Under the light of the lanterns and with the music playing, she felt more carefree than she had in a long time.

After a while she said, "My head is spinning. I need to catch my breath." "*Complimenti!* You are a good dancer."

"So are you!"

He smiled and reached for her hand. "Ready for more?"

The spell of romance was undeniable. They danced all night, till the musicians finally packed up their instruments and the waiters were clearing the tables.

When Paolo finally dropped them off around one in the morning, it was "*Buona notte, tutti,*" and everyone headed for bed, with dance melodies still playing in their heads.

The next morning at breakfast, James couldn't help teasing Erika about Paolo. "What's wrong with you? I think he'd be perfect for you. He's good looking, smart, and speaks your language perfectly. He obviously adores you. And you both have a connection that an idiot can see. When you two talk, you forget that others are still in the room."

"James, he works for me. And I need him to keep working for me. I could put the business in jeopardy if it didn't work. And as I have just learned with Craig, sometimes things don't work."

"I understand that. But you have so much in common, and last night at Livernano, the two of you danced the night away. It's just a thought."

Todd broke in. "Enough about Paolo, darling. What shall we do today?"

"I have to go to work."

"But we're only here for a few more days—please spend some time with us today. Is there a spa nearby? That would do you good!"

"I'm not sure. I'll call Elisa and find out."

Erika made the phone call and reported back. "There's one with hot springs an hour away."

"That's perfect," said Todd. "Are you in, James?"

"Of course."

Todd had to tease Erika one more time. "You should ask Paolo to come." Then he relented. "No, I'm just kidding. Let's get our stuff."

The spa day was just what everyone needed—massages, soaks in the hot springs, a facial for Erika. They drove home relaxed and renewed.

"Should we stop for dinner?" James asked.

Erika thought about it for a minute, then said, "Let's not. We have so much food at home. There's still the eggplant parmigiana that I made the other day. I'll call Doris, and everything will be ready when we get back to the house."

They had just gotten back and Erika was with Doris in the kitchen when Massimo walked in.

"What a pleasant surprise!" she said. "Will you stay for dinner? My friends, Todd and James, are here from New York, and I'd like you to meet them."

"What a perfect welcome," Massimo said. "Yes, I'd like to stay. What have you all been doing?"

"We went to the spa today, the one with the hot springs. Now I think they're wandering around the property till dinner is ready. Come sit outside and have a glass of our white wine. I remember you liked it. How is Milan?"

"Same as ever. Very hot at the moment, so I came home for a few days."

She interrupted him to introduce Todd and James, who had walked in. "And this is my cousin Massimo."

"I can see beauty runs in the family," said Todd.

"Don't mind him," Erika said. "He's a touch eccentric when it comes to speaking his mind."

"I like him already," said Massimo.

As Doris motioned them all to the table, Erika asked, "Does Paolo know you're here?"

"No, it was a spur-of-the-moment decision. I'll call him later. I have some days off, and I thought I might go to the beach tomorrow. Do you all want to come?"

"Yes," said Todd. "See, James, I knew we should have stayed for two weeks. There is so much to do here."

"Can't you stay?"

"No, James has to be back at work on Tuesday, and so do I. But we'll be back for sure. Will Paolo come to the beach too?"

"Yes, if it's okay with the boss," said Massimo, gesturing at Erika.

"I think I can let him off work," she said, smiling. "Just this once."

Todd winked at her.

"No music tonight, Erika?" Massimo asked.

"I'll put some on," she said. "It's been so much fun having you here," she added to James. "I'll miss you."

"We will miss you too," said James. "But for now we are here. No thinking of departure is allowed."

She raised her glass. "To friends and relatives. *Salute!*"

They lingered over dinner, then sat and talked some more till Erika suddenly said, "Oh, look at the time. It's eleven, and I'm worn out. I'm going to bed. You boys have fun, and I'll see you in the morning. Oh, what time do you want to leave tomorrow, Massimo?"

"Is ten thirty okay?"

"Perfect. And you two . . . don't stay up too late. *Ciao!*" But as she rounded the corner, she couldn't help but linger as the conversation turned to her.

"Is she not amazing?" Todd asked Massimo.

"Yes, and from what I hear from Paolo, she's a quick learner and smart as can be. How long have you known each other?"

"Since college. But after she got engaged to Craig, we hardly saw each other anymore."

"Paolo told me a little about that. He must have been a handful."

"That is putting it mildly, Massimo. He was so controlling and demanding. I kept asking James what she saw in him. But she had to find out on her own. I was so happy when I heard about her accepting the terms of the will."

"Everyone here was surprised that she decided to stay. But we're all very happy. Paolo was worried the most, especially when she first arrived. You probably don't understand what it means to us to keep Casalvento going. The property had been in our family for generations. To give it up and sell it to a foreigner would have been a disaster to us all and the whole community. Most people in Radda work for Livernano or Casalvento. And Paolo is really taken by her," Massimo added. "Did you know he was engaged in the States?"

"Yes," said James. "He told us a little about that."

"That's unusual. He normally does not talk about that time. He was heartbroken when he came home. It took him a while to get over the girl. But ever since Erika arrived, he's been different."

"I told James they would make a handsome couple," said Todd.

"That would be great for Paolo," Massimo said. "Do you know if she likes him?"

"From what I can see—and James agrees with me—they are already in love with each other. Erika just doesn't know it yet. Or won't admit to it. We all need to work on that."

"Let's drink to them!" said Massimo. "*Salute!*"

XXXIV

———

$\mathcal{T}$HE NEXT DAY, EVERYONE WAS READY by the time Paolo and Massimo arrived to take them to the beach. Doris had packed snacks, and there were plenty of towels and some chilled wine as well. They piled into the car, with Paolo driving, James in the front seat, and Todd, Erika, and Massimo in the back. The hour's drive passed quickly as they carried on conversations despite competition from the radio. Luckily, Paolo located a parking space close to the *spiaggia*, the public beach.

"You find a place to spread out your towels," Massimo said. "I'll walk over to the trattoria and make a reservation for later. I know this place. It's not fancy, but it's good and lots of locals eat here. You're in for a treat. We can bring our own wine, too."

He returned just as Erika was about to put her things down next to Todd. "Erika, do you mind sitting over here with Paolo?" Massimo quickly redirected her. "I'd like to talk to Todd and James, and I don't want to talk over you in the middle."

Though it was still early in the summer, the scene was lively, with boats in the water, people swimming, and kids playing football on the beach, which was more like tiny pebbles than soft sand.

"The sea smells completely different here," said Erika, "with more salt in the air. I can smell the pine trees, too."

Intent on their conversation, Todd, James, and Massimo seemed to ignore her, but they all had grins on their faces, as though they were sharing some secret plan. She turned to Paolo and said, "It looks like we are the fifth wheel on the car here. Do you want to go for a swim? I need some exercise before we eat."

"Yes, great idea. Let them be."

He got up and ran into the ocean with Erika close behind him. Then the two of them ventured out farther, matching each other stroke for stroke. Paolo finally paused and floated for a minute, and Erika copied him.

"Are you okay?" he asked. "You seem a little different these last few days."

"What do you mean?"

"I'm not sure, exactly. It's just something I sense."

"I guess it's having my old friends around," she said. "I've been so happy to see them, but they also bring back scenes of New York and my life there. It makes me think of Craig, for one thing. I was with him for so long, and breaking up with him was so sudden. Every once in a while, I question that decision. I wonder, too, if I've just thrown myself into things here too suddenly. But I'm happy at Casalvento, and I like being able to explore Tuscany. I guess I just have to wait and see what fate has in store."

Paolo looked at her. "At least I have a better sense of what's bothering you," he said. "There have been so many changes for you. And yes, it's probably best to simply play everything by ear and see what comes. For now, let's swim back—it must be time for lunch."

Todd, James, and Massimo were already at the trattoria. "You finally made it," said Massimo. "We ordered some food to share, and we opened the white wine we brought."

After lunch, they sunbathed, swam, took a walk, sunbathed, and swam some more. They finally made it home just after nine, and Paolo and Massimo came into the house with them.

"I'm going to bed," Erika said. "I feel like it's been a long day."

"That's not allowed," said James. "We are only here for a couple more days."

"You can keep the party going without me," she said as Paolo turned some music on, Massimo opened a bottle of wine, and Todd and James continued to joke with them.

"Paolo, you're taking them antiquing tomorrow, right?"

"Yes, did you want to come?"

"I don't think so. But I'll see you in the morning. *Ciao*."

Erika lingered in bed the next morning. But when she turned over and looked out the window, the beauty of the day got her moving. She made herself coffee and took the cup out onto the balcony.

Todd and James were leaving in two days, and she would be alone again. Well, not totally alone. There was Paolo. But she didn't know what to think about that. He was everything she liked in a man, but he was still her employee.

She suddenly realized that the house was very quiet. Where were Todd and James? What time was it? She checked her cell phone. Ten minutes to eleven—oh boy, she had overslept again. They probably left with Paolo hours ago.

She put on a robe and went downstairs to make herself some ham and eggs. *Look at me*, she thought. *I'm cooking breakfast!* She smiled at the realization.

She spent the day taking pictures and lounging at the pool until she heard a car coming into the driveway, and she went to greet the shoppers.

"You're back! You left me alone all day. That wasn't very nice."

"We did ask you last night if you wanted to come," said Paolo.

"I know, I'm just teasing. Anyone up for a swim? The water's nice and refreshing."

"Maybe a little later," James replied. "We're thirsty for an ice-cold beer. Plus, I found out Paolo plays backgammon. He claims to be better than me. We'll see."

Erika went upstairs to shower and change and returned to join the others. Todd was in the living room.

"How was the antique market?" she asked him.

"Not so much my style, but we had fun. I brought back some pots and pans for you and an olive-wood salad bowl with utensils. It looks cool. I left it on the kitchen table."

"You are really trying to domesticate me."

"We're just trying to prepare you for the future." He winked. "By the way, Paolo bought you something too."

She went outside to the patio, where Paolo and James were deep in their backgammon game at a small side table. "So, who's winning?"

"It's one to one," said Paolo, glancing up. "You look nice. Do you want to sit with us?"

"Sure. Let me get a glass of wine. Do you need anything?"

"Do you have any of the chips we like?"

"I'll see what we have to snack on."

When she returned with a bowl of chips and popped one in her mouth, James turned to Paolo with a grin and said, "Can you see how she's changed? She would never have eaten chips or done anything in the kitchen. I like what you Italians have done with her."

"More beer?" Erika asked extra cheerfully, playing along.

"Yes, another beer for me," said James.

"Paolo, what about you?"

"No beer. May I have a glass of your white wine?"

"*Our* white wine," she said. "Of course."

She poured him a glass and asked James, "What should we do for dinner tonight?"

"See what Todd wants to do. This game is requiring all my brain power, it seems."

Todd was still in the living room. "You know, Erika, you could use a little lifting in here. We still have a little time—I could help."

"No, Todd. That's sweet, but I like it like this. For me, it's perfect as is. What I really want to know is what you want for dinner."

"What should we make? We could see what the garden has to offer!"

They went to the garden and got fresh tomatoes. With mozzarella and olives from the refrigerator, they had the makings of a perfect appetizer. Erika also found another pan of eggplant parmigiana in the fridge and pulled that out as well. She turned the oven on medium heat and placed the dish inside.

"Twenty minutes should do, right? What do you think?"

"That should be fine," he said, adding, "All this cooking is exhausting!"

"Todd, we are not cooking—we are just reheating."

"Oh, well, darling, for me it is cooking."

"Where's Massimo?" Erika asked. "Didn't he go with you today?"

"Yes, but we dropped him off. He had something to take care of. He'll be here around six."

As Erika was carrying place settings to the patio, she saw James with his head in his hands. Evidently, he had lost the game. "Oh, Paolo," Erika scolded with a grin, "you should have let our guest win."

"Oh, no! That game was hard—I just got lucky. One more?" he asked James.

"Okay, but I warn you, I'll be tougher this time."

As they started the next game, Massimo arrived. "I'll play the winner," he announced. This time, James prevailed, and Massimo took Paolo's seat.

"Paolo, can you get us some wine for tonight's dinner?" asked Erika.

"Yes. And if it's okay, I'll go to the cantina and get a magnum of Janus 2007. It's a lovely wine and will go perfectly with dinner."

"What a beautiful night," Erika mused aloud. "Why are the evenings so different here than in New York or the Hamptons?"

"I think it's the clean air," said Todd. "And no air traffic. I've been sleeping so much better here—like a log, though the wine might have something to do with that."

By the time Paolo returned from the cantina, the dishes and glasses were on the table, along with the appetizers and the eggplant parmigiana. At the sight of the magnum, Todd's eyes opened wide. "I've got to take a picture of that—and the food. Everything looks so delicious!"

Erika put on music in the background, and they gathered at the table. Just two more nights, and her friends would be gone. She looked at Paolo, who was talking with his whole body, like an Italian. His eyes met hers, and he smiled.

After dinner, Paolo and Todd helped her clean the kitchen, while James and Massimo played another game. *I wish it could be like this all the time*, she thought.

"Paolo," she said, "Doris brought some *semifreddo* yesterday. We should have it for dessert."

"Have you tried our Casalvento's sweet wine yet?" he asked. "It's called Monk Monk."

"I had no idea we made sweet wine."

"Yes, we do, but not very much. I'll go down to the cellar and see if you have some here."

Finally, the backgammon game was over, and the group sat down to dessert and a glass of the sweet wine.

"This is amazing," said James, "the dessert, the wine. Before we leave, we need to buy wines to ship home. That way we can share them with friends and remember these wonderful ten days here."

"Hanna should be in the tasting room tomorrow," said Erika. "She'll be able to help you."

Todd and James went back outside to sip Cognac and smoke cigars, and Paolo and Massimo joined them. Erika looked at the scene and quietly slipped up to her room. She sat on the balcony for a while as conflicting emotions washed through her—happiness for her friends, sadness that they were leaving, unexpected warmth at the thought of Paolo's killer smile, and curiosity about the days to come.

XXXV

———

FTER SATURDAY'S LATE NIGHT, Sunday morning was subdued. James was making breakfast and Erika was setting the table outside when Todd finally found his way downstairs. "Man, my head hurts," he said. "Erika, do you have something for my headache? And is there black coffee?"

She nodded. "I'll get it for you."

"James, can you make the eggs like you do at home?"

James laughed. "So now you like my eggs?"

"They're the best thing for a hangover," Todd said, adding, "What time did we go to bed last night?"

"I think it was about two. We had way too much Cognac."

Erika handed Todd the aspirin and coffee. "Maybe you should go for a quick swim before breakfast?"

"I don't want to move," Todd said. "And has anybody seen my shades? The sun is so bright today."

"I think they're upstairs," said James. "But wait, the eggs will be ready in a minute."

"Thank you," said Todd. "But as soon as I finish, I think I'll go back to bed."

"We'll let you recuperate today," said Erika. "I just can't believe you guys are leaving tomorrow. The time went by so fast."

"I know. I wish we could stay longer," James said, passing Todd a plate of steaming eggs. "We'll try to come back for the harvest. That would be fun."

"There are so many places we never got to," said Erika. "I wanted to explore more of Tuscany with you and Todd."

"Well, you can go with Paolo, can't you?" James said. He refilled Todd's coffee, a smile on his face.

"Why do you keep talking about Paolo? I know what you and Todd are trying to do!"

Neither James nor Todd said anything, but Todd laughed a little more vigorously than a typical hangover would allow. "Feeling better?" Erika teased him.

"Yes, the aspirin is doing the trick. And these eggs! Plus, I don't want to sleep away my last day here. Look at what a beautiful place you have. You should say thank you every morning. We have to go back to city life, while you stay here in paradise."

"Speaking of which, we have to start packing," said James. "Who's taking us tomorrow morning?"

"Luca will be at the house at three. He knows the way, and that will give you plenty of time. While you pack, I'll be at the pool. When you're finished, we can spend the afternoon there."

A couple of hours later, the three of them were chilling out, lazing on rafts in the water. "Do you guys want something to drink?" James asked. "I'm thirsty. How about white wine?"

"That sounds lovely," said Erika. "Can you get it? You can turn the music on while you're there. And maybe bring some snacks back."

"Anything else, *Signorina*?" James smiled.

"No, that should do it . . . Or would you rather get dressed and go to Castellina for ice cream?"

"No, let's just hang out here with a glass of wine," said Todd. "Tell me again, when is the harvest? I want to make sure we get our tickets."

"The white wine will be harvested beginning in September, the red from the end of September until mid-October. I think you should come back around the last week of September."

James walked up with his hands full, balancing the wine and glasses along with the snacks.

"You found everything?" asked Erika.

"Of course. By now I should know where everything is."

"You really did settle in," she said. "And knowing that you'll be back in a few months will make it easier to say goodbye tomorrow morning. For now, though, let's go back to the house and get dressed—we can take James over to the cantina to arrange for the wine shipment."

A little while later, they returned to the patio for another glass of white wine. Erika sat down next to Todd while James went to get glasses for them. "And bring back some olives," Todd called after him. "Now, what's for dinner tonight?" he asked Erika.

"I don't feel like cooking. We could go to La Villa—they have a great fish restaurant."

"Sunday and fish? No, Erika."

"I can see what the refrigerator holds. And we have so many vegetables in the garden. I can make us something."

"No, I don't want you to cook—it's our last night. What about a pizza?"

She thought about that for a moment. "You know what, I can call Mirella and ask her to order one for us—Luca can pick it up."

She made the call and reported back: "Mirella is ordering a *pizza quattro stagioni*. It's got black olives, artichokes, red peppers, ham, and cheese, and we should have it in forty-five minutes." As she poured herself a little more white wine, she said, "This visit has been just wonderful."

"Well," said Todd, "we'll be back in September. Maybe it will even coincide with when you take over the properties. Then we could organize a party with balloons and fireworks!"

"A small party would be nice, but nothing crazy."

"You know what we need?" said Todd. "Let's have some music—great Italian '70s music! And maybe it's time to switch to red wine . . ."

"All right," said Erika. "I'll be the disc jockey, but you can set the table."

Luca drove up with the pizza, and they all dived in.

"Remember, Erika," said James. "You're living in paradise. Enjoy every moment, watch the stars, and live the days. You look happy here. Stay that way."

They heard another car pull into the driveway. This time it was Paolo. "*Ciao, tutti,*" he said. "I just wanted to stop by to say goodbye."

"Thanks," said Todd. "Come sit with us and get yourself a glass. Do you want some pizza?"

"No, *grazie*. I already ate. But I will take a glass of wine. And I wanted you to know that everything is organized for Luca to pick you up tomorrow morning. Also, Todd, don't forget to let me know when the furniture will come from Berlin so I can take care of the container."

"Thanks, Paolo. Just make sure you take good care of my darling here."

"Of course. We still have a long way to go, but everything looks promising for a good year. Let's keep our fingers crossed that it stays like that. I wish you all a good trip back."

Erika stayed up with Todd and James a while after Paolo left. At the close of their last evening together, she told them, "If it's okay with you, I don't want to say goodbye. I'll just say good night." She hugged them both. "*Buona notte.* I miss you already!"

XXXVI

———

*T*HE GOOD WEATHER LEFT Tuscany along with Todd and James. It had rained nonstop for a week when Erika got a phone call from Bernardo. "*Ciao*, Erika," he greeted her warmly. "I just wanted to let you know that I will be close by Casalvento tomorrow. Did you want to have lunch with me? I have another letter to give you."

"Yes, Bernardo. I would love to see you. I'll be in the cantina tomorrow. Do you want to come there? Or should I meet you somewhere?"

"You know, it's probably better if we meet at the bar in Radda. Let's say twelve thirty?"

"Okay, *ci vediamo domani.*"

"So you're learning Italian! Good for you."

"I'm trying! I'll see you tomorrow."

"*Ciao*, Erika."

After a pleasant lunch with Bernardo, Erika was with Paolo and Elisa in the cantina going over the inventory and the budget. It was hard for her to concentrate on business. Bernardo had given her the third letter with his usual admonition to wait to read it until she was at home alone. Though Paolo had done a great job with cutting costs, and she wanted to focus on that, her mind was elsewhere. She couldn't wait to read the letter.

She looked out the window and noticed a red Fiat approaching the cantina. That surprised her. Because of the rain, she hadn't expected many visitors. When she saw a man getting out of the car, though, her heart almost stopped. "No, it can't be him!" she gasped. "That's impossible. He hates to fly. Why would he come here?" But she knew she wasn't mistaken. "Paolo—it's Craig."

"I thought you broke up with him, and the wedding was canceled."

"I did! It was! I don't know what he's doing here or what he wants. I'm going to the tasting room to find out."

When Erika opened the door to the cantina, Craig was rapidly approaching, until he stepped into a mud puddle. He didn't look happy. "What kind of a place is this?" he growled.

"*Benvenuto*, Craig. Welcome to Tuscany. Sorry about the weather. Unfortunately, you can't just push a button for sunshine, and we needed that rain."

"Erika, what on earth are you wearing?"

"Jeans, rubber boots, a sweater, and a rain jacket. The perfect gear for weather like this."

"You look like a farmer."

"Craig, you came all the way from New York—uninvited, I might add—and the only words that come out of your mouth are insults. I suggest you turn yourself right back around and return to where you came from." She turned around to walk away.

"Wait, Erika. I'm sorry. I didn't mean it."

"I'm sure you didn't, Craig. You just can't help yourself."

She tried to leave, but he followed her.

"Honey, please let me explain."

"Explain what, Craig? You and I are over. I don't understand why you had to come here, but I'll say it again. We're finished. You made this trip for nothing, and I'm not changing my mind. I actually love it here, and I'm going to make it my home."

"Erika, is this person bothering you?" Paolo asked. He had moved closer to her.

"No, it's okay, Paolo."

"Who is this, Erika?" asked Craig.

"This is Paolo, the vineyard manager and my right-hand man."

"You're sure he's not something else?"

"What difference would that make? And in any case, I don't need to explain myself to you."

"Erika, I don't want to fight. Is there a place where I can take a shower and change and get comfortable and have a drink? I flew all the way from New York to see you and to talk to you."

"You can do whatever you want, Craig. But you're not staying in my house. Go find room and board elsewhere."

"You can't be serious, Erika."

"I'm about as serious as I can get," she said. She turned on her heel and went back to her office, calling over her shoulder, "Goodbye, Craig. Paolo, please make sure he leaves."

"You heard my boss," said Paolo. "When you get to the gate, turn right. That will take you to Radda. I'm sure you'll find a room there."

Furious, Craig walked out the door. "I'm not finished with this," he said, but Erika remained quiet.

"He's gone, Erika," Paolo said.

"I'm sure his mother's behind all of this. He would never have come on his own. I just hope he goes back to New York right away. Paolo, I need to call it a day," she added. "Bernardo gave me another letter at lunch, and I want to go up to the house and read it before you come up for dinner. You are coming tonight, right?"

"Yes. I'll be there around seven, if it's okay with you?"

"Perfect."

The rain had stopped, and the sky was Tuscan blue again. To clear her mind, Erika decided to detour to the chapel before going home. Once there, she said a short prayer. "Grandfather," she said softly. "I've found love, peace, and a wonderful life here. I'm not letting anyone take this away from me."

As she walked back to the house, she made a mental list of things she needed to do. First, she had to talk to Tiffany and find out how things were going with Mr. Levine's company. Tomorrow, first thing, she'd email Molly and catch up.

The air smelled so fresh after the rain. *It's been good for the grapes*, she thought. *We needed it.* She went into the house and went upstairs to change her clothes and freshen up. Then she walked up the stairs to the office and opened the third letter.

XXXVII

Dear Erika,

I hope that the past few months you've been in Italy have brought joy and a little time for you to think about what you will do with Casalvento and Livernano. I also hope that Paolo has shown you around. Maybe he has taken you to see Florence and Siena. Siena was always my favorite. I went to school there. It brings back happy moments that are so long ago. But, for now, back to my story. Where did I stop? Oh, I remember. That everything was prepared for Concetta and Roberto to join me in Italy.

By then, we had phones installed in Casalvento and in New York. I called Concetta many times until I finally caught her. We spoke, and I told her that I was ready for them to come. That is when she told me that she couldn't do it. I tried to explain to her that she and my son belonged here with me. She insisted that she had no ties to Italy, that she was born in New York, did not speak the language, and did not want to leave her home. I tried to reason with her. But the conversation never changed her mind. She told me that she no longer wanted to be married to me. My world caved in right in front of me. When we hung up, I called my lawyer and friend, Bernardo. Our lawyer. He told me I could go back and claim my boy, but he wasn't familiar with American law and advised me to use a lawyer from New York.

Bernardo helped me find one, and that lawyer contacted Concetta. She insisted on having the marriage annulled. I did not want to accept that, but then I found out that she had met someone else and wanted to be free. Her new husband also wanted to adopt Roberto.

In the end, I gave her what she wanted under one condition, that the new man in her life would not adopt Roberto and that Roberto would keep my name. She agreed. I also asked that she send Roberto to Italy during the summer when he got older. She agreed to that as well, and I believed her.

But, of course, that never happened.

Until he was twelve, Roberto thought that the man his mother was married to was his father. When he got older, though, he asked Concetta why his last name was different from hers. Concetta told Roberto that his real father had left them behind and went back to Italy. Of course, he was upset and did not want to have anything to do with me. It was useless for me to try to contact him. I assume Concetta never gave Roberto the letters I sent over the years, and I never heard from my only son.

I was powerless. To understand why, I need to tell you more about how I got to America in the first place. I had immigrated illegally in 1953. Now I know it was not the smartest thing to do, but at that time I was afraid. Could I have done it differently? I'm not sure. It was a difficult time back then.

I was working in the kitchen of a container ship, and I had with me the little money I had saved. I was very sad when I left Italy, and I was hoping for a prosperity-filled future. My only worry at that time was how to stay in the States. The captain understood my situation. He gave the crew a one-day pass, and I, like all the others, was supposed to be back on board at the end of the day. But the plan was for me to get out and not to come back. Only the captain knew.

I never returned to the ship. The captain covered for me, and the boat left without me. Meanwhile, I found my uncle, who welcomed me with open arms. He and my aunt and his children were all so gracious to me. His kids hardly spoke Italian, but we got along. I shared a room with my cousin Maurizio—Mau—and he became my best friend. We worked together in my uncle's business. I worked hard. I wanted him to be proud of me. Mau had a band, and I started to play the bass.

When I wasn't working or playing in Mau's band, I hung out with the old men. They still spoke Italian. I'd smoke cigarillos with them, play cards, and drink some homemade wine. Oh, Erika. I have to smile when I think about what we drank. They called it wine, but it was very different from what I was used to. On Sundays, as in Italy, all the families got together, and we cooked, talked, and drank. We had fun. Life had a meaning again.

It was a whole new world, and I began to like it. Especially when I met Concetta. Who would have ever thought it would end like it did?

It was not easy for me to forgive her for taking my only son away from me, but I finally forgave her. My life here in Tuscany was very difficult after I realized that Concetta and Roberto would not be joining me. But, over the years, the wounds start to heal. My passion for my music stayed with me. I loved to play the bass, and I played until I got arthritis.

Although reading the letter made Erika sad, she also took great pleasure in getting to know more of her grandfather's story. She realized how kind a man he was and how much she had missed by never meeting him. At least she now knew where his unmarked grave was.

She hadn't quite finished the letter, but she needed a break and went downstairs to talk to Doris in the kitchen.

"I think tonight Paolo and I will cook our own dinner," she said.

"Does he know that?"

"No, not yet. But I'm sure we'll be able to manage. Do you think it's warm enough to eat outside?"

"It should be fine. I'll set the table before I go. *Buona sera*, Erika."

"*Buona sera*, Doris." Erika poured herself a glass of red wine and took it up to the office to finish reading the letter. She picked up where she had left off.

Maurizio was the first one to come and visit me in Tuscany. It is always nice to have visitors. I hope you have invited some of your good friends from the States. Maurizio updated me on how Concetta and Roberto were.

Eventually Concetta sold the townhouse and moved away. Then she broke off all contact with my side of the family. The only thing I know for certain is she had no more children with her husband.

I never remarried. You may not want to hear this, but I want you to know everything. I did have a lady friend from Austria. She was a painter, and she came to Livernano for a vacation with a girlfriend. We became close, and eventually she came twice each year for a couple of weeks. She painted all the paintings in the church. I liked her a lot, but it was not love the way I had loved Concetta.

I enjoyed reading my books. I planted the garden to resemble an English garden I once saw. The roses are very rare, and so are some of the trees. The vineyards also became my life and passion. Paolo and his family were a great help and a part of rebuilding Livernano. Erika, you will find that the wine business is a tough business. I don't want to sugarcoat it. Your yield each year is up to God. Also, you need to understand that you are in a business that is dominated by men who don't much like the idea of a woman running an estate like ours.

We are not big like so many others around us. But we are known for our quality. Paolo understands how I liked to run things. I wanted to experiment, to make new wines. Like the Sangiovese that we planted in Livernano some years ago. The clones did not come from our area—they were from Brunello.

Our wines are not typical for the Chianti region. They are more rounded in the mouth and not as tart as many others. Let Paolo take you around to other wineries and teach you to taste the difference.

The grapes should be developing now. Go through the fields each day, touch the vines, and watch how they grow. Take pictures of the process, if you can. You will see it's amazing. I hope that you will continue to enjoy the countryside with all its beauty. The flowers must be in full bloom by now. I hope Doris decorated the house with our sunflowers. Make sure you give them plenty of water. They are very thirsty.

On a different note, in the living room is a gramophone from your great-grandparents. It is still working. Try it. And when you turn it on, think of me, my darling Erika. Be sure to enjoy the evenings. Sunset was always my favorite time of the day. Especially after we'd worked hard in the field or in the cellar.

And be sure to have parties and entertain. Casalvento was always alive with friends coming and going. I hope Massimo is visiting. He is a good boy. And I also hope that you have fun with Paolo. He has a good soul! Cook with him. Otherwise he will just work all the time.

Now I will say goodbye for today. Wishing you happiness in your life, and don't forget to smell the roses!

Sending you un abbraccio.

Your grandpa,
Umberto

Erika looked up at the ceiling and blew him a kiss. *Un abbraccio anche per te, Nonno.*

She sat for a moment, then heard Paolo's voice calling her name. "Paolo, I'm up at the office," she called down. "I'll be done in a flash." She stopped in the bathroom to apply some rouge and lipstick and put her hair in a ponytail.

Paolo had put on some music, and as she came down the stairs, she noticed the old gramophone. Why didn't she see that before? And now the bass in the corner also took on a different meaning. And it was true that Doris had placed sunflowers everywhere in the house.

Erika suddenly got a chill. How could her grandfather have known about the sunflowers? In fact, it seemed like he knew everything that was going on!

Maybe it was because of the time of year, she thought, shrugging away her puzzlement as she turned to say hello to Paolo.

XXXVIII

"ERIKA, I OPENED A BOTTLE of your wine," said Paolo. "I hope you don't mind."

She smiled at him. "Not at all. You can pour me a glass as well."

"Is Doris cooking tonight?"

"No, I thought maybe you and I could cook together. I'm not sure what we can make. But in one of his letters, Grandpa told me that you like to cook. Do you mind?"

"No, not at all."

Paolo looked so handsome at that moment, so at home in the room, that Erika blew him a kiss, startling both of them. Then she brought her mind back to dinner. "How do we start?"

"First, we go to the garden and see what we can harvest, then we can see what treasures the refrigerator holds."

There were some zucchini and peppers in the garden, and they brought those in. Doris had stocked the kitchen well with tomatoes, eggplant, onions, and anything else they might need. Paolo assessed the bounty on the counter like a general surveying his troops. Then he started giving Erika step-by-step instructions.

"Please get the large frying pan. Under the stove, in that cabinet," he said, pointing.

She put it on the burner as Paolo continued. "Pour a little olive oil in. I'll have some garlic and the onions chopped and ready in a flash. Go ahead and turn on the stove."

As the oil warmed, he added the garlic and onions to the pan. "You are in charge of stirring," he told her. "Remember how my mother put an apron on you and gave you the wooden spoon? I will never forget the look on your face."

"I was so surprised," she said. "I had no idea what she was saying, but I kept stirring. It's funny to think about that now."

Paolo brought over the cutting board with more chopped vegetables— red and yellow peppers, zucchini, and potatoes—and put them in the frying pan. When they began to sizzle, he told Erika, "Now let's add some tomato sauce, salt, and pepper. After it cooks a while, we can put in the *aubergine*. You probably call it eggplant. Don't forget to keep stirring."

They sipped wine as the sauce cooked, laughing comfortably in each other's presence. After about twenty minutes, he said, "Here, add a little water and chicken stock, and let's turn down the heat and let it simmer. You don't have to stir it every minute. Do you want to eat it like this? Or we could put it over pasta?"

"What do you normally do?"

"The first day just like this, then the next day we add pasta."

"Then let's have it like this," Erika said. "I'll set the table." She was about to get the plates when she heard a noise. "Paolo, did you hear that?"

"Yes. Stay here. I'll go outside and see what is going on. Can you lower the music?"

He went out slowly but returned quickly with Santo, who was holding Craig by the arm. "Look who's here!" said Paolo. "Santo was doing his rounds and found this intruder looking through the windows into the kitchen.

"Craig? What are you doing here?" demanded Erika.

"I knew you had something going with this guy," snarled Craig. "I knew better than to trust him. I saw it all."

"Whatever you saw, Craig, it does not concern you."

Furious, Craig tried to twist his way out of Santo's grip, to no avail. "She is my fiancée, and I have all the right to be here," he shouted.

Paolo reacted coolly but firmly. "I thought you understood that Erika does not want you here."

Erika stared at the interloper, full of emotion, as scenes from her life in New York collided in her mind with everything she'd experienced in Tuscany. Finally, she calmed down enough to say, "Craig, I don't need to explain myself to you anymore. Paolo, please call the *carabinieri*. He is trespassing!"

Craig couldn't believe what he was hearing. "The police? No, Erika, you can't."

"Oh, yes, I can. This is my property."

"Erika," said Paolo, "if we call the *carabinieri*, they will lock him up."

Craig stopped struggling, his body going slack. "Okay, I'm leaving. Don't call the cops. I can't believe I listened to my mother and came here. What a stupid idea. But one day you'll be sorry. Throwing away a life of luxury in New York to become a farmer in Italy. Dropping me! You've lost your mind, that much is clear."

"Promise that you'll leave Radda first thing tomorrow morning," said Erika, ignoring his rant. "And, Craig, I want you to pack everything of mine that's still in the apartment. I'll have Todd and James pick it up. Santo, please make sure he gets off the property."

"*Si, Signora.*"

Craig was still fuming as Santo led him away.

"Are you okay, Erika?" asked Paolo.

Tears were running down her face, and she was finding it hard to master her feelings. "Yes, I'm just realizing I spent more than a decade with someone I don't even recognize anymore. It makes me sad and angry all at the same time."

"But he's gone now. Try to calm down a little. Come here." Paolo put his arm around her shoulder and pulled her close. He held her face and brushed the tears away. "Feeling better?"

"Yes, much better, thank you." She remembered their dinner. "And he interrupted our cooking, too!"

"I see you're getting your sense of humor back," Paolo said, giving her a kiss on the forehead and softly brushing her hair back. "If it would make you feel safer, I could stay overnight in the guest room. Just in case he returns."

"Thank you. Yes, I would like that."

"I'm still hungry, aren't you? Let's go have dinner."

It wasn't long before everything was back to normal. They were sitting outside eating the dinner they had cooked and sipping wine. "I know it hasn't been easy with me," Erika said. "It's just been a lot for me. I just hope you don't find me negative."

"No, I don't. And I can see you becoming a different person. Your grandpa is proud of you."

"What do you mean he is proud of me? He's dead."

"But I'm sure he can see you," Paolo said. "We spent so much time together, I guess I feel he's still here. He taught me everything I know, and after my breakup, he brought me back home."

"Tell me about it."

"There's nothing to tell. I wasn't good enough for her father. That's all there is."

"That can't be the whole story."

"But it is. Let's talk about happier things."

"Do you still love her?"

He leaned back. "No, it's in the past."

"Are you dating someone now?"

He looked at her ruefully. "With you here, there's no time for dating." He raised his glass to her. "*Salute!*"

"Where in California were you?"

"I thought we were finished talking about that."

"I just want to know where in California you were."

"Okay . . . This was ten years ago. Your grandfather thought it would be good for me to go to the States and work on a vineyard. He wanted me to have that experience, but he also wanted to perfect the white wines we made. California white wines are much better than Tuscany's, so he sent me there to learn. I went to a winery in the Russian River area and worked there for three years—everywhere from the fields to the cellar. I loved my time there, but I missed my Italy. Tara, the owner's daughter, also worked at the vineyards. She did the marketing."

"What was she like?"

"Do you really want to know?"

Erika nodded.

"To me, she was like an angel. Tall and slender with long blond curly hair and blue eyes. She had the best laugh. I fell in love with her from the first moment. We had it quite difficult in the beginning—my English was not the best. But we managed. I wanted to spend my life with her. I proposed to her, and she accepted, but when her father found out, things went sideways. He was a very different kind of a person than she was. He knew that we went out together, but I guess he thought it was not serious. After he made us break up, I could not stay with the company. Then your grandfather told me to come back. I was hoping Tara would come with me, but I was wrong. Now it's all in the past. You learn to forget."

"Your story has that in common with my grandfather's story. Today, I read that he played the bass, and I guess the keyboard, too."

"Yes, he loved his music. He was not so good on the keyboard. I'm the one who played it. He loved jazz, and so do I. We had some great jam sessions together."

"Paolo, you surprise me again and again."

"You surprise me too. Erika, I would have never thought that you could fit in here as quickly as you have. You really seem to love what we're doing here. I can feel it."

"Yes, I do, very much. And I love the people here."

Unexpectedly, before she really considered it, Erika leaned over and kissed him softly. "Thanks for everything today."

Paolo just stared at her. He looked unsure of how to react, and she quickly defused the moment and rose to her feet. "Let's go and clean up," she said, starting to clear the table. "Do you want to help me . . . or are you just going to sit here?"

Without a word, he carried the rest of the dishes into the kitchen.

"Do you want anything else tonight?" she asked him.

"No, Erika. I'm good."

"So I'll see you tomorrow for breakfast?"

"No, I have to get up early and go to the cellar."

"But tomorrow is Saturday."

"Yes, but we are pushing the leaves up on each row in Livernano. We already did that in Casalvento. I have to take the *squadre*—the crew—to the vineyard."

"Do you want me to come with you tomorrow?"

"No. There wouldn't be anything for you to do."

"Okay, good night then."

"*Buona notte*, Erika."

She went upstairs and got ready for bed, but she wasn't sleepy. She turned off the light, went out onto the balcony, and just sat there in the dark. She could hear Paolo in the guest room.

He had been shocked when she kissed him, that much was clear. Maybe he didn't like it. No, she couldn't believe that, but she also never knew what he was thinking. Sometimes he had this look on his face, like he knew something she didn't know.

I have to say the kiss was nice, though. Especially after that mess with Craig.

Thinking about Craig and New York made her numb. She had loved being there and always imagined she would grow old and gray there. And now she couldn't imagine living there. *But life changes. People change.* She had changed.

XXXIX

*W*HEN ERIKA WOKE UP, the whole house was quiet. She realized Paolo must have already left for the cantina. Too bad—she would have liked to have had breakfast with him and maybe have taken a drive around Tuscany to taste some different wines. A little disappointed, she got out of bed and started the coffee machine. After brushing her teeth and washing her face, she took her coffee and went downstairs. Something smelled good. Was Doris already there?

No, it was Paolo.

"Good morning, Erika."

"I'm surprised to see you! I thought you had to take the workers to Livernano?"

"That was at six this morning. The weather is changing again, and it will be a very hot day today, so we started early. I stopped in Radda and got us some fresh rolls and pastry. I was not sure what you like for breakfast, so I bought one of each."

She smiled at him, unsure if she could—or should—give him a hug.

"By the way, you look cute in your polka dots."

She realized she was still in her pajamas. "Sorry, I did not know you'd be here, or I would have dressed up."

Paolo leaned over and gave her a kiss. Short but sweet. *What's come over us?* she wondered to herself. Had they moved to some new kind of relationship?

The moment passed before anything else happened.

"Let's have breakfast," Paolo said.

She followed him to the table, which he had decorated with sunflowers.

"How did you sleep?" he asked her. "You had quite a stressful day yesterday."

"I slept. Do you think Craig left?"

"I'm sure he did. I think the idea of the *carabinieri* really scared him. They would have never locked him up."

"You made that up?"

"Of course. What else could I have done? I wanted to get back to my dinner with you. And it was a nice dinner, too. Now what do you want to do today?"

"You don't have to go back to work?"

Paolo shook his head.

"Then I thought I'd like to drive around Chianti and stop at a few wineries."

"We can do that. It would be good for you to know some of our competitors. Why don't you get dressed? I'll clean up in here."

"Thank you for breakfast, Paolo. It was a nice surprise."

Erika took a little time getting ready. She stared at her open closet, trying to decide what to wear. He always saw her in pants—maybe it was time for something different. She chose a loose white shirt and a light brown skirt and put on white ballerina slippers, then smiled at herself in the mirror. She sprayed a little perfume on, grabbed her handbag, and went downstairs.

"Wow, you look great," Paolo said. "Let's go, but I want to stop at my house and get my other car. I want to take you around Chianti in my little treasure."

He drove the short distance, parked, and opened the door to his garage. Inside, Erika saw a small red Fiat.

"What is this?"

"It's a 1966 Cinquecento."

"This car is older than me!" she exclaimed.

Paolo patted the little auto. "This was Italy's most famous car, besides the Ferrari, of course. It was the first city car. Fiat started building them in 1957, and it became famous because of all the Italian movies it was in. It's a fun car. And it has a lot of memories for me. This was the first car I ever owned."

Erika looked sideways at the vehicle. "I don't think I'll fit in this."

"*Cara*, if I fit, you will. Come on, get in." He opened the door for her, and she got into the passenger seat. Then he got behind the wheel. "*Sei pronto?*"

"*Sì!* But where are we going?"

"It's a little too early to start tasting wines. I thought we'd go to Gaiole first. It's not far. And there's a castle and a pretty church. There's a lot of history there. Gaiole is one of the four original *comune* of the Chianti Classico region."

"How many wineries are there in Chianti? "

"If you include all of Chianti—Empoli, Pisa, Siena, Florence, Arezzo, and so on—there are around a thousand. Just in Chianti Classico, there are about three hundred and fifty wineries registered. Tuscany has forty-two *Denominazioni di Origine Controllata* and eleven *Denominazioni di Origine Controllata e Garantita.*"

"Oh, there's so much to remember," Erika lamented.

They spent the next couple of hours exploring Gaiole and driving around. Finally, the heat and the constant winding roads got to Erika. "Paolo, when will we stop for lunch?" she asked. "I'm getting hot, and I'm thirsty, too."

"We're heading to La Villa now. It's a small village with an amazing seafood restaurant. You'll like it. We can sit outside under a tree with plenty of shade."

He parked the car, and they walked to a restaurant with a sign proclaiming its name: Osteria la Piazza. It was an unpretentious place with a garden, but the owner, a tall skinny man wearing a white apron, recognized Paolo right away and came out to greet them. While Erika went to freshen up, Paolo talked to the owner.

"What did you order?" she asked when she returned.

"Alessandro said he'd surprise us. And I ordered our white wine. I hope that's okay with you."

"Of course, we have to support them. But tell me, Paolo, what does *osteria* mean in English?"

"It's the old name for a place that served simple food and local wines. The owner was an *oste*, and the shop was called an *osteria*. The name stuck. You can see the place is very casual and simple. But the food is actually sophisticated."

The waitress came over with some water and the wine, then a few minutes later she brought an appetizer of *bruschetta con pomodoro fresco*. Fresh olive oil and balsamic vinegar were already on the table. *"Buon appetito,"* she said.

Paolo leaned over to Erika. "She is the owner's wife. They run the restaurant with the whole family. He uses ingredients and flavors that are traditionally Mediterranean. You will be surprised."

The waitress came back, this time with an assortment of *antipasti*—stuffed artichokes, fried rice balls, asparagus with pancetta, and a plate of mixed seafood. Erika couldn't believe the number of dishes. "Paolo, who will eat all this food?"

"Just eat what you can," he told her, "but try something from each dish. We don't want to insult the chef!"

"The food is delicious," she said, nibbling her way through the offerings. They were still enjoying the *antipasti* when the waitress placed a large pan in the center of the table and gave each of them a fresh plate. "I've got to take a picture," said Erika, bringing out her phone. "This looks amazing. What is it?"

"Spaghetti con frutti di mare—spaghetti with fruits of the sea." Paolo pointed out the ingredients. "Calamari, shrimps, mussels, *aragosta*—that's lobster—and here are razor clams. You will like those. It's all in a light sauce with fresh herbs and cherry tomatoes."

As they dived in, Alessandro came over to see how they liked his creation. He had a glass of wine with them while Erika couldn't stop praising the meal. In the end, he wouldn't accept any money for it, though they offered several times.

"Paolo, let's just bring him more wine," Erika suggested.

"That's a great idea. We will do that. Now let's go taste some other wines."

They spent the rest of the afternoon visiting wineries, where Paolo introduced Erika to his old friends and schoolmates who now ran the vineyards.

Maybe one day she would have lots of friends here. *And I'll be able to invite them to Casalvento or Livernano for parties. I'll be fluent in Italian, too.*

At each place they stopped, she bought some wine for the house, and by seven they were back at Casalvento.

"I can't eat anything for dinner," Erika said as Paolo dropped her off. "I'm still full from lunch, but, if you want, you could come in for something."

"I would love to, but I have to see how the work went over at Livernano. Will you feel safe alone in the house tonight?"

"I'm sure I'll be fine. That was a beautiful day, Paolo. Thank you!"

"I enjoyed it too."

He leaned down to her and gave her a light kiss, then another more passionate one. Abruptly, he let go. "You have beautiful eyes and very soft lips," he told her. "Lips meant to be kissed."

Flustered, Erika didn't say anything for a minute, then finally managed to ask, "Are you sure you don't want to come in for a little while?"

"No, Erika. I told you my story yesterday. I can't . . . I don't want anything like that to happen again."

She looked at him and nodded. "I understand, Paolo. Oh, wait a minute. The wine is still in your car."

He opened the trunk and carried the boxes of wine to the cellar, and she wished him good night as he was leaving. He turned around once more before he got back into the car. "If you wanted to, Erika, you could come to our family luncheon tomorrow. You'd be very welcome."

"Thanks, but I think I will pass for now."

"If you change your mind, we start at one."

Erika went into the house and up the stairs to her room. She changed her clothes and went out to the balcony to think. More than anything she wanted to talk to a friend. She got her phone and dialed Todd's number, but the call went to voicemail. Back inside, she tried to read, but she fell asleep in the chair. When she woke up, it was still dark, and she realized she'd forgotten to close the house. She went through all the rooms, closing windows, locking the doors. *I can't be so careless*, she told herself.

As she lay in bed, confused thoughts swirled in her head. She knew how she felt about Craig. That was over, definitely over. But then there was Paolo. Was she really ready to start a romance with him? Given what he had just told her, he didn't seem ready—and perhaps never would be. California was a long time ago, and he was still not over that girl.

She remembered the handsome tourist she met when she first came to Tuscany. What was his name? Oh, yes, Max. They had a fun dinner. But what was the point of even thinking about him? He was good looking and sexy, but he lived in New York, and he was married to his job. It would never have worked between them.

Everything is so new here now. I'm afraid I could make some wrong decision that will affect my whole life.

Erika wondered what her parents would think about all this. It was sad how much her father had missed out on. Would he have loved it here? And it pained her to know that her father and grandfather never really knew each other. Of course, now it was too late for her to know him too, though at least she got a glimpse through his letters. Overwhelmed by these feelings, she finally fell asleep.

When she woke up, though, she felt strangely refreshed and determined. All doubts and worries were gone. She suddenly knew what she wanted, and it was here before her in Tuscany.

She opened the house to let the fresh Sunday air in, turned on some music, and made a cup of coffee to drink on the balcony.

I can't get enough of looking at the vineyards, she thought. Every day the grapes seemed bigger, the leaves greener. Even the rose bush below the balcony was sending out blooms the size of small plates. Doris had told her that the rose was called Crimson Glory, and if you didn't know better, you'd think it was fake. The fragrance was so strong she could smell it up where she sat on the balcony.

Erika remembered the notes she'd found that her grandfather had made about the garden—trees he liked, roses he planted, even what the best fertilizers were. She smiled to think about those. For the roses, he had used fish heads that he would bury under the bushes. In winter, he covered the roses and strawberries with sawdust.

She would have to remember that when winter came, though probably Mirella would know what to do. There was still so much to learn and remember. *I better begin to make lists for the fall. And I have to reorganize the whole office. Maybe I can start today.*

And, at that moment, Erika understood that she had made her decision about the estates and her life. Her work and her future would be here in Tuscany.

XL

———

Y THE BEGINNING OF JULY, summer in Tuscany was in full swing. The weather was hot, with thunderstorms rolling in almost every afternoon and cooling things off temporarily. When Erika took her morning walks, she would see Santo and the others working in the fields. They started at six, then took a four-hour lunch break to escape the heat of the afternoon.

The grapes seemed to be changing color and maturing day by day, and Erika documented the process with her camera, filling an album already thick with photographs. The green grapes at Casalvento had already been pruned, and Paolo was now overseeing the team at Livernano.

Todd and James had retrieved the rest of her belongings from Craig's apartment and sent a few boxes to Tuscany. Craig had chosen to be absent when they came, but there was not much to gather up. Erika had not accumulated much during those years. But there were pictures of her mother and father, and she was glad to have them around her in Casalvento. She had rearranged the office as well, organizing and cataloging the papers and books and truly creating her own space.

She had also been in frequent contact with her office in New York, though that business seemed ever more distant. She emailed and occasionally called to check in with Tiffany, who was working with Molly to wrap up the Levine deal. Erika was looking forward to closing that aspect of her life, too.

Summer had brought its share of tourists to the cantina, and Erika was now pitching in and selling wines more and more often, especially on days when Hanna was off. Coming to work each day was a pleasure for her. It was fun to interact with customers from around the world, but she especially enjoyed meeting those from the United States, since she could speak English with them, and she liked that both the American and Italian flags flew in front of the building. Her Italian was getting much better too. She wasn't quite ready to lead tours of the winery, but Elisa or Paolo were able to jump in if necessary.

As she stood at the counter of the cantina on an early July afternoon, she couldn't help but be gratified at how well they all worked together there. Her first impressions had been way off the mark. But that seemed so long ago now.

Time had gone by so quickly. Tomorrow was already the fourth of July, and Paolo had told her there would be music and fireworks in Radda in honor of the American holiday. He wanted her to go with him, and maybe Massimo would come as well—she hadn't seen him since Todd and James left.

She sighed at the thought of Massimo's brother. Vincenzo didn't want to have any contact with her, and she wasn't sure if it was because of the land problem or if he just didn't like her. Bernardo promised her it would all be taken care of after the transfer of the properties, but she hated the idea of having an unhappy neighbor. And there was still the issue of the contractor to deal with.

At that moment Paolo walked in the door. "*Ciao*, Erika. How were the sales today?"

"Super. I sold four packages, all for the States—New York, Maine, California, and Florida. I love doing it."

"Are you ready for tomorrow's festivities in Radda?"

She nodded. "I'm looking forward to it."

"I'll pick you up at the house at around six. I have a table reserved at Michaele's for dinner at eight, and the fireworks start at ten. We can watch from Radda or from the cantina."

"I'm not sure where the best view is."

"Let's play it by ear then. We've finished for the day at Livernano. Do you want to go to Castellina and have the most famous ice cream in Tuscany?"

"Why not? Let me go up to the house and change."

"Erika, for ice cream you don't need to change. We can just go as we are."

The line at the *gelateria* was long. "They must be really famous here," said Erika.

"Yes, everyone knows about this place. People come from all over. If you want, you can take a seat, and I'll stand in line. What flavor do you want?"

"I don't care, just nothing with raisins."

"Raisins are just grapes, and you like wine."

She smiled. "Yes, I do, but I don't like grapes dried out."

Paolo shook his head. "You're funny, Erika. Cup or cone?"

"Cone, please."

Twenty minutes later, Paolo was back with two cones in his hands, each holding a colorful tower of several flavors.

"You want me to eat this mountain of ice cream?" Erika asked. "What are these?"

"There's chocolate, lemon, pistachio, and *fragola*—strawberry. Just eat what you can."

To her surprise, she finished every bite.

By eight, they were back in Casalvento.

"Do you want to come in, Paolo?" Erika asked, still sitting in his car.

"No, *cara*, not tonight. I had a very early start, and I'm really tired. I want to be fit for tomorrow night."

She leaned over and gave him a quick kiss and was about to say good night when he put his arm around her, drew her close, and kissed her back. He smiled. "*Buona notte, cara.*"

"*Ciao*, Paolo."

She got out of the car, waved goodbye, and went into the house, still thinking about the kiss as she closed up for the night.

The next morning, Erika stood in front of her closet with a cup of coffee, planning what to wear to Radda. She finally chose a white dress with a red belt, red shoes, a bag, and a blue scarf and laid the outfit on her bed—she threw on some shorts and a cotton shirt for the morning. For the next few hours, she would be helping make tomato sauce with Doris and Mirella.

"*Buongiorno, tutte,*" she said as she came down to the kitchen.

"*Buongiorno, Signora. Siamo pronte.* We're ready," said Doris.

Erika turned on some music and wrapped herself in the apron that Todd and James had given her. The two women already had everything organized. It was obvious that they had been doing this for many years.

There were two stations. Doris was on the left washing glass jars and lids and placing them in the dishwasher to be sterilized. At a double sink on the other side of the kitchen, Mirella was washing mounds of tomatoes. She showed Erika how to take them one by one, cut them into quarters, and then squeeze the juice out. The cut tomatoes went into a plastic bucket. It was slow and messy, but Erika took her time and eventually took over that step completely.

When the bucket was full, Mirella turned the contents into a giant pot on the stove, boiling the tomatoes and slowly stirring them with a wooden spoon the size of a paddle. Meanwhile, Santo came by to set up a machine on the patio that would separate the seeds and skin from the cooked tomatoes.

When the tomatoes were done, Mirella and Doris carried the pot outside and emptied the contents into the machine. Erika watched as the strained sauce flowed out the front into plastic containers. Then the huge pot was washed and placed back onto the stove, and the sauce was poured back in and brought to a boil again. Doris added some herbs and seasonings, and after the sauce had thickened, she filled the jars one by one and put on the lids. She took the hot glass jars and placed them upside down on the kitchen counter, which had been covered with a heavy wool blanket. When all glass jars were filled, she covered the array with another wool blanket. From time to time, Erika could hear the lids popping.

"Doris, why do you turn the jars upside down?"

"It's the old way to vacuum-seal them. Simple and easy."

Exhausted but happy to have taken part, Erika finally excused herself. "Ladies, I have to go. I need to get ready for tonight's *festa.*"

"*Si, Signora. Non ce problema,*" said Mirella.

"Enjoy yourself!" added Doris as Erika went upstairs to change.

She was dressed in her patriotic outfit and waiting for Paolo when he drove up in his red car, punctual as always.

"*Ciao,* Paolo."

"*Ciao, bella.* Get in. We need to hurry so that we get a good parking space close to town."

"Surely you won't have any trouble with this little car."

"Do you think I'm the only one with a Cinquecento here? A lot of people have them. They are collectors' items. But I heard you helped make tomato sauce today," he said. "Impressive!"

"News travels fast! Or are you keeping tabs on me?"

"I like to know what you're doing, that's all. *Eccola!*"

When they arrived, he spotted a parking space and pulled in. "Now we can just walk around. There are lots of stands with local products to sample."

Families and couples were strolling around the piazza. Erika was surprised by all the kiosks with bites of food. "We could just eat our way from one to the other. We don't even need to go for dinner."

Paolo put a small piece of cheese in her mouth. "That will slow down your talking."

"Are you saying I talk too much?"

"Maybe from time to time, yes. But you're serious, and I like that." He pointed her in a different direction. "Now for some wine. We each buy a glass, and then we can go from one producer to another and taste their wines."

"What an interesting idea! Why aren't we represented here tonight?"

"Your grandfather was not a fan of events like this. He said it didn't bring anything to our brand."

Paolo stopped at a booth where there was a familiar face.

"*Ciao*, Vincenzo," Erika greeted her cousin, but he did not return her greeting.

"Vincenzo, let us taste your Chianti Riserva," said Paolo. When Vincenzo put just a drop in Erika's glass, Paolo chided him. "Come on, Vincenzo, give your cousin a nice pour."

The winemaker poured in a bit more Chianti and, without saying a word, went on to the next person in line.

"Let's move on," Erika said. "What a grim, unhappy person he is."

Paolo nodded. "It's impossible to change him. We've all tried. I guess he likes being this way, but it's really too bad."

At the edge of the piazza were stands with clothes, scarves, belts, and even shoes and handbags. Erika steered Paolo in that direction, and she bought a couple of scarves she liked.

"Oh, Erika, that reminds me . . . I bought you a handbag when I was antique shopping with Todd and James. I forgot to give it to you. I'll bring it to the house."

"I can't wait to see it."

The band was starting to play, and the two of them walked over to the city fountain and sat on the edge to listen till it was time for dinner. At the restaurant, the owner greeted them warmly, and Paolo introduced Erika. "This is Umberto's granddaughter."

"*Una bella ragazza.* I'm Michaele, one of your grandfather's best friends. We went hunting together all the time."

"I didn't know he hunted. I learn something about him every day."

Michaele showed them to a table in the corner. "It won't be so noisy over here." Moments later, he returned with a bottle of Casalvento's Chianti Classico and three glasses of Prosecco. He raised his glass. "Let's have a toast! To you, Erika, and to Casalvento. *Salute!*"

Michaele emptied his glass and asked, "Do you know what you want to eat?"

Erika was perplexed. "We haven't seen any menu."

"You don't need one." Michaele took a chair, turned it around, and sat down. "I have the menu in my head: insalata, pasta pesto, and steak Florentine."

"What else?" Erika asked.

"That's it!"

"Yes," Paolo chimed in. "That's the whole menu, but it's the best, believe me."

"Then I'll take the insalata, pasta pesto, and the steak."

"Good choice," said Paolo. "I'll have the same, but we'll share the steak, Michaele."

Michaele nodded and smiled as he went to take care of their order.

"Wait till you taste the steak," Paolo said as he poured the Chianti. "Michaele is known for it. He actually raises his own cows for the meat."

When the meal was over and Paolo had paid the bill, Michaele came back to say goodbye. He caught Erika in a big hug and kissed both her cheeks. As they left, she saw him wink at Paolo.

"What was that?"

"What?"

"The wink he gave you."

"I didn't see anything," Paolo insisted. "And now it's almost dark enough for the fireworks. Do you want to go back to the piazza, or do you want to see them from your house?"

"Let's go to the house."

"Okay, but we'll have to hurry. We don't want to miss the beginning."

XLI

HEY MADE IT HOME just in time to settle themselves on the stone wall, where they had a perfect view of the colorful rockets soaring into the now-dark sky. For half an hour, they marveled as the display went on and on. There were silvery sprays and red, white, and blue rockets and an explosive, noisy multicolored finish. When it was over, they went over to the kitchen and sat on the patio, not talking much, just enjoying the quiet.

Finally, Erika broke the silence. "Why don't I turn on some music? And can you get us a little more wine?"

When she came back from the living room, Paolo was there with a bottle of Chianti, two glasses, and the opener. He watched her for a second, then opened the bottle and poured the wine.

"Is everything okay, Paolo?"

"Erika, *cara*, there's something I've been meaning to ask you. I need to know."

"What is it?"

He kept staring into his glass.

"Come on, Paolo. Stop this suspense."

"I guess I need to know that you're serious about staying here in Tuscany. That you have no regrets about Craig or your life and business in New York. That you're committed to Casalvento and what we've been building with the vineyards and the estates."

"How can you ask me that, Paolo? You saw me with Craig. I'll never change my mind about him. And I've said over and over that I want to stay here and honor my grandfather's wishes."

"And is that the only reason you want to do this?"

"What are you really asking, Paolo? What are you afraid of?"

"Erika, this is hard for me. You know my story, and you know it wasn't easy for me to tell you about it. I fell in love with a woman at a winery once before, and our breakup was hard. My disappointment lasted a long time, and though that's definitely in the past, I'm afraid to have something like that happen again. I have strong feelings for you, Erika, but you're also my boss, and that complicates things a lot."

"Paolo, you don't have to worry about me leaving Casalvento. I like it here . . . I love it here, and I'm going to stay. As for the rest, let's not worry about that now. Besides, you have Todd and James on your side!"

He took her hand and softly stroked it with his thumb. For someone who was a farmer, his hands were surprisingly soft. Like his lips.

"We had a fun day," Paolo told her, "and I enjoyed it very much. And I hope we have others. That reminds me, when we were in Siena, you mentioned that you'd like to go to the Palio. I asked Massimo if he could help me find tickets. We need good ones, in a place with a balcony, otherwise it's better to watch it on TV. Massimo reminded me that the owner of the trattoria in Siena has a room upstairs that he rents out. It has a balcony, and it faces the Piazza del Campo. I called him, and he had four tickets left. I bought them for us."

"That's great. Thank you for thinking of it. Tell me the date again."

"August sixteenth."

"Who are the other tickets for?"

"I thought Massimo would come with his girlfriend."

"He has a girlfriend?"

"Yes, it's an on-again, off-again relationship. She's a doctor too, and they're both very stubborn. But personally, I think they're perfect for each other."

He looked at his watch. "It's late. I better go. Happy Fourth of July, Erika."

Erika was startled by Paolo's abrupt departure, and after he left, she suddenly was overcome by a sadness she couldn't quite identify. Was she ready for another serious relationship?

She took the glasses inside, rinsed them, and put them in the dishwasher, then locked the doors. In the living room, she put a record on the old gramophone. It was a sad song, and the sound was scratchy, but she liked hearing it. When it was over, she turned off the lights and went upstairs. Tired and a little confused, she simply fell into bed without washing her face or getting undressed.

She woke up in the middle of the night, and it suddenly hit her. It was true what Todd and James had been saying. She *was* in love with Paolo. All her doubts were silly. She took off her clothes and got back into bed and was swiftly asleep.

It was midmorning by the time she woke up and made herself some coffee. As she sipped it on the balcony, she saw Santo wiping down the table.

"*Buongiorno,*" she called down.

He looked up. "*Buongiorno, Signora.*"

She went over her to-do list in her head. First, she needed to call Bernardo. He had mentioned there was another letter from her grandfather, but they'd never made plans to meet. She also needed to connect with Todd about when they'd return for the harvest. And because it was Friday, maybe Doris could get some mussels and clams, and she could make Paolo his favorite dish. It still bothered her that he had left so suddenly.

When she had showered and dressed, she went down to find Doris, who was in the kitchen.

"*Buongiorno*, Ms. Erika."

"Buongiorno, Doris. Could you run back to Radda and see if you can find some mussels and clams for dinner?"

"I think that it will be too late. The truck leaves at noon. Can we do it next week?"

"Yes, of course." Erika was disappointed, but there was no choice. A call to Bernardo was next. It turned out he was away for a week on a business trip. Erika then called Paolo.

"*Pronto.*"

"*Ciao*, Paolo. I wanted to thank you for yesterday. I had a lot of fun. I still can't get over that steak at Michaele's and the fireworks display."

"I had a good time as well. Are you coming to the cantina today?"

"I don't think so. I have some calls to make. Can you come here for lunch?"

"I can't. We have a lot going on. There are a lot of tourists here today."

"Should I come and help?"

"No, we can manage."

"Okay, I'll check in with you later."

There was still no word from Todd, so Erika took out her grandfather's letters and reread them. But it was hard for her to concentrate. She kept thinking about Paolo and their talk the previous night. Maybe taking some pictures would help. She grabbed her camera and went down the stairs again. She was about to go out to the garden when she saw a brown paper bag on the table.

"What is this, Doris?"

"Paolo came by for a few minutes while you were upstairs, and he left this for you, Ms. Erika."

That was strange—he had just told her how busy he was. She opened the bag and took out the gift, holding it up for Doris to see. It was an exquisite handbag—light brown with dark leather trimming. "This must be the one he bought with Todd and James."

"Oh, Ms. Erika, it's beautiful."

"What a surprise! I need to thank him. Do you know where he is, Doris?"

"Yes, he told me to tell you that he was going to the chapel."

"That's odd. I wonder what he's doing up there—he said there was so much to do at the cantina."

Erika went to the garage and got the John Deere and drove it up the hill. Paolo was waiting near the cypress trees in front of the chapel. "Thank you for the beautiful present," she told him. "I love it and couldn't wait to tell you!"

"I'm glad you like it, Erika. Todd helped me pick it out. I have another surprise for you, too."

He took her hand as she got out of the little tractor. "Now close your eyes, please. I'll tell you when to open them again." He led her around to the other side of the chapel, helping her step carefully on the uneven ground. "Okay, you can open your eyes now."

There, with a panorama of Tuscan hills and vineyards in front of them, Paolo had prepared a beautiful picnic in the grass. Bread, cheeses, olives, cold cuts, and wine. She couldn't quite believe the scene. "Paolo, this is beautiful, but what's the occasion?"

"We had such a great time yesterday, then I left so quickly. I wanted to make up for the way the day ended. Will you forgive me?"

"Of course."

He held out his arms and pulled Erika close, as if to say he'd never let her go. Then he kissed her. "Are you hungry?"

"Yes, but this is a very nice appetizer."

Paolo laughed and let her go. "Come on. Let's sit down."

"You know, Paolo, I can't shake this strange feeling that my *nonno* wants us to be together. In his letters, he's always giving me little hints about you, talking about all your good qualities."

"He loved you a lot, and I loved him too. He was always good to me. And he always had these great stories. Once in the winter, he was with the band in New York City, and they didn't realize there was a blizzard outside. They had some drinks, and when they left, they couldn't find their car. The snow had completely covered it, and they didn't remember where they had parked. They had to uncover five different cars before they found the right one, and then it wouldn't start. They ended up on the subway and didn't get back to the Bronx until six in the morning, almost frozen. The way your grandfather told it, you had to laugh out loud. He had so many stories."

"I want to hear them all," said Erika. "But not just this second." She leaned over to Paolo, who took the hint and kissed her.

XLII

———

*T*HE MONTH OF JULY was slowly coming to an end. Erika had settled into a routine. She continued to put in time at the cantina and made rounds of the fields in the John Deere in the evening. She learned to cook new dishes and frequently made dinner with Paolo. They used the time to get to know each other better, telling stories about growing up and places they'd been.

Other things were still uncertain, though. Todd and James kept changing their minds about scheduling their harvest visit, and Erika was beginning to wonder if they were serious about coming.

One morning, while enjoying her morning coffee on the balcony, she realized she had never connected with Bernardo, either. The situations with Vincenzo and the contractor still made her uneasy, and she wondered about the next letter the lawyer had promised to bring. She got her phone and dialed his office number.

A recording declared that the office would be closed for the next three weeks. *Three weeks?* she thought. *How can that be?*

She called Paolo next, and he picked up instantly.

"I just tried to call Bernardo," she told him, "but the office is closed for the whole month of August. Is that possible?"

"Oh, yes. August is the month when most Italians are on vacation. Everyone looks forward to it, and there's a big holiday on August fifteenth called *Ferragosto*. The name comes from Latin—*Feriae Augusti*, the festival of Emperor Augustus. Schools are all closed. The beaches are packed. Traffic is bumper to bumper. It's a crazy time in Italy."

"Oh, I see."

"You sound disappointed, Erika. What's wrong?"

"I thought I would get another letter. I guess I'll just have to wait. On another subject, do you want to have dinner with me tonight?"

"I'm sorry, Erika. I'm busy with some friends."

"Is Massimo in town?"

"I don't know if he came this weekend or not. You have his number—call him."

Paolo's annoyance at Erika's questions was audible in his voice. "Is everything all right?" she asked carefully.

"Yes." He paused, and she felt as if he was choosing his words carefully. "But it sometimes seems like you have trouble being alone."

"Oh. I didn't realize," she said.

"I can't come for dinner," he said, his voice more gentle now, "but can I come up in the afternoon for a second? I have something here I need to give you."

"Sure. I'll see you later." She hung up, feeling worse than before. She considered her options. She no longer wanted to call Massimo. It was just nine thirty in the morning, and it was already hot, too hot for a walk. At least the thick walls and closed shutters of the house kept the place cool inside.

She tried to think of what Paolo had told her a while back, when she had complained of the heat and humidity after a particularly heavy rain. "Without the sun and rain, we would not have wine," he had said.

Perhaps she complained too much? Had she done something to fall out of Paolo's favor?

Maybe a swim was the answer, she thought. She changed into her bathing suit and went downstairs, still grumpy.

"Is everything okay?" Doris asked, once they'd exchanged their greetings.

"No, not really. But I'll be fine—I'm going for a swim."

She took some towels out and put them on a lounge chair by the pool, took off her cover-up, and dived into the pool. The cool water was refreshing and took the edge off her gloomy mood. As she swam laps, she tried to put Bernardo and Paolo out of her mind. Time slipped away, and she was surprised to see Doris walking up to the pool. "I made you a fresh salad with tomato and mozzarella," she told her.

"Thank you, Doris. You're an angel."

"Are you sure you are okay, Ms. Erika?"

"I'm fine. I just have to do some thinking and sort out a few things, that's all."

"If you would like to talk, I'm here."

"Thank you very much, Doris, but I have to do this on my own. I'll be there for lunch in a few minutes."

She got out of the water and sat down at the patio table. When she saw the salad, she wished she had her camera with her—she'd never seen a simple dish look so amazing. The tomato slices were the size of a hamburger bun, and the basil leaves that garnished them were huge. The balsamic vinegar was sweet. *Well, it's ours,* she thought proudly, *and it's been aged for fifteen years.* Paolo had said that the vintage that year was so bad you really could not make good wine. But the balsamic was heavenly.

Between the swim and the fresh food, her bad mood finally lifted.

After lunch, she went back to the pool, put on sunscreen, along with a baseball cap and dark glasses, and stretched out on her stomach on a raft. Then she just let her mind and body drift. Her eyes were closed and she was fully relaxed when Paolo came by. For a while, he just stood and watched her, saying nothing, while Erika pretended to be asleep. She was enjoying looking at Paolo from behind her dark glasses, knowing he couldn't see her eyes. It was flattering to see how he appraised her body and a little fun to guess at the perplexed look on his face. But when he started to leave, she rolled off the raft into the water.

Paolo heard the splash and looked back at her. "Are you okay, Erika?"

"Of course, just fine!" she laughed. "I was just resting with my eyes closed. Did I fool you?"

"You did." Paolo smiled at last. "I didn't want to disturb you. I had something to give you, and Doris told me you were here at the pool."

She saw the envelope in his hand but asked anyway, "What did you bring?"

"Bernardo knew that he'd be at the seaside in August with his family. So when he came the last time, he gave me the next letter. He said to give it to you when I thought the moment was right. When you told me you called Bernardo's office today, I could hear your disappointment that it was closed. Here is the fourth letter for you."

"Oh, Paolo. This has made my day. Thank you!"

She reached out to take the envelope from him, but he said, "Erika, your hands are wet. Where do you want me to put it?"

"Give me a minute. I'm coming out." She swam over to the edge, climbed out, and wrapped herself in a towel. "I've had enough sun for today. Let's go back to the house."

They walked back to the patio together silently. She wasn't sure what to say. She had wanted him to have dinner, but he'd refused, and she wasn't sure why or what he expected of her. When they got to the kitchen door, she finally spoke. "I'm going to put some clothes on. Please wait for me?"

Paolo nodded.

She dashed upstairs and changed into white cotton pants and a cotton sweater, murmuring a prayer as she did so: "Grandpa, help me. If you want me and Paolo to get together, please send me a sign on how to do it. I'm not getting through to him. What does he think the last three weeks have meant? Why did he make that wonderful picnic if he didn't want anything more to do with me? He suddenly seems so different. So cold. I don't know what else I can do."

Paolo was sitting there with the envelope in his hand when she came back down.

"Paolo, would you like a glass of wine?"

"No, Erika. I can't stay. Here is your letter. I'll talk to you tomorrow."

Paolo walked away, leaving Erika speechless and confused and staring at the envelope in her hand.

XLIII

———

$\mathcal{E}$RIKA TOOK THE ENVELOPE up to her room. She was tired from the ups and downs of the day, but she couldn't rest till she knew what was in the letter.

Cara *Erika*,

Come stai, mia cara Erika? *I hope this fourth letter finds you well. It should be almost August by now—a very hot time in Tuscany. The grapes are turning red, and we can't really do anything at all except watch them develop. I hope you are taking pictures. I'm sure Paolo is preparing for the harvest, checking that all the machines are working. The white wine from Livernano should be ready to be picked by the end of the month. This will be your first harvest. Make sure that Paolo explains the whole process. Stay with him while the grapes are picked.*

But now I need to tell you more of my story.

When Maurizio finally came to visit me in Tuscany, he told me that Concetta and my son had moved and no one knew where they had gone. She did not keep her word about staying in touch, and that upset me very much. With Maurizio's help, I hired a private investigator to find her. A month later, the investigator was successful. They had moved to Florida, and I called her with the number the investigator had provided. I knew Roberto was old enough to be able to travel, and Maurizio had offered to go to Florida and pick him up and fly with him to Europe.

When Concetta picked up the phone, she was truly surprised. We spoke for a long time. She told me about Roberto, who had just celebrated his tenth birthday. She said he was a good student and liked sports. He had had a difficult time adapting to his new environment in the beginning. But he was doing much better and had many new friends. I was happy to hear that.

When I asked her if Roberto had asked about me, however, the phone went silent. Then Concetta told me that my son did not know anything about me and that he thought her husband was his father.

It was like someone stabbed me in the heart. I asked how she could do this to me. She tried to explain, but it did not make any sense. She had completely wiped me out of her life and my son's life. After I hung up with her, I called Maurizio in New York. Like me, he was shocked but not totally surprised. He offered to go to Florida on my behalf and demand to see my son and talk to him. He left for Florida a week later and went to Concetta's house with no warning. You can imagine how surprised she was to see him. But she let him into the house.

They talked for a while, and she pleaded that he not tell Roberto the truth. She kept saying that he was still young and that her husband was very good to him and treated Roberto like his own son. She promised that when Roberto finally questioned why he had a different last name than his supposed father, she would tell the boy the truth.

When that day came, however, and Roberto asked about his name, she told him that I had abandoned the family when he was an infant, that I had gone back to Europe and left them behind.

When Roberto was older, I managed to contact him, but when we finally talked, he did not want anything to do with me. It was my word against his mother's. It didn't matter that I had sent money every month until Roberto turned eighteen to make sure that he had everything he needed. Concetta had also kept the source of the money from him. After my call, Roberto became angry at his mother and was estranged from her, too. Concetta blamed me for that, of course.

He went to college in New York, where he met your mother. Concetta was not invited to his wedding, and when you were born, he did not share that news with her, either.

You know how it all ended. You never got to meet any relatives. Not your grandmother or me. You never even knew that we existed. Dear

Erika, even after all these years, writing my story still hurts. I hope that, as you read this, you will come to understand me. My letters to you are of great importance, but I don't want them to make you sad.

Maurizio passed some years back, as did his wife, but he had five children, and they all live in New York. They came to visit many times, and we all became close. Bernardo has their names and numbers so you can contact them. I am sure they would love to meet you.

Writing this letter takes a lot of energy from an old man. My eyes are not what they used to be.

I hope you have tried the gramophone and listened to the old records. There are more of them in the office. And be good to Paolo. He did not deserve what he had to go through in California and is still saddened by it, though he says it is in the past. I believe it is hard for him to trust. I hope you can change his mind.

Sending you un abbraccio,

Your nonno,
Umberto

When Erika had finished reading the letter, she read it again, and then again. She barely ate any dinner and was reading it one more time when she finally fell asleep.

XLIV

―――――

*W*HEN ERIKA AWOKE the next morning, it was as if all the clouds had drifted off, and with them her dark mood had also gone away. She felt hopeful and happy.

She turned on the coffee machine and called down, "*Buongiorno*, Doris."

"Good morning, Ms. Erika," she heard in return.

"Can you please turn the music on? You know my favorite station."

The music filled the house, and Erika took her coffee out to the balcony to greet the day. Mirella was watering the flowers and Santo was cleaning the fountain, and she waved to both of them.

As she sipped her coffee, she thought more about the newest letter. Her grandfather had insisted that she not be sad, and she was determined to follow that advice. Now that she knew his story, she could do everything she could to erase the pain of the past. She could start by contacting Maurizio's children, the New York cousins that she never knew about. She would invite them to visit her in Tuscany.

And then there were his comments about Paolo . . . that he was a good guy but was uncertain about trusting himself to love.

Erika looked out to the view, which she had come to love. The sun was already unrelenting. There were beads of sweat on her forehead. It would be another hot day.

She showered, dressed, and got her phone. She needed to call Paolo and get things back on track with him, but before she could dial his number, her phone rang. Paolo's name was on the screen.

"*Pronto.*"

"Erika, I'm sorry for yesterday. I don't know why I left so suddenly."

"Well, I wasn't in a very good mood either. Are you at the cantina?"

"Yes."

"Why don't you come up here? We can talk a little."

Five minutes later, he was at the house. They found a shady spot on the patio, and she told him about the contents of the fourth letter.

"You know, Paolo, I've told you before that I have the feeling that my grandfather wanted us to be together. He always writes little hints about you, though I don't quite understand how he knew what kind of person I'd like."

"He knew me well, and perhaps he had an intuition about the kind of person you would be. Maybe he simply thought we would be a good team, here at the vineyard. I can't speak for him. What I will say is that it was fun hanging out with him . . . cooking and making music. I liked his stories, and I didn't even mind when he repeated them. They were funny and interesting. There were stories about Maurizio and his band. When he was young, I guess Maurizio was something of a ladies' man. I had to laugh, and there were always more stories to listen to. I'll try to remember them for you."

"And what about the Palio? Are you excited about going?"

"Yes, I can't wait to see what it's like. Is Massimo coming with his girlfriend?"

"He said he would, but with him you never know. If not, then it's just the two of us. You don't mind, do you?"

"No, not at all. You know I enjoy spending time with you. And we don't have to wait for the Palio to go somewhere. We could go to the seaside tomorrow."

"I'm not sure that's a good idea. The beaches are packed right now, and the traffic coming home will be terrible."

"What about hanging out with me at the pool then?"

"Erika, I'm not really a pool kind of a guy. Do you want to go to Brunello di Montalcino?"

"But you just told me there's a lot of traffic."

"Yes, to the beach, but not to the countryside."

"I don't know. Let's see how we feel tomorrow."

Paolo laughed. "I know why you want me at the beach or the pool. You just want to see my handsome body in a speedo!"

"Is that so bad?"

He looked at her closely, and she couldn't quite read his expression. "Erika, I need to go back to the cantina for a while."

"Do you want to come back for a late lunch?"

"*Si, cara. A dopo.*"

He was back a few hours later. Doris had made a beautiful salad and a little pasta, and he and Erika ate quietly. She was aware of the romantic undercurrent and feeling shy about that. There were questions in the back of her mind. Should they greet each other with a hug? A kiss? Why were they so awkward all of a sudden?

Erika remembered her grandfather's encouragement and decided that she needed to make a first move. "Paulo," she said, "let's take some water and a bottle of white wine and drive up to the chapel."

"Sure, that sounds good," he told her. "I'll get the wine. Why don't you find a blanket and then bring the John Deere around?"

By the time she came up with the little tractor, Paolo was standing there with a basket filled with the drinks and glasses. When they got up to the chapel, they walked to the spot where they'd had their picnic. Erika unfolded the blanket, and when they had settled themselves comfortably under a tree, Paolo opened the wine and poured them each a glass.

Before Erika could take a sip, though, he leaned over and kissed her. "To us," he said before he kissed her again.

The awkwardness was finally gone. They talked and sipped the wine, and eventually Erika stretched out and put her head in Paolo's lap and fell asleep. She woke up with him stroking her hair softly.

"How long was I asleep?" she asked.

"I don't know. You looked so peaceful like that. I think I fell asleep for a few minutes too. Look how beautiful the view is from here. The day is so clear you can see the towers of Siena. It's amazing." He pointed at the towers, but then abruptly dropped his hand and looked to her. His dark eyes looked wet. "I have to ask you. Erika . . . could you imagine living in Italy?"

"Yes. I love it here. I just need to get better with the language."

"That will come, Erika—I promise you. You should watch Italian movies. We could watch them together."

"I don't know . . . I haven't turned on the TV in weeks. I love the quiet.

The evenings are so amazingly beautiful. No sunset is the same as another. And when I walk around Casalvento, even if I take the same route, I always see something new. The smell of the woods, the vineyards, the flowers—it's all so astonishing. When I wake up in the morning, I'm smiling and happy. It's overwhelmingly beautiful, especially when you are around." She looked at him and laughed. "You know, when I first heard of this estate, I had no idea what I could do with it. The only thing that came to mind was to sell it as fast as I could. Then, when I arrived, I could not believe what I had inherited. That I had to stay here was the best thing that ever happened to me. Somehow my grandfather knew in his heart that I was not in the right place—somehow he knew where I truly belonged. I guess sometimes people have to be forced to find happiness."

"You could not be more right," Paolo told her. He looked at her as he continued stroking her hair and her face. "I never believed I could love again," he said. "I will do my best to believe that this is what you want, because it would make me the happiest man on earth."

He leaned down and kissed her again, and all her doubts vanished.

Part FOUR

XLV

—

ON AUGUST 16, THE DAY of the Palio, Erika waited for Paolo to pick her up and thought again about her feelings for him. The last few weeks had been pleasurable, full of embraces and delicious kisses, but nothing more. She was beginning to wish that he would take things a step further. She didn't quite understand his hesitancy, but she supposed all she could do was wait until he was ready . . . even if things were normally the other way around.

By the time they arrived in Siena's inner city, it was around noon, and the crowds were already gathering. Paolo parked the car at a friend's office, and the two of them made their way to the Piazza del Campo. It seemed that thousands of people were packed into the center of the square, behind a fence. Around them was the track that the horses would follow. Erika could see the horses as well, decorated with the flags of each *contrada*. When she looked up, she saw that flags were also draped over the balconies and from the windows of the surrounding buildings, showing support for the various teams. It was a colorful, crazy spectacle.

"Stay next to me," Paolo shouted to her over the noise of the crowd. "If I lose you, we won't be able to find each other."

"Paolo, isn't it dangerous for the people in the center? They're like sardines in there."

"We've never had any real problems, but people do underestimate the heat. After the last run, there's a lot of partying and drinking, especially among the younger crowd. You have no idea how many people don't make it home, especially if their team wins. You can see people sleeping everywhere—even inside the church on the benches." He took her hand and pointed with his other hand. "We have to make it over there. Use your elbows if you have to."

Finally, after about fifteen minutes—and after covering what normally would have been a three-minute walk—they got to the entrance of the restaurant. The owner took them up to the fourth floor, where the room opened to a panorama of the piazza. A table was set up with drinks and finger food, and a handful of people were already milling around, introducing themselves to each other. Only Paolo was from Italy; the others were visitors from other countries.

Erika had brought her camera, and she went to the balcony and began to zoom in on the horses and the expectant faces of the spectators. "This is amazing," she told Paolo. "Thank you for bringing me here. But where is Massimo?"

"He had to come directly from Milan with his girlfriend, Sofia. I'm calling him now to let him know where to park and where to go. They should be joining us soon."

"Paolo, there's so much going on. How do the races work?"

"Siena is divided into seventeen *contrade*, and each of them has their own flag. The festivities actually started three days ago with different kinds of competitions and parties and formal banquets. Right now they're having the *prova*, a trial run. At five, there's the procession of the *Cero Votivo*, the Votive Candle. And at a quarter past seven, we have the *Prova Generale*. After that, each *contrada* has a dinner—the singing, dancing, and drumming goes on for hours." Paolo looked toward the door. "And here are Massimo and Sofia now!"

Massimo walked in with a stunning woman behind him. Sofia was tall with dark hair, blue eyes, and strong facial features. She hugged Erika as they were introduced and kissed her on both cheeks. Massimo gave Erika a hug and kisses as well, then stood back to look at her.

"My darling cousin," he greeted her, "you look more beautiful every time I see you." He looked over to Paolo and back at Erika. "Do I see a new spark?"

Erika blushed a little, but Paolo just took Massimo by the arm. "Why don't you and I get Erika and Sofia a glass of wine," he said, leaving Erika alone with Sofia.

"I'm sorry," said Sofia, "but my English is not very good. Do you speak French?"

"No, *mi dispiace*. Just a little Italian. I'm learning, but it's a slow process."

"Any new language is hard, even more when you never had it in school. We can help each other. You help with my English, and I will do the same with your Italian?"

"I would like that very much."

Just as Paolo and Massimo returned with the drinks, the noise from the piazza quieted down.

"The *generale* will start in a minute," said Paolo. "They are sealing off the Palio."

The crowd below became totally silent, intent on the beginning of the race. There were a few false starts, then suddenly the horses were off. Three laps and ninety seconds of frenzied running later, it was over. A couple of the horses were riderless as they crossed the finish line, but it seemed that no one got hurt. The crowd went wild as the flag of the victorious *contrada* was waved from every corner and balcony of the piazza. The winning horse and rider took a celebration lap, and the crowd started to disperse.

"That was it?" Erika asked.

Paolo smiled and hugged her. "That was it!"

"So what happens now?"

"We party along with everyone else. Let's go. I made a reservation at Paolo's. Same name as me! It's my friend's pizzeria."

"Is there a restaurant owner you don't know?"

"What can I say? I'm a likable guy."

The four of them went down the stairs and managed to navigate through the supporters of rival *contrade* as confetti rained down from the balconies around the piazza.

The restaurant proved to be a quaint hole-in-the-wall with just twelve tables. Shelves lined with bottles of wine decorated the walls. Wine bottles had been converted to lamps, too, and that added a nice glow to the cozy space. A *pizzaiolo* was working at the pizza oven, and at the back of the room was a prosciutto station with sausages and salamis hanging from racks. The little kitchen seemed to have just one person—the chef and owner himself.

"Why don't you sit down here," Paolo said, "while I go and say hello. Is it okay with you if he decides for us what to order?"

"Not at all," Erika said, and Sofia nodded agreeably.

Massimo led them to a table near the back, and the lone waiter immediately brought water, then returned a moment later with a carafe of red wine and small glass cups—it all felt very rustic. Wearing black pants, an apron, and a burgundy polo shirt with the logo of the restaurant, the waiter fit perfectly in the environment.

Paolo returned from the kitchen. "I don't think we'll leave hungry."

"I love this place," Erika told him as he sat down.

"I thought you would." Paolo reached over to pour the wine, and two pizzas arrived, a *pizza bianca* and *pizza margherita*. They were closer to flatbread than the round pies Erika was used to, but they tasted excellent. Afterward, the waiter brought a plate of prosciutto and wild boar ham, followed by pasta with sausages. The food just kept coming, until Erika and Sofia protested that they couldn't eat another bite. The evening ended with the restaurant owner joining them for after-dinner drinks of his house-made limoncello.

For Erika, the rest of the night was a blur.

She woke up in bed the next morning, wearing only her underwear and with a terrible headache. As she turned over, she realized Paolo was lying next to her, still asleep.

Her first thoughts were *Oh, my gosh! What did I do, or not do?*

She couldn't remember anything. And she really needed an aspirin. She lay there for a little while, then, with a glance to make sure Paolo was still sleeping, got out of bed and tiptoed to the bathroom. She washed her face and combed her hair, took off her underwear, and grabbed the robe that was hanging behind the door. When she opened the door, Paolo was standing there in a T-shirt and shorts.

"Paolo, you just scared the sugar out of me!"

"I scared the sugar out of you? That's an expression I never heard before." He smiled and asked, "How are you, *cara*?"

"Me? I'm feeling great."

"You don't have even a little hangover after all the limoncello you consumed last night?"

"No, should I?" Erika asked innocently.

"Ready for coffee?" Paolo was grinning as if he knew a secret but said nothing as he went to start the coffee. A few minutes later, he called over to her, "*Cara*, how do you like your coffee?"

"Two spoonfuls of milk, no sugar."

He handed her the cup, and they went out to the balcony. Erika could only wonder exactly what had gone on the night before but couldn't find the right words to ask the question. Finally Paolo put her mind at ease.

"You don't have to worry, Erika—nothing happened last night between you and me."

She didn't know whether to be relieved or disappointed.

"We left the restaurant, and as soon as we got into my car, you fell asleep. You were still sleeping when we arrived at the house, so I carried you upstairs and, yes, I undressed you—which I rather enjoyed—and put you in bed. As I covered you, you reached out for my hand and didn't seem to want to let it go, so I lay down next to you. By the way, did you know that you talk in your sleep?"

"How should I know that? I'm sleeping."

"Very funny. Are you ready for breakfast?"

"Yes, please, and some aspirin."

"So you *do* have a hangover?"

"Yes, I admit it. I think I had much more limoncello than I should have."

"Come on. I'll make you something that will fix your headache." He leaned over and kissed her softly.

After breakfast, he was washing the dishes in the sink, and Erika decided it was about time one of them had to act. Standing behind him, she put her arms around his waist and pressed her body against his back. She knew he could feel every curve of her through the thin robe. He dropped the sponge into the sink and turned around, taking her in his arms. He stroked her cheek and kissed her hard as they both gave in to the passion that had been building for weeks. Backing away for a second, he looked at her closely, then he kissed her again, and they went back upstairs.

All reticence was gone as they fell into the bed. Paolo pushed the robe off Erika's shoulders, and she tugged his T-shirt over his head. Time stopped for them as they explored each other's bodies hungrily with lips, fingers, everything. When they finally made love, Paolo began slowly, sensually, sweeping her with him as the force of their emotions and their physical desire for each other became overwhelming.

Afterward they lay there quietly, with Paolo watching Erika's face as he stroked her side, her arm, her back with the tips of his fingers. "I want to savor this moment," he told her.

"The day is young, Paolo, and we have all the time in the world."

They rested for some time, dozing, and she woke to him kissing her eyelids, then her neck, and, as his lips brushed the more intimate parts of her body, she soon felt the electricity of that touch, and they made love once again. It was more sweetly romantic the second time, as they came to know each other's rhythms and pleasures, reveling in the new sensations they called up in one another.

They dozed for a while, sleeping wrapped in each other's arms, reluctant to let go.

Later in the afternoon, as the breeze came through the open window, Erika stirred first. She nuzzled his neck, waking him gently. Sleepily, he pulled her up and wrapped his legs around her body, bringing her to his chest and whispering in her ear, "Are you happy?"

"Must you even ask? I don't think I ever felt so in tune with someone before." She leaned into him and caressed the arms that circled her. And as her hair brushed his shoulder, he kissed her neck and said, "Let's have a glass of wine and toast to what just happened between us."

"Yes, but let's make it champagne."

They put on robes and made their way downstairs. Paolo opened the champagne, and they took their glasses out by the pool. The sun was lower in the sky, bathing the landscape with gold. Erika looked over at Paolo and reached for his hand.

"I love it here," she told him. "My grandfather knew this would happen—somehow, he knew. I only wish he were here so I could tell him myself."

Paolo thought for a moment, sipped the champagne, and raised his glass. "To Umberto . . . and to you. Do you want some dinner? We can make it together."

Erika smiled at him and nodded. "But first, maybe a little dessert?"

XLVI

———

*A*s THE WEEKS WENT BY, it was clear that the season was beginning to change. The days were still very warm, but the nights were
getting colder, perfect for the ripening grapes. Paolo checked the sugar in
the white grapes each day, trying to gauge the perfect moment to begin
that harvest.

Everything was ready. The destemming machine was in position, and
the press for the grapes was clean, as were the steel tanks for fermenting the
white wine. The *cassette*, the plastic crates, were washed and trucked over
to Livernano. The *squadra* was on standby. There would be two hectares of
white grapes to be picked by hand, destemmed, pressed, and put into the
tanks, all in the same day.

Erika was both excited and a bit daunted by everything that needed to
happen. She was determined to learn as much as she could, both by taking
part and by using her camera to document the process. Doris helped her
get the clothes and gear she would need—special shoes, gloves, and clippers, for starters.

Erika also started working on closing her New York business. She
emailed Tiffany with details and called every few days to follow up on the
contract to buy out the company. While the calls were cordial and the deal
was going through without any problems, she could detect a new tone in
Tiffany's conversations. Something had changed, and she couldn't help but
wonder if Tiffany and Craig had gotten together again. Well, good for them
if they had—she had her own lover to make her happy.

Even with all the work of harvest looming, she and Paolo were reveling
in their new closeness, finding moments to be alone to sneak a kiss or just

brush against each other. Paolo insisted on staying at his own house during the week, saying he needed to stay focused on the harvest, but he came to cook dinner with Erika every day, letting Doris go home earlier. And he was there on weekends, sharing the days and nights with Erika.

She had started to put an album together, collecting her pictures from the last few months and writing her impressions. So much had changed and was still changing; she wanted to make sure she would never forget all that she had learned and experienced.

In a month, she would be officially taking over the properties, and another new chapter would begin. The business was thriving with the popular wine tours and luncheons, and guests were filling the suites at Livernano, which had also hosted quite a few weddings. In a few days, she'd meet with Bernardo again. She needed to talk to him about placating Franco, the contractor, who continued to stop by the office and complain. Bernardo had said that he also had one more envelope for her. She couldn't wait to find out what was in it.

One weekday morning, Erika woke early and went down to the kitchen to get some water and was surprised to see Paolo there.

"*Ciao, cara.* I just came by to get you. We are ready to pick the white grapes at Livernano today—starting with Sauvignon Blanc and then Chardonnay."

"Oh, this is exciting! Let me just get dressed and grab what I need."

Five minutes later, she was back downstairs and ready to go.

As he drove them to Livernano, Paolo said, "Why don't you help to pick one row, so you know how it's done? I can only stay until noon. I have to be at Casalvento when the first tractor transports the grapes there, so I can weigh each *cassetta*. We can see how you feel at noon. You may want to come back with me."

There were a dozen people waiting at Livernano when Paolo drove up. They waited while he marked the beginning of each row of Sauvignon Blanc with a red ribbon, then assigned each person, including Erika, to a row. As the others got busy, he showed Erika what to do.

"This is how it works. One *cassetta* is tied to you, then five others are piled on top. Will you be able to pull them?"

She tried it and nodded.

Paolo continued. "When you move, make sure you hold on to the top *cassetta* with one hand. We don't want the crates to fall over or the grapes to get dirty." He knelt down with the clippers in his hand. "Watch me closely. You hold the grapes in one hand, and then cut the stem like this. Don't throw the grapes into the *cassetta*. We don't want the skin to break. If you have leaves or anything else that is not a grape, throw it away. When the top *cassetta* is full, place it in your row close to the vine. Santo will collect them with the tractor, and he needs to be able to pass through the rows. Now try it, so I can see how you do it."

Erika put on her gloves and started to work.

"You're a natural, *cara*. I'll be back in a little while." He leaned over and gave her a quick kiss on the cheek, then left to check on the others.

For the next two hours, Erika worked her way up the steep row, filling three *cassette*. It was hot, back-bending work, and she was tired and thirsty by the time Paolo reappeared at the top of the vineyard hill. She waved at him, and he signaled her to come up. She untied the *cassetta*, stood up straight to stretch, and slowly walked up to join him.

"Oh, Erika, your face is as red as a tomato. Did you forget to use sunblock? I have some water in the truck."

"Thank you!" She took the water, drank some, and splashed her face with it as well.

"I knew it would be hard, Paolo, but it's important for me to learn about every step, even if it hurts."

"That's great, Erika, but I think it's enough for one morning. You're a good sport." He kissed her forehead, and they got into the car and drove back to Casalvento. "Why don't you go up to the house and rest a little."

"No way, Paolo—I need to watch what comes next. I'm just going to wash up a little, then I'll walk over to the cantina."

When she got there, Hanna was giving a wine tour to clients, who were amazed by the winery work that was taking place around them.

The first tractor had arrived with the *cassette* filled with white grapes, and Mirella was using a forklift to unload them. After Paolo carefully weighed each crate and recorded the numbers, Luca emptied the *cassette* into the destemming machine. The stems fell out one side, leaving only the loose grapes, which were transported to the press and crushed. Tubes carried the juice to another machine that would remove the skins several hours later. Finally, the juice would go into the tanks.

Erika watched it all for a long time, marveling at the complexity of everything that went into making wine. Finally, she asked, "Paolo, how much longer will you be here?"

He stopped what he was doing and wiped at his brow with a towel. "There's one more load coming, and we have to crush it. I would say another two hours."

"Okay. I'll go up and have some dinner ready for you when you are done."

"Thanks, *cara*. I should be up around eight. We have to wash everything down, then Mirella and Santo will clean up after."

When Erika got back to the house, she was grateful that Doris was preparing dinner.

"Oh, Doris, thank you! Paolo will be here later to eat with me. Please set the table outside. I'm going to shower and maybe lie down for a few minutes. I had no idea how labor intensive the harvest would be."

She was still asleep when Paolo woke her with a kiss a couple of hours later. "Oh, Paolo, I guess I was more tired than I realized!"

"Don't worry. Can I take a quick shower here? I'm dirty and sticky from the grapes. Normally, I shower in the cantina, but I thought it would be okay. I brought up some clean clothes."

"Of course," she told him. "Did things wrap up well?"

"Yes. We're having quite a good harvest—twenty percent more grapes than last year. I checked the books just before I came up here."

Once Paolo had showered and dressed, they sat outside and sipped white wine with the pasta and fresh tomato salad that Doris had made.

"I can't believe I helped pick grapes today and then was there for the crushing. If only Todd or James could have seen me!"

"You did well, Erika. You're finding out what being a winery owner is really all about. I'm proud of you."

"Thanks, that means a lot. Will you stay tonight?"

"Erika, I would love to, but we need to start early on the Chardonnay. I need to go home and get some sleep. If I stay, well . . ." He shrugged and smiled at her.

She laughed. "Okay, I'll see you tomorrow. Thank you for everything, Paolo."

The next morning, Erika's muscles were still aching, so instead of heading to the fields, she went up to her office, replied to emails, and signed some contracts for Tiffany. At noon, she walked over to the cantina.

"*Ciao, tutti*," she greeted everyone. The harvest work was again in full swing, and the first truckload had already arrived. "Things are happening fast today," she said to Paolo, who was weighing *cassette* of grapes.

"We have almost eighteen people picking today. We need to work quickly. There's rain in the forecast, and we can't pick when it's raining. Oh, Erika, before I forget, Bernardo will be here tomorrow. He has to prepare some documents for the takeover, and he needs some more information and signatures from you."

"It'll be nice to see him again. Are you coming up for dinner tonight?"

"I don't think so. We'll be here until midnight for sure. We'll have some panini."

"Is everyone staying that late?"

"Yes, those of us from Casalvento."

"Why don't Doris and I make something simple and bring it down for you all."

"You would do that? That would be great."

At seven, Erika and Doris loaded the John Deere with the goodies they had made: *pasta fagioli*, zucchini frittata, cold cuts and cheeses, bread, beer, and a bottle of white wine for Paolo and her. They used the loading platform of the little tractor as a table, and everyone sat around on the plastic crates. Erika's Italian was now good enough to carry on a simple conversation with Mirella, though Santo's rustic dialect was still beyond her. Still, she felt as if she belonged, as if she was truly part of the Casalvento family.

"This is like the old days with your grandpa," said Paolo. "We did this all the time."

After dinner, the crew went back to work, and, as Doris and Erika were cleaning up, Paolo came over and said quietly, "*Cara*, if you want, I'll come up later."

"I'd love that. If I'm already in my room, just come upstairs."

He kissed her quickly. "*A dopo*."

She was already asleep when Paolo got under the covers and put his arm around her. She stirred a little, barely aware of his presence, but before she could answer, Paolo was dead to the world.

They were still like that, side by side, as the sunlight brightened the room the next morning.

Erika turned over and looked into Paolo's eyes, which were open. "You're up?"

"I didn't want to wake you, so I just waited. I had a very beautiful woman to look at."

He kissed her and ran his fingers lightly over her face and body, and she responded with touches and caresses that quickly brought them both fully and passionately awake. They made love with an intensity that surprised and delighted her. Afterward, as he rested with his head on her chest, she ran her fingers through his hair, which had a faint aroma of grapes.

Eventually, he said, "*Cara*, I would like to stay like this forever, but I have to go to work, and you need to get up too. Bernardo will be coming."

Erika looked at him and gave him a quick kiss. "I love harvest time."

XLVII

─────────

*E*RIKA WAS ALREADY AT THE CANTINA when Bernardo arrived the next morning at eleven. Well dressed and gentlemanly as always, he greeted her with a hug and a kiss on each cheek.

"You look amazing, Erika. Paolo told me how you've helped with the harvest, both in the fields and in the cellar. *Brava*, well done!"

"Oh, Bernardo, it's been hard work but also fun. I have a whole new perspective about wines. I drink them now with respect."

"You should, Erika. Winemaking is a passion, sometimes even an obsession. It's a form of art. The wine usually reflects the character of the owner. Each bottle that you see here in the cellar is a reflection of your grandfather and Paolo. They were the perfect team. Now, this will be yours and Paolo's first vintage together."

Erika was touched by what Bernardo said, especially in light of her growing love for Paolo. Some of that love had indeed gone into the vintage. "You are right, Bernardo. This is a new beginning for Casalvento and Livernano—not only for the wine but also for Paolo and me."

"I am happy to hear it! But enough wine talk," he said. "There is much paperwork to get signed."

Erika held up a finger. "Before we do that, Bernardo, I want to talk to you about Franco Stucco. He hasn't come back to the house, but he's returned to Livernano several times, always grousing about my grandfather's will. I have an idea, and I want to know what you think. What about giving Franco some kind of award from Livernano that acknowledges his work and the importance of his contribution? It would include some sort of generous financial award—you'll have to consider how much would be best—and we could even put up a plaque somewhere, in his honor. My grandfather left the properties to me, but I don't want to have someone so unhappy coming by all the time and upsetting the guests. Maybe some recognition will make Franco feel more comfortable with me as the new owner."

Bernardo considered the idea for a few minutes before he finally said, "I think that's not a bad idea, Erika. It's a little unusual for Tuscany, but then you're an American, so it's okay. And, yes, it may help to make Franco less angry. Let's go ahead and plan a little ceremony for after you've taken over the winery officially. And speaking of the takeover, please sit down. I have to explain how it will work, and it will take a little time."

Erika sat down and listened carefully to what Bernardo had to say.

"So, if I understand right," she finally said, "you want me to sign one percent of the company over to Paolo?"

"Yes. The reason is that you are an American citizen, not an Italian resident and not a farmer. If you give Paolo one percent, you'll get government funding for certain things, for example, a new tractor or any kind of machinery or construction. It will help a lot."

"Did you speak to Paolo about this?"

"No. I wanted to talk to you first, to get your approval to draw up the paperwork."

"I have no problem with it, Bernardo. That can only help the company. But I'd like to talk to Paolo about it myself. I can do that tonight, if it's okay with you."

"Of course, Erika. That would be good—we have to transfer all the bank documents into your name, and I need to know if you want to give Paolo the authority to sign the winery accounts as well."

"Bernardo, please, you can decide about that. I'll do whatever you think is best for the company. I trust you."

"Thank you, and I take that as a great compliment. Are you sure you're ready to take this all on?"

"Oh, yes!"

"Good. Now, here is the letter from your grandfather that I promised. The last one."

"Thank you. This means a great deal to me. Did you want to stay for lunch?"

"Sorry, I have to go to my next appointment, and I'm late already. But please put on your calendar the appointment with the notary. It's set for October seventh at ten a.m. in Siena. I know it's a week earlier than we planned, but that was the only time available."

"That's fine, and I'm glad that it's all set. Thank you again."

Bernardo left her with another kiss on each cheek and a wave as he left. Erika waved back and then looked at the envelope in her hand. She couldn't wait to read it and immediately headed for the house. Doris was in the kitchen as she came in.

"Back so soon, Ms. Erika?"

"Yes, I'll be up at the office if you need me."

Erika made herself comfortable in the heavy old wooden chair and looked around the room. *How simple and strong everything is here,* she thought. *This place must have so many stories to tell.* She would have loved to have heard them from her grandfather but was still determined to find out as much as she could. Every drawer held some secret about her existence or her grandfather's past. The only thing she needed to do was put it all together.

She unfolded the letter.

Cara *Erika,*

When this letter reaches you, my darling granddaughter, you will be close to receiving your inheritance. I'm so proud that you have had the courage and the stamina to stay and carry through with my wishes. Not that I would have thought otherwise. You are my blood and my soul, and I imagine you have inherited my stubbornness as well. After all, you are a Germoglio, which means "bud" in English. The bud of a grape is a germoglio. Growing grapes for wine, like drinking it, is in our blood.

Cara, I hope that, even after all the years we missed, you have come to know me—who I was, how I lived, what I believed in, and the history of our family. It is important to me that we carry our tradition forward into the next generation. And that I made you see something of that.

Life is never easy, and we all have our paths to follow. I hope that I have helped you see yours. Now, when you walk through our property, perhaps you can see the beauty of the land and its culture like I did. Be proud and stand tall.

After these months in Italy, I'm sure you have become a different person from the woman you were when you left New York. Maybe being here has helped you see life in a much happier way. That the sun not only gives us light during the day but also makes the grass green, the roses bloom, the vegetables grow, the vines and trees bloom and bear fruit. And puts us in a happy mood as well!

When the day gives way to the night, the moon and the constellations are beautiful, and the animals can come out from their hiding places and find nourishment. I hope that you will sleep well and have wonderful dreams—with a person next to you that you love and want to share your life with. I want you to enjoy life with all its glory. I wish for you to find love and happiness. It would mean the world to me if you found that in Tuscany.

I wish for you to experience all of this. If you can, then I have done what I was sent to do, what I felt was the right thing to do. Then I have found my path . . . and you have found yours!

I embrace you!

> Un grande abbraccio,
> *Your* nonno,
> *Umberto*

As Erika came to the end of the letter, tears ran down her cheeks. Yes, she had found her path, and her grandfather had helped her. She would carry the tradition on and show her children the beauty of their land, and she would tell them how wonderful their great-grandfather was and what he had to go through to find his own path. And she truly wanted to break the curse of unhappiness and unkindness between brothers and family.

Her grandfather had helped her to see life in a totally different way. She could smell the roses now. She could see the different colors that made up the beautiful landscape, and she could hear the music in the wind. And she had learned what love and happiness felt like.

As she put the letter aside, it occurred to her how fitting the name

Casalvento was for the house. In English, the word meant "House of the Wind," and it was true—the house stood on a hill with no other house in sight, wrapped in the wind.

She put the letter in the box with all the others and stroked the lid as she closed it. She left the office feeling more lighthearted, with a smile on her face. She needed to go up to the chapel, to bring her grandfather some flowers but also her high spirits. She wanted to feel as close to him as possible right now.

Along the way, Erika felt a light breeze and listened for the music it carried. She couldn't help noticing how the leaves were changing color. The sunflowers were all gone, their glory days over for the season. The tomatoes were almost gone too, but the pumpkins were swelling, and the harvest for the red grapes was about to begin. It was almost fall. Every season had something to offer, she knew.

She came to the cypress trees and saw the small chapel in front of her. She stopped to admire the view, which never failed to amaze her. Down at the cantina, she could see the cars coming and going. September was always one of the best months for tourists in Tuscany, though now most were coming without kids, who were back in school.

She took a deep breath and inhaled the fresh air, trying to listen to the nature all around her. She said her prayer there, then took the flowers she'd brought into the chapel and placed them in the vase on the altar.

"For you, Grandfather," she murmured.

XLVIII

———

$\mathcal{L}$ATER THAT AFTERNOON, Erika was helping Doris prepare dinner when her cell phone rang. Todd's name was on the screen. Despite her wet hands, Erika managed to answer it.

"Todd! Hello! It's good to hear from you."

"Darling, how are you?"

"Things couldn't be any better. How's New York? And how's your project coming?"

"Slowly, I must admit. The client's still a handful, but in the end I think the place will be beautiful. Darling, is Paolo with you?"

"No. Why?"

"I wanted to thank him. The container came and cleared customs without a problem. I was so worried about the taxes. But nothing. They just started to unload it, and nothing broken so far. Paolo did a great job. I'm so happy. I don't know how he did it."

"I'm glad to hear all went well. I'll tell him later. He's busy right now with the harvest. We already brought in the white grapes."

"Yes, I saw the pictures you sent. When will you start on the red?"

"I think this weekend. Are you guys coming? It would be fun to have you here."

"That was my second reason for the call. I spoke to James, and my office assistant checked the flights. We could arrive on September twenty-eighth and leave on October tenth. If that's okay with you, we'll go ahead and get the tickets."

"That would be amazing! It means you would be here when I take over the properties. We can celebrate afterward."

"We would love that. Believe me, darling, it was not easy to get James out of his office, but I told him that we promised. We'll see you in a couple of weeks."

"Bring warm clothes with you. It's getting cool at night."

"Will do, darling. Before I go, how is your love life going?"

"Oh, Todd, you were right about Paolo. He is amazing, and I think we're good together, and a good team, too."

"I'm glad you listened to us. I want to hear all the details when we arrive. Oh, darling . . . one more thing. We heard through the grapevine— and you will not believe this—Craig is dating Tiffany. I guess they started seeing each other after he came back from Tuscany. James and I ran into them at a restaurant on the Upper East Side a couple of days ago."

"Good for them. I had a feeling. I've been dealing with Tiffany and Molly. I'm selling her my shares of the business."

"You are?"

"Yes, I'm not going back to my life in New York. And I wouldn't be able to work with Tiffany. That would be too weird."

"No, I understand. I'm sure you have everything under control. We'll see you soon, darling. Kisses!"

"*Ciao*, Todd."

She put the phone down and turned to Doris, who was wiping down the dining table. "They're really coming back," she told her. "Todd said they'll arrive in two weeks."

Doris smiled at the news. "I'll start getting the room ready for them."

Moments later, Paolo came through the door.

"*Ciao, cara. Ciao,* Doris." He walked over and gave Erika a kiss.

"Todd just called hoping to speak to you," she told him. "The container arrived, and everything went smoothly. He was so happy and wanted to thank you himself. Plus he and James are coming back to Tuscany. They arrive on the twenty-eighth of September for two weeks. That means they'll be here when I take the properties over."

"That must make you very happy."

"Yes, they are my closest friends. And guess what? Craig is dating Tiffany!"

"Does that bother you, *cara?*"

"Not at all. I already guessed there was something going on with them.

On a different note, though, I need to speak with you about something important. Do you have time now? We can have a glass of wine and talk."

Paolo got a bottle of Chianti and glasses and followed Erika into the living room. She sat near the fireplace.

"I can't wait for the cold winter nights. It'll be nice to have a fire here again."

"Those will come soon enough. But keep your fingers crossed that the weather stays nice for a while—I think we'll start to pick the Merlot in Casalvento this coming weekend. It will be a lot of work to get all the grapes in. But tell me what is on your mind."

"Well, you know that Bernardo needed to talk to me. He told me that it would be in the best interest of the company if I signed over one percent of the shares to you. It would benefit us tremendously. Will you agree to that, Paolo?"

"Of course. I know it will save us money and help with government funding. How could I say no? Did Bernardo say when the big day will be?"

"The appointment is set for ten a.m. on the seventh," Erika told him. "With the notary in Siena."

"That's coming up soon. Are you excited?"

"I can hardly wait, but I'm a little nervous." She set her wine glass down on the coffee table. "At least having you here with me, in this new chapter of my life, helps, and it makes me happy."

In response, Paolo reached out and took her in his arms.

She kissed him, then asked, "Are you hungry? Dinner is almost ready."

"I'm hungry for you, *cara*. But, yes, let's eat."

The harvest continued over the next couple of weeks as the days got shorter. The Merlot from Casalvento had all been brought in, and Erika and Doris continued to load the John Deere with food and drive it down to the cantina in the evenings. It eased the difficulty of working the long hours and made the end of the day seem like a little family party.

Erika also kept taking pictures of the harvest, documenting every stage of the process. Crushing the red grapes was the same as for the white ones, but the fermentation took place in wood instead, some in barrels and some in tanks. Paolo showed Erika how to sample the juice each day so she could taste the transformation into wine.

Meanwhile, she had signed the paperwork for the sale of her share of the New York company. She thought she might have to return to the States in November to finalize everything and retrieve the last of her possessions from storage, but it seemed like that would be a fun time to do some Christmas shopping and say goodbye to the city.

Before that, though, there was still much to be done. As the end of September neared, visitors were still coming to taste wines at the cantina, where Hanna was busy with tours. With the weather holding up, Livernano was almost full, and the Merlot there was now ready to be harvested.

And Todd and James were finally due to arrive. Luca went to pick them up at the airport, while Erika, dressed in work clothes and rubber boots, was spending the morning helping at the cantina. She had asked Luca to bring her friends there before taking them to the house.

I want Todd and James to see me at work, she thought as she squeezed through the small opening in one of the wooden tanks to clean it. *They'd never believe it otherwise*. Once inside, she had plenty of room to stand up, and she was still in there when she heard Todd calling her name.

"Todd, I'm over here, inside the tank," she answered. As he walked over, he saw her emerging from the huge wooden container and rushed over to give her a hug, then stood back in mock horror.

"James, you've got to come here and see this," Todd called out. "You won't believe it."

James laughed. "We have to take a picture. What is that all over you?"

"It's grape skins, from the inside of the tank. How was your trip?"

"It was fine, darling," said Todd. "And it's wonderful to see you, even looking like this!"

"I'm so glad you're here," Erika said. "Why don't you go up to the house with Luca. Doris is there waiting for you. I'll walk over, and while you get settled in, I'll take a shower."

An hour later, they were all at the table on the patio, toasting their reunion and having snacks. Erika filled them in on everything that had happened over the summer. Finally, she asked about Craig and Tiffany.

"Honey," said James, "those two are made for each other. Total soul-mates." He cringed a little in mock disgust.

Erika laughed. "Good for them. I mean it! It has all worked out for the best, and I dare say I am grateful to Tiffany for the intervention."

At that moment, Paolo walked up and greeted Todd and James with a warm hug each, then sat down to join the party.

"I want to thank you again," Todd told him, "for arranging the container so well. And for taking such good care of our friend here. Erika has been giving us all the details."

"About what?"

"Everything!" James exclaimed. "We're happy you took our advice."

Paolo laughed with them. "Well, I have to say it wasn't easy. I think the handbag finally convinced her."

"Stop it, Paolo—you know that's not true," said Erika. "It was your killer looks that had me smitten."

The joking and laughter went on all evening as the four of them enjoyed dinner and wine, played music, and reminisced.

Later when Paolo and Erika were in bed, he asked her, "So, it was my killer looks that finally got to you?"

"Yes, that, and your eyes, and your smile, and your kisses . . ."

"What about my lovemaking?"

"Hm . . . I'm not sure. Remind me?"

The next morning, Paolo had already left and Todd and James were having breakfast on the patio by the time Erika got up.

"You boys are up early."

"Yes, we didn't want to waste an hour of our time in Italy!" James said. "Are you going to the cantina today?"

"No, I'm staying home with you guys. It's still warm. We can hang out by the pool and go for a ride later. Paolo will be back for dinner. I thought we might go over to Livernano."

"No," said Todd. "Let's stay here tonight. We want you and Paolo to cook for us."

James chimed in. "It's much more fun. We can drink wine, and we don't need to drive."

Over the next ten days, Erika spent as much time as she could with her friends as the harvest drew to a close. The three of them went shopping and wine tasting and explored some of the little towns Erika hadn't had time to see.

The day before the meeting with the notary, Todd and James told her she needed to relax, and they took her to the spa. Paolo had made dinner reservations at L'Antica Macelleria Cecchini in Panzano—the owner, Dario Cecchini, was a butcher and a bit of a local celebrity. The meal was a performance that started with Dario reciting poetry. Then, with music blasting, and as everyone watched and took pictures, Dario cut two steaks with a nine-inch knife that he juggled between cutting the pieces of meat. After the show, the diners applauded and were ushered upstairs and seated around an open grill.

The four of them ordered the steaks the restaurant was known for, and Paolo opened a bottle of wine they'd brought with them. Todd stood up and raised his glass.

"Let's drink to Erika and her big day tomorrow!"

"Salute!" they all sang out, and Erika was beset with a welter of emotions—excitement, trepidation, curiosity about what tomorrow would bring, and, as she looked around at her oldest friends and the man she loved, a feeling of warmth washed over her.

XLIX

———

ERIKA BARELY SLEPT THAT NIGHT. Paolo kept trying to calm her as she restlessly tossed and turned, contemplating the big day. She could hardly believe that the moment for the takeover of the properties had finally arrived. As she got dressed, she kept replaying the last few months in her head. She thought back to her birthday dinner with Craig. He had given her that huge engagement ring and set a date for the wedding. Everything had seemed so perfect. Then, when she went to work on that Monday morning, she'd received a simple registered letter, and nothing had been the same since. A little more than five months later, she had left her old self behind. Nothing that she thought was important then had much meaning to her now.

Here in Tuscany, she now had a purpose. She glanced out the window. The day was overcast, but even clouds couldn't ruin the beauty of the landscape.

Erika stood in front of the mirror and looked at the outfit she'd chosen. It had been a long time since she had put on clothes like these—a crisp white blouse, a black designer skirt, a black jacket, and high heels. She pulled her hair back in a bun and added earrings and a little makeup. Her New York uniform. It was time to retire this look—it made her look old. These days, she was more comfortable in jeans, a simple blouse, and sneakers or boots.

She heard Paolo call from downstairs, "Erika, are you ready? We don't want to be late."

"I'll be down in a minute." She grabbed her handbag and lucky pen and went to join the group that was waiting for her downstairs. Todd, James, Doris, and Paolo were all in the living room.

Paolo stared at her. "The last time I saw you dressed like that," he said, "was when you first arrived in Casalvento."

"I know, Paolo. I put it on just for this occasion. It'll probably be the last time I wear something like this. Before we go, though, do we have time to play one song on the gramophone? I want to hear my favorite old tune in honor of my grandfather."

"Of course," Paolo said. "I think we have about five minutes."

She turned on the song and hummed along, brushing away a few tears. Playing the gramophone always reminded her that she had never known Umberto. She swallowed bitterly, wishing he could see this moment. She comforted herself with the fact that perhaps he could. She had felt his presence all along. When the song was over, she looked at everyone and said, "Okay. Let's go."

As she and Paolo walked out the door, Todd gave her a hug and wished her luck. "We'll be waiting here for you with champagne when you come back," James said.

Paolo took Umberto's Lincoln Continental out of the garage. He had polished it so that it gleamed, and Erika couldn't resist running her hand along the side, admiring the old vehicle as she climbed into the front seat. Paolo drove slowly up the hill to the gate. While he waited for it to open, he turned to her.

"Are you ready?"

Erika took a deep breath and nodded.

They were quiet for most of the ride, just listening to the radio. Erika watched the scenery and remembered the first appointment she had had with Bernardo and the notary. "Paolo, did you bring all your paperwork?"

"Yes, plus Bernardo has copies as well."

As they drove into Siena, the Continental attracted plenty of stares. It seemed gigantic, especially when Paolo gingerly navigated the narrow streets of the city center. When he pulled up to the notary's office, he paused in front of the columned entrance to the building's courtyard.

Erika gave him a quizzical look. "Do you think the car will fit through this?"

"It will be tight. Look out your side, and make sure I'm not getting too close."

"Okay. How will we turn around once we're inside?"

"Let's worry about that later. Just make sure I don't hit the gate now."

Paolo parked the car in the middle of the courtyard, blocking some of the parked vehicles.

"What happens if some of the cars parked here need to leave?" Erika asked him.

"We will deal with it then. You worry too much."

Paolo helped her out of the car and held her hand as he accompanied her into the building and up to the third floor. Bernardo was already there in the waiting area, and as Paolo stopped to talk to the receptionist, Erika greeted the lawyer with a warm hug and a kiss on each cheek. "*Ciao*, Bernardo."

"*Ciao*, Erika. *Come va?*"

"*Bene*. A little nervous, though."

"You don't have to be. This will all go smoothly. The notary is running a little behind, though. You have all your documents with you?"

"Yes, I do. And Paolo has his too."

"Will you be staying in Italy, Erika?"

"Yes, of course I will. But I do have to go back to the States at the beginning of November. I sold the shares of my consulting firm to my partner, Tiffany. Everything is ready for her to take over the business. We just have to sign the final documents."

"You look so different today in your New York clothes. It reminds me how well you've settled in here. I know I've said it before, but I will say it again—I am so proud of everything you've done at the winery and at Livernano. I'm sure it was not easy."

"It was a learning process, but I surprised myself. At first, I didn't know how I'd last all these months, but I'm so grateful to the people who worked for my grandfather. They supported me in every way, and I've learned so much. Even cooking. Before I came here, I couldn't boil an egg! You and your wife should come for dinner, and I'll show you."

Paolo walked up to them and hugged the lawyer as well. "*Ciao*, Bernardo, *come va? Tutto organizzato?*"

"*Si*, Paolo! Everything is ready." Bernardo turned back to Erika. "Would you like some water?"

"Oh, yes, please. How much longer do you think we'll have to wait? I'm more nervous than I realized."

"The notary has another client behind that wooden door to your left. I guess that meeting is taking a little longer than he expected."

The receptionist handed Erika some water, and she sat down next to Paolo and took his hand. Finally, the wooden door opened, and the notary came out to the waiting room, quickly shutting the door behind him.

"*Ciao*, Bernardo, Paolo, *Signora*." He took Erika's hand and lightly kissed it. "*Siamo pronti?*"

"*Si, Dottore*," Erika murmured, and they all trooped into another room, where the notary took his seat at the head of a long table with several stacks of papers.

Erika and Bernardo sat down on one side, with Paolo opposite them, and the lawyer explained what would happen. "First, we sign the properties over to you, Erika, and later we'll sign the one percent to Paolo. I'll need your passport and driver's license."

She gave them to Bernardo, who handed them to an assistant who made copies. Then she watched as the notary stamped page after page. *Bump, bump, bump*—the sound echoed off the walls and high ceiling, filling the silence. From time to time, the notary would read a document aloud, and Bernardo would translate. Each time, Erika agreed, "*Si, si, si*," and added her signature with her lucky pen. After an hour, she was finished. She leaned back in her chair and sighed with relief.

Then it was Paolo's turn to follow the same procedure. Finally, it was Erika's turn to sign those documents as well. At two in the afternoon, they were finally done.

"*Auguri, Signora*," the notary said, shaking Erika's hand as he left the room. Paolo got up as well and moved toward the door. Before he went out, though, he turned back to Bernardo with a serious look that puzzled Erika.

The lawyer took Erika's hand. "How do you feel now?"

"I'm a little tired, Bernardo. This has been a life-changing experience. I'm a different person than I was, and I owe it all to my grandfather."

"That was his wish. And now there is one more thing I have to do. What I'm about to say is difficult and may even be a little shocking to you. But it must be done. You have to believe we had no other choice."

Erika held her breath for a moment. "What are you talking about? Is everything okay? Have I made the wrong decision? Please tell me, Bernardo. What is it?"

"Everything's fine, but please keep an open mind. You have to realize that we thought this was the only way to get you to come to Italy and help you understand your grandfather and his family. Believe me when I say he wanted nothing more than to be a part of his son's life and later to be part of yours. Over the years he suffered a lot, but he didn't know how to reach you."

"Yes, I see that, Bernardo. I was happy to have those letters, but now you're scaring me."

"Yes, about those letters . . . Did you notice that they had no date?"

"Yes, of course, but I didn't think too much about it. Should I have?"

"The fact is, those letters were not written in the past. They were written during the time you've been in Tuscany."

Erika suddenly felt a chill. "What do you mean?"

"Erika, your grandfather is not dead. He is alive and in that room behind the wooden door. He signed the documents over to you right before you came today. You are now the rightful owner of both properties. And Umberto is definitely living."

Erika stopped breathing for a moment, and a shudder went through her body. The room seemed to spin around her.

"Are you all right?"

"I think I'm in shock. You're saying that my grandfather has been alive all this time? How is that possible?"

"It's true. It's why Paolo told you the story about the unmarked grave. Umberto was the one who came to Casalvento when you first arrived. He wanted to see how you were doing, to see a glimpse of you. He didn't mean to frighten you, but when you said you were scared, Paolo asked him to stay away."

"Where has he been for all these months?"

"He was with Paolo's parents."

"They all knew? I cannot believe this, Bernardo. I'm so confused and . . . angry. How could you all keep a secret like this?"

"I know it's hard to understand, Erika. But please think about it. Umberto is an old man. He just wanted for you to understand him, to get to know him. He was convinced that this was the only way he could get you to come to Tuscany." Bernard straightened. He reached forward to pat her hand. "Now, I will leave you for a couple of minutes. You have to decide whether you want to meet Umberto or not. The decision is yours to make, and yours only. He will accept whatever you decide. It's up to you. I'll wait for you outside."

Bernardo left the room and shut the door behind him.

Erika just sat there, overcome by the unexpected news. She tried to stand up, but her legs felt too weak, and she sank back into the chair. But the room suddenly seemed so hot that she forced herself to get up and open a window.

Don't panic, she told herself. *And try not to cry.*

The fresh air revived her, and she sat down and drank some water. She took a deep breath and just sat there.

Her grandfather was next door. Did she want to meet him or not?

Once again, she thought back over the last five months and all the changes in her life. All because of Umberto. She thought of the letters and how much he had endured over the decades, all the things he had gone through. She remembered how many times she had wished she had a chance to spend time with him and really know him. And now that was a possibility. He was an old man, eighty-nine years old.

She opened the door. Bernardo and Paolo looked at her expectantly. She had made her decision.

L

ERIKA WALKED OVER TO the lawyer and took his hand. "Take me to him, Bernardo."

He stood up and hugged her, and she could feel how the relief of her decision had relaxed his body. Paolo came over to her too, kissed her, and squeezed her shoulder as he whispered, "Don't be afraid, *cara*. He loves you."

Erika smiled weakly and tried not to show her emotions as Bernardo opened the heavy wooden door. Standing at the window, with his back to her, was a tall man with silver hair but a strong, straight body despite the cane he was holding. He was dressed well in a brown leather jacket over gray pants. When he heard people entering the room, he slowly turned around. The lines on his face betrayed his age, and it was clear his eyes had seen a great many things in his day. He looked intensely at Erika, locking on to her eyes as if to engrave her in his mind.

Suddenly, Erika realized she had seen him once before—he was the one they called "the mentor" at the Sunday family lunch at Paolo's house, soon after she had arrived. That day, she had never heard his voice.

This time, he said simply, "Erika," and, smiling a little, opened his arms to her.

She let go of Bernardo and walked into her grandfather's embrace, tears flowing down her face. Umberto could not hold back his tears either, and the two of them seemed to cling to each other for dear life. For a long time, neither moved nor said another word. Finally, Umberto took a step back and looked at Erika's face earnestly. He pulled out a handkerchief and wiped her tears, then mopped his own eyes as well.

"*Nonno*, let's go home," Erika said.

His face lit up with happiness, and he put his arm around her, pulling her tight. "*Si, cara*. My dear granddaughter. My blood, my life, my love! I thank God for allowing this wish to come true. *Andiamo a casa*."

When Paolo saw the two of them emerge from the room, he hurried over to hug them both, and he too broke down in tears. "Bernardo left a little while ago," Paolo told them. "I think the emotion got to be too much for him."

They went downstairs, and when Umberto saw his old Lincoln Continental, he grinned from ear to ear and patted the hood. He got in front, and Erika took the back seat. She held her breath as Paolo eased the car around and backed out the front gate slowly, leaving without a scratch.

On the ride home, Erika kept reaching to the front, touching her grandfather's shoulder, as if to convince herself that he really was sitting in front of her.

"*Nonno*, I have a question."

Her grandfather turned his weathered profile toward her. "*Cara*," he said, "I'm sure you have many. Start with your first one."

"Why didn't you just call me up in New York? Why all this charade?"

"Erika, from what I could find out, you had your perfect life. Your business, your friends, planning your wedding. You had never heard of me. Do you really think if I called you out of the blue and said I'm your grandfather and I want you to come to Italy and take over my properties, you would have left everything behind? Would you have come all this way to get to know me and learn about my life?"

"No, probably not." Her grandfather was right—even from so far away, and without ever meeting her, he had known her heart. "No, I would have never come here."

"I know it was not fair, and we tried to think of other ways to get you to come, but in the end, this seemed best. That is why we came up with the idea of the unmarked grave and the letters. It was important to me that you find out about my story before you met me."

"*Nonno*, I guess I understand, and I know it was important for me to understand all the family history, but it's still hard for me to believe. And it makes me angry, but right now I'm too happy to think about that. Paolo,

I can't believe that you could keep a secret like this from me. Promise me, from now on, you'll always tell me the truth."

Erika looked at her watch. "It's almost five. Why are we going so slowly?"

Paolo looked in the rearview mirror. "The gas tank is almost empty, and I want to make sure we make it home."

When Paolo finally pulled up to the driveway of the house, everything seemed unusually quiet. Where were Todd and James? Paolo helped Umberto out of the car, and she thought she saw the old man slip him something, but just then he reached out and patted the car again.

"She still runs well after all these years, don't you think, Paolo? Isn't she a fine machine?"

Erika took her grandfather by the arm, and they were walking down the steps to the kitchen when she saw a crowd of people coming around the corner. Bernardo was there with his wife and Doris, and Mirella, Santo, Luca, and Robby were hurrying up from behind. Erika looked around. As she stepped forward, she saw many people standing in the garden, their faces turned toward her and smiling. She recognized Paolo's family—parents, brothers, and sisters and their husbands and wives. Elisa, Hanna, and Constantina were there. Massimo was standing with Sofia, and even Vincenzo had come and was smiling. That was a good sign. Maybe the unhappiness between neighbors had finally come to an end.

Erika saw Todd and James. "Did you know all about this?"

"Not before today," said Todd. "But Paolo called us in New York and made it clear that we had to be here at this time, so we knew something was up."

"And, Doris," said Erika, "how could you keep a secret like this for so many months?"

"It wasn't easy, Ms. Erika. In fact, it was very, very difficult. I'm sorry I couldn't let you know the truth. But I was happy when Paolo called us from Siena and said that you had agreed to meet your grandfather, and we could go ahead and let everyone know. That's why everyone is here."

Doris, Mirella, and Paolo's sisters had set up a long table overlooking the vineyard and prepared a feast. Lanterns were hanging in the trees along with bright yellow balloons.

Umberto took a seat at the head of the table, with Erika on his left side and Paolo on his right. The three of them kept staring at each other and reaching out to touch hands as the sound of laughter and conversation filled the air. Course after course came out from the kitchen—plates of *antipasti*, pastas, steak, and lamb.

Wine flowed like water as there was one toast after another. It was a joyous celebration, not only of Erika's new ownership status but also of Umberto's return from the dead.

But suddenly, the electricity went out, and the lights in the trees went dark.

"Paolo, what's going on?" Erika called across the table. "Why now? Will the generator kick in soon? And, *Nonno*, are you okay?"

"Yes, *cara*, I'm fine. I'm sure it will come back on soon."

There was a sound from the kitchen, and Luca came out carrying a huge cake with candles. Around the table, everyone started to sing:

"*Buon compleanno a te . . .*"

"Grandpa, is today your birthday?"

"Yes, my darling, it is. The happiest birthday ever!"

He blew out the candles, and the lights came back on. Erika kissed Umberto, then looked over at Paolo and blew him a kiss. He stood up and came over to take her by the hand.

"Will you come over here, Erika? Just for a moment."

She followed him to the fountain and caught her breath as he got down on one knee.

She realized what was happening, and her heart was beating so fast that she barely heard what he said. Even before he finished the sentence, she had started to cry again.

"Erika, *cara*, don't cry. I love you! Can you imagine spending your life with me? Will you marry me?"

"Yes, I can. And yes. I love you. You know that."

Paolo pulled a little box out of his pocket and opened it to reveal a red velvet lining with a delicate ring shaped like a sunflower. He slipped it on her finger.

"This ring was given to me by your grandfather. It belonged to your great-grandmother."

Paolo stood up and held her face in both hands and kissed her. Then he kissed her again. She hadn't noticed that everyone had left the table and was now close by, smiling and clapping.

Umberto held up his wine glass. "*Saluti tutti!* To love, life, and happiness! And lots of children! Don't wait. I won't live forever."

RECIPES

————

PENNE DELLA NONNA

- ❏ 1 pound penne pasta
- ❏ 3 whole red peppers, seeded
- ❏ Extra virgin olive oil
- ❏ 1 cup heavy cream
- ❏ 1 cup Parmigiano-Reggiano cheese
- ❏ Salt and pepper to taste
- ❏ Flat-leaf parsley for garnish
- ❏ ½ cup diced boiled ham

Cut red peppers into pieces and puree in a food processor. In a saucepan, add olive oil to coat pan. When the oil is hot, add the pureed peppers and cook for a few minutes. Add the cream and stir until incorporated, for about 10 minutes over a high flame. When the sauce becomes thick, add Parmigiano-Reggiano and salt and pepper to taste.

Boil the pasta until al dente. Add cooked pasta to the sauce and toss until the pasta is covered. Sprinkle with parsley.

Add the diced ham and toss again.

Serve immediately.

Wine pairing recommendation: Livernano L'Anima

PASTA E FAGIOLI

- ❑ 2 tablespoons olive oil
- ❑ ½ pound Italian sausage, spicy or sweet
- ❑ 1 small red onion, finely chopped
- ❑ 2 small carrots, finely chopped
- ❑ 2 stalks celery, finely chopped
- ❑ 4 cloves garlic, minced
- ❑ Salt
- ❑ Pepper
- ❑ ½ pound dried white beans, soaked in water overnight
- ❑ 5 medium tomatoes, diced
- ❑ 1 cup of chicken broth
- ❑ 2 sprigs of rosemary, finely chopped
- ❑ 1½ pounds small pasta, any shape
- ❑ Freshly grated Parmesan, to garnish
- ❑ Freshly chopped parsley, to garnish
- ❑ Splash of flavored vinegar

In a large, deep pot over medium heat, heat the olive oil. Add sausage and cook, breaking up with a wooden spoon, until cooked through, about 5 minutes. Stir in onion, carrots, and celery, and cook until slightly softened, about another 5 minutes.

Add garlic and cook until fragrant, 1 minute or more. Season with salt and pepper, then add the chicken broth, beans, diced tomatoes, rosemary, and a little of the parsley.

Bring the mixture to a boil, then stir in the pasta. Reduce heat to medium and cook until pasta is al dente and the beans soft, about another 10 minutes. Taste and adjust seasoning if necessary.

Serve in a soup bowl, and garnish with parsley and Parmesan. Add a splash of olive oil and vinegar.

Wine pairing recommendation: Casalvento Chianti Classico

LINGUINE CON COZZE E VONGOLE
(Linguine with mussels and clams)

- ☐ 1 pound linguine
- ☐ Half a stick of butter
- ☐ ¼ cup chopped fresh parsley
- ☐ ½ cup chopped scallions
- ☐ ¼ cup olive oil
- ☐ 2 cups white wine
- ☐ ½ pound mussels
- ☐ ½ pound clams
- ☐ 3 strips of prosciutto, chopped
- ☐ Salt and pepper
- ☐ Peperoncino, chopped, if desired

Clean the mussels. Five hours before eating, place the clams in a deep dish with sea salt and place in a cool place or in the refrigerator.

Add olive oil and butter in a large skillet and heat, then add the scallions. When lightly browned, add white wine, half the parsley, prosciutto, salt and pepper, and peperoncino, if using. Let mixture boil for 5 minutes, then turn stove off. The sauce gets better if you make it 3 hours before eating.

Boil water and add linguine. Cook al dente, and strain.

Heat the sauce, then add clams and mussels and turn the heat to high and cover. Three minutes later add the pasta and stir into the sauce. Lower the heat and cover again. Cook for 5 minutes. Discard any clams and mussels that have not opened.

Serve in a deep dish, garnished with the rest of the parsley and a hint of olive oil.

Wine pairing recommendation: Livernano L'Anima

AUTHOR'S NOTE

—

EACH LIFE HAS ITS OWN STORY. Coming from Austria and living in Palm Beach, I moved in two very different worlds.

When I came up with the story for my book, I invented another person with other experiences, but I soon realized that some of what I wrote shadowed onto my own life.

I married an American born in the Bronx. His parents were two Italian immigrants who met on the ship coming to their land of dreams. America!

My husband grew up so poor that he got his first pair of new shoes when he went to the navy. But he was a self-made success and as a result was able to buy a property in Tuscany. As we renovated the property and planted the vineyards, I became fascinated with the process of winemaking and life in Italy. It was the most amazing time . . . and still is! I wanted to do my best to bring part of my experience into this novel. And I hope that others can enjoy it with me.

Casalvento and Livernano both exist. Casalvento is my personal home and also where the winery is located. Livernano is a 1,500-year-old hamlet that was abandoned in 1953. We bought it in 2002 and have restored it over the years. Today it functions as a hotel.

I would like to thank all the people who have been with us through all those years. They have given my husband and me the beauty and pleasure that Tuscany has to offer.

And I want to especially thank my late husband, Bob, who always told me, "Life is too short to drink bad wine."

ABOUT THE AUTHOR

GUDRUN CUILLO is a graduate of the very prestigious all-girl Catholic academy and preparatory school of Leibnitz, Austria. Soon after graduation, with her instinctive artistic flair, she joined the opera as an artist-in-residence for stage scenery and makeup. That work eventually took Gudrun to New York to continue her education.

While enjoying traveling throughout the U.S., Gudrun came to Florida, where she fell in love with a successful entrepreneur and Broadway producer, Robert Cuillo, who was also Italian American. They married, and in the ensuing years, they established Casalvento Winery in Radda, Chianti Siena, Italy, and restored Livernano, a nearby medieval village, to its original splendor.

Gudrun has had two career passions: winemaking, which has garnered numerous awards and much recognition for Casalvento Winery, and writing. In her debut novel, Gudrun combines her life experience with her gift for storytelling.

Gudrun spends her time between Austria, Italy, and Palm Beach, Florida.